DISCOVERY OF THE BLOOD

Discovery of the Blood

The Bonds of Blood Trilogy: Book One

The Blood & Shadows Series: Book One

J.A. CALLIN & WOLFGANG JACOBS

Tredeciverse Studios LLC

Please contact info@tredeciverse.com for general queries and permissions.

https://tredeciverse.com for more information or

https://tredeciverse.store to order.

DISCOVERY OF THE BLOOD
The Bonds of Blood Trilogy: Book 1
The Blood & Shadows Series: Book 1

ISBN 979-8-9931704-0-4   Paperback
      979-8-99311704-1-1   Ebook
      979-8-9931704-2-8.   Audiobook

1 2 3 4 5 6 7 8 9 10

Dedication

J.A.: To my mother and father. Without your encouragement, I might never have set pen to paper. Thank you both for everything — and I hope we see each other again someday.

Wolfgang: To my father, my personal Wall, thank you for everything you did for me. All the lessons, all the encouragement, and all of the love and pain you shared showed me that the human experience is full indeed. I miss you every day and look forward to that day when we can sit down together, and you can tell me, "You did the best you could, son. I'm proud of you for that."

To my mother, my loving and protective mother, the one who goes to battle for me every day. Thank you for everything you do for me. Thank you for never giving up on me, even when it was difficult. This is a dream come true, and, without your fighting spirit, it would still be a dream.

Contents

Prologue: Becoming a Martyr

May 13, 2007: A Cabin in Central Pennsylvania

The old man knew this day would come.

It had been a long time coming, too. William Andrew Wolfe-Wall had made no shortage of enemies in his life. He had once been an intelligence agent and had danced with some of the most feared enemies of his country during that career. Now, he fronted an investigation into those who would threaten the world. He had ruffled many proverbial feathers, asked too many probing questions, and stood against those with power, wealth, and influence. The man known as 'The Wall' to his enemies had done so much in his efforts to stymie his global foes, to save those they had threatened the most.

In retaliation, he'd been threatened, fired, and forced on the run.

That his enemies would have finally decided to end him didn't surprise the old man. He was surprised that they'd taken so long to make that decision, especially given what else he had discovered. Still, the decision itself was a foregone conclusion.

He might have fought against it, fled to one of those places he considered safe, if not for the news he'd received. William chuckled to himself, the sound mirthless, as he set down the schedule his doctors had given him earlier in the week.

Weeks of aggressive chemotherapy, he thought with a shake of his head. *Not to mention immunotherapy and who knows what else, for what? Another year at most, if I'm lucky.*

He sighed, then turned back to where his computer waited, with

1

one last email waiting to be sent. Once he sent these final instructions, he could meet his end with a peaceful heart.

One click, and the email went into the digital outbox. *Such amazing technology we have nowadays. Even the thought of this would have been nothing but science fiction when I was a boy.*

Of course, many things had been different back then, not just the technology. Growing up during the Great Depression and experiencing many of the hardships prevalent at the time had prepared William for several of life's harsher realities. It just hadn't been enough to prepare him for the life he would lead. Back then, he and his siblings were still innocent, not yet acquainted with the horrible things people could do.

Now, at eighty years old, William could no longer call himself innocent. Thanks in part to his former career, The Wall had become far too used to dealing with true evil. He had witnessed many heart-wrenching events and experienced all manner of despicable acts while in the field. His current activities had allowed him to see and hear even more.

Maybe it's a good thing that I won't be around for much longer, William thought as he saw his email disappear from the outbox. *Considering what's coming.*

The beginnings of a humorless smile turned the corners of his lips upward. A moment later, with a few clicks and a typed-in command, he opened up a new program. His grandchildren would have been surprised to learn that William knew programs like this one even existed. Still, they were all convinced that he barely knew how to turn his computer on.

Silly little ones. William once again shook his head. *Ah, well. Let 'em have their delusions while they still can. They're the ones that'll have to face the future, not me.*

He took a deep breath, then typed in the final command, the one that would cause his computer to destroy itself. He hated having to do it, but it was better than letting his enemies have even the slightest chance of stopping what he had set into motion against them.

Check, he thought with a grim smile. *And, with luck... Checkmate.*

Switching off the monitor, William stood up from the old office chair. His knees creaked, and he loosed a tired breath as he glanced at the digital clock that sat on the nearby end table, which proved that it was almost ten o'clock at night.

They'll be here soon. William reached for the handgun he always kept beside himself, then the information from his doctors. *Time for me to get into position.*

Slowly, he began the walk to the kitchen. The distance was short, mere steps, but it felt like an eternity.

William took the time, too, to pause by each of the frames that lined the short hallway. There were no landscapes, no impressionist pieces, or any other art style. Those belonged to a different life, the one he had shared with his Lucille.

Here, now, there were only photographs of the people who mattered the most to him. His parents, Henry and Ethel, had been gone for years now, but William still missed them. His sisters, Anna and Julia-Jean, were also gone, as were their husbands. William still loved them, and seeing their old portraits, together with his mother's and father's, never failed to bring a sad smile to his face.

Their absences from his life still left him with a hollowness in his chest. Time had dulled the grief that came with each passing, but it had never entirely erased it.

As hard as it was to mourn them, it was nothing compared to the loss of his brother. William's gaze settled upon the three photos he had of Walter Nicholas Wolfe-Wall. One was of Walter with William and their sisters, back when they were children; another was of Walter with their parents; and one, William's favorite, was of Walter alone. He was dressed in the army uniform of the early 1940s, smiling as though he didn't have a care in the world.

William's smile came and went with the flicker of memory. He'd envied Walter so much back then. William himself had been too young to enlist and had been unable to fight at Walter's side in the Second World War. William had thought, with the naivety of youth, that the War would be a grand adventure, a glorious fight.

Walter's disappearance had taught him otherwise. War was anything but glorious. Loss was its only guarantee.

William had spent his life forever trying to fill his brother's place, to protect the family Walter had once watched over with such care. People said that he had succeeded. William had become an operative of the Special Intelligence Network, or SIN, protecting the so-called free world from its enemies to the absolute best of his abilities. He had traveled the globe, both with and without his beloved wife and their children, and had done

4

everything he could to try to make the world they lived in safe.

Perhaps he had, but one failure still taunted him, refusing to let him go even now. His voice dropped to a whisper as he stared at the picture of his brother.

"I could never find you, Walt," he murmured. "I could never bring you home."

The words hung in the still air like ash. William knew his failure to do so would follow him into the grave.

His eyes drifted then, and William found his favorite photograph of his wife. It had been taken when they were both young, both experiencing the full force of their fledgling love. Lucille Clancy's light red hair had been pulled back to cascade down and frame her young face. Brilliant, silver-gray eyes laughed at the camera and its operator.

He felt another weight slide onto his heart at the sight. That photograph had been taken before William had been recruited into SIN's ranks. That was before he participated in the Cold War. That was before the long, slow theft of Lucille's life, before the cancer hollowed her out to leave her a mere shell of the girl William had known and loved, before he'd been left with only memories in an empty house.

"I should have been there, with you," he whispered. "You always stood with me."

Yet he had not done the same. There had always been another assignment, another dangerous dance for him to take the lead in. He had barely made it back to his wife in time, at her end.

William felt the beginnings of tears form, and he needed to blink them back as he whispered, "I'll be seeing you again soon, my Light."

He took another step forward. Two, then three.

Unbidden, his feet halted at the photographs of his two children. His lips curled upward in a wistful smile at the sight of their then-young faces, which were both bright and happy. Quetta was married now, with three children of her own and a mostly good man as her husband. Henry walked the same dangerous path that William himself had once carved through the shadows.

They didn't know everything, but that would soon change. The old man had made sure of their inheritance in more ways than one.

His hand paused on the door that separated his private spaces from the rest of the cabin. William breathed deep, feeling the exhaustion that came with age, with illness, and with the time he'd spent preparing for what would come in the next hour or two.

Did they honestly think I'd run? He almost snorted at the idea. If his enemies had learned anything about him by now, it was that he only ran when he had no other options. If he chose to stand firm?

Without warning, he coughed. The sound proved harsh. His chest hurt, too, when he finished. William's lips thinned. A slow death held no appeal for him, but something quick? He could work with that.

Taking another deep breath, William forced himself to straighten. The old resolve returned iron to his spine.

This will not be your victory, he promised his enemies in the silence. *It will only be the beginning of your downfall.*

6

Another small smile, this one vicious, spread over William's lips. His enemies had made their greatest mistake years ago. They didn't know it yet, but his death would be the final match. His children and grandchildren would become the flame of justice.

Twisting the doorknob, he headed out into the living room. Only his immediate family knew about this cabin, but they rarely ever visited. It was why he had returned to it to await his executioners. Here, in the vacation home he had purchased as a younger man, he could enjoy the memories of his life. At the same time, he awaited his death, and he could also make certain no one else would be harmed, either by his would-be killers or by what he'd done to prepare for them. They and their masters were merciless, and William had no desire to endanger any innocent.

He reached the tiny kitchen. Glancing about reassured him that almost everything was set. Once he concealed the door to the cabin's cellar, all he would need to do was sit and wait.

With that done, William placed the medical schedule and his gun on the table, then went to a small cabinet to take out a few glasses, as well as a small bottle of rare whiskey. A moment later, he took the seat facing the door.

He didn't, however, pour himself a glass right away. Instead, his eyes slid upward to glance at the old clock, which was illuminated by the soft moonlight coming in from the small windows. He blinked when he saw that it was fifteen minutes past ten already. It was surprising that his killers hadn't shown up yet. William had almost expected to greet them when he'd opened the hallway door.

Well, he *had* only turned out the lights a mere twenty, maybe twenty-five minutes ago. Perhaps they wished to kill him as he slept?

It didn't matter. They would be there soon enough. In the meantime, William could use whatever time he had left to continue to reminisce.

His eyes slid back down from the clock to land on the collage of photographs that had been hung below it. Another softer smile touched his lips. These were some of his favorites, all being of the young woman he'd considered to be a second daughter, alongside her child—William's first grandchild.

He sighed at the thought of them. Katherine Rose Kincaid had been one of William's favorite students back during his brief time as a recruiter and instructor for potential SIN operatives. Katherine had been selected for the program due to her gift with languages, and she'd been on track to not only join William in his line of work but to marry William's son, Henry. She had been a beautiful and vivacious girl back then, intelligent and passionate about life and justice, wanting nothing more than to make a positive difference in the world, no matter how small.

However, Katherine had also been a stubborn creature. Whenever she had made up her mind on something, very little could change it. Henry had had many battles with her, both large and small, during their relationship. William himself had also experienced it a few times before 'unhappy events', which had caused Katherine to leave both the training program and William's son.

She had kept all knowledge of her son from his father, too. She would have kept the boy's existence from William himself, had he not demanded an explanation for her decision to abandon Henry, her schooling, and her would-be career.

Another sigh escaped his throat. William had never been able to convince Katherine of how wrong she'd been to keep her child a secret. Unfortunately, she had extracted William's vow of silence before she would explain anything. That decision haunted William even now. He could still hear the quaver in Katherine's voice when she had finally confided in him about the deaths—the *murders*—of her father, her mother, and her two brothers. She hadn't believed the official report and had wanted, *needed*, to return home so that she could find out the truth.

It was a need that he understood only too well.

It was why he had agreed to keep her secrets after getting her to promise that she would keep in touch. William had believed they could revisit the topic of introducing her son to Henry after Katherine had come to terms with everything and had hopefully brought the people responsible for her family's untimely deaths to justice.

Katherine, however, had not only proven herself too stubborn to admit that she was in the wrong, but she had also discovered that the murders of her family members were just the tip of an enormous, very nasty iceberg of criminal activity in her hometown. Such things had been occurring there for not just one, two, or even five or ten years. They had, instead, been going on for *decades*.

"And you couldn't let it go," William murmured into the darkness. "No matter what I said to try to convince you to let *me* take care of it."

He had begged her to allow him to do that. He had *pleaded* with her to let him take the risks instead, so he could finish the investigation she had begun. She hadn't just uncovered the identities of the perpetrators, the ones *truly* responsible for her family's deaths. She had also started to discover those responsible for some of the worst series of crimes, both in her home city and across the globe. It hadn't been just herself who she had been placing in harm's way, after all, but her *son*.

William winced at the thought of him. Robert William Henry Nicholas Alastor Kincaid took after both of his parents in so many ways. However, back then, he'd still been a bright and happy, innocent child. He'd been a genuine treasure, at least in William's admittedly jaded point of view.

He would have given anything for Robbie, as the boy had preferred to be called back then, to have remained that way. William had wanted Robbie never to know genuine fear, or sorrow, or hatred, or anger. Perhaps that hadn't been entirely realistic, but thanks to his mother's stubborn refusal to give up her investigation, Robbie had learned those things far sooner than he should have.

And so much more.

William blew out an unhappy breath. Yes, he had understood Katherine's near-obsession to end the worst nightmares the people of her home city had suffered. He had even applauded her for wanting to bring accountability to those who more than deserved it.

What he could *not* understand was why it had taken precedence over her child's safety and well-being. Katherine had placed Robbie in grave danger. As both a father and a grandfather, William could neither condone it nor forgive her for it. He had always done his absolute best to eliminate the dangers his career had posed to his wife and children. Why had Katherine not felt the need to do the same?

Worse, Katherine hadn't been nearly as careful as she had believed she'd been, and the scenario William had most feared came to pass.

Sitting in the darkness of his kitchen, William shook his head. A deep breath, full of sorrow, escaped his lungs. Yes, Katherine had been reckless. Yes, William's fears had been realized. Yes, Katherine had been killed, and her son had indeed been taken by the perpetrators, who had thought to use the boy to force William to hand over the evidence against them, back when they had believed him to be nothing more than a 'kindly older gentleman'. The three weeks it had taken him to track Robbie's kidnappers down had been some of the most terrifying moments of his life back then, but William had *succeeded*. He *had* saved Robbie from the absolute worst of what those bastards had planned to do to the boy.

The old man's shoulders slumped a moment later. While he had managed to rescue Robbie from the worst of what had been planned, the things that had already been done had proven to be more than enough to change his grandchild.

A noise from outside caught William's attention, distracting him. He turned his head, listening with an intensity few could rival. Was it time?

Apparently not. William shook his head again when he heard his closest neighbor's cat meow. Why did it always travel the half-mile between them to come and visit, and why couldn't its owners learn to keep the silly thing inside?

And should he consider it rude that his executioners were making him wait?

Maybe, but he thought he should instead be grateful that they were delaying his reunion with Katherine, if only for a few minutes more. William did not doubt that he would answer to her for the path her son had chosen, and he hoped she had noticed that William had tried his best to talk Robbie out of it.

"I *did* try, Katherine," he whispered to the surrounding air. "I really did."

The problem was that Robbie wasn't just his mother's son, but his father's. William knew just how stubborn Henry could be, and Robbie had inherited a potent combination of his parents' tenacity. Being forced to witness his mother's murder and then being kidnapped by her killers had been the catalyst to transform the friendly, happy boy Robbie had been into the angry and determined young man he had become.

William couldn't blame Robbie for who and what he had become. It was why William had done his best to give Robbie every tool and advantage he could, even while trying to persuade the boy that there were other, better paths for him to follow. Robbie had needed to be able to protect himself, at the very least, and he'd also be able to avenge his mother, if he so chose.

William had little doubt that Robbie wouldn't try to avenge him as well, once he heard about William's death. If Robbie combined forces with Henry...

Yet another mirthless chuckle made its way past William's lips. If their enemies had thought that he, The Wall, had been hard to deal with, he could only imagine the sort of hell they would find themselves in once William's son and grandson went after them, especially if they decided to work together. He almost wished he could be around to see it.

But he wouldn't. The near-inaudible scraping he heard at the front door, coming as someone attempted to pick the lock, made sure of it.

A hardened smile turned the corners of William's lips back upward. *Showtime.*

The door opened soon after. Two men walked in. William recognized them both.

Connor Shelley had been a recruit of SIN and William's student for a brief time. The other man he knew as both Mister Mulryan and as Echo.

"Gentlemen." William smiled at them. "Welcome. Let's have a chat."

Connor blinked, his light blue eyes widening as his gun lowered a moment. It was apparent he had not expected William to be awake, let alone sitting at his kitchen table, waiting for them.

Mister Mulryan, too, looked surprised. He just covered it up better. His hand had automatically dropped to the weapon he had concealed before he realized what he was doing. He schooled his face a moment later into a mask of civility.

"Mister Wall." He spoke in a congenial manner despite his shock. "We did not realize you would be expecting us."

Connor did not yet speak. Instead, he raised the gun again, aiming directly for William's heart. He didn't shoot, though, as William responded.

"If I hadn't wanted us to talk, don't you think you'd already be dead?" William looked almost disappointed. "Really, Mister Mulryan. I know that Connor's never been that quick on the uptake, but with your reputation?"

Mister Mulryan inclined his head in acknowledgment of the criticism. Connor's look sharpened, his eyes snapping with sudden anger.

"Push the gun away," he grated. "Slowly."

William did so, making sure to push the doctor's schedule along with it. He wanted to shake his head again, but knew how Connor would take it. *He was never the sharpest knife in the drawer. I'd almost pity Mister Mulryan if I didn't know what would be happening soon. Having Connor as a student was an experience, to say the least.*

Connor came forward to take the gun and frowned at the piece of paper beside it. A moment later, his mouth all but fell open as he read the words that were on it.

"Stage 4?" he managed to whisper before once more meeting William's gaze. "I... We had no idea."

"Of course you didn't," William told him, also seeing Mister Mulryan's look of realization. "It wasn't something I chose to advertise."

"Understandable," Mister Mulryan's voice softened, just a fraction. "Is this why you're not fighting back?"

William inclined his head. "Any sane man would prefer the quickness of a bullet to the head instead of wasting slowly away, don't you agree?"

"Indeed." Mister Mulryan nodded.

14

"Before I go, though," William said. "There are a couple of things I think you should be made aware of."

"Oh?"

Mister Mulryan's face settled into something vaguely inquisitive. Connor, on the other hand, looked wary. William's expression seemed to be both smug and calculating.

"Why aren't we just killing him?" Connor asked, glancing at his companion. "Why are we wasting time talking?"

William shared a look with Mister Mulryan before shaking his head. "You know there's a reason he washed out of SIN's training program."

"So I have been informed." Mister Mulryan breathed out a small sigh. "You have been told, repeatedly as I recall, Mister Shelley, that we never waste an opportunity to gather information. Mister Wall has things we wish to know, as I am sure we have things he wishes to know before his end."

Connor grumbled something that neither of the other men wished to hear. William once again shook his head before dismissing the younger man and turning his full attention to Mister Mulryan.

"If you're hoping I'm just going to give up the information your Masters on that Council of yours were hoping you'd find and destroy when they sent you out here," he said. "Then I'm afraid you're a little late. It's not here." He saw the flicker of dismay that crossed Mister Mulryan's face. "It's already in the hands of another, and I do not doubt that the one I sent it to is *not* going to be happy when the reason why I sent it when I did is discovered. Oh, and don't bother with the computer. It's already been wiped."

The corners of Mister Mulryan's lips turned downward as he considered what William had said. Connor, however, snorted.

"We have others going after your second," he said in a derisive voice. "And I seriously doubt that a *boy* in a *coma* will be much trouble."

"Who says I sent it to them?" William retorted in a congenial tone. "After all, if *I* knew you were coming, why wouldn't my second know about the team being sent for him?" Connor's eyes widened in sudden fear, while Mister Mulryan's lips pressed together in a thin, unhappy line. "As for the other, why would I send anything to him? As you've said, he's in a coma."

Or so I want them to continue believing. William had to smile, both at the thought and at the way Mister Mulryan's brow furrowed in thought, while Connor just stared at him in consternation. *The ones they answer to are going to have a hell of a shock in the not-too-distant future. Several shocks, most likely.*

But those things were, again, in the future, and William wouldn't be around to see the fallout. He, or rather the two before him, had seen to it. The moment they had picked the lock on his door and entered the cabin, the timer had been set. The clock above them ticked merrily away, and in just a few more minutes, all of William's problems on Earth would be over, as would his two companions'.

For an instant, he wondered how the ones who had sent them would spin everything. Mister Mulryan was a known member of the Red Sword, but Connor Shelley was not. The

16

younger man had, as William had stated, washed out of the Special Intelligence Network's training program. Would he now become a double agent, at least on paper? If so, William could almost feel sorry for whatever family the young man might have had, if any.

But that's the life he chose, he reminded himself. *It's not your fault, Will, that Connor washed out, any more than it's your fault now that he's here, ready to kill you.*

"Perhaps," Mister Mulryan said, recapturing William's attention. "We shall need to have a chat with your son."

William laughed lightly to conceal his sudden unease. His relationship to his son and fellow agent wasn't that well-known to those who were outside of the Special Intelligence Network, for the simple fact that it would have placed both of them in far too much danger for anyone's comfort. For Mister Mulryan to know about Henry?

That begged a pair of uncomfortable questions. How had Mister Mulryan discovered the relationship William had with Henry? Had someone within SIN told him?

"Who says I would have sent anything to him, either?" William at last managed to retort. If someone from SIN *had* told Mister Mulryan certain things, then some of the more troubling things William had been discovering were, unfortunately, proven true. "He believes I'm retired, after all."

He chuckled once more, seeking to distract them from possibly putting any other pieces of the puzzle together, and reached for the bottle of whiskey he'd put out earlier. Turning it as he picked it up, so that Mister Mulryan could see the label, William was rewarded when his distraction appeared to work.

"Is that truly a bottle of...." Mister Mulryan's voice trailed off in near-palpable shock. "I didn't think more than a handful were left."

"It is, and you are correct." William nodded confirmation, seeing the others' admiration and envy, and gestured to the glasses. "Care to join me?"

Connor would have reached for a glass without thinking twice. Mister Mulryan, however, thought a moment before shaking his head.

"As much as *we* might like to," he said with a glance at Connor. "We have a mission to finish first. Perhaps we may indulge once it's over?"

William covered his slight pang of regret with another chuckle. "Whatever you want. It's not like I'll be able to argue against it then." He poured himself three fingers' worth into the glass he'd taken to use and held it up to catch a beam of moonlight in an apparent toast. *You had your chance, and you'll never so much as get a single sip of it now.* "But I warn you, and Mister Shelley in particular. This stuff stings on the way down, and the afterburn's a killer. I find that's meant to be *savored*, however. You know what I mean?"

"Of course." Mister Mulryan bowed his head ever so slightly. "In the meantime, perhaps we might continue our conversation."

No doubt in the hopes that I'll let something slip. William shrugged, hiding a shark's grin behind the rim of his glass. The gentle sip he took burned a thin line down his throat to pool in

18

his stomach. *Not that it'll matter if I do.*

The clock ticked merrily away as a chair across from him scraped against the floor, and William saw Mister Mulryan taking a seat. They eyed each other for a moment before Mister Mulryan spoke.

"You and yours have created quite a bit of trouble for my employers," he said.

William couldn't help his smile. "I'm glad we could be of service."

Connor rolled his eyes. William stifled the urge to sigh in disappointment. The boy was no longer his student, after all.

Mister Mulryan kept his focus, at least. Of course, William had expected him to do so. He had gained a fearsome reputation in the field, and for good reason.

"I must admit to curiosity," Mister Mulryan said at last. "Regarding the reason why you would go to such lengths for Katherine Kincaid's son."

"She was a former student," William said. "Much like Mister Shelley here, except *much* more intelligent and talented."

Connor snarled. Mister Mulryan glanced at him, mouth once again a thin line.

"Another outburst such as that, Mister Shelley," he said, his tone containing an arctic chill. "And I may advise your mentors to rescind your full membership for another year at least, so that you may learn *patience.*" He returned his attention to William. "I apologize, Mister Wall."

William waved it away. "No need, Echo. I attempted teaching him once myself, remember."

"Indeed."

"As for Katherine and her son," William said. "I will admit I

19

thought of her as a daughter. Her son might as well have been my grandson."

Mister Mulryan eyed him. "A daughter? Perhaps she was to *be* your daughter, through marriage?" He saw William's lips thin, just perceptibly. "Come now, Mister Wall. It's been suspected for some time. Either she was to be married to your son, or perhaps you had an interest in her yourself."

"I'm a little too old to be fathering children, don't you think?"

William didn't like giving away any information. Still, it wasn't as if Mister Mulryan or Connor would be leaving to share it with anyone. A swift glance at the clock proved their time was winding down. They didn't realize it, of course, and William's final act on Earth would be to make sure they didn't until it was too late. *Let them think they've won, Will. Them and their Masters.*

"You say that you destroyed all of the information that you were holding," Mister Mulryan continued after another moment, watching as William took another swallow of his drink. "I've danced with you enough times, Mister Wall, to know that you would have made hard copies of everything. That makes me wonder whom you would have sent them to, if not your second."

"You'll be finding out," William told him. "Probably a lot sooner than you realize."

"Oh? Would you care to explain?"

William chuckled. "That's a puzzle for you and your people to enjoy."

20

The corners of Mister Mulryan's lips turned downward. "I'm afraid I'm not so fond of puzzles. I leave those to Mind Twister. He does so enjoy figuring out ways of turning your people to our side."

Mind Twister? William inclined his head. *That's someone I haven't heard of before. If he's actively turning SIN's agent against them, then he must be embedded in the recruitment department. I wonder...*

"Who's that?" He took the chance to ask it directly. "It's not like I'm going to be able to tell anyone."

Not personally, at least, but then, there was a reason he had made certain the door to the cellar had been concealed.

Unfortunately, Mister Mulryan wouldn't be cooperative. Instead, his faint frown became a small smile. "Just as I must puzzle some things out, so must you."

"It was worth a shot," William downed another sip. "Although if this Mind Twister is the one responsible for bringing Mister Shelley to you, I'm not so sure you should be thanking him."

Connor growled before spitting, "At least *I* joined the winning side."

"Peace, Mister Shelley." Mister Mulryan chuckled, shaking his head. "Although you do have a point, Mister Wall."

"I know," William said, smiling a little. "I have to admit, I find myself a bit disappointed with you, Echo. I would have thought you would be the type who enjoyed solving a mystery or two. Of course, I've always enjoyed puzzling out the identities of those your Council has working for them. I may not know them all, but I do know more than a few."

"And if you know them, then your second knows them as well." Mister Mulryan drew in a deep breath, then sniffed. "While that may be true, I think the unknown ones shall be the undoing of those closest to you. Your son is in more danger than you know, in fact. It is quite unfortunate that you won't be able to warn him."

He grinned maliciously. William's eyes snapped, but he kept his voice level.

"I have all faith in my son's abilities," he said before permitting himself to smile. *My son's, my daughter's, my grandchildren's, and my son-in-law's.* "In fact, he may just become the thorn in your side after this."

Mister Mulryan's lips pursed again, and he watched as William drained the rest of his glass. "One last question. Your second is very efficient, and he fulfills his purpose more than adequately. However, he lacks the skills and the time to handle everything you need done." He tilted his head. "Since you were direct, allow me to be so as well. Who else is in your employ?"

"You mean to tell me that, despite all of your Council's vaunted connections, you haven't already figured them all out? Really, Echo. Again, I feel disappointed."

"Them?" Mister Mulryan arched an eyebrow. "So you have multiple people in your employ."

"Given everything that we've handled? That should have been obvious."

"A point," Mister Mulryan conceded before asking, "Are there any within our organizations? Any of them?"

William's mind automatically began to form a face. He shook his head, replacing the face with the image of a bird. The bird's form was compact and sturdy, with a long, slightly curved

22

bill. Two tufts of feathers stood up on its head like tiny horns. The lark concealed the would-be mental face, and he almost smiled at it before putting down the empty glass in front of him to hide the fact that it had become too heavy for him to hold. He could feel the poison within the alcohol working swiftly, and another swift glance at the clock revealed there were only a few more seconds left.

"That's another puzzle for you to enjoy," he said.

"Of course." Mister Mulryan stood and nodded to Connor. "Mister Wall, it has been a pleasure to have this one last chat. Mister Shelley, you have the honors."

William closed his eyes, listening to Connor draw out the process of checking his weapon. He whispered a final *good-bye* in his mind, the poison having relaxed him to the point of near-insensibility, when Connor's voice reached him without warning.

"Hey, wait a sec. There's a picture that's miss—"

He never completed his sentence, just as neither he nor Mister Mulryan managed to use the weapons they'd brought. Instead, the wall next to them, along with the rest of the cabin, *exploded.*

Chapter One: A Funeral and a Letter

May 22, 2007: A Central Pennsylvania Cemetery

The day William Andrew Wolfe-Wall was laid to his final rest proved to be gloomy in more ways than one. The skies were cloudy and overcast, with the sun seldom daring to peek out from behind the gray clouds. A few scattered drops of rain fell from time to time, too, almost as if the world itself was struggling to hold back tears of grief.

The service itself had been kept small. Only William's son, his daughter, her family, and the current Director of the Special Intelligence Network were in attendance. Given the nature of William's former work, it would be best to keep things as low-key and unadvertised as possible.

The man who called himself Victor Wolfe stared at the dark-colored casket that held his father's remains. He had known this day would one day come. It had come for his mother many years earlier, so why wouldn't it come for his father, too?

Victor just hadn't thought it would come this soon.

Clenching his jaw, he did his best to remain stoic, though his dazed, even lost, expression betrayed the inner turmoil he felt. Victor had been influenced in so many ways by his father to the point that he had chosen to follow in William Wolfe-Wall's footsteps and had joined the ranks that made up the Special Intelligence Network, which was a semi-covert agency of the United States Federal Government that handled certain types of situations that were both foreign and domestic. Victor had discovered his father's occupation quite by accident as a child, and he could well remember the argument he'd had with William about his decision to join. William had not been happy about it, but he'd also done his level best to teach Victor everything he could once Victor had proven he would not be swayed from the choice.

He'd made sure that Victor knew, too, just how proud he'd been of him. It was all Victor could ponder while attending William's funeral, watching as his father's casket was placed before him and before his sister. For the man known to most as The Dire Wolfe, it was more than just the ending to an era. He and his sister were now both orphans, bereft of the rock their father had been for them during his life.

The quiet sniffling next to him caused Victor to slide his silver-gray eyes over to the right. His sister, Jacquetta Allison Wolfe-Wall, now Jacquetta Thorne, stood next to him, sandwiched between her brother and her husband, Frederick Augustus Thorne. Her expression seemed impassive, save for the stray tears that made their way down her pale cheeks from watery blue eyes. The sound hadn't come from her or her stone-faced husband. It had, instead, come from her daughter, seventeen-year-old Emma Sophia Thorne, who stood on her father's other side and leaned into his comforting, one-armed embrace. Emma's tears flowed freely, unlike her father's or her two brothers'. Nineteen-year-old Charles Sebastian Thorne was doing his best to emulate his father's unmoved façade. However, one could see his tears swimming in his hazel eyes. Emma's twin, Josiah Harrison, had squeezed his own eyes shut as though in denial of the sight before him. His expression was one of pain, of anguish, and he flinched whenever a stray drop of rain fell upon him.

Victor wished he could follow Josiah's example, closing his eyes to block out the sight, if not the reality, of the casket before them. He didn't, however. As much as he sometimes hated it, Victor usually preferred taking reality head-on and dealing with it as it came to him.

Reality was one of the reasons Victor was grateful to have his Director there. Arnold Kingston not only represented the Special Intelligence Network on this day, but he could also help keep an eye out for potential trouble. William Andrew Wolfe-Wall had once had many enemies, just as Victor himself did, and it was not unreasonable that one or more might show up if only to make sure The Wall was indeed dead. As not many knew William had had a family, seeing Jacquetta with her husband and children, as well as Victor himself, might be enough to clue them in and place them all in danger.

Such was the life of an agent of SIN, both past and present.

Victor had attempted, back at the start of the funeral, to split his attention between service and watching for enemies, but it had proven an impossibility. He was still somewhat in shock, and not just from his father's unexpected passing. The way William Andrew Wolfe-Wall had died haunted Victor to no end. Having his Director at the funeral relieved him of further burden, and Victor couldn't help but feel grateful.

At last, the minister finished speaking. There were no eulogies, no final words from either Victor, Jacquetta, or the others, as no one wanted to alert any potential enemy watchers to the nature of the attendees' relationships. It was simply over.

Victor felt a gentle hand resting upon his left shoulder, one that prevented him from following his sister and her family over to speak with the minister. He looked over to see his Director holding him in place.

"You have my sincerest condolences for your loss, Agent Wolfe," Arnold said in a quiet voice. "I know that The Wall wasn't just your father but your first teacher and mentor when you joined our ranks. That will make his loss even harder for you to bear, I suspect."

Victor didn't argue with him, even as he spoke. "Thank you, Director. I...I don't doubt that you're right."

Arnold offered him the barest ghost of a smile. "Most of the time, Agent Wolfe, our people are granted up to a week, sometimes two, for bereavement leave. In your case, however, I will extend that time by at least two weeks. You rarely, if ever, take leave of any sort, even when it's been recommended. Given the circumstances of The Wall's passing, I daresay you'll need the time to come to terms with everything and grieve."

Victor almost blinked, taken aback by the offer. "I thank you, Director, but I don't think—"

Arnold held up a hand, forestalling the rest of what Victor had been about to say. "I am not being altruistic, Agent

Wolfe. Not entirely, at least. Again, you will need to come to terms with not only the fact that your father is gone but the manner in which he 'departed.' You have also, again, accrued more than enough vacation time to be granted the additional leave. However, there is also the fact that we are investigating the circumstances surrounding your father's passing, and you cannot be underfoot until we've finished."

"I—" Victor's shoulders slumped as he gave Arnold's words a few moments of consideration. The man was forced to acknowledge and speak the simple truth, and as the head of Victor's agency, he had the power to enforce his edict. Victor also felt as though he had no energy to argue. "Thank you, Director."

"Of course." Arnold inclined his head. "This does not mean we won't be keeping you in the loop of our investigation, Agent Wolfe. It simply means you won't be an active participant."

"I understand." Victor hesitated. "May I ask, though, who the chief suspects are?"

"I think you already know," Arnold said before giving in to the look he received. "We have the Red Sword, of course. He danced with them often enough and spoiled enough of their schemes for them to go after him, even after his retirement. There's also the Xiomar Cartel, as your father was instrumental in putting a good many of their higher-ups into prison, if not eliminating them from this world. The last suspects, at least at the moment, are various members of The Commission, all of whom had cause to want your father removed, even now."

"If I—"

"No, Agent Wolfe." Arnold shook his head, anticipating what Victor had been about to offer. "As much as I appreciate you wanting to help, we need this done by the book." He nodded to where Victor's sister, along with her husband and their children, stood conversing with the minister. "Go. Spend some time with your sister and her family. Take a vacation. Clear your head. Come to terms with your father's passing, and let *us* do our jobs."

"And now I know how some of our other agents have felt when something similar happened to them," Victor muttered before his shoulders slumped. He blew out a saddened breath. "Did you see anyone here?"

Arnold hesitated before admitting, "One person was watching us, but I didn't recognize who it was. If he or she *was* one of our enemies, sent to make sure of things, then they must be new to the ranks of whichever organization sent them."

"Or they could have simply been someone they paid to keep watch." Victor watched as Arnold nodded. "You'll keep me informed?"

"I believe I said I would," Arnold said and nodded once more to where Jacquetta and her family now stood alone. "Go, Agent Wolfe. Be with your family. Help them, and let them help you."

"I—" Victor glanced over at his sister. "I will, Director. Thank you."

"Of course." Arnold followed his glance. "Give my condolences to your sister and her family for me, will you? I want to make one last sweep before I return to the office."

"I will, sir. Thank you for coming."

"You're more than welcome," Arnold said. "The Wall was once one of our best agents, and it's only right that I attend." He offered another small smile. "Take care during your leave, Agent Wolfe."

"Yes, sir."

Victor watched as his Director stepped away, then turned to make his way over to where the others waited. Jacquetta embraced her brother the moment he joined, while her husband, who preferred to be called Rick, gave him a half-hearted smile.

"How're you holding up, Victor?" he asked quietly.

"Doing about as well as expected, Rick," Victor told him, his voice and face both reflecting his sorrow as he returned his sister's embrace. While he and Rick couldn't always be said to get along, they had mutual respect and had even managed to develop something of a friendship. "The Director has offered us his condolences, and he's also given me more than the standard amount of time for leave."

"As well he should," Jacquetta murmured. She had never liked the Special Intelligence Network, hating how it had placed her and her family in near-constant danger during her youth. She had come to hate it even more since her brother had joined its ranks. "You've always done far more than you needed to for them, just like Dad did."

"I know you feel that way, Quet," Victor said. "But—"

"Your decision. I know." She tilted her head to look up at him. "Have you given any more thought about staying with us for a while? It'd be better than you rattling around in that apartment of yours all by yourself."

Her tone suggested there could be only one correct answer, and, truth be told, Victor didn't want to be alone at the moment. "As long as it's all right with you, too, Rick."

"Of course, it's all right," Rick said. "Especially since I'll have to be going back to work in another day or two. This way, neither you nor Quet nor the kids will be left alone."

"Thank you, then," Victor said. "I'll need to grab a few things before I head over. It'll take me about two, maybe two and a half hours to get home, get the stuff I want, and go."

"That's fine, as it'll take us about the same amount of time." Jacquetta gave him a small, pleased smile. "We'll be expecting you about an hour or so after that, then."

Victor nodded, returning her smile with the slightest hint of his own. They talked for another minute before separating, with Victor heading for his small two-door sports coupe. Victor didn't remember much of the drive back to the little, two-bedroom apartment near Philadelphia that he called home. He barely remembered parking, and it felt as though it took everything he had to make the short journey up to his apartment's door.

With slow, almost mechanical steps, the man with the brown hair that was starting to become gray managed to unlock his door and enter the tiny foyer. Somehow, he also managed to get to his living room, where he collapsed onto the small couch.

He still couldn't believe that his father was gone, that

William Andrew Wolfe-Wall wouldn't find a way to come back this time. The pain of it, though still not fully realized, cut more profoundly than any knife or bullet ever could. Losing his mother had been bad enough. To lose his father, too?

Victor breathed deeply, closing his eyes as he leaned back against the couch cushions. While The Dire Wolfe and The Wall hadn't always had the best of relationships, Victor still loved and respected William Wolfe-Wall. His old man had been Victor's hero since Victor was a boy. As Victor aged, he came to see his father as someone to rely on, no matter the issue. Now, The Dire Wolfe slowly realized he would never again be able to see his father, talk to him, and get his advice.

Someone knocked at his front door, startling Victor and derailing those thoughts. His eyes flew open, and he looked over his shoulder, the beginnings of a frown appearing on his lips. His neighbors all believed him to be little more than a businessman who traveled a lot and who, while friendly enough, preferred to keep to himself. As a result, they almost never bothered him, not even when he came home for a 'vacation.'

So, who could be at his door?

He inclined his head, then hauled himself to his feet at another, more insistent knock that seemed sharp yet oddly... delicate, like the tap of a spoon on porcelain. There could be only one way to find out.

Opening the door, he found a woman standing there in a plain navy postal uniform. The uniform itself wasn't wrinkled, but also wasn't spotless, as Victor spied the small, faded stain on her collar. Her satchel bore the weight of long familiarity, and her name tag read *V. Lark* in blocky embroidery.

It was the glasses that caught his attention, in any case. They were cat's eye frames, slim and deliberate, the color of tarnished silver. They had the effect of turning her face into a mask, drawing his eyes to hers, and causing Victor to blink. Her eyes were unusual and piercing, a shade of gray so pale that it was almost translucent.

They reminded him of his mother's eyes, in a way, causing him to stand frozen before her. He even missed the moment she spoke, until she repeated herself.

"Special delivery for a Mister Wolfe?" she said.

Victor blinked again. "Yeah. Uh, that's me."

"Good." She didn't ask for an ID as she handed over the envelope, then tapped the small screen of her tablet. "Signature?"

Her voice had proved warm, but there seemed to be a strange undercurrent as she handed over the tablet. It wasn't nervousness or indifference. Instead, it seemed to be something more measured, something which Victor couldn't—yet— identify.

He shook the fluttering of suspicion away as she offered him the stylus. "I wasn't expecting anything."

She offered up the faintest smile as he signed. "That's usually when it matters the most."

What an odd thing to say. Victor frowned, looking up, only to see her already walking away. He hadn't heard the telltale sound of boots on pavement when she'd moved, and the trees lining the curb soon swallowed up her silhouette.

How in the hell had he missed the moment she'd turned to leave?

His lips became a thin line. Obviously, the events of the morning had clouded his thinking. *No wonder the Director insisted I take a vacation. I definitely need one.*

Breathing deep, he glanced back down at the envelope and froze. His eyes became fixed on the name of the sender.

W. A. W-Wolfe.

He had no memory of shutting the door or of moving back to his couch. He would never remember the moment he sat back down.

Instead, the envelope in his hand held the full weight of his attention. Under almost any other set of circumstances, Victor would have exercised far more caution than he did now in opening up an apparent piece of mail. He hadn't gained the high rank he now held in the Special Intelligence Network by being stupid. Victor Wolfe had many enemies, including some who were supposed to be his colleagues, and he had no desire to become their victim.

But, coming as this letter did right after the funeral of its sender? Victor would later believe he could be forgiven for tearing it open without so much as holding it up to a light source to see if it actually *was* a letter and not something more deadly.

Fortune favored him, however, in the sense that it did indeed happen to be nothing more than a letter and, to Victor's surprise, a key. With hands that were beginning to tremble, Victor unfolded the letter and began to read the last message his father and fellow agent of SIN had written to him.

Henry,

Well, you'd prefer it if I didn't call you that, but it was the name your mother and I gave to you, so I hope you'll forgive your old man his quirks. No doubt, if you're reading this, then I've shuffled off this mortal coil, most likely at the hands of my enemies.

Don't worry about them, in any case. They'll get what's coming to them soon enough, and they aren't the reason I've taken the trouble of writing this. What Katherine kept from you is.

I know you've wondered for some time about why she left. Perhaps you even wondered where she was at my funeral, if I happened to have one. There's no easy way for me to put this, Henry. Katherine couldn't come to my funeral because I had already gone to hers.

No, it wasn't cancer or anything like that. It wasn't a natural death at all.

Katherine, like her parents and brothers before her, was murdered. Bringing the bastards who killed them to justice was part of the reason she left. It's part of why I was forced to go, and I have no doubt it was also partly responsible for my untimely demise. Katherine's family was stepping on some well-connected toes in her hometown. When she dug into it, she found out the truth about what happened to them and to others with her shared heritage. With the knowledge she now possessed, the Powers That Be couldn't let her live. Unfortunately for them, she'd already shared what she'd found with me.

The key I included in this letter belongs to a safety deposit box that I registered at our favorite hometown bank under the name of Robert Pupp. Ask for Mister Eppes when you go, use that name, and show him that key. It's how you'll gain entry—Eppes owes me, and it's how we set it up, should the worst ever happen.

The safety deposit box to which the key belongs contains copies of some of the evidence Katherine gathered, along with other, more personal items. The originals, the remainder of what she had, plus what I added, are being held by a group of trusted friends. They'll let you see it, maybe even read you into everything if you impress them, but they will not let you have it.

No doubt you're wondering why I didn't go to the Special Intelligence Network, or why I don't want you to go to them with this information? The answer is simple. I did go to SIN. I tried to get their backing for an investigation, only to discover that our agency is more likely to confiscate and destroy the evidence than to be of any help.

I learned far too late just how deep the rot of corruption goes, Henry. It's in SIN, other agencies, corporations, entire organizations, and networks. If you take this up as I did, Henry, then you'll have to be very careful and not just for yourself.

But for your son.

Yes, Henry. You and Katherine had a son. I never agreed with her decision to keep him from you, but she was adamant that you shouldn't have to give up your dreams in order to play house with her. She was sure it would cause resentment, no matter what I said to convince her otherwise. Nonetheless, you knew Katherine far better than I did, and you know her stubbornness knew no bounds.

I should have told you about him right after her death, but, at the time, I'm afraid I was a little preoccupied with rescuing him and then keeping him both safe and alive. He witnessed his mother's murder and what those bastards planned to do to him... I could not allow that to happen.

The blood on my hands from that rescue was well-earned. Once Robbie was in a place of safety, I made the mistake of going to SIN for help.

As I said, I never knew its core was so tainted. My going to the Director almost ended with the evidence Katherine had collected being taken from me. It also almost ended with her son being handed back over to the very people who had killed her. I couldn't let that happen any more than I could let them destroy the evidence of their sister agency's wrongdoing.

Fortunately, Robbie had convinced me to take some precautions.

Your son has quite the suspicious streak, Henry. I can't really blame him, considering where and how he was raised, not to mention what had happened, and that suspicious nature he's got served us both well that day. Oh, SIN made sure to fire my ass. They probably thought I'd roll over with the threatened loss of my pension, only to make it official when I refused. A few weak threats were also made regarding you and your sister, and I didn't win any friends when I pointed out how quickly that would raise suspicions from my allies, who would no doubt start to investigate. It's why I was allowed to walk out that day with the evidence safe and secure, and with enough time to get both Robbie and myself out of the country.

Our family's wealth and my investments kept us solvent and alive. I continued keeping Robbie out of our enemies' hands and kept them from learning just who Robbie's father happened to be. Believe me when I say, son, our enemies would love to see him and everyone even remotely connected to him dead, even now. Well, they probably wouldn't kill him until after they learn just where all the evidence is and who it's with. His guardians are doing their best to make sure no one can step even a single _foot_ near Robbie without every alarm in their city going off.

But only a fool believes in absolutes. It's why I held off on telling you anything until now. I didn't want to risk Robbie's life or yours any more than necessary.

The Department of Mid-Western Island Affairs _hates_

the fact that they've been stonewalled up to this point in regard to Robert Kincaid, and they're doing everything they can to bring those proverbial walls down. So far, they've been held off, but his home city's delicate power balance could shift and bring the entire island down around his ears.

Again, <u>if</u> you pursue this the way I have, you'll have to be highly guarded. Many people like what Island Affairs can get for them, and they won't appreciate someone with even your record trying to expose them. That said, I know for a fact that Robbie would love to finally get to know his father. It's one thing he's wanted in life more than having his mother back. I've done my best by him, but I fear I've made a poor substitute.

Regardless of what you decide, though, I do ask two things.

One—try to keep the existence of both the information in this letter and the key I've given you to yourself. You may share it with your sister, as her husband may be of some help to you in this, but unless there is someone else you feel you can trust <u>completely</u> (with the exception of any agents of SIN), then do not take the chance. SIN is not to be trusted. Not at all. The same can be said for those within any alphabet soup agency you care to name. Yes, the corruption infests many corners of our government. Yes, they will stop at absolutely nothing to destroy the evidence and your son. He has become the constant irritation they want removed.

Two—regarding Robbie. Please, don't believe everything you might read or hear about him. Not everything is as it seems with the life he now leads. Keep him <u>safe</u>, if you can.

And keep yourself safe, too.

Dad

Nemini Crede.

"Trust no one," Victor whispered the translation, which

confirmed that the letter was a real one, before supplying the rest of what William Wolfe-Wall had been so fond of saying. "Verify everything."

The question, of course, was *how*.

His mind whirled as shock, anger, and grief all vied for dominance. The idea that his father would have turned on the agency he'd once served to the detriment of everything else, the same agency that Victor himself now served, stymied him, but that somehow seemed less astonishing in comparison to the fact that Katherine, *his* Katherine, was dead and that he, Victor Wolfe, had *fathered* a *child* with her.

He stood, abruptly restless, and headed into his bedroom. Given all of the events of the day, plus what he had just learned, Victor found that he needed to hit something. Right *now*.

Dropping the letter, together with its envelope and the key it had contained, onto the nightstand beside his bed, he went to stand before the punching bag that sat in the corner of his bedroom. Secure in the fact that he was alone, Victor cut loose.

He didn't pull his punches, either, as he usually would have. In fact, he barely registered the fact that he was hitting the bag at all. Instead, he focused on Katherine and his unknown child.

To be honest, it had been some time since Victor had permitted himself to even think of *her*. Even now, in his mind's eye, he could still see Katherine Rose Kincaid as she'd been, the last time he had seen her. Her fiery red hair had been loose and dancing about in the breeze. She'd been laughing at some joke he'd told her, although her blue-green eyes had shimmered with the sadness of the knowledge that he would soon leave.

Victor hadn't thought their separation would last for very long. Just a year or two. That's how long he'd been told that it would take back then for him to complete his apprenticeship as a field agent for the Special Intelligence Network. Then, once Katherine had finished her apprenticeship, he and she would be back together again.

Except that it hadn't worked out that way. By the time Victor had returned, Katherine had gone. Resigned from the initiates' program due to an unspecified medical condition and fled to who knew where. Victor had wanted to search for her, to find and help her.

His father, however, had forbidden him to do so.

Victor hadn't understood it back then. Now? When the letter revealed that Katherine had had a son—*his* son?

For a man who had all but given up on ever having a wife and child of his own, in part due to the nature of his profession but also because he had never found another woman who could compare with his Katherine, the shock of being told, even by letter, that he had a child rendered Victor almost incapable of even the most basic thoughts.

He raged at the universe for having separated them, then at his father for having kept them that way. Why had William Wolfe-Wall allowed it?

But had he?

The question caused Victor to all but freeze in his hits as

he recalled a portion of his father's letter. *She was adamant that you shouldn't have to give up your dreams in order to play house with her. She was sure it would cause resentment, no matter what I said to convince her otherwise. Nonetheless, you knew Katherine far better than I did, and you know her stubbornness knew no bounds.*

He barked out a humorless laugh. Oh, yes. Victor well remembered Katherine's tenacity. Hers had equaled his own in many ways, and they'd had a fair number of arguments because of it.

Memories once again tickled at the edges of his mind, but Victor pushed them all back in favor of what was, for him, the biggest revelation. He had a son, *a child.*

If the information had come from anyone else, Victor would never have believed it. Still, it wasn't just anyone who had written the letter he held. It had been his *father,* and Victor felt as if he had no choice but to believe.

The idea elated him. It also terrified him. There had been a time when Victor had dreamed of becoming a father, a time when he had believed he would have Katherine at his side not only as his partner in SIN but as his wife and as the mother of his dream children, but that had been before she'd left. That had been before the reality of being an agent of SIN had crashed down upon him, and he'd learned that family, while desired, was often a danger.

He took a deep breath. The life of a covert operative could be a perilous one. It didn't matter what sort of agency one served; an operative tended to make some genuinely nasty enemies. Victor was no exception, any more than his father had been, and to realize that he now had a *child* who could be used against him was quickly accentuated by a shot of genuine, unadulterated fear lancing through him.

What could happen if the word got out that The Dire Wolfe had a child? Had family? Would Victor's enemies attempt to find his son and hurt him in order to avenge themselves for Victor's actions against them? Or would they try to use Victor's son against him to lure Victor to his death? Or would they do something else, something that could end up pitting him against his son, his child?

Victor didn't know, just as he didn't know how Katherine could have kept something like this from him, how his father could have done so!

I never agreed with her decision to keep him from you.

That single line from the letter resurfaced in his memory, and a little of Victor's sudden, icy anger towards his father melted away. Katherine had no doubt extracted his father's promise not to say anything, and William Wolfe-Wall had always done his best to keep the promises he made. Between that and Katherine's belief that Victor would have resented her if she'd made him 'play house' with her...

A small, sad smile formed on his lips as he whispered, "I wouldn't have, Katherine. I swear it to you."

His father had managed to juggle somehow being an agent of SIN with having a family, after all. Victor would have done his best to emulate William Wolfe-Wall's example.

He just wished Katherine had given him the chance. Perhaps he could have even prevented whatever had happened to her if she had allowed him to stay with her.

But just what *had* happened? Victor knew that Katherine had been close to her family. They had come to the university she'd attended on more than one occasion, and she'd gone back home almost every summer and winter break. To find out that her mother and her father, along with her older and younger brother, were *all* gone? That an *entire* family had been wiped out?

Why? And why would William Wolfe-Wall have believed that it would have contributed to his own passing?

Silver-gray eyes flashed, grief once again mixing with the anger. Katherine had supposedly given Victor's father evidence, which he claimed that the Special Intelligence Network had attempted to confiscate and destroy. William Wolfe-Wall had also contended that SIN had even tried to turn over Katherine's son, *Victor's* son, to the same people who had killed her.

Again, why? How could they or anyone else have even considered such a thing?

Victor didn't want to believe it. Yes, he knew that SIN didn't have the best of reputations. Granted, they weren't as bad as some of the other alphabet soup agencies out there, but there was a definite reason the Special Intelligence Network had the reputation it did. Still, the idea that they would have handed over a *child* to the same people who had murdered said child's mother boggled Victor's mind. It was unfathomable!

He struck at the bag one last time, unleashing raw, angry energy into it. To his shock, the bag all but disintegrated before him.

Victor stood, staring at the broken mess before him, before unexpected pain called his attention to his hands. The knuckles of both were raw, red, and even bruised. How long, he wondered, had he been there?

A quick glance at the time caused his eyebrows to rocket upward. It had been a full forty-five minutes since he'd last glanced at a clock. Jacquetta would most likely have expected him to be on the road already, heading over.

Well, hopefully she'd forgive him for running a bit late. Victor breathed out a quiet, calming sigh before deciding to clean everything up, including himself.

Close to twenty minutes later, after disposing of the badly-abused punching bag, Victor stepped into the shower. The rain of water striking his exposed skin acted like a balm, allowing him to refocus on something more pleasant—namely, his unknown son.

He had a nickname for the boy, as well as an alias. What else did he know?

To Victor's chagrin, the answer was almost nothing. He only knew that *Robbie* was in danger and that he could make it worse.

But what was Robbie like? How old did he happen to be? Given how long ago it had been since Victor had last shared Katherine's bed, shower, transportation, and other things, Robbie had to be in his twenties. That meant he wasn't a boy but a young man. What did he look like? Did Robbie take more after

44

Victor or after Katherine? What did he like? What *didn't* he like? What were his favorite foods, and which foods were avoided? What did he want to do for fun? What was his goal in life, and what were the plans to achieve such goals?

And just what had William Wolfe-Wall meant when he'd cautioned Victor to 'not believe everything' about whatever Robbie was doing? That everything was not 'as it seems'?

Again, Victor didn't yet know. He planned to find out, but would his son genuinely *want* to meet with him? Yes, Victor's father had seemed confident, but Victor couldn't help feeling the opposite. Why would *his son* wish to meet with a man who could upend his life, however it happened? Who could put the young man in extreme danger, maybe even put his actual life at risk?

Except that again, according to the letter in Victor's hands, his son's life was *already* at risk. It had been in danger, most likely from the moment Katherine had started looking into the things that had cost her her life.

And, somehow, the Special Intelligence Network had contributed to that risk. William Wolfe-Wall had claimed that they had gone so far as to fire Victor's father from his position in their agency—something Victor had never known about. He had, instead, always been told that William Wolfe-Wall had finally accepted retirement, not that he'd been forced out!

"Why the hell didn't you *tell* me, Dad?" he finally voiced the question, placing one hand against the wall as he bowed his head. *"Why?* I could have *helped* you somehow!"

He had no idea about the length of time he had stood

there in the shower, letting the water hit his back and then his face. If a few stray tears happened to mix in... Well, who would notice?

At last, with the water having turned cold some time ago, Victor stepped out. He scrubbed at his face before heading back into his bedroom to change.

Dropping down onto his bed shortly after pulling on a pair of simple blue jeans and an old t-shirt, Victor paused in putting on his socks and a pair of older boots to stare at the letter and the key that had come with it. He had so many questions, and it seems there was only one way to begin answering them.

He stood as soon as he finished tying his boots' laces, ready to head out the door to pay the bank in question a visit, only to stop at the sight of the digital clock that was also on his nightstand. No bank he knew of stayed open past five o'clock, and it now happened to be almost a half-hour after that. Just the journey to his hometown would take the better part of two and a half hours, or even three.

And wasn't he supposed to be heading over to Jacquetta's at that moment?

"Tomorrow, then," he whispered to himself. "I'll go tomorrow."

For now, he had some packing to do. He started for his closet, only to be waylaid by the sound of his phone ringing. Victor blinked and headed back over to the nightstand. Looking at the number, he answered it.

"Hey, Quet," he greeted his sister in a rough voice. "I'm not on the road yet. I thought I would be, but—"

"It's fine, Vic," Jacquetta assured him quietly, in an unusual tone. Victor almost frowned. He expected the sadness, but now he thought he also heard disbelief. "Will you be heading over here soon, though?"

"Planning to, yes." He hesitated, glancing down at the letter and the key he still held. "I might need to talk to you and your husband about something when I get there."

"Oh?"

He could tell her interest had been piqued, but again, there was something else in her voice. Victor almost asked if she, too, had gotten a letter from their father before deciding he could wait to find out. His phone lines weren't secured, after all, and the last thing he wanted right now was to give anyone from his or any other agency a heads-up if they happened to be listening in.

"Yes," he said at last. "I'll fill you both in after I get to your house."

"Sounds good," she said before she attempted to lighten her voice. "What would you like for dinner, by the way? None of us feels like cooking, so we're going to order something."

"Whatever you want to order will be fine by me, Quet."

"So you'd like some creamed spinach, steamed broccoli, and Brussels sprouts?"

"Quet!"

"Relax, big brother." She laughed a bit at the abrupt fear in Victor's voice. "I wouldn't do that to you. Not unless you *really* upset me." Another laugh escaped at his exaggerated sigh of relief. "I'll let you get on the road. See you soon, Vic."

Hanging up, Victor resumed the journey to his closet. It was a short trip, but it allowed him to regain control over his emotions and put on a stoic mask. Pulling out a single suitcase, he went through the motions of selecting enough clothing for at least a week's stay at his sister's place. Victor didn't know how long he'd be over there, but that didn't matter. Getting the answers he now so desperately needed did.

Chapter Two: Disclosures

On the Road to the Thorne Residence

Victor felt his mind whirling as he headed out to the suburbs of Philadelphia. While most of his thoughts were on the letter and the key he'd received, a small and insidious part of his brain had turned to what Arnold Kingston had said to him.

Had it been simple kindness, combined with efficiency, that prompted his director to grant him an extended leave? Going over what Arnold had said produced no proverbial red flags. Still, after having read his father's letter, Victor couldn't help but question what his director had said. If the highest levels of the Special Intelligence Network were indeed compromised, then he had to wonder if his extra leave had been given so that Victor himself could be watched more easily.

He didn't know. Not yet. Victor knew it could be that his father had simply become a bit more paranoid as he'd aged, but he'd been killed. Murdered. *Was* it really paranoia, Victor had to wonder, when 'they' really were out to get you?

And just who was responsible for his father's death? Arnold had listed the three organizations that were most likely to have had a hand in it. The Red Sword was a group of international terrorists that had become infamous for striking without prominent warning or pattern. The Xiomar Cartel was a criminal enterprise that spanned the globe and gave governments fits whenever it appeared. The Commission was a league of criminal powers that operated much like the American version of *La Cosa Nostra* once did, while remaining so far back in the shadows that some doubted the group even existed. Victor's father had dealt with all three at several points in his career, and each organization would have had reason to want The Wall gone, even after he'd left SIN.

But were any of them, or any of the others William Wolfe-Wall had danced with on occasion, in reality responsible for what had happened? Had it, instead, been someone far closer to home? Someone within SIN itself, or maybe one of their sister agencies?

Again, Victor didn't know. The letter he'd received had given him ideas but nothing concrete, at least not yet. Perhaps when he visited the safety deposit box spoken about, he'd find the evidence, but until then, speculation accomplished nothing.

Victor blew out a breath. He didn't want to take chances. Not with this.

So what *did* he know? The Special Intelligence Network, like any other government agency, faced a number of risks, including double and triple-agents, power-hungry superiors, Congressional oversight committees, and slashed funding. Victor knew that many things were often kept concealed, if not outright buried. Between that and what William Wolfe-Wall had alleged, Victor knew it was best to keep what he knew to himself, at least until he knew for sure whom he could trust.

His eyes slid to his rear-view mirror out of habit, and abruptly, Victor frowned. The car behind him had been there for some time. Not quite an abnormal amount, but close enough to warrant some suspicion.

A look at the driver set off a muted set of alarm bells in Victor's mind. He'd seen the man behind him before.

But where?

Before he could think further, the car turned right onto a side street. Victor might have breathed a sigh of relief had another car not quickly replaced the first. The female driver also seemed familiar, though Victor couldn't place her any more than he could remember the first one.

Several streets passed before she, too, turned off and was replaced. Victor's lips became a thin line. His eyes narrowed at the sight of his new follower.

Seth Yago was a newer agent of SIN, just barely out of training, and had been assigned to one of Victor's former partners for mentoring. Victor had spoken with him several times during the past few months and knew him well enough to recognize him on sight. What was he doing, following Victor and apparently trying his best not to be noticed as he allowed another car to slip in between his and Victor's own?

Well, Victor knew of at least two quick and efficient ways to find out. A quick glance at his car's fuel gauge made him smile. No one would suspect him of anything if he stopped off at a gas station, would they?

A few intersections later, Victor pulled into one that also had a small convenience store. Parking his car next to an open pump, he got out and headed inside, not only to pay for some gas but also to hopefully lure in his current tail. Victor didn't think it would work, and if it didn't, he'd make a single, simple phone call.

Much as he had halfway expected, Seth did not follow him inside, even though he found a nearby parking spot. From what Victor knew, the kid had all the makings of a good agent of SIN, and this seemed to prove it.

But what was he doing, following Victor around? Well, if Seth wasn't going to provide the answers himself, then Victor had a call to make.

Several minutes later, as he waited for his car's tank to fill, Victor took out his cell phone and dialed. A few transfers and connections later, he heard Arnold Kingston's voice.

"You are not coming back to work, Victor," Arnold chuckled as he spoke. "Not unless it's a world-ending emergency."

Victor chuckled back, knowing he had more than earned his reputation as a workaholic. "No, sir. That's not why I'm calling. I do, however, have a question."

"Oh? Fire away, then."

"Are the people following me doing so on your orders? Or should I be asking for backup?"

Arnold groaned. "I *told* them to be discreet."

Victor almost smiled and kept his tone deliberately light. There weren't many reasons for his director to order agents to watch another agent, he knew. Given what his father's letter had said, however?

"You may want to have them look up the word, then, sir," he said. "So, is this a training exercise for some of our newer agents? Or is there something more going on?"

"Officially? Training, something from what you've told me, they definitely need."

Victor breathed out a near-inaudible sigh and tried to keep his tone carefully modulated so as not to betray the suspicions he now had. "And *un*officially?"

Silence answered him for a moment before he heard a tired sigh echo over the phone line. "There's no use in trying to keep anything from you, is there?"

"Sir?" Victor felt the corners of his lips turn down at the beginning of another frown.

Arnold sighed again. "It's just a precaution, Victor. There are concerns that The Wall's death would be a beginning."

If he hadn't read his father's final letter, Victor might have been touched by this pretense of worry for his safety and survival. Still, he played along, knowing how he would be expected to react. "Have threats been made?"

"Not in so many words," Arnold said. "But you and he... While most were unaware of your familial relationship, some *did* know, and it's been theorized that one of your father's enemies would like to make a clean sweep."

Fear of a different sort swept through Victor's spine. A 'clean sweep' of William Wolfe-Wall's family wouldn't mean *just* him.

"My sister—" He started to say.

"I know, Victor." Arnold proved swift to reassure him. "I'll be having someone watch her and her family as well. If anything happens, she and her family will be protected."

Victor blew out a breath of heartfelt relief. "Thank you, sir."

"Of course. Like I said, too, this is just a precaution. Again, most did not know about your relationship with The Wall. Even fewer people knew he had a daughter as well as a son, especially since she chose not to follow in his footsteps."

The way I did. Victor almost nodded, knowing it was the truth.

Yet, there was *some*thing in Arnold's voice that did not sit right with Victor. He couldn't put his finger on what it was, but he knew he couldn't ignore it. Victor had learned long ago to rely on his instincts. He'd also known Arnold Kingston for a long time. While he considered the current Director of SIN a friend, Victor had learned long ago not to trust him. Not completely. Arnold Kingston could lie right to someone's face, and that person would never know about it until it was too late.

Not unless Arnold wanted them to know.

Victor would assuredly have to postpone paying a visit to his father's *favorite* hometown bank. He hated the idea, but what else could he do?

The beginnings of a plan formed in his mind. While he wanted and needed to find out what was in his father's safety deposit box, he knew he couldn't take the risk while he was being watched. Who knew how long that might last? However, the thought of his sister brought back a portion of his father's letter.

You may share it with your sister, as her husband may be

Her husband. Rick Thorne. A man who was widely believed to be one of the best private investigators in the business.

The corners of Victor's lips curved back upward, although he made sure his tone held nothing but the right amount of concern. "I was planning on following your advice to visit with her and her family for a bit. I'd planned to stay for a week, but I can always stretch it out, so long as they don't mind."

Arnold's voice contained more than a hint of relief. "It might be wise, and it would certainly make things easier. I can assign the ones I have watching you to her as well, along with their mentors."

"You could, yes," Victor agreed, swallowing back another sigh of relief before a potential complication struck him. Seth's mentor was, again, one of Victor's former partners, whom Victor himself trusted, but what about the others? "But who are they? How do you know if we can trust them with this information?"

A flash of rare humor entered Arnold's tone. "You mean to say you wouldn't trust your former partners? Especially when you told them this information yourself?"

"My former partners?" Victor grinned abruptly. Were they *all* being mentored by Victor's former partners? "You mean you dragged Maria, Ron, and Phillipe out of the field for this?"

"Who better to keep watch on you? And who better to help them train their recruits?" Arnold chuckled. "I have no doubt you, your sister, and her family will give them all the training they need. *Especially* those children of Jacquetta's."

Victor blinked and began to chuckle as well. It seemed the reputation of his sister's family preceded them. Victor could only hope they would not end up on the most wanted wall one day.

"I do not doubt that they'll be delighted to help," he said.

"Of course they will." Arnold chuckled back. "Those three take after their grandfather a little *too* much sometimes, if you ask me. Could you please do me one favor, though? Tell those young people not to scar those new operatives of mine too badly? The idea that a trio of teenagers could run rings around them might make them rethink a few of their life choices."

"I can try, but you know probably as well as I do that they'd take it as a challenge."

"No doubt." Arnold chuckled again before seeming to sober. "Do you know if their father is handling any cases at the moment?"

"I do not," Victor said. *At least, not yet.* "If he is, I can tell him to be extra careful, but you know him, sir. Anything short of an apocalypse won't stop him from working a case he's accepted. And I'm not entirely sure an apocalypse would slow him down either."

"Yes. Unfortunately, I do know."

Arnold's voice held a resigned note. Victor understood why, too. The Special Intelligence Network had attempted on innumerable occasions to recruit Victor's brother-in-law but had been rebuffed each time. While Frederick Augustus Thorne might agree to do the Special Intelligence Network a favor every once in a while, he would never belong to them.

"See if you can't explain things to him," Arnold said at length. "Perhaps it will help convince him to remain home in order to protect his family if the need should arise. We don't currently have the people to spare to help keep watch over him otherwise. Barring that, it may be a good thing if you can remain with your sister and her children for a time."

"I have no problem with that, sir," Victor said. "I'm on my way over there now, in fact."

"Very good. I'll let you go on with your drive, then, and will have some *mostly* kind words with the people I assigned to watch you."

"Yes, sir." Under other circumstances, Victor might have pitied Seth and the other two who had tailed him. Still, it was better that they learn the needed lessons now rather than wait for the day they might be captured by one of SIN's many enemies. Given what Arnold had said earlier about training them, Victor could not hide his smirk. "I'll let my sister and her family know what you'd like us to do, too, sir. Is there anything special you'd like us to impart to our students?"

Arnold groaned again. "You're going to let your niece and nephews have entirely too much fun with them. Aren't you?"

"It's a definite possibility, sir."

Another groan echoed over his cell phone's speaker. "Just don't break them, Agent Wolfe. *Please.*"

Chuckling to himself, Victor ended the call. A minute later, he was back on the road, with Seth still following him.

Just over half an hour later, Victor drove his car up the driveway to his sister's house. The large colonial-style farmhouse, which came complete with a wrap-around porch, a stone front, and white fencing along the property's extensive borderline, had been a gift from William Wolfe-Wall to his daughter when she'd married Frederick Thorne. While close enough to the city to let the Thorne Family enjoy many of the benefits that came from city living, they were also far enough away to keep them safe, at least in theory.

That last was, for both Jacquetta and her husband, the most important. Frederick Thorne's profession, however, sometimes made that an impossibility. Again, he was one of the best private investigators in the business. He was also a former Philadelphia police detective. He'd made any number of enemies in the course of his career, and some of those enemies wouldn't hesitate to track him down and attempt to use his family against him.

Of course, those few who had tried had quickly come to regret their decision. While Victor's sister had chosen not to follow in her father's footsteps, she had still learned as much as she could from him and could more than take care of herself most of the time. William Wolfe-Wall had also taught her children how to defend themselves, which meant that any would-be kidnappers were in for the shock of their lives if they tried to take any one, two, or even all three of Frederick and Jacquetta's children to use as bargaining chips against their parents.

Dimly, Victor wondered if his father had also taught

Katherine's son before shaking his head as he parked his car outside the front door. If William Wolfe-Wall had taught his daughter's children, why wouldn't he have taught his son's child? Especially given what had ultimately happened to Katherine.

Exiting his car, he grabbed his suitcase and made his way up to the front door. Before he could raise a hand to knock, it opened to reveal his sister.

Jacquetta once again moved to embrace her brother, and he put down his suitcase to accept it willingly. There could be no mistaking their relationship as brother and sister. Both had brown hair, just starting to go gray. Both were on the taller side and had a naturally athletic build. They both had oval faces, similar chins, and even had the same kind of nose.

Jacquetta, however, had blue eyes instead of gray. She also possessed a more fiery temper than her brother. Jacquetta ruled her household with an iron grip, usually wrapped in a velvet glove. It had often amused Victor to witness how her husband, who had dealt with some of the worst dregs that humanity had to offer, would go out of his way to avoid Jacquetta's notice whenever she happened to be angry about something.

Right now, though, her normal fire had been doused with the tears Victor could see still swimming in Jacquetta's eyes. It was the reason he returned her embrace with equal ferocity.

Only when they separated did Jacquetta look up at her brother's face. She inclined her head a moment after.

"Are you all right?"

The question, simple and expected though it was, still

froze Victor. His face began to tighten, the mask of an agent of SIN slipping back into place.

Jacquetta stopped it with a gentle smile that spoke of her own sorrow. "I'm hurting, too, Vic."

His lips thinned as he fought back sudden tears, and he leaned into another, more comforting embrace. "I know."

"Come inside," she told him quietly when they again separated. "We ordered pizza, and we're all waiting in the living room."

He didn't argue; he just allowed her to lead him. When they appeared in the archway, Rick stood up from where he'd been sitting and crossed the short distance to greet them.

"It's good to see you again, Victor," he said, eyeing his brother-in-law and seeing the emotions that swirled within Victor's silver eyes. "Quet's prepared the guest room already."

"Thank you," Victor said, his eyes flicking over to where he could see the three younger faces of his niece and nephews. "Hey, kids."

"Hey, Uncle Vic."

Only Emma spoke, although Charlie and Josiah both waved. They had each changed from their more formal clothing into jeans, t-shirts, and sweatpants, but all still wore somber expressions.

Rick glanced between them and his wife, then spoke. "Why don't we sit down in my office for a bit, Victor? You, me, and Quet. Kids, do us a favor and listen for the door. Let us know when the pizza gets here."

"Will do, Dad." Charlie said, nodding in agreement with his brother and sister.

A few moments later, they were ensconced in Rick's home office. The dark-paneled room didn't seem all that special to anyone just glancing in. It had filing cabinets, a pair of tall, older-looking bookcases crammed full of binders and books, a normal-looking desk with an equally normal-looking computer, telephone, desk lamp, and an all-in-one fax machine, scanner, and printer.

The office, however, had a secret. It was a Sensitive Compartmented Information Facility, or SCIF, room.

Most police departments and private investigators would never have had access to such a place. Only a few government officials, military personnel, and certain intelligence agencies were supposed to possess them, but, again, Rick Thorne had performed several favors for the Special Intelligence Network and other similar agencies. They had made his office into a SCIF room not only to pay for his services but also so he could continue assisting them occasionally. Now, secure in the knowledge that no one could listen in or otherwise discover what he had to say, Victor intended to use the office to ask for his family's help.

The question was where to begin. With the fact that the family would be watched over the next several days to make sure that no one would try to murder them, the way William Wolfe-Wall had been? Or with the letter that Victor had received, the one that announced the existence of his son?

Jacquetta gave him the answer by asking a question. "Did

you get a letter from Dad?"

Victor blinked, then looked at his sister in surprise. "You got one as well?"

"We both did," Rick said. "As did the kids." He took in Victor's shocked look and reached into the topmost center drawer of his desk. "Take a look."

Victor picked up the one addressed to his sister first. It was shorter than his letter had been, but that didn't matter nearly as much as the fact that it was their father's words.

> My Dearest Quetta,
>
> First of all, I want to thank you. For what, I hear you ask? I thank you for simply being my daughter. It means more to me than you might know, even with you having a girl of your own. Second, and more importantly, for being you constantly and unapologetically. You have a gift, Quetta, for being able to stick to your principles, no matter what backlash or punishment you might face or whatever the prevailing situation might be. You take after your mother in that, and it was something I've always admired about her and you, my girl. You will continue being able to stick to your guns no matter what in the coming days, weeks, and, hopefully, years ahead.
>
> Trust me, your gift will be needed.
>
> Bad things are coming, Quetta. I know that for a fact. You and yours, together with so many others around you, will face significant changes and challenges before much longer, but I know you. Even when barely out of diapers, you had a tenacity most did not.
>
> You've also always had compassion. Remember that kitten you found back when you were five? It was hurt, sick, and clawed you up something fierce when you tried to help it, but you refused to give up on it. You insisted we take it to the

62

vet and try to save it. You dedicated yourself, at five, to its care and refused to give up on it. You became its mother in every way imaginable. Miss Fluff repaid you for that when you won her over by becoming your protector—much to the dismay of me, your mother, and your brother at times.

Victor looked up at his sister. "I hated that cat, you know."

"I do." She inclined her head, smiling softly. "But I loved her." She nodded at the letter. "Finish it."

You'll need both that strength of will and that ability to be kind even in the direst of circumstances in the years ahead. As I said, bad things are coming, and your family is going to need those qualities of yours to withstand everything. Your brother, your husband, and all of the kids will need you to remind them of what's essential so they don't lose themselves in the coming battles. Your role will no doubt be critical to winning the fight ahead.

That said, there will be some good surprises, too, a few of which you'll be finding out in the not-too-distant future. Never forget that I love you, Quetta. I am also so very proud of you. You were as much my Light as your mother was, and I'm not lying when I say you brought me back, time and again, from the darkness. Be the Lioness of Light that I know you to be. Guide your family, care for them, and give them the strength and hope they'll need in the war ahead.

Manet Petram Qui Salvet

Your Loving Father

Nemini Crede. Quin Omnia.

Victor felt tears sting his eyes, but he shook his head, blinking them away to focus on the letter he had in his hand. Were bad things coming?

The memory of what Victor had read in his letter resurfaced. Between the accusations of corruption, murder, and other crimes, one could indeed say that 'bad things' were coming, especially if Victor took up where his father had left off.

And when he informed them of the existence of *his son*...

Well, there could be no time like the present. Victor took a steadying breath, then looked up.

"You remember how I said I had something to talk to you about?" he said. "Back when you called just before I left to come here?"

Jacquetta nodded. Rick thought a moment, then inclined his head.

"Quet told me something to that effect," he said. "And you said you got a letter of your own?"

"I did." Victor drew in another deep and uneasy breath. How, he wondered, would his sister and her husband react to this? "In it, Dad says that I have a *son*."

Jacquetta rocked back in her seat with a gasp. Rick stared at him in equal shock before realization dawned in his eyes.

"That's what he meant," he murmured.

Victor stared back at him in sudden disbelief. Jacquetta looked from him to her husband.

"Your letter?" she asked. "The surprise Dad mentioned?"

Rick nodded and slid another letter over to where Victor now sat. "Read it."

With hands that were beginning to tremble, Victor

picked the piece of paper up. Again, like Jacquetta's, it was shorter than the one Victor had received. The words that had been written, however, struck him in a way the other two had not.

Frederick,

I know you hate that name, but let me use it this once.

When you first approached me to ask for my permission to marry my daughter, I'll admit I wasn't thrilled. I used my connections to vet you thoroughly when you first started dating, and while you mainly were clean (we won't discuss your short time in Vegas), I still had my doubts.

Victor looked up with raised eyebrows, momentarily letting himself become distracted. "Vegas?"

Rick almost smirked, even as he rolled his eyes. "We don't talk about that."

"No." Jacquetta's iron tone was enough to dissuade any more questions. "We do not."

"Ah." Victor nodded, acknowledging his sister's warning, and returned to Rick's letter. "Okay."

That said, I knew Quetta's mind was made up, so I gave you what you asked while preparing for any fallout.

You surprised me then by remaining so steadfast. You've become Quetta's shield, and your relationship with her reminds me greatly of the one I shared with my wife—never have I been so glad to have my doubts proven wrong.

Again, Victor looked up, this time inquisitive. "I didn't know he didn't approve of you at first."

Rick shrugged and glanced at Jacquetta with a small smile. "I'm just glad I changed his mind. Read on, Victor, and try to finish before the pizza gets here."

"Right."

You're an intelligent man, Rick, and you're also usually a good judge of character. Yes, you've made mistakes, but you consistently work to rectify them once you're aware of them, and you never give up on the essential things.

That is why this letter, while not as emotional as the others I'll write, is the most important.

You are the Keeper and Defender of Truth. You are both constant and consistent in seeking out the reality of a matter, no matter what it is. Granted, that's part of the job you've chosen as your career, but it's also become one of your most defining characteristics. Your desire to seek out what is evil and expose its truth will become one of the most critical talents we have in the coming fight. In the weeks, months, and even years ahead, you will find out many things that have been hidden away. I am entrusting you with ensuring that we receive these pieces of information in a timely manner and in an unadulterated form. I say 'we,' Rick, but I don't mean it in an entirely spiritual sense. I have taught many people the skills we will all need, not only to survive but to thrive in the world to come. You, on the other hand, have learned most of what you know on your own. I've helped on occasion, but between your willingness to pursue knowledge and your persistence in accomplishing a goal, I can both trust and rely on you to see things through.

First, please do whatever my children and grandchildren need you to do. Henry has quite a surprise coming and will need help processing what he learns and locating everything associated with it.

Victor looked up once more. "He wasn't kidding."

"I take it you never knew?" Rick asked.

"No." Victor shook his head. "I did not."

Rick nodded and held up a hand, forestalling the rest of what Victor wanted to say. "Finish the letter, then we can talk."

> Jacquetta, as you know, acts as the Rock of our family, the one everyone clings to in a storm, but she will need your strength to help her endure. Charlie has a bright future ahead of him, so long as he can remember to focus on that which is most important. Emma is both loving and talented, and I do not doubt that she will go far, regardless of what happens. Josiah is Gifted but wrestles with many doubts and insecurities, and I have no doubt that he'll need his family's support once everything is revealed.
>
> You, Frederick Augustus Thorne, have the skills and the mindset to complete what is needed. You may not be my Heir, but you are my surviving will. As that will, you are the only one I will say this to.
>
> You know that I live by Nemini Crede, Quin Omnia. I want to give you a different message from the one I've given Henry and Jacquetta, however. For you, it's Fide Modo Veritati. I hope you will understand it when the time comes.
>
> William

Victor almost frowned as he looked up for the final time. "Faith only in the truth?"

"I don't know what, exactly, he meant by that," Rick said. "But I intend to live up to it." He eyed his brother-in-law with some sympathy. "It must have come as quite a shock for you to be told you have a son."

"Oh, you have *no* idea, Rick." Victor let out an unsteady

breath. "The two of you *know* me. There are more than a few reasons that I stopped thinking about getting married and having my own kids. You both know the circles I deal with, and the chances of having my wife or children be used against me were just too great for me to consider." He swallowed hard at the thought. "To find out, from *Dad* of all people, that I have a son?"

"You're worried that you would put this child in danger?" Rick guessed with some ease. He often worried about his own family, and the ones he usually dealt with were nowhere near as dangerous as the ones Victor dealt with.

Victor hesitated, then pulled out the letter. "According to this, he's already in danger." He paused before plunging forward. "Dad insinuates that there may be more to his death than it first seems. He goes so far as to suggest that SIN itself might have had something to do with it."

Rick's lips formed an 'o' while Jacquetta's eyes flashed. Neither one had ever liked or trusted the Special Intelligence Network, although the reasons each had were different. Rick thought SIN tended to be too cautious in most situations it handled. At the same time, he also believed the majority of its agents were too headstrong and far too prone to using the types of violence that Rick himself frowned upon. Jacquetta, on the other hand, despised SIN for taking her father and then her brother away from their family and putting them all into near-constant danger throughout her childhood and beyond.

But neither one would have even *considered* the possibility of SIN turning on one of its own.

68

"Do you have any sort of proof?" Rick wanted to know.

"I might." Victor hesitated, then held out his letter. "Read it."

Rick took the letter with some trepidation before he and Jacquetta did just that. Discovering the extent of Victor's relationship with Katherine Kincaid—his sister could remember him dating her, but she hadn't known back then just how involved Victor had been with her—was merely the pleasant tip of an otherwise large and ugly iceberg. The idea that the Special Intelligence Network would cover for a corrupt sister agency, which Rick and Jacquetta both assumed was the Department of Mid-Western Island Affairs mentioned in their father's letter, did not sit well with either of them. That SIN would also have fired William Wolfe-Wall for attempting to expose that corruption, and for trying to confiscate evidence so they could destroy it, was bad enough. For SIN's people to try handing over a *child* to the same people who had murdered that child's mother? To the people who would likely kill said child as well?

And when that child happened to be Victor's son, at least according to the letter?

Jacquetta glanced up from where she'd perched beside her husband's chair in order to read said letter with him. "Have you been to this safety deposit box Dad mentions?"

"Not yet. I'd planned to check it out," Victor said. "But that was before I discovered I was being watched. When I called the director, he claimed there were worries that what had happened with Dad was just the beginning and that he had assigned a few agents to watch me as a result." He eyed his sister, almost dreading her reaction. "They're now watching you and yours, too."

"Are they now?"

He winced at Jacquetta's frosty tone before offering what he hoped she would see as a peace offering. "Yes, but Mister Kingston is rather hoping that you and the kids will consent to help me train them."

"*Train* them?" Rick's eyebrows rose.

Victor nodded and gave both him and Jacquetta the ghost of a mischievous smile. "Yes. It seems that three of our watchers are newer agents who could use some extra experience. The only other thing Mister Kingston asked was for the kids not to scar them too badly. Of course, since their mentors are all my former partners..."

"You mean we're being watched by Maria, Ron, and Phillipe?" Jacquetta smiled back, her expression holding a shark's joy. "Oh, this should be *fun*, then."

Rick almost chuckled. "I almost pity the kids they're supposed to be teaching." He inclined his head before asking, "Am I expected to join in on the training, too?"

"As much as my director would like you to," Victor spoke with some caution. At last, he'd come to the proverbial meat of the matter. "I'd actually prefer that you didn't."

Rick arched an eyebrow before he understood. He'd never been called stupid. "You want me to check out the deposit box, then?"

70

"To start with, yes." Victor nodded. "If it were just Ron and Maria and Phillipe who were watching, I'd talk to them and let them know what I wanted to do. They'd let me and not tell anyone. Even the director does not command that kind of loyalty, and all I'd need to do is ask." He reached into his right-hand pocket to grab the key that had come with the letter. "But they've got recruits, and the fewer people who know about this, the better. Director Kingston also told me they didn't have the people to keep watch on you if you didn't stay home with everyone else, so you should be able to visit without anyone following. This is the key Dad sent. If you're not too busy, I'd like you to head out to the bank Dad spoke of sometime in the next day or two. Take out whatever the safety deposit box holds if you're allowed. If not, I'd like you to make a record of everything that we can use to go over whatever's in there."

"I can do that," Rick said. "I'll stop in at the office and talk with my partners first, then head out. Just tell me which branch your father's favorite is."

"I would appreciate it." Victor sighed in relief. "Thank you, Rick."

"Of course." Rick gave him a small, sad half-smile. "Finding out what your father was investigating, along with Ms. Kincaid, takes precedence over a businessman's unfaithful wife and the wrap-up of a minor fraud case, at least it does for me." His smile lightened a fraction. "We'll also be glad to help you with whatever else you might need." When Victor looked at him in puzzlement, he added, "You said yourself that you never expected to be a parent."

"And you and Quet both have the experience I lack?" Victor let loose a weak chuckle. "I just hope my kid doesn't cause me half the amount of trouble your three do."

"You only have the one, according to the letter," Jacquetta said with a faint smile. "So we can hope." Her smile dissolved. "Of course, this presumes you *want* to be a father to your son?"

She and Rick both saw Victor wince, then draw in a deep breath. His following words were quiet and full of uncertainty, but they also heard the longing deep within his voice.

"I do, Quet," he said. "I really do. I just don't know if I *should.* It's been years since his mother and I were together. Over twenty years now. This isn't a little boy we're talking about, but a young man. He's lived his entire life without knowing me, and until this letter, I didn't know about him. I know what Dad says, but why should my son *want* to know me?"

Jacquetta glanced at her husband and saw him flick his eyes back to her in surprise. Rick wouldn't have expected that talk from Victor, but she'd known her brother all of her life. Despite being almost six years younger, Jacquetta was all too familiar with Victor's insecurities. More than half were the result of being their father's children, she believed. When she considered the simple fact that Victor had never expected to become a father at all, the family's matron could understand his trepidation.

"Right now," she said, keeping her voice soft. "Since we have nothing else to go on, we'll take Dad at his word. He says the one thing your son has always wanted is to know his father. To

72

know *you*."

"I know, Quet," he said. "But what if he's *wrong?*"

Fear, Jacquetta thought, *does not look good on my brother's face.* "You won't know unless you take the chance, Vic."

Victor blinked at her. "This is no time for platitudes, Quet."

"It's not a platitude," Rick told him, "when it's true."

They watched Victor's lips pursed before inclining his head. The fear on his face, however, didn't lessen.

It was, they thought, understandable. Henry Victor Wolfe-Wall was used to dealing not only with his fellow agents of SIN but also the acolytes of The Red Sword, members of the Xiomar Cartel, and associates of The Commission, among others. The closest he'd ever come to dealing with children on a regular basis was when he visited his niece and nephews. Granted, Charlie, Emma, and Josiah Thorne were a handful, even for well-trained government agents, thanks to the training they'd received from their grandfather, but things were always different, as Jacquetta and Rick knew from personal experience, when one needed to face one's children. Victor had never had to do so before.

He was also correct to point out that his son wasn't a boy but a full-grown man. On the one hand, it could make communication easier. On the other hand, Victor's son hadn't grown up with him and hadn't been raised by him. How would the young man view his father, based on that? Would he accept the fact that his father hadn't even known of his existence? Or would he somehow blame his father for not knowing?

And what of the boy's mother? What had she said regarding Victor? For that matter, had the boy's grandfather—Victor's and Jacquetta's father—said anything? What did the boy know, if anything, about *any* of them?

Jacquetta bit back a sigh. Yes, William Wolfe-Wall had had good intentions, considering he'd kept the secret of Victor's son in order to safeguard the boy's life and Victor's. That didn't mean she agreed with her father's decision.

Still, what was done was done.

"He also points out," Victor said, his voice becoming little more than a whisper, "that my son's life is in danger. If I go to seek him out, he could become an even greater target."

It was true. The three of them knew it. Victor's enemies were many, and most weren't adverse to using violence. If any of them were to discover the fact that The Dire Wolfe had a *child* to use against him, the number who wouldn't take the opportunity could easily be counted on a single hand.

"Which is all the more reason for you to try at least to find him," Rick said, leaning forward. "You could protect him better that way. Stay in the shadows at first if that's what you want. Doing that would let you get to know him a little more, too. Once you know him, you can decide whether or not you should introduce yourself."

Victor thought about it, his gray eyes becoming stormy. "What if he *doesn't* want to know me, though? If I do decide to meet with him and..."

74

He couldn't finish his sentence. Jacquetta winced, knowing what he wanted to ask.

"We'll worry about that if and when it happens," Rick said. "If it does, then at least you'll have tried. So long as you keep the proverbial door open, too, then there's always the chance that your son will reach out to you in the future. This could be as much a shock for him as it was for you."

"It could?" Victor blinked at the thought, and the sudden realization made him grimace. "I hadn't even thought about that."

Rick didn't doubt it, and he could see that his wife hadn't thought about it, either. Granted, under more normal circumstances, both Jacquetta and Victor would have, but between learning of their father's murder, attending his funeral, Victor receiving the letter he had and *then* reading its contents, which informed them not only of the existence of Victor's son but of an investigation that might have led to their father's death; plus who knew how long ago it had been since both his wife and her brother had had a whole night's sleep. Rick rather suspected they were both running on mere fumes at this point.

"Let's not worry about it yet," he said. "We'll deal with it if and when it happens. There are a lot of factors you and he will have to consider, too. Yes, Victor, there's your job and everything that goes along with it, but there's also whatever your son might be doing. Depending on his line of work, the people he has as friends, and whether he's dating right now, the possibilities are endless."

"Or he could even be married already." Victor blanched

without warning. "I could be a *grandfather* and not even know it!"

Rick and Jacquetta again glanced at each other, uncertain if they should laugh or sympathize. Rick decided to shake his head instead.

"Let's not get ahead of ourselves, Victor," he said. "Let me find out what's in this safety deposit box first, and we can go on from there."

"Agreed."

Victor drew in a deep, shaky breath just as they heard a quiet knock on the office's door. Charlie poked his brown head inside a moment later.

"The pizza's here," he said before taking in the expressions his parents and uncle wore. "Is everything okay?"

"Everything's fine, Charlie," Rick told his oldest son. "Or about as well as they can be after your grandfather's funeral."

"Ah." Charlie glanced at his mother and uncle again, then nodded. "Sy and Emma already took the pizzas to the kitchen."

"Then we'd better hurry up and go there ourselves," Rick said, standing up. Jacquetta and Victor were close behind in following suit. "If we don't, your brother might eat everything himself." He flicked his eyes back to his wife and brother-in-law. "After we finish eating, though, I want everyone to gather back in here. We'll have some things to discuss." He drew an unsteady breath of his own. "And I have something to give to you and your brother and sister from your grandfather."

"Oh?" Charlie moved to step forward but stopped at his

76

father's shake of the head.

"After we eat," Rick said. "Not before. All right?"

Despite looking somewhat disappointed, Charlie nodded. The group left the office and went to the kitchen.

Dinner proved to be a somber event. Despite having two large plain pies, one large pepperoni, and another medium veggie, no one had much of an appetite. The loss of their family member had not only killed much of their desire for food but also kept their usual conversation quiet and reserved.

Not even Josiah, well-known for his ability to eat an entire large pizza or two by himself, seemed all that hungry.

Afterward, the whole family gathered in Rick's office. Victor settled himself on the chair he was offered and took the time to study his sister's three children as they, too, arranged themselves and made themselves comfortable.

Charles Sebastian Thorne, at nineteen, was the oldest. He had Jacquetta's brown hair, Rick's hazel eyes, and a laid-back, studious personality that matched his father's. Charlie enjoyed school for the most part, as he loved learning and excelled in subjects like math, science, martial arts, and computer technology. Rick's first son had also proven himself to be a mostly steady sort of young man, one who hoped to either follow in his father's footsteps by becoming a private investigator himself or somehow turning his passion for unusual pets into a full-time career.

Seventeen-year-old Emma Sophia Thorne possessed the light red hair of her maternal grandmother and brilliant, sea-green eyes that were a near-perfect match to her paternal grandfather.

Like both her mother and her father, Emma tended to be an active girl who loved playing softball and riding horses, as well as dancing and practicing self-defense. She also had a fantastic head for numbers, which she hoped to one day put to use for her father's business.

Her fraternal twin, Josiah Harrison Thorne, had the same light brown hair as his father, along with his mother's blue eyes and her fiery temper. He far preferred being outdoors to sitting in a classroom or office, whether it meant playing football or baseball, working on his family's various cars, or indulging his creative gifts through painting or drawing. He, too, hoped to put his multiple talents somehow to work for his father's business. Truth be told, he also dreamed of becoming a world-famous artist.

A small smile formed on Victor's face. Charlie, Emma, and Josiah were all good kids, and they each took after their parents in specific ways. Rick and Jacquetta had every reason to be proud of them.

How would his own son be in comparison? Victor didn't yet know, any more than he knew how Charlie, Emma, and Josiah would react to the news that they were cousins.

He would soon discover the answer to that last uncertainty. Rick informed the three about their *other* visitors about what they, their mother, and their uncle would be doing in the next few days. Charlie, Emma, and Josiah took the news in their stride—it was, to be honest, far from the first time they'd been in a sort of protective custody—but they did question where their father planned to be, if not with them.

"I'll be doing your uncle a favor," Rick told them before glancing at Victor, his eyebrows rising.

Victor understood the implied question and took a deep breath. "Before we go on, understand that we cannot discuss this anywhere else. This can *not* get out, not right now and perhaps not for some time." He speared each of them with a serious look, one that he hoped brought home the gravity of the potential situation. "Too much may be at stake for us to take the risk."

His nephews and niece glanced at each other before nodding in understanding. Again, they'd been through similar situations before when they'd been asked to keep certain secrets. Victor had no doubt they would keep this one, too.

Especially when they learned just how personal it was. Taking a deep breath, Victor made the revelation. "It seems that I have a son."

Emma's eyes went wide. Charlie blinked in disbelief. Josiah glanced between his father and mother, then looked at Victor.

"We have a cousin?" he asked, incredulous.

"Yes." Victor nodded in confirmation. "You do."

Their shocked silence reigned for close to a full minute. Both boys looked to their mother for confirmation, while Emma looked to her father. She recovered quicker than either Charlie or Josiah did, too.

"Why didn't you..." She broke off, eyeing her uncle. "Oh. You didn't know?"

"No." Victor shook his head. "I didn't. Not until I received a letter from your grandfather."

"A letter?" Charlie frowned. "When did you get it?"

"After the funeral," Victor confirmed it with a nod. "As you might expect, I was caught off guard."

"By getting the letter?" Josiah wanted to know. "Or by the news that you've got a kid?"

Victor almost smiled. "Both."

"According to your grandfather's letter," Rick said. "There are some things he's left in a safety deposit box for your uncle. As Victor would like to keep this a secret for the time being, I'll be going in his place to check it out and maybe even retrieve whatever your grandfather left there. The rest of you will keep our other *guests* entertained."

"And distracted, am I right?" Charlie had always been quick on the uptake. "So that way, they don't suspect anything out of the ordinary?

"You guessed it." Jacquetta nodded at her son, offering him a small smile before sweetening the proverbial pot. "And, since it's well-known that your grandfather just passed, no one will be expecting you back at school for another few days."

"Cool." Charlie glanced at his siblings and saw them both grin before returning his mother's smile. "We'd be happy to help out."

"I don't doubt it."

Rick also grinned as he spoke. Missing a few days' worth of school wouldn't hurt any of his three, he thought, especially

80

when given the reasons. Having helped raise them, Rick Thorne had complete confidence in his children's abilities, not only to catch up on their education and keep certain things secret, but also to drive their watchers up the proverbial wall. Even the most well-trained agent of SIN was, he believed, no match for any one of *his* children—a consequence of having The Wall as a grandfather, The Dire Wolfe as an uncle, and both him and his wife as parents.

"We can consider this a tribute to your grandfather, too, I think," he said. "There was nothing he seemed to love more than educating people that first impressions are not always right." Rick held their gazes for an instant longer before reaching back into his desk. "And, speaking of your grandfather, he left each of you a letter, too."

"A letter?" Emma said, her eyes widening a little. "When?"

"They arrived via today's mail," Jacquetta told her daughter. "Remember the certified post I signed for? Each of us received one."

"Just like your uncle did before he came over," Rick told them and slid each of the unopened envelopes over. "Take them, read them, and if you want to talk, just say the word."

Chapter Three: An Investigation Begins

May 23, 2007: Early Morning

Despite what Rick had been told about SIN supposedly not having the manpower to keep watch on him if he left his family's home, he still went through the trouble of appearing to keep to his routine. It never hurt to be *too* careful in his line of work, after all.

He didn't see anyone following him, though, as he drove to the city office of Cross, Thorne, and Zeal Investigations. His appearance surprised the only person visible upon crossing the office threshold.

"Rick!" Helena Cross-LeMaire, acting as receptionist, stared at him in disbelief. "What are you doing here? You're not supposed to be back until next week!"

"Had something come up, Lena," he told her. "Your brother and Chris both in?"

"They are," she said. "How are Quet and the kids doing?"

"About as well as can be expected," Rick told her. "Is Miss Lin here as well?"

Helena nodded. "They're all here, Rick, and most likely in the conference room. They said something about going over the Long case."

"Still?" Rick almost sighed. "That thing's Long in name and long in the time it's been taking us to complete." Another sigh left his lips, and he shook his head. "Never mind. I've got something to talk to them about."

"Do you want me to call them up here?"

"No. I'll head back."

He heard them long before he finished walking the short distance back to the conference room. Chris Zeal's excitable tenor mixed with the quieter baritone of Edgar Cross, and neither sounded happy. In fact, Rick thought Chris sounded somewhat exasperated. At the same time, Ed had notes of dry frustration and irritation mixing in his voice.

It didn't surprise him, given the file they were supposed to be working on. The Long case had proven itself to be *quite* the issue and in more ways than one.

He paused by the door, deciding to listen to the conversation before joining.

"...and so, Chris, we can't use that information," Edgar Cross said, the strained patience in his voice indicating that he was doing his best to explain things. As a former defense attorney who had known his clients were guilty, Ed had quit and refused to, as he'd put it, sell his soul. He knew both the law and the tactics that the opposition could use. "And that's according to the law."

"Oh, come *on*, Ed!" Chris snapped back. "This took me *ages* to hack, and the only reason we got it is that the head of security for Longinus, Incorporated, is an idiot who kept his password in his glove box!"

"That doesn't matter," Ed told him. "We cannot legally use that information in a courtroom. We'll have to see if we can't use it to find something else, something that we *can* use instead."

The sound of a pen or pencil skittering across the table reached Rick's ears. His eyebrows went up. It took a lot to get Chris Zeal angry or upset. Even when he and Rick were in junior high school, Chris had developed a reputation for being happy-go-lucky and excitable, especially when dealing with a new piece of technology. In all of his interactions with others, he seemed almost unflappable. For him to display any temper was a sign that he was close to, if not at, his breaking point.

His following words confirmed it. "This company is *really* starting to piss me off."

"Just *now?*" Ed's dry voice asked. "I've been annoyed with them since our second week of dealing with them."

It was as good a time as any to make his appearance. Rick pushed open the door.

"Having a good time, gentlemen?" he asked as he walked inside the conference room.

"Rick!" Chris looked over, his dark blue eyes lighting up. "What're *you* doing here?"

"I work here, remember?" Rick said with the slightest trace of his usual grin.

"Not at the moment, you don't," Ed said, standing up to eye the other. His brown eyes were warm with concern as he searched Rick's face. "You're supposed to be home with your wife and kids right now. How're they doing?"

"As I told your sister, they're as well as can be expected," Rick said. "Quet's brother is over, and he's with them." He

84

glanced about the room. "Where's Miss Lin?"

"She escaped to the file room," Ed said, appearing to relax at Rick's explanation. "Not that I can blame her."

"I heard the two of you talking as I came in," Rick said. "The Long case?"

"Yeah." Chris nodded, irritation flashing over his face. "According to Ed here, we're gonna have to go back to the drawing board. Everything we've gotten on what his so-called wife and partner have been doin' within Mister Long's company is now *useless* because of some obscure law they passed two weeks ago. It's *infuriating*."

Ed sighed, rolling his eyes. "I keep telling you, Chris, that I don't write the laws. I simply make sure we operate within them so our cases can't be shot to hell by some hotshot lawyer or a donkey judge."

Rick glanced between them. This was an old argument, one he didn't feel like revisiting. "Has anyone contacted Mister Long about this?"

"Oh, hell, no." Chris shook his head. "I want to give him *good* news, not devastate him."

"We may not have a choice, though," Ed said. "Unless we can somehow get someone to flip on the wife or the partner or figure out a different angle to make a break, we're simply spending way too much time and money spinning our wheels on this."

Rick held up a hand and headed over to where everything was spread out on the table. He wasn't the tech guru that Chris was or the lawyer that Ed happened to be, but he *had* been a detective and was still an investigator. He also had a fresher set of eyes. "Hold on, guys. Lemme see what you've got right now."

"Be our guest," Ed said. "Please."

It would take him close to half an hour to find something that the others could use. Rick couldn't blame either man for not having seen it first—it was a tiny, almost insignificant detail in the grand scheme of things. The Long case had proven to be a massive, tangled web, focusing on their client's wife and his leading business partner. Mister Long had suspected the two of having an affair and, thanks to the prenup that had been signed, wanted evidence. When Rick, Chris, and Ed accepted the case, they envisioned it taking no more than a few weeks to deliver what Mister Long wanted.

Instead, they had uncovered evidence suggesting that the two had also embezzled money. Going to Mister Long with their suspicions had given them the green light to find out what, exactly, was going on within *Longinus, Incorporated*, as well as with Mister Long's wife and partner. The information found hinted at many things, none of which were good.

The problem was proving it. Mister Long's business partner, in particular, had proven to be quite careful. For Chris to finally find any proof, only to be told it wouldn't be helpful in a courtroom, was devastating for their client. It was beyond frustrating for each of them.

But with Rick's mind and eyes having been elsewhere for the past few days, his looking at the documents now allowed him to see one small but glaring error. "Look at this. Right there. Do the two of you see that discrepancy in the access logs?"

Chris bent down, studying what Rick had pointed out. A wide smile spread across his face. "Oh, *yeah*. Rick, you beautiful genius, we've *got* them!"

Ed frowned, glancing between the two. "What is it? What'd we miss?"

"You remember that access log, Ed?" Chris said, looking up. "The one that shows that this file was last saved two weeks ago?" At Ed's nod, he continued, "Look at the date of it."

Ed did his best not to sigh in exasperation. "The date hasn't changed, gentlemen."

"Not on *this* access log file," Chris said. "Look at the date it was saved on the *server*."

Ed blinked and looked. Exasperation turned to confusion. "It was saved over a year ago there. What the hell?"

"I've seen stuff like that before," Rick said. "It means that this file was accessed and then resaved locally with a later date to try to make it appear as if the file was newer than it actually is. The original, however, was stored on the file server, complete with the original date it was created. That means that *this* information?" He tapped the paper that showed the discrepancy. "It's been falsified."

"Huh." The beginnings of a shark's grin appeared on Ed's face. "That law I was talking about earlier, Chris? It does not apply retroactively."

"Which means?" Chris eyed him in expectation.

"It's admissible, and we can use it."

"Yes!" Chris pumped the air in exultation. "Rick, we are back in business!"

"I'm glad to hear it." Rick gave him a slight, brief grin. "But the Long case isn't why I'm in today."

"Oh?"

Both Chris and Ed turned to look at him. Chris looked curious. Ed inclined his head, eyes narrowing, and his expression becoming shrewd.

"You said your brother-in-law is staying with your wife and kids at the moment," he said. "He the reason you're here right now?"

"He is." Rick nodded in confirmation. "Victor received a letter recently that claims he has a son. He asked me to look into the possibility."

"Oh, wow." Chris's eyes went wide. A guarded look appeared on his face. "Is that a good or a bad thing?"

"He's choosing to see it as something good, at least for right now," Rick said. "The letter he received claims that there's a safety deposit box in his hometown with evidence and information. I'll be heading over there to collect it, but I wanted to give the two of you a heads-up on what I'll be doing."

"Plus, you might need help afterward?" Ed asked with a knowing look.

"Might," Rick said, nodding. "It'll depend on what's in the box."

Ed and Chris glanced at each other, then nodded back.

They had each faced similar situations with their own families before. There was a reason Helena now worked in their office and a reason Chris had asked the question he had.

"Just say the word, Rick," Ed told him, and Chris agreed. "We'll help where and when we can."

"Thank you." Rick gave them both a grateful smile. "It's why I asked where Miss Lin is—I may be borrowing her to do some research. We'll play it by ear afterward."

Neither one argued, and soon after, Rick returned to his car and the road. Again, he kept an eye out as he traveled the almost three hours it took to reach the bank in question. Victor had told him during one of their conversations the previous night that it had been William Wolfe-Wall's favorite hometown bank, and Rick had made it there just after one in the afternoon.

As he exited his car, he made certain once more that he had the safety deposit box key that Victor had given him before heading inside. A young lady, well-dressed and wearing a pleasant expression, greeted him as he entered the lobby. Rick offered her a polite smile in return.

"I'd like to speak with Mister Eppes," he told her.

"Of course, sir. If you have a seat, I'll inform him that you're here, Mister...?"

"Robert Pupp."

Rick watched her face closely to see what sort of reaction she might have, but saw nothing as she nodded and directed him to a comfortable, nearby chair. What kind of evidence, he wondered as he watched the young lady walk towards the back of the bank, would be in the safety deposit box? What else, if anything, might he find alongside that evidence? His father-in-law had been the sentimental sort, at least while visiting his family, and Rick had to wonder if William Wolfe-Wall had left any personal mementos for Victor or even for Jacquetta. Would there be anything at all about Victor's son?

A thin and nervous-looking middle-aged gentleman with light blond hair and pale green eyes approached him at that moment, breaking his train of thought. "M-mister Pupp?"

Rick rose to his feet, inclining his head in acknowledgment. "Yes. Mister Eppes?"

"Yes." He glanced at the door. "Shall we go to my office, sir?"

Rick gave him a slight nod and followed the man to a small but well-appointed room. Much to Rick's surprise, there were no windows, only two works of uninspired art, and a small collection of filing cabinets that sat on the farthest wall, near a plain but functional desk. Two armchairs were waiting in front of that desk, while a simple coat rack stood nearest the glass door.

The office was a far cry from what Rick would have envisioned for a bank manager. No matter how small the bank branch was, most managers had the most prominent office available.

Mister Eppes noticed his surprise. "It may be smaller than most of the offices here, sir, but it's the best protected. No one can overhear us or even see us without us seeing them. I alone have the key, so no one can get in without my authorization, and

90

my door happens to be bullet-resistant glass. I have my own way out, too." He offered Rick a small, sad smile. "Mister Wall did everything he could to ensure my safety. Can I assume by virtue of the fact that *you* are here instead of him that he didn't take as much care with his own?"

"He did his best," Rick said quietly as he remembered the letter Victor had allowed him to read. "But it wasn't enough."

"I warned him to be careful," Mister Eppes said with a sorrowful sigh. "The people that we're up against hate being brought to account for their crimes by those they see as beneath them." Another more profound sigh escaped him. "I take it you're here to collect what's in the box?"

Rick tamped down on the surprise he felt, even as he nodded. "I am, yes."

"I'll admit, I half-expected his grandson to be the one to show up if anything happened," Mister Eppes said, startling Rick further. "But I'm glad that you were chosen to come instead. Mister Wall's grandson is rather distinctive in his appearance." He nodded to one of the chairs, missing the glint of curiosity that appeared in Rick's eyes. "If you'll take a seat and hand me the key, I can get the box."

"Of course."

Forcing back a surge of strange impatience, Rick sat down to wait for Mister Eppes' return. What, he wondered, had Mister Eppes meant by *'chosen to come'*? The letter Victor possessed had mentioned a *'**group of trusted friends**.'* Perhaps Mister Eppes believed him to be one of them?

And had he indeed met Victor's son?

A few moments later, Mister Eppes was back. He locked his office door before placing the large, fifteen-by-twenty-two-inch metal box on the desk in front of Rick.

"As far as anyone else is concerned, this is just the itemization that needs to be done following the death of the box's owner," Mister Eppes said. "Mister, uh, Pupp Senior is said to have kept a collection of semi-valuable coins, as well as a few personal mementos—that's what the report I'll put into my records will state, at least. Mister Wall gave me a list of what his, uh, heir would, uh, find when the time came."

Rick wanted to frown at the idea of having fraud essentially committed before him. Still, when he considered what was actually supposed to be in the safety deposit box, as well as William Wolfe-Wall's death and Mister Eppes' own words, he found he couldn't blame them for setting things up that way. It was the reason he let himself nod in agreement as Mister Eppes opened the box.

The first object to greet them was a miniature, framed portrait, placed face down as though to hide the rest of the box's contents. Rick carefully and gently extracted it, turning it over more out of curiosity than anything else.

The painted faces of a woman and a child, who looked to be about nine or ten years of age, met Rick's eyes. There could be no mistaking the fact that they were mother and son. They looked too much alike, with the boy having his mother's straight nose and high cheekbones, and sharing his mother's large, round eyes. Both

92

also possessed fair skin and red hair, although the mother's hair happened to be a more fiery shade, while the boy's proved to be a darker, more coppery red. Another notable difference? The mother had blue-green eyes, while her son's eyes were blue-gray.

They were a slightly different shade, Rick realized, of Victor Wolfe's own silvery-gray eyes. Without question, and just as he'd realized that the woman in the painting happened to be the boy's mother, Rick knew that the boy couldn't be anyone other than the son of The Dire Wolfe. The shape of the boy's face, his thin lips, his square chin, and the set of his jaw, together with the color of his eyes, left the private investigator in no doubt.

He also couldn't deny the reason Mister Eppes had called William Wolfe-Wall's grandson *distinctive*. If the child in the portrait happened to be him, and if the painting itself happened to be in any way accurate, the boy couldn't help but stand out, thanks to his looks.

Something that the boy had not inherited from his father, Victor. Rick almost chuckled at the thought. Victor Wolfe could blend in with virtually any sort of crowd he happened to be with, thanks in large part to his mostly nondescript appearance. His training as an agent of the Special Intelligence Network had only increased that ability.

Setting aside the portrait, Rick discovered a few more personal mementos resting underneath. The copy of what Rick assumed was the boy's birth certificate caused the private investigator's eyebrows to rise when he saw the child's full name. The tiny photo album and little scrapbook made him smile more than once when the investigator glanced through them. He set aside the collection of letters that appeared to be from both mother and son—that would, Rick believed, be for Victor to go through first—and found his smile widening ever so slightly when his eye was caught by the eight-by-eleven-inch photograph that showed Rick's father-in-law holding a younger version of the boy from the portrait. A chuckle escaped soon after when he saw the three small pieces of artwork, all done in a child's hand and addressed to 'Grampy Will.'

Unfortunately, those happier moments would be the only ones Rick would get to enjoy. Underneath the collection of keepsakes were three binders, all filled with a variety of newspaper clippings, reports from both doctors and medical examiners, more photographs that Rick recognized as surveillance photos, and others that had clearly been taken while someone was undercover. Two composition books were also found, each one being filled with notes, even in their small margins. A single ledger made up the bottom, filled with names and a single letter beside each name. Some had E, others had S, L, O, D, P, or X.

The threads that connected all of the notebooks, the binders, and the ledger? Everything that had been collected had taken place within a location that Rick had never heard of—the Mid-Superior Islands. Everything was also of or about children. To be more specific, they were all *kidnapped* children.

It took Rick a bare minute to realize what all of the evidence before him seemed to suggest. Ice lanced through his spine, alongside memories he would have preferred not to have.

94

God in Heaven, this is not what I expected or wanted to discover.

Rick knew that kidnapping rings existed. He also knew that human trafficking happened far more frequently than most realized, thanks to his time as a detective with Philadelphia's Police Force. He knew it on a personal level, too, as each of his children had become targets on occasion because of his work. The perpetrators of such crimes, be they buyers, sellers, or 'procurers,' were all scum of the Earth, in Rick's opinion.

He drew in a deep breath as he looked through everything the safety deposit box contained. One of the biggest obstacles to bringing such people to justice was that many of them appeared to be ordinary. There weren't any unique patterns of behavior, like with serial killers or other potential offenders. Unique birthmarks or signs did not forewarn of savagery and evil. The people involved could literally be anyone, from business people, priests, stay-at-home moms, teachers, cashiers, actors, and even fellow police officers, up to and including some of the very rich, the famous, and the very powerful. Those people were some of the worst, in fact, as they could make specific problems disappear without a single trace.

If Katherine Kincaid and William Wolfe-Wall had discovered an exceptionally well-connected ring of kidnappers and traffickers, it was no wonder that they were both dead now. If Victor's son had happened to get involved, even peripherally, then it boded ill for his future.

He saw what happened to his mother....

The memory of that piece of William Wolfe-Wall's letter

to Victor came back to Rick at that moment, and he felt his blood begin to boil. There could be no question that Victor's son had gotten involved, which meant that the question of finding him turned into not only a matter of locating him but of protecting him so that he could help reveal the people who were responsible for the crimes that both his mother and grandfather had investigated.

Or had he already done so? The '*group of trusted friends*' mentioned in Victor's letter... Hadn't the letter claimed that they, whoever they were, happened to be in possession of the evidence already? And weren't they already protecting Victor's son from those who would do him harm?

Rick's eyes flicked back up to where Mister Eppes waited patiently for him to finish his inspection. While he would have loved to question the bank manager, Rick didn't think he could dare. So far, Mister Eppes had been willing to believe that Rick had been sent on behalf of William Wolfe-Wall's grandson. He couldn't jeopardize the bank manager's continued cooperation by asking questions that would almost certainly guarantee the other becoming suspicious.

Victor would most likely never forgive him if he screwed this up. Jacquetta might not, either.

Which left Rick with one option. He'd have to puzzle over it with them when he showed them everything. "Do you have a secure way for me to move all of this?"

Mister Eppes nodded. "Of course."

A few minutes later, Rick walked out of the bank with

everything in a large, opaque canvas bag. He kept his face blank, not letting either the shock or the anger underneath make it to his surface. It wasn't easy. That there were some out there in the larger world who would harm children was bad enough. To know that a group of so-called people had apparently *collected* children for the sole purpose of harming them was beyond infuriating.

He would definitely hug his three children when he got home and give simple thanks that he was still able to do so.

Grabbing several deep breaths after sitting back in the driver's seat of his car, Rick glanced outside. The sun still sat high up in the sky, which would allow him to get at least most of the way back before dark. He thought a moment more before deciding to go home instead of the office. He'd have to sort through things with Victor before reading in his partners and Miss Lin. No one would question him coming home a little early, either, not with his father-in-law's loss so fresh. With luck, the drive would allow him to gather his thoughts, calm his emotions, and then let him mentally review everything he'd so far found.

Human trafficking was an ugly crime, with those who dealt with children being the worst of the worst. Unfortunately, it was also highly profitable, and many professional traffickers were able to escape public notice, thanks to the money, the influence, and the power their more well-placed clients liked to use as weapons. Unlike auto theft, homicide, and other similar crimes, there were no federal statistics to consult, thereby helping to keep the more law-abiding public in the dark. Rick knew for a fact that the cases of abducted children that were seen on television were merely the ripples on a surface that concealed an otherwise large, dark, and ugly underworld. Most cases went unreported by the media, and to get anywhere close to the factual numbers in *just* the United States, one had to call up the individual states and add up their results.

The total, Rick knew, was staggering. The implications of that total were genuinely disgusting.

He shook his head, not wanting to think about it. Not yet. He could dwell on it later, as he had the feeling it would all come into play.

Until then, he had a number of other things to ponder. The evidence he'd seen so far would be damning for the perpetrators, whomever they were. Again, according to the letter that Victor had received, what Rick had taken from the safety deposit box happened to be the mere tip of an enormous, very nasty iceberg. Just the little bit of information he had learned so far had already led to a number of questions.

What, for example, was the Department of Mid-Western Island Affairs? In his letter, William Wolfe-Wall mentioned that the members of this Department were trying to reach Victor's son and weren't happy that their efforts were being stymied. Why? What did they fear? Were they involved in the crimes that had cost Katherine Kincaid her life?

And what were the Mid-Superior Islands? Where were they? Rick had traveled extensively, but he couldn't recall having ever heard of such an island chain before.

What had Mister Eppes meant, too, when he'd claimed

that William Wolfe-Wall had done everything he could to ensure Mister Eppes' safety? What did Mister Eppes himself know, and why would Rick's father-in-law have gone to such lengths to protect him?

"'The people we're up against,'" Rick murmured the words Mister Eppes had spoken. "Who are they, and what did you mean when you said that they don't take well to being called out by those they think of as being beneath them?"

Of course, Rick knew from long experience that many criminals tended to be arrogant. That's how more than a few of them were caught. Serial killers, assassins, and others like them rarely thought of their victims as anything other than objects. In contrast, some business people, politicians, dictators, and other leaders thought anyone who didn't move in their circles was subhuman at best and mere property at worst. When the two types were combined into a single group...Rick's anger threatened to break his cool logic again.

His lips thinned. Given what Mister Eppes had said, the evidence Rick had so far seen, and then what William Wolfe-Wall had insinuated in the letter he'd sent to Victor, it wouldn't have been surprising to find out that they were dealing with just such a group. To be able to infiltrate the uppermost levels of the Special Intelligence Network, among other federal entities? That took a lot of *money*, quite a bit of *power*, and massive amounts of *influence*—far more than what most people could even dream of attaining.

Which meant that he and Victor would be treading on

perilous ground. It was no small wonder that William Wolfe-Wall had warned Victor to be careful if that did indeed happen to be the case. They would *all* need to be, for however long they pursued this.

Rick didn't doubt that they *would* pursue it, too. He knew his brother-in-law well enough to know that Victor would want to do everything he could to help his son, to protect him, and to bring the people who had murdered his son's mother to justice. How many times had Victor helped Rick preserve his own family, even when his agency would have preferred he go on assignment instead? How often had Victor put himself in jeopardy to make sure that Jacquetta, Charlie, Emma, Josiah, and even Rick himself were kept safe from those who sought to do them harm?

If for no other reason than that, Rick would now return those favors.

At last, just as the sun began to set, he turned into his driveway. The time had come to show Victor what he'd found.

Chapter Four: First Report

Thorne Residence

Rick slid his eyes back and forth as he drove up towards his front door, trying to find even a hint of the people watching his home and family. He didn't think he would see anything, as each of Victor's former partners had proven to be excellent at their jobs. Ronald Kohler was a former cop recruited by the Special Intelligence Network. Maria Fuentes had been a sharpshooter and computer specialist working for the military before entering SIN's service. Phillipe Depardeux, on the other hand, had been a security and melee combat specialist for Interpol before transferring to SIN. Rick had met each of them before and knew how good they were at their jobs.

He didn't know if he would be able to say the same thing about their apprentices. Seth Yago, Annette Prior, and Korey Smithson were all young and unknown to him. The fact that they had made it into SIN's apprenticeship program spoke well of their abilities, but Rick knew nothing beyond that. As such, he wanted to take the time to be on the proverbial lookout.

Much to his satisfaction, however, he saw nothing. There were no hints of anyone or anything watching him or his home.

He almost smiled before parking the car and looking up to see Jacquetta and Victor both waiting for him at the door. The would-be smile vanished.

Getting out of the car with the canvas bag, he headed up the front steps and into the house. He didn't let either of them speak.

"Let's head to my office," he said, just as Victor's mouth opened.

Jacquetta's eyebrows rose at his tone, while Victor looked taken aback. Still, neither one of them argued, and soon they were in the safety of Rick's office. Jacquetta perched on the arm of Rick's chair, while Victor took the seat on the opposite side of the desk.

"Where's the kids?" Rick asked before anyone else could speak.

"Outside, assisting in various training exercises with my former partners' apprentices," Victor answered shortly. "We gave them instructions to keep everyone busy while we talk."

"Good."

Rick nodded, then took a deep, preparatory breath. He didn't know how Victor would react to most of the information he'd brought back. William Wolfe-Wall hadn't hinted at the nature of what sort of evidence he had been collecting, only that it had cost Katherine Kincaid and likely William himself their lives. When Victor saw what Rick had found and realized what his former lover and his father had been investigating...

It was the reason he hesitated to answer when Victor asked, "What did you find?"

Rick glanced at him but made no move at first to unzip the bag he'd laid on his desk. Jacquetta frowned at his uncertain pause.

"What is it?" she wanted to know.

"Which would you prefer to start with, Victor?" Rick asked after a moment, deciding it would be best to leave it in Victor's hands. "Your son? Or with what his mother and your father were collecting?"

Jacquetta glanced at her brother, noting how his brow furrowed with thought. His head inclined, and his eyes were fastened on Rick's face.

No doubt Victor could also see the apprehension dancing in Rick's eyes, as well as hear the hint of dread that laced his voice.

Under other circumstances, Victor would have dismissed the question to dive headfirst into the bad news. He dealt with the evils that human beings were able to do and justify, just as Rick himself did. Victor had likely seen as much, if not more, of it than Rick himself had, in fact. Thinking about his own career as both a decorated detective with the Philadelphia police and then as a private investigator, Rick could only imagine the depths of depravity Victor would have seen before recoiling in disgust.

But right at this moment? When the muck and mire had to do with events that had killed both Victor's former lover and then his father? When the information had something to do with the son Victor had never known he'd had?

For once, Victor shied away from the news he knew he wouldn't like to hear, at least for a moment. "My son. *Definitely* my son."

Rick gave him the ghost of a smile, and the tension in his shoulders loosened a little. It wouldn't, he knew, be more than a temporary distraction from the rest of what he had, but he'd take it. *And, best of all, I know just the thing to start with.*

Unzipping the bag, Rick reached in and brought out the portrait. The look that came over Victor's face when Rick handed it to him said everything.

Victor's eyes began to swim as he stared at the picture. His right hand seemed to move almost of its own accord, coming up to gently touch Katherine Kincaid's painted face before sliding down to the boy's. A single tear fell down his cheek a moment later.

How long the three of them sat there, with Victor staring at the painting of his former lover and her—*his*—son, Rick had no idea. Time itself almost seemed not to exist, and he nearly started when Jacquetta leaned towards him.

"Did you get his name?" She whispered.

"I did," Rick confirmed, glancing at Victor. Although the other man's eyes never moved from the portrait in front of him, his head inclined just enough to let Rick believe that Victor was listening. "Robert William Henry Nicholas Alastor Kincaid."

Jacquetta blinked, incredulity making an appearance. "Come again?"

Stifling the urge to smile, Rick repeated the name. The ghost of a grin flickered on Victor's lips as Jacquetta shook her head in disbelief.

"Katherine never did anything by halves," Victor murmured. "Poor kid...I can't say that I'm surprised, though."

"You're not?" his sister asked.

"No." Victor shook his head. "Robert was the name of Katherine's father, Quet. William was not only the name of our own father but the oldest of Katherine's two brothers. Henry, of course, was me. Nicholas was our uncle's middle name. Do you remember what Dad said about his older brother?"

"Older brother? Oh!" She nodded as the memories came to mind. "Uncle Walter, who went missing near the end of World War II. His middle name was Nicholas?"

"It was," Victor confirmed.

"I'm surprised she didn't use his first name, then," Jacquetta said.

Rick almost smiled. "Look at the birth certificate, Quet."

She leaned over and did as her husband asked. Her lips turned upward in a sudden smile. "He was born on December 24. Your Katherine not only used Nicholas in honor of our uncle but also the Christmas Saint."

"No doubt." Victor agreed. "Especially considering how much Katherine always loved Christmas."

"What about Alastor?" Rick asked.

"That was Katherine's other brother." Victor chuckled, but the sound seemed more saddened than amused. "She named my son for all of us."

He gazed at the portrait a moment more before, with great reluctance, setting it aside. "Is there anything else about him?"

"A photo album," Rich said. "Also, a scrapbook, the copy of his birth certificate, a few other pictures, and even some letters from both him and his mother."

Digging into the bag, Rick brought them all out, and both he and Jacquetta needed to fight back the amused grins that threatened to appear when Victor all but snatched the items. The agent of SIN opened the photo album in the next heartbeat, and an amazed smile appeared on his face soon after. His smile only grew as he began to leaf through the album's pages.

"Quet, look," he said, turning it so she and Rick could see what he did.

There were three pictures on the pages facing them. Each one featured a young boy with blazing red hair at various stages in his life. Two of the photographs also featured William Wolfe-Wall, while the third had only the boy. The first showed a toddler, either two or three years old, at what looked like a petting zoo, with William Wolfe-Wall helping the child feed a goat. In the second, the boy now appeared to be around five or six and wore a broad smile and a backpack, signifying his first day of school. The third showed the same boy once again, this time around nine or ten years in age, with William Wolfe-Wall next to what looked like a little fishing boat. Both wore blue jeans and t-shirts, and both held fishing poles while posing with their apparent catches, a pair of nice-sized trout.

Rick couldn't help but smile at that particular photograph. He'd spent several small vacations with William Wolfe-Wall, doing the exact same thing. Of course, part of those vacations had been more about William teaching him various things before they went fishing. However, the memories still brought him quiet joy.

Jacquetta had reason to smile as well, although hers was due more to the way Victor beamed at them. It seemed clear to her that her brother had embraced the idea of being a father. He had always been a good uncle, and Jacquetta had no doubt that Victor would make an excellent dad.

And if there happened to be a mistiness to his eyes, or hers, or even Rick's own... Well, they could each attribute some of that to seeing the image of a happy William Wolfe-Wall alongside that of Victor's son.

Rick hated the fact that it couldn't last, but the album in question was a small one. The scrapbook happened to be, as well. Victor had also never been one to run and hide from the ugly realities of life. His father had been murdered. His former lover, too, had been killed. His son, according to the letter he'd received, was in danger from the ones who had committed those murders.

Once he came to the last page of the album and then the scrapbook, he drew in a deep breath. Setting the items aside, along with

106

the letters and other mementos, he allowed his gaze to linger on them for the briefest moment before turning back to Rick.

The tone of his voice held nothing except foreboding. "What else did you find?"

It was Rick's turn to take a deep, preparatory breath. Reaching back into the bag, he pulled out the ledger, binders, and composition books. Victor's brow furrowed, and a frown began.

"That's it?" he asked. "That's everything?"

"Everything that was in the safety deposit box," Rick told him. "But if what your letter says is true, and these things are only a portion of what your son's mother and your father were collecting?" His lips became a thin, unhappy line. "We're going to be treading some hazardous waters."

Victor's frown deepened as he reached for, then opened, the first binder. It didn't take long for his expression to become stormy. His eyes flashed with silver lightning.

"Vic?" Jacquetta eyed her brother in concern. "What is it?"

"Traffickers." Ice coated Victor's voice.

Jacquetta drew in a sharp breath. Rick nodded, his expression becoming grim.

"Yes," he said. "Wealthy and influential ones, at that. They'd have to be to make all of *these*—" He tapped the binders. "And others possibly disappear, as well as murder anyone who threatens to expose them."

"Like Dad and Katherine," Victor muttered a curse. "Whoever they are, they'd have to be extraordinarily well-heeled to be able to influence any of the higher-ups at SIN."

"Without question." Rick nodded. He didn't mince his words. "And it's most likely not just monetarily. Is it possible for someone to pull

107

off all of this and *then* have whoever the Director was back then try to confiscate and destroy the evidence? *That* takes quite a bit of power and influence, even more than money."

Victor's head came up. His eyes had become almost black with rising rage. His jaw became set dangerously.

Jacquetta could see the oncoming storm and sought to head it off. "Downstairs, Victor. Now."

Rick almost blinked, but the way his brother-in-law surged from his seat propelled him from his own. Victor looked very much like a grizzly bear who was about to attack. Rick didn't, couldn't, blame him, especially not when he remembered all of the information that sat inside the binders, but he had never before seen his brother-in-law looking so ready to commit homicide. Rick wanted to get between him and Jacquetta, just in case the SIN agent lost it.

Victor didn't, however. Instead, he obeyed his sister and left the office. Jacquetta followed close behind, alongside Rick.

The moment they reached the basement gymnasium, Jacquetta pointed her brother in the direction of the large punching bag in the center of the room. Victor, again, didn't argue. He simply headed towards it.

Rick almost swallowed when Victor began to strike the bag. He had never seen Victor in such a full-fledged rage before, and it unnerved him, to say the least. The blows Victor dealt the bag were full of fury, making it swing and quake ominously.

It was nothing, however, in comparison to the look Jacquetta gave him. Her blue eyes smoldered with a different sort of rage, one that was tempered both by grief and dark memories.

"These traffickers," she said, voice low and demanding. "Do you believe them to be in the same league as the ones Norman and his Councilman friends were involved with?"

"Worse," Rick said, his own voice almost inaudible. *"Much* worse. The group Norman and his Councilman buddies ran with fell apart the moment Norman flipped on 'em. These people, whoever they are, probably have layers of protection that those Councilmen never even dreamed of. Again, Quet. If we can believe what your father wrote in that letter to your brother, then the highest levels of SIN were compromised. That's far beyond the sort of influence those Councilmen thought they could wield."

She nodded, her expression darkening further. "Bastards like them cost the innocence of far too many children, almost including our own. If they also cost my father his life, Rick..."

He heard the anger in her voice mix with anguish. His arms opened in the next heartbeat to envelope her in a comforting embrace.

"We'll get them, Quetta," Rick promised. "We'll make them pay."

She said nothing more, leaning in and returning his embrace. Rick felt his wife's tears wet through his thin shirt. It ignited an anger of his own, and he prayed he'd be able to keep the promise he'd made.

A savage yell recaptured both his and Jacquetta's attention just a moment later. They looked up as the punching bag fell to the floor, splitting open as it hit. Victor stood next to it, breathing heavy. The anger still lurked within his eyes, but his expression had begun to clear.

Jacquetta half-smiled. Rick stared in disbelief.

"You murdered my bag," he said.

"What?" Victor blinked, looked at the broken piece of equipment, and blew out a breath. "Oh. Yeah. I broke mine, too.

Yesterday."

"Feel better?" Jacquetta wanted to know.

"Not really," Victor told his sister. "But I also no longer feel like actually killing something." He took a second, longer look at her, noting the reddened eyes. His voice gentled. "Are you alright?"

"I will be." She inclined her head. "Feel up to finishing our discussion?"

Victor let loose another breath before nodding. "Head back up to the office?"

Rick glanced again at the bag, then nodded. "I'll have to order a new one, so that sounds like a plan."

"Sorry." Victor had the grace to look a bit chagrined. "I can pay for it."

"We can discuss that, along with everything else," Rick said, summoning up a half-smile. Grief, he knew, did things to people. Losing a punching bag would be a small price to pay in the long run if it helped Victor deal, no matter how unexpected it was. "Come on."

Five minutes later, they were once more sitting in Rick's office. Victor once again produced his now well-read letter. His eyes narrowed at one of the lines as he tried to transition to the unflappable agent of SIN.

"Dad said there were a lot of people who like what this Department of Mid-Western Island Affairs can get for them." He spoke in a quiet, measured tone, his training as both an agent and as a Wolfe-Wall once again taking hold. "Do you think *that* is what he meant?"

He gestured to the binders and notebooks. Jacquetta's eyes darkened when she glanced at them. Rick heaved a sigh, dark memories rising.

110

"It wouldn't," he said at last, "surprise me in the least. There are a surprising number of people out there who prey on children, and some of them have the money and the connections to get what they want, no matter what it is." His tone became bitter. "Those are also the sort of people who almost never suffer the consequences of their crimes, even if they do get caught."

Victor frowned at Rick's words, which held the weight of experience. He turned a quizzical look on his sister, only to blanch at her fierce expression.

"Am I missing something here?" he asked.

"Just before Rick left his department to become a private investigator, he was part of a task force that went after those predators who prey on children," Jacquetta told him, her voice filled with a mother's wrath. "Some of the very last people anyone would have suspected of being *that* way were caught up in their net, including teachers, doctors, priests, business people, even fellow *police officers.*"

She all but spat those last words. Rick glanced at her, reaching over to lay a gentle hand on her knee, then looked back at Victor.

"One of the guys I knew, another detective, happened to be one of the people we caught," Rick said. "We'd considered him a friend, had him over, and everything. We never once suspected."

"Sy never liked him," Jacquetta said. "But he would never say why."

Victor sat up, eyes blazing once more. His voice became a dangerous growl. "He didn't—"

"No." Rick shook his head, cutting Victor off with a chopped hand. "He never touched any of ours. Sy said he just never liked how he would watch him, Charlie, and Emma." He breathed out another sigh in a visible attempt to keep himself calm. "Anyway, of the close to one hundred people we caught, three *walked.* All of the charges against them were dropped, despite the evidence we had against them."

"*What?*" Victor snarled.

"As it turned out," Rick continued, nodding at him. "Two of the people who walked were politicians on the rise, who somehow had the clout to make even the smallest hint of an allegation disappear. The third happened to be a pharmacist who also had connections to some very wealthy, influential people." Hazel eyes became a burnished, angry gold. "It didn't help that the victims of each of the three *vanished,* as they'd never existed."

Victor gaped in disbelief. "Are you *serious,* Rick? Didn't anyone make the connection?"

"Of course we did," Rick told him. "But we were flat-out ordered not to say or do anything. Our higher-ups told us that the politicians were simply the victims of a setup. The pharmacist was supposedly an asset of the intelligence community." He blew out a rage-filled breath. "Everything we had gathered against them was destroyed, and the allegations were swept under the rug. We couldn't touch them, not then."

Victor's eyes narrowed at his brother-in-law. He knew Rick well enough to know... "You didn't like that."

Rick's face proved a mask of stone, but his eyes were troubled. "No. I didn't."

"It's part of the reason he left the police force," Jacquetta said. "And it's the reason he went into business for himself."

"When I worked for the force, I had to do what I was told, even when it was to stop an investigation," Rick said. A small, shark-like smile swam over his lips. "Now, people can tell me all they want to back off on something, but I don't have to listen."

"And the deputy director wonders why you refuse all of SIN's job offers." Victor chuckled before arching an eyebrow at the other man. Another thing he knew firsthand about his brother-in-law was just how tenacious he could be. "Did you ever make those bastards pay?"

Rick's smile widened. "Oh, yeah. It took me a while, and I had a lot of help, but I can cheerfully say that not even one of them walks the streets now."

"What about their backers or whatever they were?"

Jacquetta also smiled. "He put them away, too, with some help from Dad. Dad was the one, by the way, who encouraged Rick to become a private investigator."

"He did?" Victor felt surprised for a second before wondering if he should be. If William Wolfe-Wall happened to be already aware of certain things, thanks to Katherine...

"Yes." Jacquetta nodded in affirmation. "He was only too happy to help, in fact." A shadow passed over her face. "Compared to someone who can influence a Director of the Special Intelligence Network, however, those people Rick went after, as well as their backers, were probably small potatoes."

"Without question." Rick's eyes went to the letter Victor held. "When was your current director appointed?"

"Only about two, maybe three years ago," Victor said. "Depending on when Dad wrote this, it could be that Mister Kingston wasn't aware of it."

113

"Perhaps." Rick preferred that option without question, but he knew there was at least one other, far less optimal possibility. "Or it could be that he is aware of it and was appointed to his position as the Director of SIN based on his willingness to play proverbial ball with whoever is responsible for all of this."

He motioned again to the collection of binders and notebooks. Victor's gaze fell back upon them, as did Jacquetta's, before moving to the photo album and scrapbook that had been filled with snippets of Victor's son's young life.

When Victor looked back up, his eyes had become pure ice. His tone proved to be just as cold.

"I want to find out," he said. "I also want to discover who these *others* Dad spoke of are. I want to see the rest of whatever evidence they have and find out what I can do to help bring the perpetrators of *this*, whoever they are, down."

Rick nodded his understanding, feeling a new fire rising from deep within him. A single glance at Jacquetta allowed him to see his thoughts reflected back at him.

"And that's," he said, "exactly what we're going to do, Victor."

"We?" Victor looked at him, somewhat taken aback by the quiet darkness he heard in Rick's voice. "What do you—"

"Do you really think we'd let you do this alone, Vic?" Rick tilted his head and arched an eyebrow at him.

Victor blinked, staring at him. "I didn't... I mean, are you *sure?*"

"Yes." Rick didn't hesitate to answer. Steel lined his voice. "I told you last night that I would help in whatever way you needed me. To have the chance to bring a bunch of people who hurt kids to justice? To hold the bastards responsible for all *this*," his finger stabbed at the files, "accountable for their crimes and maybe even give some children their childhoods back?"

"You won't be able to get rid of us until we do," Jacquetta agreed.

"Quet—" Victor began.

"No, Vic." She shook her head at her brother, eyes and voice unyielding and stifling any protest, even as she smiled at him. "Neither Rick nor I will allow you to do this by yourself. Dad..." She breathed deep, the grief she felt over William Andrew Wolfe-Wall's death threatening to overcome her for a moment. "Dad would want you to have some back-up you know you can trust."

Victor knew she was right, but something nagged at him. "What about your kids? If we start ruffling feathers, they could become targets."

It was the truth. Rick and Jacquetta both knew it.

They shared another look before Jacquetta spoke in a soft voice. "As much as Rick and I might hate it, it wouldn't be the first time. They'll understand if we explain it to them."

"Are you *sure-?*"

"We are." Rick cut his brother-in-law off and sighed at Victor's surprised expression. "As Quet said, it wouldn't be the first time. As much as I hate it, my career has put all of them in danger more than once. The kids can handle it." He hesitated, then plowed ahead. "What's more, they might be able to help."

"Help?" Victor eyed him in consternation. "Rick—"

Again, Rick cut him off. "According to your father's letter, your boy's been at risk for some time. He might want someone closer to his age to talk about certain things, and, as I said, Charlie, Sy, and Emma have all been through this before, on more than one occasion."

"It'll also give us a way to keep tabs on them," Jacquetta said and shrugged when her brother turned his look on her. "If we don't give them a way to help, chances are only too good that they'll look for one on their own, and *that* could land them in the sort of trouble we'd prefer to keep them out of, as we both know only too well."

She gave her husband a wry smile. He returned it with one of his own and lifted his right shoulder in a half-shrug.

"Unfortunately," Rick said. "Quet's right. They're all curious about the cousin they've never known, and, given what we've learned, the last thing we want is for them to take things into their own hands in an attempt to help both him and us."

Victor almost winced at the thought. He wanted to deny their words. There was an urge to deny his sister, brother-in-law, nephews, and niece even the opportunity to help.

But he couldn't. He had no one else to turn to, and he'd already asked for Rick's help. Jacquetta wouldn't allow him to keep her away based on that alone. As for Charlie, Josiah, and Emma? Victor had already seen the three in action on more than one occasion. He knew their parents spoke nothing but the truth when they said that their sons and daughter would look for trouble if not given the chance to assist in a more official capacity.

"All right," he said, at last, the words being dragged past his lips with the greatest reluctance. "As much as I hate to admit it, I know that you're right."

He breathed out a resigned, unhappy sigh. If anything happened to a member of his family, *any* of them, Victor would never forgive himself.

Rick knew it and understood. "We'll lay down some rules, Vic, and do our best to keep everyone safe."

He offered his brother-in-law a lopsided grin that did in no way conceal his worry. Jacquetta gave Victor her sweetest smile, which still managed to convey the promise of retribution if anything happened to any of them.

It would, Victor decided, have to be good enough. "So, where do we begin? How do we go about finding out what we want to know?"

"We start with what your father gave us," Rick said. "We have three binders and two notebooks of possible evidence. We also have the letter he gave you."

"What about this, Mister Eppes?" Jacquetta asked. "What did he tell you?"

"I didn't question him too closely," Rick said before filling them in on his visit to the bank and concluding with, "I didn't want him becoming suspicious of me and not giving me all of this."

"Smart thinking." Victor's eyes fell back to his father's letter. A moment later, his eyes found and fastened on a single sentence. "Dad mentions a Department of Mid-Western Island Affairs being stonewalled regarding my son. I've never heard of such an agency before, so what is it? What does it do, and what is it supposed to be doing? More importantly, how does it relate to my son?"

Those were all, Rick thought, excellent questions. "I don't know, at least not yet. I *do* think I know where we can start getting some answers, though."

"Oh?"

"Yes."

Rick nodded as he held back the small smile that mixed faint incredulity with a bit of sad amusement at Victor's lack of realization. Under other, more normal circumstances, he knew his brother-in-law would have already thought of this himself, but between learning of his father's death, making arrangements for the funeral, the funeral itself, then learning of his former lover's death, the fact that he happened to be a father and that his unknown child happened to be in danger...Rick believed Victor could be forgiven for being a little slower on the uptake than usual.

It was the reason he tapped one of the binders. "Everything here happened in a single location: the Mid-Superior Islands. That's where we'll begin."

"Ah." Victor thought a moment before he, too, nodded. "That sounds good, but where would these islands be, Rick? I've been all over the globe, just as Quet has, and I can't recall hearing anything about something like them before."

"Nor can I," Jacquetta agreed.

Rick's brow furrowed. "What about your Katherine?"

"She never talked about islands, at least not that I remember. She and the rest of her family said they were from Michigan, I think."

"Michigan?" Rick reached over to where Victor's son's birth certificate had been placed. "That's the state listed as your son's place of birth." He held it up to point it out. "See? The state of Michigan, the city of Sulivan." He felt the corners of his mouth turn down. "It's only got the one 'L,' which is odd."

"It's probably just a typo." Jacquetta dismissed it. All records, even official ones, weren't immune to a mistake or two. "Right now, let's take a

118

look at what we have. There's a Department of Mid-Western Island Affairs. We also have the Mid-Superior Islands. Your son's birth certificate, Vic, puts him in the state of Michigan, which is also where Katherine and her family told you they were from." She glanced from her brother to her husband and back. "To the best of my knowledge, there's exactly one body of water in the Midwestern United States, by the state of Michigan, that has *Superior* in its name."

"The Great Lake." Victor nodded agreement after a moment's thought. "Which has quite a few islands, if I'm not mistaken."

"You're not," Rick said, his mind racing. He stood up, walking over to his desk to pull out an old-fashioned phone and address book. "I have a small number of contacts out in that area. I can get in touch with them and see what they can tell us." He saw Victor look over, a worried look on his face. "Relax, Victor. No one has to know anything beyond the fact that I'm looking for the previously unknown son of a client. That's the story I told my partners about why I'll be busy over the next few days. Ed and Chris do know that you are my client, though."

Victor's face clouded further. "I don't know if I like the idea of them knowing."

"It's *all* they know," Rick said. "At least for right now, and it not only keeps them from asking too many follow-up questions but lets me ask them for some help if I need it."

"You think you might?"

"It's possible," Rick said before holding up a hand to forestall any would-be protests Victor could make. "I trust them, Victor. Your father also vetted the two of them before we became business partners. I won't tell them anything they don't absolutely need to know to help me track down your son."

Victor eyed him a moment before offering up a somewhat sheepish smile. "All right. You say you trust them, and if they passed Dad's checks, that'll have to do. I don't want to put my son in any more danger than I absolutely must. Until we know more about what's going on and who's involved, I'd like to keep my part in everything quiet." He made a face a moment later. "Of course, that begs the question of what we're going to do if and when you *do* find my son." Gray eyes rose once more to meet hazel, apprehension returning to glitter in their depths. "How are we going to arrange a meet if my son decides he wants that without me confessing things to my director and maybe others?"

"We can worry about that when the time comes," Rick said. "For now, let's just concentrate on the immediate task of finding your son. Everything else can come after that."

Victor hesitated, then gave a nod of agreement. His gaze turned to steel. His voice took on a knife's edge. "Do whatever it is you need to do, then, Rick. I want answers."

"And you'll have them." Rick glanced at Jacquetta. "While I'm working on this, I take it you'll be continuing as you all did today?"

"If that's all right with you and Quet," Victor said. "I told the director we would be leading our watchers on a merry dance to help *train* them." His eyes narrowed. "But maybe we can do a little more without anyone in SIN being the wiser."

Jacquetta eyed him. "Such as?"

"*If* my Director is involved, then he would need people at his side whom he could trust to help cover everything up. If he *isn't*, then there would have to be people at or close to the top who could run interference

120

whenever necessary while getting things done." Victor chewed on his lower lip. "Maybe it's time I started taking a closer look at the people giving me and my fellow operatives of SIN orders. Aside from Director Kingston, we have his second-in-command, Ryan Dominick. He's been the Deputy Director of SIN for the past eight, maybe nine years now. It's said the only reason he wasn't appointed to the top job was because of the politics involved. He doesn't always like to play nice, even with those who control the purse strings."

"That'd be a good reason to keep him where he is, then," Jacquetta said. "In theory, at least." She tilted her head. "Will you be asking your former partners to help out?"

"No. Not yet. I want to do my research first and maybe confirm a few things before even trying to involve them."

"Good idea," Rick said. "I've dealt with both Dominick and your director before, but who else is there for you to look into?"

Victor breathed a sigh as he thought. "We have Vera-Faye West. She's the Chief of Staff and Special Counsel, appointed to her position about five years ago. No one wants to get on her bad side, as their careers have a nasty tendency to stall out if they do. She reminds me of a beautiful cobra. Philip Evander is next after her and is basically the CFO of SIN. Dexter Ibarra is the head of training. He has an outstanding reputation, and I think he's above suspicion, unlike Marcus Kraft and Rolanda Brogan. They're also at the top of SIN's hierarchy and are known to be difficult to deal with. Each one has a number of powerful connections who could be lending their influence to keep people from looking too closely at whatever might be going on—and again, that's just the ones at the very top. There are at least two or three dozen more just below them who have their connections, their influence, their power, and their own unpleasant reputations."

"Which means you'll need to be more than a little careful when checking them all out," Rick said.

"Dad insinuated the same thing in his letter," Victor said. "I can't ignore this, in any case. I *refuse* to."

Rick and Jacquetta nodded their grim agreement. They wouldn't—couldn't—ignore this, either.

But first, they had some parenting to do.

"Let's call the kids in," Jacquetta said after glancing at the clock that hung by the office door. "We'll have dinner, and after that, we can make up a plan of how we're going to handle things for the next few days. And Vic?" Her brother looked at her as they each rose from their respective seats. "Don't worry. We'll get to the bottom of this, one way or another."

Chapter Five: Finding Leads

May 24, 2007: Offices of Cross, Thorne, and Zeal Investigations

The following day, Rick found himself back at his work office. Chris and Ed were again in the conference room, going over some more of what they'd discovered about the Long case. They had waved Rick away when he had offered to help, leaving him time to focus on finding out more about Victor's son and the city they assumed the young man called his home.

His first step, as he'd told Victor and Jacquetta the previous night, would be to get as much information as he could about the Mid-Superior Islands and the Department of Mid-Western Island Affairs. Despite having never heard of either before, Rick didn't think it would take *too* long to find something.

Oh, how wrong he was.

His first step was a simple internet search, which yielded nothing. Rick could feel a frown forming as he scrolled down the results page. More and more, he went down, searching for something-anything-that might qualify as information. There were pages about the scenic trails around Lake Superior, more about the Apostle Islands, Caribou Island, Isle Royale, Grand Island, and others, and still more pages about the animals, geology, tourism, and more.

There was nothing, however, about the Mid-Superior Islands.

It surprised Rick, but didn't yet frustrate him. Perhaps the Mid-Superior Islands were only called that by the locals?

Picking up his phone, he thought to find out. During the next two to three hours, he called as many of his contacts in the Lake Superior area as he could. Much to his amazement, he heard the same impossible thing over and over again. No matter whom he spoke to in Michigan, Wisconsin, Minnesota, and even the Canadian province of Ontario, each person claimed never to have heard of the Mid-Superior Islands.

As he hung up from his last contact, Rick felt dazed, even bewildered. How was it possible that *no one* around the Lake Superior area had heard of these islands even once?

His lips became a thin line, and his brow furrowed with thought before clearing as an idea struck him. Perhaps he had talked to the wrong people? Almost all of Rick's contacts were in Toronto, Detroit, Lansing, Grand Rapids, Ann Arbor, Milwaukee, Green Bay, and Minneapolis-St. Paul's areas. None of those cities was close to Lake Superior. Instead, if they were by any of the Great Lakes, they were by Lake Michigan, Lake Huron, Lake Erie, and Lake Ontario.

He nodded to himself. No doubt that happened to be it. If the Mid-Superior Islands *were* known only to the locals, then it made sense that none of his contacts in that area would have heard of them. He just needed to think of another way to get the information he wanted.

"Mister Thorne?"

He looked up to see Xiao Lin poking her head inside his office. "What is it?"

"It is almost one o'clock," she said. "Mister Cross and Mister Zeal are planning to order lunch and would like to know if you want anything?"

"Oh." Rick blinked and glanced at the clock. "Wow. I didn't realize it was already this late. They say where they were ordering from?"

124

"They are still discussing it, I believe," she said, eyeing him. "Forgive me for asking, Mister Thorne. Normally, you would be working with them, not on something else, so..."

"What am I doing?"

He smiled at her as she gave him a slight nod. Xiao Lin, or Miss Lin as she was more commonly called at the office, was a college student who had taken the position of assistant to earn more money and get some valuable experience for her planned degree in criminal justice. She seemed mousy at first glance, but could become quite talkative, even brash, after one got to know her. She liked things that made her *think,* she had said in her interview. She was also known for the habit of spouting the most esoteric bits of knowledge at the least expected moment.

Chris loved the fact that she could come at things from different angles than the rest of them, while she reminded Ed of his daughters, and he liked how eager she was to learn. Rick appreciated her sharp mind and the fact that she put one hundred percent into both her job and her college work. She enjoyed learning in general, had proven herself quite observant, and never appeared to mind the odd hours a private investigations firm could work.

She had also learned the routines of Ed, Chris, and Rick, as well as Helena's, and how unusual it was for any of them not to follow their habits. Considering how rarely Rick himself deviated from what he considered normal, he found he couldn't blame her for being curious.

"I'm helping out my brother-in-law," he told her. "He just found out by letter that he has a son and wants the chance to get to know him."

"Ah!" Lin smiled brightly. "Good for him. I hope you find the boy."

"I hope so, too. I'm just having a problem finding the kid's supposed hometown." Rick waved at his computer. "According to what my brother-in-law remembers about the boy's mom, she lived somewhere by Michigan and Lake Superior. To be more specific, she was supposed to live on an island on the lake itself."

Lin inclined her head. "Which one?"

"That's my main problem at the moment," Rick told her. "I'd never heard of the Mid-Superior Islands before now, let alone the city of Sulivan."

"The Mid-Superior Islands? The city of Sulivan?" Lin stared at him with suddenly wide eyes. It was a look of shocked recognition, something Rick had not expected, and her following words proved even more surprising. "Is that with one 'L' or two?"

He stared back, almost unable to process what he'd heard. *How in the world?* "One. We thought it was a typo on the document the city's name was on, but do *you* know of these Mid-Superior Islands, Miss Lin? Of Sulivan?"

"They are mentioned in a blog that I follow," she said. "Quite frequently, too." She had palmed her ever-present tablet in the next instant. "Let me find it."

It took only moments before she crowed in triumph and placed the tablet in front of Rick. He almost frowned, picking it up. There, on the screen, in rudimentary green text on a black background that reminded Rick of early terminals in the bullpen:

```
Project Enigma
Post # 342
```

126

Written by The Haunted

Title: Island Affairs

Ever since I arrived in the Mid-Superior
Islands, I've been aware of the
Department of Mid-Western Island
Affairs. How could I not be? Their
presence, though usually subtle, is
everywhere, even more than the DBJF.
Island Affairs is supposed to be a
bridge. Since the Mids are, on record,
a dependent sovereign nation, Island
Affairs is meant to be the agency that
spans the gap between the local and
federal governments, with the closest
example being the Bureau of Indian
Affairs.
But what role does it actually play?
To hear the local-born people of
Sulivan, in particular, tell it, the
Department of Mid-Western Island
Affairs exists strictly to try and
control them. One cannot take a job
outside the Mids or attend an outside
university without the express
permission of Island Affairs. One can
travel between the Mid-Superior
Islands, but not beyond without
permission. Until recently, one could
not even come into the waters
surrounding the Mids, either, without

Island Affairs' express say-so. Not even
cargo ships, despite the Mids' proximity
to the shipping lanes that crisscross
Lake Superior, had permission. It's been
said that Island Affairs even attempted
to prevent the DBJF Alliance
Corporation, which was founded within
the borders of the Mid-Superior Islands
and Sulivan, from going public until an
agreement between them was reached.

Rick's eyes went wide, and he suppressed the urge to let out a low whistle. The *DBJF Alliance Corporation* was not a business to take lightly. While rumor had it that the company had started as nothing more than a partnership between specialized contractors, it had grown into something far more and, within only four years, had become a literal corporate powerhouse. Thanks to the owners' shared love of tinkering, inventing, and improving existing products, as well as a fortuitous meeting with government agents, the *DBJF,* as the business was more commonly known, had grown and expanded. It had a variety of government contracts now, as well as civilian ones, and it wasn't just concerned with garden-variety construction. No, the DBJF had gone into creating various electronics, armor, weaponry, and even clothing, with many of their inventions seeming almost out of this world. The DBJF Alliance Corporation no longer had just one or two regional offices but was in virtually every state in the United States and a number of the Canadian provinces, and had even moved across the oceans to set up shop within Europe and Japan.

Was this Department of Mid-Western Island Affairs the

'government agents' that had given the DBJF its needed break? If so, and if this blog post happened to be truthful, then what had been in the agreement between the DBJF and Island Affairs that had permitted it?

He thought a moment, then turned his attention back to the blog. He could think about the connections later. There was more to read.

```
On the other hand, Island Affairs is
rumored to be the one responsible for
letting in the former heads of The
Pasquale Family, which is one of the
leading sources of crime within Sulivan.
Island Affairs is said to be responsible
for the Scordato Family arriving in the
city of Babineaux Island Affairs is also
reputed to have brought the Ferra Family
within Logan and saddled Talfryn with
the Tafano Crime Family. Worse, it's
been said that Island Affairs has
actively covered up the crimes of each
organization, which range from
kidnapping to extortion to racketeering
to outright murder.
```

Rick's eyes skimmed over the rest, taking note of various examples that the author of the blog provided. The ending example made him sit up in shock, as it happened to be nothing less than the murder of Katherine Kincaid and the disappearance of her son, Robert.

This case might be even more difficult than I first imagined. Rick's lips pursed at the thought. *What was it that Victor's letter said?* **Many people like what Island Affairs can get for them.** He inclined his head. *Is that* *due to the DBJF or something else?*

And how was it that Miss Lin had found the blog when he hadn't been able to?

She looked mildly uncomfortable when he asked. "I... do not always use the more mainstream search engines. Sometimes, the usual methods don't work, and I need to use things like the Dark Web to find anything."

"The Dark Web?" Rick's eyebrows went up.

Miss Lin nodded, still uncomfortable. "I do not like using it, but sometimes it alone has the information I need. If it's something the so-called Powers That Be want to keep hidden, chances are I can still find out about it there."

Ah. Rick nodded slowly. *Someone wants to keep these Mid-Superior Islands hidden for some reason. But why?*

Exhaling a slow breath, he let his eyes drift up. The names of the other open tabs caught his attention, and abruptly, he glanced at Lin.

"Prepping?" he asked.

Lin snatched the tablet back. "Hey, it's not as out there as you and so many others might think. Some people actually believe that being prepared for something like an invasion is necessary!"

Rick fought the urge to snicker, even as he held up his hands in an attempt to placate her. "Everyone's entitled to their beliefs, Miss Lin. I'm just surprised that this would be one of yours."

She shrugged, a self-conscious look flitting over her face. "Being prepared is what allowed my grandparents and their families to escape Mao's Revolution when it began. While I don't necessarily think something like that would ever happen here, I don't want to leave anything up to chance, if possible."

Rick's face softened. "Understandable. That sort of thing can leave a mark."

"Even generations later," she said, giving him a thin smile. "Is there anything else I can help with?"

Shaking his head, Rick let her go after giving her an idea of what he'd like for lunch, then turned back to his computer. He had a lead now—the DBJF Alliance Corporation.

Finding their website proved easy. Finding anything else useful proved considerably more difficult for Rick, who spent a few hours scouring the website for information. At any other time, Rick would have been impressed by everything the DBJF's website had listed, from their products to their offices to even their Research and Development page. When he was attempting to find an entry point to the Mid-Superior Island City of Sulivan, however?

Not even the 'about us' page had the information Rick wanted and needed. He clicked and scrolled, clicked and scrolled, coming up empty-handed each time.

Until he grasped at the straw that was the 'Miscellaneous' page and scrolled down to its very bottom. There, at last, he saw the link he'd been hoping to find. When he clicked on it, Rick couldn't help voicing both relief and victory.

Granted, the city of Sulivan's Government website wasn't anything special. It simply provided a list of phone numbers, internet links, and email addresses. Rick scrolled through the list, ignoring the information for Sulivan's Mayor, deputy mayor, city attorney, public works director, economic planning director, finance director, police chief,

131

and fire chief. A small shark's smile swam over his lips when he finally saw the listing for the Department of Mid-Western Island Affairs.

"Finally," he muttered. "Pay dirt."

The site, like the others, didn't seem special. There was a simple mission statement, which claimed the Department was there to help facilitate interactions between the United States Federal Government and the local City Government; a list of essential personnel, including the director, deputy director, and Sulivan City Supervisor; and a list of phone numbers and email addresses for the various Federal Liaison Officers. Grabbing a sheet of paper and a pen, Rick began jotting down as many as he thought might be to help him on his case before freezing on a single name that, much to his surprise, he actually knew.

Grabbing his phone once again, Rick dialed. Two and a half rings later, he heard the familiar voice.

"Ethan Plumber."

No amount of professionalism, Rick thought, could ever disguise a person's boredom. "Ethan, it's Rick Thorne."

"Rick?" Immediate, happy surprise filled the other man's voice, obliterating his previous apathy. "Man, I haven't heard from you in *ages*. How the hell did you find me? And what can I do for you?"

"Who says I need you to do anything?" Rick asked, fighting hard to hold in the smile that Ethan couldn't see. "And, to be honest, I wasn't expecting your name to come up in my research."

He wasn't lying. Ethan Plumber was, or had been, an agent with the Federal Bureau of Investigation. Rick had worked with him a few times, first during his time as a detective with the Philadelphia police force and later as a private investigator, and he'd never heard anything but praise

132

for the other man.

So, what could Ethan be doing in a place like *Sulivan?* What had caused him to go to work for the Department of Mid-Western Island Affairs as a 'Liaison Officer'?

"Yeah, that doesn't surprise me," Ethan said. Rick could almost see the other man's knowing grin. "What are you lookin' into?"

"I have a client who's looking for his son," Rick said, choosing to omit Victor's identity for the moment. He also stifled his curiosity regarding the reason behind Ethan's being in Sulivan. "This son was born in the Mid-Superior Island City of Sulivan and, during my investigation..."

"You came upon the Department of Mid-Western Island Affairs?" A strange, guarded note entered Ethan's voice.

"Yes," Rick confirmed it while wondering at the other's sudden and unusual wariness. "I'd never heard of it, any more than I'd heard of these Mid-Superior Islands or of Sulivan before now, and when I saw your name listed on the website, I thought I should call."

"Yeah." Ethan went silent for a moment before he said, "Let me call you right back, Rick."

Alarm bells began to ring in Rick's mind. "Ethan?"

"Give me fifteen, maybe twenty minutes."

"Ethan—"

"I'll explain when I call you back!"

He hung up before Rick could say another word. The private investigator felt a frown cross his lips as he put his phone down. Ethan Plumber had never, from what Rick remembered, acted so *impolitely.* He'd always kept up the mask of "The Agent" during the times Rick had worked with him before.

The few exceptions to that rule, which Rick could count on one hand, had always been when something 'more' happened to be going on.

Again, the words from William Wolfe-Wall's letter drifted through Rick's mind. Hadn't his father-in-law mentioned a '*group of trusted friends*'? Could Ethan be one of them? If so, what was he doing in this Department of Mid-Western Island Affairs? Had he been planted there, undercover? If not, what had happened to land Ethan in his current position?

What was going on?

Stewing in his seat, wondering what he'd do if Ethan *didn't* call back, Rick began to look again at his list of names. If he had to find someone else to help track down Victor's unknown son, he would. He had just been lucky to see a name he already knew.

Nineteen minutes later, the phone rang. Rick snatched it up.

"Sorry 'bout that, Rick," Ethan's voice echoed in his ear. "I just wanted to get out of the office before going any further so my supposed boss can't overhear anything."

"Not a problem," Rick said, even as his eyes narrowed. Ethan didn't want his *boss* eavesdropping? Did that mean he'd been planted into this Island Affairs? "I take it that now he won't?"

"Nope." Ethan's voice now held a distinctive playful cheeriness that was at complete odds with how he'd sounded before. "I also wanted to see if you'd recognize *this* guy."

"This—?"

Before Rick could finish his sentence, another entered into the conversation. "Remember me, Thorne?"

It took Rick almost a full minute to place that semi-familiar light tenor. When he did, he nearly wanted to deny it. There could be *no* way! "Ray? Raymond Douglas? Is that really *you?*"

"Damn it, Rick!" The other man groaned in mock dismay. Ethan, on the other hand, laughed and crowed, "Ha! Told ya he hadn't forgotten 'bout you! Gimme the ten bucks!"

Rick's mind whirled, even as he laughed alongside Ethan. Ray Douglas had been part of Ethan's squad in the FBI, and the two often partnered up together. They had a similar sense of humor and the same attitude towards their workload. Ray could be a bit more on the sarcastic side than Ethan. Yet he was just as methodical, professional, and diligent. Little had escaped Ray's notice during the cases Rick had worked with him, and for *Ray* to also be in the Mid-Superior Islands?

What, Rick had to ask again, was going on?

Before he could speak those words, Ray again spoke. "Ethan tells me you're looking for a missing child?"

"More like a young man and, so far as I know, he's not actually missing," Rick said. "His father didn't know he was a father until recently, and would simply like the chance to connect with his son if it's possible."

"Oh." Ray, strangely, sounded as though he'd winced. "Well, if we can help out, we will."

"I'd appreciate that," Rick said, frowning. Why would Ray *wince* at that idea? Raymond Douglas was a family man—wouldn't *he* want to know if he had a child he'd never known about? "The young man I'm looking for is about twenty-four years old and, like I told Ethan, was born in the Mid-Superior Island City of Sulivan. His mother, from what I understand, was a native."

"What were their names?" Ethan asked. "I doubt we'll have heard

135

of them, but we can always run them through the computer systems we have here and see if anything pops up."

"Sounds good," Rick said. "The mother was Katherine Kincaid, and her son would be Robert Kincaid."

"Kin*caid*?" Ray's voice seemed to rise an octave. When he next spoke, his voice again held an odd edge. "Could you spell that for me?"

Rick did so, alarms once again beginning to go off in the back of his mind. His befuddlement would only increase, too, when he heard Ethan gasp.

"Holy *shit.*" Ray whistled. "A *Kincaid?!*"

"Ray?" Rick knew he sounded incredulous. "What are you—?"

"Anywhere else," Ray cut him off. "And that particular surname probably wouldn't mean much. Here in the Mids? In the city of *Sulivan?*" He could be heard exhaling. "The Kincaids were one of what are called The Old Families, which were descendants of the original settlers that founded the cities and towns of the Mid-Superior Islands."

Ah. Rick thought he understood. "I take it these Old Families, including the Kincaids, have power over there?"

"They did," Ray told him. "Not so much anymore, though, thanks to the fact that most, if not all, of them have been wiped out."

"*What?*" Rick sat up in his seat as another portion of William Wolfe-Wall's letter came to him. ***Katherine, like her parents and brothers before her, was murdered.*** An entire family being killed was nothing less than a tragedy. Still, if he understood what Ray seemed to be saying, this was multiple families and a large stack of homicides. This case was becoming even more dangerous the more information he collected. "As in murdered?"

136

"As in taken out and killed off by those who wanted their power," Ethan told him, his voice grim. "It was, from what I've read and heard, Sulivan's Night of the Long Knives."

"Only instead of it being a single night, it happened in the passage of several weeks and months," Ray said. "And instead of knives being used, there were drive-by shootings, random explosions, and unquestionable assassinations."

Rick almost gaped. "Are you *serious?*"

"Unfortunately." Ray's tone became dark. "Of the Families who were targeted, few managed to survive. Those who did are believed to have either moved away or changed their names and gone to ground."

The unspoken implication couldn't have been made more evident. Neither Ray nor Ethan believed that Victor's son would still be in Sulivan. Not if he was still alive.

If Rick hadn't read the letter Victor had been sent, he might have come to the same conclusion. "I have reason to believe the young man I'm searching for is in Sulivan. If he's not using his mother's surname of Kincaid, he might be using Robert Pupp, with two 'p's, Robert Wall, or even Robert Wolfe, with an 'e.'"

"Robert Pupp, with two 'p's, Robert Wall, or Robert Wolfe, with an 'e,' you say?" Ray went silent for a moment. "Hold on a minute, if you would, Rick. I'm going to put those names into my work computer. If anyone with those names received so much as a traffic ticket in the past ten or so years, it'll be listed."

"Whoa." Rick felt his eyebrows go up. "Your systems can do that?"

"Believe it or not," Ray said. "The DBJF Alliance Corporation has made Sulivan its primary headquarters, and they supplied most of the city's computer systems. The one used by our local office is the same one used by Island Affairs and the local police department, and it's all interlinked— sort of our little version of a combined NCIC and VICAP. Since I'm the Special Agent In Charge out here, I've got full system access."

"So if my client's son had even the most minor scrape with the law, chances are you'd have a record of him that you can access. No matter what name he might use." Rick grinned. "I wish we had something like that out here."

"You said it," Ray chuckled. Rick could hear tapping as the agent typed on a keyboard. About a minute later, he reported, "I don't have anything on either a Robert Pupp or a Robert Wall, but I *do* have one report on a Robert Wolfe, with an 'e.' It's about seven years old, and his occupation at the time was 'student.'"

The slight snicker from the other end that Rick heard prompted him to ask, "What did he do?"

"It seems Mister Wolfe was at a student party that got out of hand. Mid-Lake University wasn't all that large back then, but its students could still get a bit rowdy. According to the report, though, he had little, if anything, to do with the issue but got caught up in the sweep that campus security, aided by some regular officers, did. It seems a couple of friends of his had dragged him along to the party in question, and since he was sober, he was let go with only a warning."

"Anything else?"

"Not according to this," Ray told him after a few more moments.

"And that was seven years ago?"

"Close to it, yes. If this *is* your boy, then he's either kept his nose clean or he's using another name."

"You're sure he wouldn't use Kincaid?" Rick asked. "Even a variation of it?"

"Not unless he wants every bell, whistle, and alarm goin' off in Island Affairs," Ethan said. "Using any form of Kincaid would be a surefire way of doin' just that, and believe me when I say, Rick, that Island Affairs does *not* want the competition, especially from the Old Families of the Mids."

Rick felt himself arching an eyebrow at Ethan's tone. "Oh?"

"Let's just say there's a *reason* a majority of the Mids' Old Families were taken out and why Island Affairs never bothered to investigate or bring anyone to justice for the crimes."

"They never investigated?" Rick thought back to William Wolfe-Wall's letter and connected the dots. "You think your Department might be responsible for what happened?"

"We do," Ethan confirmed. "Of course, the problem is proving it."

"According to the official record, the blame for what happened to a majority of the Old Families can be placed with the Pasquale Family," Ray said. "They were and are one of the major criminal elements here, and it's been said they wanted to end the hold the Old Families had on things here in Sulivan. Unofficially, though?" He could be heard to sigh. "No one would be surprised if Island Affairs happened to be involved. A number of Sulivan's native-born residents believe it, without question."

Again, the memory of his father-in-law's letter ghosted through Rick's mind. *Island Affairs hates being stonewalled...*

He leaned forward in his seat. "Well, like I said before, I'm pretty sure my client's son would still be in Sulivan or, barring that, the Mid-Superior Islands."

"Then he's either gone far underground, or he's using another name," Ethan told him. "It wouldn't matter which city or town he happened to make his home, either. If he wants to keep Island Affairs off his back, he ain't using any variation of 'Kincaid.'"

"Damn." Rick let out a sigh of his own. He didn't have a clue as to what other name or names Victor's son might use.

"Sorry, Rick." Ray understood his frustration. "I don't know what else to tell you. Of course, I've only been here for a little less than five months now, and Ethan's been here for just over three."

"So there's a lot you're still learning," Rick said, holding in a sigh. His mind whirled with thought before he came to the only conclusion he could. "I don't suppose the two of you would like some company?"

"Some company?" Ray asked. "You're thinking of coming out here?"

"If I want to have a chance at finding my client's son, or at least of finding out where he might've gone?" Rick said. "Yes."

There was silence for close to a full minute. Rick could well imagine Ray and Ethan glancing at each other, holding a silent conversation before Ray once again spoke.

"It couldn't hurt," he said. "And who knows? We may be able to help each other out."

Rick's eyebrows rose a little. "How so?"

"We'll explain when you get out of here," Ethan said. "Grab a commercial flight to the Webster A. Ryan Airport. The airport code is W, A, R. I'll send you out the paperwork tonight so you'll be able to expedite

140

the customs process."

"W, A, R. Wait. *War?*" Rick blinked. "And why would I need to go through customs?"

"Trust us, 'war' fits," Ray said dryly. "And going through the Mid-Superior Islands' version of customs is mandatory, no matter where you're coming from. Ethan and I will meet you when you get here. Just text me the time. Not Ethan, though, so his supposed boss won't find out right away."

"All right." Rick made a note. "Hopefully, I'll be seeing you soon."

"We look forward to it," Ray said, and Ethan echoed him.

A moment later, having ended the call, Rick turned back to his computer. All he needed to do was find a flight, and he could head out to the Mid-Superior Island City of Sulivan.

Chapter Six: Now Arriving in the City of Sulivan

May 25, 2007: Flying towards the Webster A. Ryan Airport

It turned out there was only one commercial flight available to take Rick to the Mid-Superior Island City of Sulivan. Rick took the train to Newark International Airport instead of Philadelphia, and as a result, feeling both bemused and bewildered. He had never heard of Mid-Lake Airlines, any more than he'd heard of the Mid-Superior Islands or the city of Sulivan, before starting this investigation, and the idea that he had to fill out customs paperwork just to be able to visit astonished him.

It had also perplexed Victor and Jacquetta when he'd told them about it not long after arriving home the previous evening. Why, they had all wondered, would he need to go through customs? Not even Hawaii required American citizens to go through customs unless they arrived by international flight.

But Hawaii is a state. Rick reminded himself. *The Mid-Superior Island Cities are a dependent sovereign nation. That could be the reason.*

Well, he'd most likely be finding out soon enough. Boarding his plane at just past noon, Rick sank into his cushioned seat with a small sigh before glancing around the cabin. Aside from the passenger plane being a little smaller and older than most of the other aircraft he had seen waiting at various gates, nothing seemed to be all that out of the ordinary. There weren't many other passengers, either, leading Rick to lean back in his seat. Fewer passengers meant fewer chances for drama and other risks, so this flight would likely be uneventful.

That was good, as it would allow him to use the two or so hours it would take to arrive in Sulivan to go over everything he knew. Taking out his ever-present notebook as soon as the plane had lifted into the air, Rick settled in to do just that.

There could be no denying that Victor's son was in danger. William's letter had made it clear, as had the little collection of binders and notebooks that Rick had found in the safety deposit box. After the phone conversation with Ethan and Ray, as well as the *Project Enigma* blog, Rick couldn't help but wonder about the difficulties he would be facing. *Had* this Department of Mid-Western Island Affairs been involved in the deaths of Katherine Kincaid and her family? The deaths of the other Old Family members, too? Was this Island Affairs the '***Powers That Be***', which William had spoken of in his letter to Victor?

And what about the '***group of trusted friends***' that William had also mentioned? Who were they? How did Rick and Victor go about getting in contact with them?

He didn't know. Not yet. Once Rick found Victor's unknown son, he guessed the right direction would be known.

Unless, of course, Ethan and Ray were already somehow part of that group? Perhaps that was what Ray had meant when he'd told Rick they'd 'be able to help each other out'? If not, then what were the two of them doing in the Mid-Superior Islands? In the city of Sulivan?

Rick felt the corners of his lips turn downward as he thought. At the moment, he had a plethora of questions and almost nothing for answers. Under other, more normal circumstances, the private eye would have salivated at the prospect of another investigation. Rick loved solving mysteries, no matter how small, and he also loved helping people alongside his partners. Right now, however? He was mostly on his own, and the

143

investigation involved his own family.

Relax, Rick, he reminded himself after a heavier sigh escaped his throat. *You'll find the answers, and when you do, it will surely make more sense.*

He breathed in at the thought. Ethan and Ray would no doubt fill him in on what had taken them both to Sulivan. With their help, and as soon as he learned the city itself, Rick could begin acquiring the information he wanted and needed. After that, he would arrange it so that his brother-in-law could fly out to meet with the son Victor had never known he'd had.

Nodding to himself, Rick at last opened his notebook. He had spent quite a bit of time going through the *Project Enigma* blog after he'd gotten off the phone the previous day. It had proven to be both an interesting and an entertaining read once he managed to get past all of the conspiracy theories the blog contained.

Apparently, according to the blog, the Department of Mid-Western Island Affairs existed solely to control the people within its jurisdiction. According to the writer, *customs* were just the beginning for outsiders. For the native-born, there were various hoops, mazes, and more to navigate in order to live a semi-normal life.

It didn't sound right. Rick wondered whether the blog's author was telling the truth. Still, he wasn't going to Sulivan to cast judgment on government entities that had over-inflated control issues. He was going there to hopefully reunite a father with his son, nothing more.

He could only hope that it would remain that way.

Just under two hours later, the voice of the plane's captain came over the speakers. "Good afternoon, ladies and gentlemen. We're about

144

fifteen to twenty minutes away from landing at our destination. Barring any unforeseen complications, we should be down on the ground and making our way to the gate. On behalf of everyone here at Mid-Lake Airlines and the DBJF Alliance Corporation, I'd like to welcome you to the Mid-Superior Island City of Sulivan. Please sit back, relax if you can, and enjoy the rest of your flight."

Rick grinned and closed his notebook. *It's time to meet with Ethan and Ray, then get to work.*

It took about another seventeen minutes for Rick to finally step inside the Webster A. Ryan airport. As he exited Gate B-3, he found two men waiting for him and felt his grin widen.

Ethan Plumber and Ray Douglas were polar opposites, at least in their appearance. Ethan was almost as broad as he was tall, being at least two or three inches over Rick's six-foot height. His skin was like dark chocolate, while champagne-brown eyes danced with both laughter and intelligence, and an equally broad smile stretched over his chiseled face. Ray, on the other hand, was almost a full head shorter than Ethan and had skin as pale as fresh milk. He had a slighter build, too, as well as sandy-brown hair that was starting to show signs that it might one day match Ethan's salt-and-pepper head. He happened to be an entire decade younger than Ethan, as well.

They shared a similar sense of humor, however, and each possessed an equal desire to see justice done. There were few better partnerships, at least in Rick's opinion, and he called over as soon as he spotted them.

"Rick!" Ray returned his greeting and started forward, his hand outstretched. His emerald green eyes were bright, and he felt the joy of a happy reunion as they shook hands. "It's good to see you again."

"Likewise, Ray," Rick said before moving also to shake Ethan's waiting hand. "You, too, Ethan."

"Shocking, too, I'll bet." Ethan chuckled. "You bring any more luggage? Or just the carry-on?"

"Just this." Rick held up the single, small duffel bag he'd brought. "I'm hoping I won't have to stay *too* long here, no matter how nice my hotel is." He caught Ethan's glance at Ray and saw the other give a slight shake of his head in response. "What?"

"First, where are you staying?" Ray asked. "And, second, it'd be best to wait until after you've gotten past customs and we're in the car before saying anything more."

Rick thought it a little odd that they wouldn't give him at least a hint of whatever happened to be going on, but he also wouldn't argue with them about it. Not yet. "Sounds good. I'm staying at the Mid-Lake Inn that's closest to the airport."

Ray nodded in approval. "Good place. We'll take you over there so you can check into your room. What do you say about heading over to my apartment after? Meg's here, and she said something about being the one to make dinner tonight."

"Your wife's here?"

Rick's grin grew exponentially at the thought, even as his suspicions about the *real* reason Ethan and Ray could be in Sulivan intensified. Yes, Ray's wife, Margaret Battaglia-Douglas, was an excellent cook. However, she was also one of the most talented freelance cyber-security experts and cryptographers in the field of investigation. While her position as a freelancer allowed her the freedom to travel with her

146

husband, her assignments rarely coincided with his.

"Yep," Ray acknowledged cheerfully. "She got here just this past weekend, in fact, after saying she was bored at home."

"Seriously?" Rick quirked an eyebrow at the other, not believing it, even as Ray gave him an all-too-innocent nod. "I'm in."

"We thought you might say that," Ethan said with a knowing look. "Got your paperwork?"

"Right here." Rick took out the customs forms.

"Good. Let's get this over with and get the show on the road."

Together, Ray and Ethan turned and began to lead Rick past the rest of the passengers, who were now heading towards the arrival customs area. Since Rick already had his paperwork, he should have been able to get through whatever procedures were in place much faster.

That was the theory, at least, and neither FBI agent seemed to think that there would be any problems. Not until they saw the Island Affairs Officer, who was on duty.

"Damn it," Ethan muttered abruptly. "I thought Glenn was supposed to be on duty here today, not Brandon."

Rick flicked a glance at him, then back to the short man with the hooked nose who seemed to be waiting for them. "Who?"

"Glenn Locke's one of the few good people in Island Affairs," Ethan told him, voice low and quiet. "Brandon Fleischmann? Not so much. He's newer and thinks he's got somethin' to prove."

"Holloway will no doubt be hearing about this a lot sooner, as a result." Ray sighed. "But it's also Friday, so hopefully, he'll be more focused on the weekend than on making trouble. Still, it's not like we've got a choice. Come on."

Almost as one, the three stepped forward. The Island Affairs Officer's dark eyes went almost comically wide at the sight of Ethan and Ray before narrowing at Rick. The private investigator presented the papers that Ray had emailed him the night before, doing his best to keep his expression as bland as possible.

"Agent Douglas," Brandon spoke in a nasal tone that grated on Rick's ears. "*Agent* Plumber. What a pleasant surprise, seeing the two of you here." His eyes shifted again to Rick, who had the sudden image of an eel that was slithering its way through muddy waters. Brandon all but oozed his following sentence. "And you must be Frederick Thorne. It's a pleasure, sir, to welcome you to this city."

Ethan looked ready to speak, only for Ray to nudge his arm in warning. Rick had to admit to being taken aback. Brandon sounded as though he *knew* him.

But how?

"I am," he finally said. "And thank you." He handed over the forms. "Here's my paperwork. It should all be in order."

"Of course." Brandon glanced through it, then looked at his clipboard. A small, malicious smile ghosted over his face. "Yes, it *mostly* seems to be correct, but I'm afraid there are a few questions I'll need to ask you before granting you entry." He gave a nod to a nearby door. "This way, if you please."

"Now, wait for just one—"

Ray stepped forward, his voice colored by worry. This time, Ethan would hold him back.

"Not here, Ray," he could be heard to mutter. "Now's not the time."

148

Ray growled before looking helplessly at Rick. "We'll be right here."

Rick nodded, biting back the urge to frown as he followed the waiting Island Affairs Officer into a small office that reminded him of an interrogation room. Brandon pointed him to a chair that sat on the other side of a small table and sat down himself before speaking.

"First question, Mister Thorne," he said. "Why have you come to this city?"

Rick's eyebrows rose just a little. He'd been to Europe twice, once to France and once to England, and both times, the questions asked by the customs officer had been simple, direct, and to the point. "You aren't going to ask 'business or pleasure,' Officer?"

Brandon's already thin lips thinned further in displeasure, and he grated, "You are correct, Mister Thorne. So which is it?"

"Business."

"A case?" Brandon looked at him through hooded eyes. "What *sort* of case?"

Rick had no desire to give any helpful answer, not to this man. "I'm afraid that's confidential."

"Hmph." Brandon's face flashed irritation. "You have a reputation, Mister Thorne, for trouble. Island Affairs is not your ordinary customs agency, and we do *not* like trouble. We prefer to cross all our 't's and dot all our 'i's. So," his eyes bored into Rick's skull. "If you please answer my question, we can move along, and I won't have to deny you entry."

It took everything Rick had not to snarl at the other. Brandon wanted to act all official? Fine. *Two can play at this game.* "As I said, sir,

I'm here on a case. Any further information is governed by client privilege, and *you* are not my client."

Brandon's glare intensified. "I see."

Rick held his gaze and was satisfied to see the other look away first. "Is there anything else?"

"How long do you plan to stay in Sulivan?" Brandon spoke through clenched teeth.

"It will depend on how long it takes me to complete my case."

It was clear that Brandon wasn't happy with that answer, but his following words gave Rick an unsettled start. "Perhaps I should give you a word of warning, then, Mister Thorne. Suppose your case, *whatever* it may be, happens to interfere even in the smallest way with my Department or anything else to do with the way these islands are being run. If that happens, you will *not* like the consequences. Our prison islands are quite uncomfortable, or so I've been told."

Rick did his best not to react, even as he wondered why this Island Affairs Officer—any officer or agent, in fact—would resort to this not-so-subtle threat. *Something else for me to look into, perhaps?*

"I'll do my best," he said at length. "Is there anything else, Officer Fleischmann? Am I free to go about my business in this city?"

Brandon leaned back. "I have just one more question for you, Mister Thorne. How are your wife and children? I believe they are named Jacquetta, Charlie, Emma, and Josiah?"

A chill ran down Rick's spine. All of the instincts he'd honed over the years began to scream. "The last I checked, they were all perfectly well. How, may I ask, do *you* know of them?"

Brandon smiled. The expression proved vicious. "I just wanted to give you a demonstration of the sort of information we can obtain, Mister Thorne. Of course, their names are a matter of public record, but..."

He made a small show of rifling through the papers on his clipboard before pulling one out. His smile widened a fraction as he slid it over to Rick. The private investigator froze at the picture he saw of his family's home. It was recent—*very* recent, judging by the fact that his entire family had on the clothing they'd worn to William Wolfe-Wall's funeral.

"Is that not your house?"

Brandon's oily, triumphant voice had Rick's eyes snapping up to his face. "How did you get that?"

"Relax, Mister Thorne." Brandon smiled again. "As I said, I only wished to demonstrate what we can lay our hands on if we so wish."

There could be no mistaking the threat. Rick made a note to let Victor and Jacquetta know as soon as he could, even as he decided that he would also look quite closely at Brandon Fleischmann—he and all who worked for the Department of Mid-Western Island Affairs.

"I understand," he bit out at last.

"I'm sure." Brandon held his gaze for a moment longer, then stood. "You are free to go, Mister Thorne. Enjoy your stay in Sulivan."

Rick rose to his feet. Ethan and Ray both saw the look on his face when he followed Brandon out, but they quickly dragged the PI away to keep the peace.

"Are you all right?" Ray demanded as soon as they were out of earshot.

"I do believe I was just threatened," Rick told him, seething. "My family and I."

"How?" Ray wanted to know.

"Not here." Rick shook his head.

"At Ray's apartment, then," Ethan said, frowning. "That was fast."

"Tell me about it." Rick took a deep breath to calm himself. It only made him fume more. "Let's get outta here."

Neither Ray nor Ethan argued, leading him away from customs into the rest of the airport. Rick looked around as they walked, on edge but also curious.

At first glance, the Webster A. Ryan Airport didn't seem like much. Compared to Philly International, Newark, JFK, LAX, and the other airports that Rick had visited in his life, it seemed ordinary. There were waiting areas, restaurants, and concession stands to accommodate those waiting to depart or pick up new arrivals. Rick's eyebrows did rise at a few of the businesses' names—the TorpeDough Bakery and the High-N-Buy were two in particular that stood out to him—but nothing appeared to be too unusual.

As they continued, however, Rick noticed a few irregularities. The arrival boards they passed listed many of the incoming planes as being 'delayed.' One, two, or even three might have been understandable, but for fifteen out of the listed twenty flights to be that way? There was also a distinct lack of security checkpoints and guards. Instead, there seemed to be an inordinate number of young men and women wandering around, all wearing matching royal blue clothes and sporting golden jewelry, ankh tattoos, and other symbols that were straight out of Egyptian mythology.

The other people in the airport, including Ray and Ethan, gave these young people a wide berth. Rick puzzled over it for a few minutes.

152

Who were those young people? Why were so many going out of their way to avoid them?

Before he could ask, he spotted something that made him halt in his literal tracks. Digital welcoming boards weren't uncommon in bigger airports. Nevertheless, the messages he saw scrolling by on *this* particular one were downright unusual, to say the least.

Welcome to the City of Sulivan! Please keep all violence to an appropriate minimum. Rick couldn't help but stare in disbelief, especially at the following words that scrolled by. *To all visitors, please Stop and Drop in case of emergency or drive-by. It is recommended that you check whether your life insurance is up to date.* Rick almost choked. Just how bad *was* this city in terms of violence? *We hope you enjoy your stay!*

"Ray?" Rick hoped he didn't sound quite as incredulous as he felt. "Ethan? You care to explain this?"

Both agents had stopped and were now regarding him with sad, sympathetic amusement. Ray's lips quirked upwards at Rick's tone while Ethan shook his head.

"Sulivanian humor," he said. "It takes some getting used to."

Rick glanced between them and the Welcome Board. Why did he have the sudden, sinking feeling that Ethan was understating the matter? "Okay...?"

"It's thrown us for a few loops, too," Ray said. "Still is, in fact."

"Just wait 'til you see the billboard that's at the end of the road leadin' away from the airport," Ethan said.

"Do I *want* to know?"

"We'll point it out to you if you don't notice it yourself." Ray chuckled. "It's kind of hard to miss, though." His eyes went past Rick

153

without warning. His tone changed in the next second. "C'mon. Let's stop acting like tourists and get you to your hotel, Rick."

A glance over his shoulder allowed Rick to see that they were being watched by two young men in blue and gold. The gazes of both weren't friendly.

Still, they did nothing more than follow the private investigator and his FBI escorts as they wound their way through the airport to the exit. Rick half-expected Ray and Ethan to relax once they were past the airport's doors, but they refused to do so until after they'd reached the parking lot and were climbing into their black SUV. Even then, however, they didn't entirely drop their guard until Ray started to drive.

"What was that all about back there, with Fleischmann and those two guys in blue?" Rick asked. "And just *what* are the two of you and Meg doing out here?"

Ray glanced back at him, but it was Ethan who spoke. "That's what happens when you piss off the wrong people."

He said it so innocently, so matter-of-fact, that Rick almost believed him. He wouldn't have even questioned it if he hadn't known Ethan and Ray as well as he did. The two men had never again been anything but professional in the time that Rick had known them.

"I'm sure," he said at last, injecting just enough sarcasm into his tone to let them know he didn't believe Ethan's words.

"What?" Ray almost grinned at him, his face becoming a mask of impeccability. "You don't think we're capable of pissing people off?"

Rick's eyes narrowed at him. "Oh, you're more than capable of *that*. I don't believe it's why you're here. I worked with the two of you before, remember? You've always been nothing less than professional, even

154

when others haven't deserved that courtesy. So what's *really* goin' on?"

Ethan and Ray glanced at each other before Ethan shook his head. He put a finger to his lips, then to one of his ears, before pointing down to the radio and mouthing the words, *'Not here.'*

Rick almost frowned. Why in the world would Ethan be concerned about listening devices? In Ray's car?

It made little sense to him, but he nodded anyway, letting the conversation turn to idle chit-chat as Ray drove away from the airport parking lot. Rick let his eyes drift outside, watching as they went over a pretty little bridge before coming to a brief rest at a stoplight. It allowed him to see the bit of wilderness that sat just across the road, as well as a single billboard.

Welcome to the City of Sulivan! Don't Forget to Duck!

Rick's eyebrows shot up. Was this, he wondered as the light turned green and Ray again began to drive, another example of 'Sulivanian humor'? Or was it indicative of something more? What sort of place *was* this city? Yes, all cities could be violent places, especially in the poorer sections, but to have so many warnings in and around just the airport?

Ethan caught his expression and grinned. "You saw the billboard?"

"As Ray said, it was kind of hard to miss."

He chuckled. "Yeah, it is. Just one more example of Sulivanian humor, at least for the most part."

"Ah." Rick inclined his head. "So I shouldn't worry too much?"

"Didn't say that," Ethan said. "Wait until we get to Ray's apartment. We can talk more about everything there."

Rick nodded, holding in a sigh as Ray made the turn onto a road that took them past two other, smaller-looking hotels. The *Rest-Your-Head Resort* stood 'in front' of the *Island Plains Hotel,* with the Resort being just two floors high. The *Island Plains* had three floors and an almost Tudor-esque appearance, in contrast with the Resort's creamy stone front.

The *Mid-Lake Inn* stood across the road from them, towering over both with no less than six floors to its main body and having two 'wings' that were three floors apiece. All were white with blue accents, as was the sign outside their front. It looked modern, spacious, and even welcoming.

Almost as welcoming, in fact, as the little strip mall that stood at the end of the road servicing the hotels. The *Sellars Island Market* seemed to have almost everything a weary traveler could want, including a *Swiftee's* Convenience Store, two different fast food places, a delicatessen with a name that made Rick's eyebrows rise a little, and a small establishment named *The Crash and Burn Bar.* While Rick mused over the names, he wondered whether any of the restaurants offered takeout or delivery.

Inside the Inn, Rick saw nothing that would put him off. The lobby proved cozy, with comfortable-looking couches and chairs scattered around a small, semi-ornate fountain. Potted plants lined the wall in front of the elevators. At the same time, the entrance to a tiny gift store, *Get Inn Gifts,* could also be seen across from the front desk, along with what looked like a small restaurant.

All in all, and again, not too different from the many hotels Rick had stayed in before, both with and without his family. Walking up to the front desk, leaving Ray and Ethan near the entrance of the gift shop, he smiled at the young woman who was on duty.

156

"Hello, ma'am," he said. "I have a reservation?"

"Of course, sir." She gave him her best professional smile that also seemed to reflect more than a bit of relief. Rick had to wonder if she'd had a bad day until then, but didn't think too much beyond that as she looked up his name, then handed over the appropriate, old-fashioned key to a room on the second floor of the main building once she processed his payment. "There you go. Enjoy your stay, sir."

"Thank you." He smiled back at her and headed for the elevators, with Ray and Ethan quickly falling into step beside him. "This isn't a bad little place."

"The Hotel District's pretty well guarded, though you still get some trouble here from time to time," Ray said. "Usually at the bar, which has a strip club attached to it."

Rick almost frowned. "Wait, I didn't see anything like that out front."

"It's kind of an open secret," Ethan said as they stepped into the elevator. *The Tempest Gentlemen's Club* keeps itself low-key, mainly because of all the families that come this way thanks to the university here, but I know quite a few guys that like comin' down here because of it."

"Including yourself?" Rick gave him a knowing grin.

Ethan shrugged, although a sly smile played at the corners of his lips. "I will neither confirm nor deny havin' met a few contacts down this way."

"Of course not," Rick smirked.

A few moments later, they were exiting the elevator and heading to Rick's room. It proved to be a nice one, spacious and pleasant in appearance, and done in shades of red and cream. Rick was quick to stow away his bag, removing only his notebook and pen.

"Let me make a quick call, then use the bathroom," he said. "Then maybe you can fill me in on why you're *really* here before we head to Ray's apartment."

"I told ya he'd never believe the official reason," Ethan said, grinning at Ray.

"I knew he wouldn't," Ray said. "And, fortunately for you, Rick, Director Martel agreed."

Rick's hazel eyes widened. Their *Director* had agreed? Rick eyed them. "So I'm right. You're not here because of some nebulous punishment or anything else to that effect."

"No," Ray confirmed, his tone turning grim. "We're not. The Director told us to read you in." He held up a hand. "Go make your call and do what else you need to do first. Then, we can head to my apartment and go over everything there."

Rick didn't argue. Instead, he headed to the bathroom and took up his cell phone to dial Jacquetta. He gave her a brief rundown of the encounter he'd had with the Island Affairs Officer as soon as she answered.

"He had a picture of *our* house?" she demanded.

"A very recent one, yes," Rick said. "I want you, your brother, and the kids to be extra careful. I know a few of your watchers are his former partners, but what do we know about the ones they're training? And who was there *before* Victor got to the house?"

"We'll find out," she said. "And yes, we'll be careful, but you'd better be so, as well. You've just arrived in that city, Rick."

"I know. Believe me, Quet."

"I do." Her voice was soft, but there was a hard edge that almost made Rick feel sorry for his brother-in-law. "I'm going to be having a conversation with Victor, and hopefully, we can get to the bottom of this. In the meantime, keep in touch, all right? And stay safe."

"I will, Quet," Rick said quietly, smiling as he spoke. "You have my word."

"And you know what will happen if you break that word."

Putting away his phone a few seconds later, Rick finished his business in the bathroom. Heading back out to rejoin Ethan and Ray, he was surprised when they didn't immediately head back to the door. Instead, Ray reached into his jacket.

"Before we head back out," he said. "We've got a little something for you."

He handed Rick not only a handgun but a concealed-carry permit. Rick's eyebrows rose. "Not that I'm arguing against them, but why?"

"Trust us," Ethan said, his tone dark. "You might need a weapon in this city, and the permit's to make sure Island Affairs can't argue or, worse, put you on a plane back home or throw you in a cell."

Rick almost smiled. He had hated leaving his weaponry back in Pennsylvania and, now, thought he could breathe a little easier. "Thanks."

"It's not a problem, Rick," Ray said. "That's one of the perks of being the SAIC out here. Now, let's head over to my place before Meg sends out a search party."

Rick nodded. They headed back out to the SUV, and less than a minute later, Ray was looping them back to the airport.

"It's quicker to take the expressway," Ray explained when asked. "And the on-ramp's back this way."

"It's safer, too, to be honest," Ethan said. "Less chance of bein' lured into an ambush, shot at, or anythin' else."

Rick stared at the back of his head. "Are you serious?"

"Unfortunately." He gave the wide-eyed private investigator a thin-lipped smile. "All of the Mids are something out of a modern wild-west show. Sulivan's no worse than Babineaux, Logan, or even Talfryn. The towns are better, but to an outsider or a tourist, they're *all* kinda nuts." Ethan glanced back. "And considerin' that you've already been threatened not even thirty minutes in?"

Ah. Rick nodded, remembering the all-too-smug look Brandon Fleischmann had worn.

"Luckily for us, though," Ray said. "We're heading towards Center Island. It's the most secure place in all of Sulivan, and that's where both of our apartments are. Not even the worst elements in this city, Island Affairs Officers included, would try anything there."

"Why?" Rick wanted to know. "Why is Center Island so secure compared to the rest of the city?"

"It's simple," Ray told him. "The DBJF Alliance has its headquarters there. Before they took over, Center Island was a crumbling, crime-ridden mess. Local PD was in over their heads, even with backup from the local FBI office and Island Affairs. The DBJF was able to come in and buy up most of Center Island's land, then revitalize not only Center Island but also the surrounding areas. Their security forces are provided by Veil-Tech Securities, and they are all very well trained. They often supplement the police presence that's been assigned to Center Island, too. Not even the worst of the gang members that make up the majority of Sulivan's criminal element want to mess with them." He glanced back at

160

Rick and offered him a small smile. "Not even our two buddies back at the airport would try it."

"Those were *gang* members?"

"Yep." Ethan nodded. "They're part of a group that calls itself The Pharaohs. Very nasty bunch that's into things like murder, extortion, and running weapons." He grimaced. "They're just one of the four main gangs that hold sway here in Sulivan."

"Only four gangs?"

Rick felt less than impressed despite being shocked. Philly, New York, Chicago, and other cities all had more than just *four* gangs for law enforcement to deal with, but most weren't as conspicuous as the ones they'd seen at the airport. In most other parts of the country, gang members were doing their best to avoid being spotted, thanks to the stepped-up efforts of law enforcement to curb gangland activities.

"That might not seem like a lot," Ray said. "But I'd be more than willing to bet that The Pharaohs, the Lords of the Wharf, the Iron Horde, and the Pasquale-Scordato Family would make most of the gangs you were used to dealing with shit themselves. They're the ones who came out on top at the end of the last round of gang warfare that hit Sulivan's streets, and *no one* wants to piss them off."

"Bad as they all are, some say that the crews that came before most of 'em were even worse." Ethan shook his head, his expression grim. "One in particular."

Rick frowned, a tingle of foreboding running down his spine. "What do you mean?"

"Wait until we get to my apartment," Ray repeated. "We'll go over everything there. For now, sit back, enjoy the ride, and see the sights."

161

Rick's frown deepened, and he considered arguing the point, but Ethan switched on the radio before he could. The music proved just loud enough to let the two up front pretend not to hear anything else he might have to say.

Well, okay, Rick thought. *I guess I'll be finding out what I need to know soon enough.* In the meantime, he'd do as Ray had suggested. Granted, he couldn't see very much from the back of a moving vehicle, especially on an expressway, but it could still give him something of an overview of the city Victor Wolfe's son called his home.

It didn't appear to be all that special. Great blocks of brick or concrete—apartment or office buildings, most likely—gave way in some places to more stylized rooftops, along with a few trees, then the sloped roofs of various row homes before changing back to a more blocky architecture. Again, nothing seemed out of the ordinary from many of the other cities that Rick had visited before.

And yet, he couldn't get the threat he'd received from Brandon Fleischmann out of his mind. The Welcoming Board's message also whirled in the back of his brain, and he couldn't help puzzling over the overt presence of at least one of the local gangs. The words of William Wolfe-Wall regarding Victor's son floated through his mind once more.

'*Considering where and how he was raised, not to mention what had happened...*' Was this what The Wall had meant? If so, Victor's son might be harder-boiled than previously thought.

The sight of a large, black tower caught his attention and derailed his thoughts. The building was massive—an enormous, obsidian monolith that lanced upward and sliced through the few clouds that were in the sky to loom over everything and everyone around it.

162

"What is that building?" he asked, leaning forward and raising his voice ever-so-slightly to make sure Ethan and Ray could hear him. "That big, black one?"

"Huh?" Ethan glanced back at him, then looked towards where Rick pointed. "Oh. That would be the DBJF's headquarters. Its official name is the Morana Building, but everyone calls it the Black Tower for obvious reasons. It was completed 'bout a year and a half ago, I think."

Rick had to admit to being impressed, both at the sight of the building and the company it represented. "Wow."

Ray glanced back to flash a quick grin at him. "Almost everyone says that when they first see it." The grin dissolved. "Except for the locals. They have *other* words they prefer to use."

"They aren't happy about it?"

"It depends on whom you ask," Ethan said before glancing at Rick as they passed one of the signs on the highway. "Make sure you don't miss the exit."

"Do you *have* to bring that up every time we come this way?"

"Yes, if only to piss you off."

Ray rolled his eyes, then met Rick's in the mirror. The corners of his lips curled upward. "Any chance you could help me convince the director to send Ethan to Alaska, Rick?"

Rick started to laugh as Ray took the upcoming exit to Sandstrom. The gentle curve of the off-ramp took them back down into the city proper, and Rick found himself almost gaping at the apparent change in atmosphere. Back at the airport, it seemed as though everyone and everything were tense, nervous, and on the lookout for trouble. Here, people seemed to be walking around without any trace of abnormal anxiety—even Ethan and Ray seemed to relax. The streets and sidewalks were cleaner, the buildings newer and sparkling in the sun.

Night into day, Rick mused, looking around as Ray made a left-hand turn. *Could a handful or two of extra security guards* really *be responsible for all of this?*

A few more minutes passed, allowing Rick to see a small park, a number of reasonably new condominium complexes, and even what looked a little like a boardwalk before Ray drove the SUV into a parking garage. "This is the closest garage to my apartment complex. It's a little bit of a walk, but it's a nice day, and Ethan needs the exercise, or he'll fail his physical readiness test."

Ethan extended his middle finger at Ray.

Rick chuckled. "I won't complain," he promised. He was pretty eager to get a closer look at what this portion of Sulivan looked like. "And I could use the chance to stretch my legs."

There wasn't, he soon discovered, all that much for him to see. They crossed the street after leaving the parking garage. Ray and Ethan took turns pointing out the various buildings and businesses. Most were modern high-rises that fit the more modern landscape, but one building stood out as different.

Rick's eyebrows rose a bit at the stone-and-brick building that sat in front of the monolithic Morana Building. It proved much shorter, being only about three stories instead of hundreds. It was also white, with a number of what appeared to be battlements lining its rooftop. Rick couldn't help but be reminded of a castle or some other similar medieval creation.

It was so out of place in comparison with the rest of Center

Island's architecture that he stopped to stare at it. Ethan and Ray stopped as well and followed his gaze.

"The City of Sulivan Crime Museum," Ray said. "At least that's what it is now."

"Oh?" Rick glanced over.

"Yep," Ethan nodded. "It used to be a police station, then sat abandoned for a little while." A shadow passed over his face. "It took a bit, but DBJF picked it up and turned it into that."

"Was it used for anything before DBJF got a hold of it?" Rick wanted to know and saw the looks that passed between Ethan and Ray. Another tingle of foreboding went down his back. "What?"

"You'll find out soon enough," Ray said after a moment. "For now, let's just get to my apartment."

Rick's lips thinned, but he said nothing more as he followed the other two to an apartment building just another block away. It was just as modern, both in age and in looks, as almost everything else on Center Island, and the interior proved no different. Ray led them over to a pair of elevators, one of which deposited them on the fifth floor, where Ray fished out his key and led them down a short hallway.

A mostly open floor plan greeted Rick's eyes as soon as Ray opened his door. Bamboo flooring stretched out before them, helping the place seem more spacious than it actually was, and Ray and his wife's simple furniture and décor helped maintain the roomier appearance.

The glorious aromas emanating from the nearby kitchen were a bonus, in Rick's opinion. *Meg always did know how to cook!*

Speaking of Meg, Margaret Battaglia-Douglas turned from where she stood next to the stove and oven to see them walking into the apartment. Rick could see happy relief shining in her deep brown eyes.

"There you all are!" she said with a teasing smile. "I was beginnin' to think you'd all gotten lost."

"Not going to happen," Ray assured her, heading to her side to steal a quick kiss. "Unless you want us to, that is."

"You, maybe," she drawled, thickening her Texas accent on purpose and grinning at her husband's mock pout. "Ethan, never." She matched Ethan's laugh with one of her own before going to greet her guest with an enormous hug. "When Ray told me you were comin', Rick, I almost asked if he'd been at the spray cheese again."

"I don't *do* spray cheese, dear," Ray said, eyes dancing with suppressed laughter. "Not when I've gotten into the Port Wine spread!"

"Glad to see you've come up in the world, love," Meg shot back, causing Ethan to laugh again and Rick to join in.

"It's nice to see that *some* things haven't changed," Rick said, grinning at them. Ray and Meg seemed to thrive on their ability to snark at each other and then laugh it off. "How're you doing, Meg?"

"Well enough, even in this crazy place," she said. "And I hope you brought your appetite because dinner's just about done." She smiled again. "Homemade cheddar-broccoli soup to start with, followed by sweet apple pork chops and green beans, then apple pie for dessert."

"Oh my," Ethan groaned with utter delight. "Marry me, goddess."

"What, a porcine object like you?" Meg laughed softly. "Go and help Ray set the table for me in the dining room, would you, Ethan, darling?"

Rick found himself chuckling. "What can I do to help?"

"You're a guest, Rick. The most I'll be asking you to do is say grace."

"I think I can handle that," he said, grinning as Ethan sputtered.

"What am I, if not a guest?" he wanted to know.

Ray also grinned. "The brother from another mother who invites himself over at every opportunity to raid our refrigerator."

"You know, just for that, I'm siccin' Aaron on you this weekend."

Rick's head snapped over to him. "Your son's here?"

"Yep." Ethan grinned. "The only good thing to come from my first marriage. He's goin' to the local university and can't decide if he wants to become an electrician or an airplane mechanic."

"Why isn't he at a trade school, then?" Rick wanted to know as Ray directed him to one of the seats around an iron-and-glass table.

"The university here has a pretty good selection of those courses, including some of the harder-to-find ones," Ethan said. "Plus, Aaron also wanted to take some of the more advanced classes that can be used to get into the DBJF. Gettin' to spend some time with his old man, now that I've joined 'im out here, is just a bonus in his eyes." Ethan's grin widened at his words, but there was a strange shadow that seemed to lurk in his eyes. "Kid graduated high school at the top of his class back home and got offers to all those Ivy Leagues, but he wanted to learn *real* work, like what his mom's dad used to do."

"You disapprove?" Rick asked. He could well remember some of the arguments he'd had—was still having, if he wanted to be honest—with his children about their potential choices of after-school life.

Ethan shook his head. "I don't have a problem with him wanting to spend time with me or learnin' what he likes, nor does his mom. The issue I have is that he had to come *here, to Sulivan.*"

"The city's not *all* bad," Ray chided. "And at least you *have* your kid with you." He sighed as he headed over to one of the kitchen cabinets, opening it to begin removing a small stack of plates. "Meg and I had to leave ours with her parents." He shook his head, passing the plates to Ethan. "The crazy laws in this city."

"What do you mean?" Rick asked, watching as Ethan headed over and disappeared into the one, walled-off room that broke up the open feeling of the apartment.

"There's a city code here that literally prevents, and I quote, the public display of children. Anyone under the age of sixteen is, believe it or not, not allowed out except at certain hours." Meg sighed as she turned back to the stove. "I don't know if I should be viewing our time in this place as a vacation or as a sort of purgatory."

Rick stared at her, aghast. "They can do something like that?"

"Believe it or not," Ray said, opening a drawer to extract some silverware. His tone darkened as he continued to speak. "They have their reasons, though, and it's part of the reason we came out here." He glanced back, shaking his head at Rick to forestall the questions that were already on the tip of the private investigator's tongue. "Not yet, Rick. Let's eat first, and then we can brief you. There's no sense in tryin' to spoil our appetites."

Rick wanted to object, but the memory of what he'd seen in William Wolfe-Wall's safety deposit box caused him to nod his agreement instead. No way did he want the potential pleasure of what smelled like a fantastic meal to be ruined.

In the little dining room, the conversation would stay light as they ate. Tales of their various families were swapped; past cases were reviewed, with endings either celebrated or denounced, and multiple hopes for the future were discussed. The food proved to taste as delicious as it had smelled, too, which should have made the entire experience one of the most joyful Rick had experienced since the death of his father-in-law.

Instead, it seemed tense, even stifled. The dark cloud of anticipation soured even the most basic of the pleasantries they exchanged.

Once the last bite of pie had been consumed and the final plate scraped off to be placed into the dishwasher, Rick saw the table become subject to a slight transformation. Place mats and table décor were all removed. Meg's laptop came out, along with a small stack of manila folders, all of which were placed at the head of the table. Ray collected cell phones and put them outside the room before returning to the table.

"We're not moving out to the living room?" Rick questioned.

Ethan shook his head. "Place is bugged. Mine, too."

Rick stared at him. "Bugged? You kidding me?"

"Unfortunately, no," Ethan said. "Their vehicles, our apartments, and even the FBI office all have listening devices installed. Ray was able to neutralize the one he found in the SAIC's office, thanks to Meg here, but it let us know that Island Affairs does *not* want to be in the dark, 'bout anything."

"That's—"

"Insane?" Ethan cut Rick off with a shrug. "That's Sulivan."

"Ethan and I found the bugs shortly after we came out here," Ray said. "We didn't want to take the chance of alerting Island Affairs that we were onto 'em, so we've left most of them in place. The one that was in here, though? Meg and I removed it, and it now resides inside Meg's little office. At the moment, she has it playing a recording we made earlier. You don't say a whole lot, but we're hoping they'll think that's due to me, Meg, and Ethan all telling you about the city." He gave a slight grin. "That, and reminiscing a little about the cases we shared. Meg had recorded a lot of our conversations back then, and she was able to work her magic with them on that computer of hers." His grin widened. "She was able to use what she learned with that one to neutralize the one in my office at work earlier last month."

"Seriously?" Rick looked at her.

"Child's play for me, Rick," she confirmed. "And it's better than lettin' certain people find out why, exactly, that you're in town."

"Ah." He tilted his head. "And why did Ray take our cell phones out of the room?"

"Probably just being paranoid," Ray told him. "But better safe than sorry, as the old saying goes, and we do *not* want to give Island Affairs any opportunities to listen in on what we're going to tell you. And, speaking of briefing you..." He leaned forward. "Before we begin, why don't you tell us what you know about Sulivan and the other Mid-Superior Islands, Rick?"

"To be honest? I know very little," Rick had to admit. "I first learned about them from a letter that my client received, which informed him about the existence of his son. He, in turn, showed it to me when I agreed to take his case. I could find nothing at first about the Mid-Superior Islands and their cities until the assistant my partners and I hired showed me a blog she'd found on the Dark Web that mentioned them. That led me to the DBJF Alliance Corporation's website, which had a link to the City of Sulivan's webpage. I found the Department of Mid-Western Island Affairs linked there."

"And you got my work number through that." Ethan nodded his understanding.

"Yes," Rick confirmed it. "That's when I called you, hoping to get more information."

"Anything else?"

"A few things," Rick hedged. "But related to my client and his son, not to Sulivan or the other Mid-Superior Islands. At least, not as far as I know."

"Understandable." Ray nodded. "Ethan and I knew nothing about the Mids ourselves, not until we were called into Director Martel's office."

"He'd only been the director a few weeks back then," Ethan said. "And he'd made a rather alarming discovery while looking into which offices needed new agents. While most offices required only one or two a year due to transfers and retirements, it seemed there were a small handful of island cities in the middle of Lake Superior that required at least twenty to thirty new agents every few months, thanks to a higher-than-normal number going missing. Worse, more than a few of the ones who went missing had the disturbing habit of turnin' up dead, and no one was bein' brought to account for the vast majority of the missing or the dead."

Rick stared at him in disbelief. "How would that be possible? Were these disappearances recent?"

"No." Ray shook his head. "They go back throughout twenty, even thirty years."

"Are you serious? No, *how* are you serious? Why didn't anyone notice this before now?"

"It's the Mids," Ethan said, aiming a look of sympathetic

understanding at Rick's incredulity. "Believe me, we asked the same question. The previous directors, however, all seemed to follow an 'out of sight, out of mind' mentality when it came to the Mid-Superior Islands and their cities. Most of the agents who were sent here were seen as mavericks or embarrassments, so who cared if they dropped off the face of the Earth?"

"Leonard Martel, though, is not cut from that type of cloth," Ray said. "He wanted to know how a bunch of agents, regardless of their former reputations, could go missing and even end up dead without anyone paying for the crimes. Given the track record Ethan and I both have, he decided to ask if we wouldn't mind going undercover here for him to find out?"

"He *asked* you?" Rick arched an eyebrow. "He didn't order it?"

"No." Ethan shook his head. "It seems that bein' sent out here is something of a death knell for a person's career, at least by most of the higher-ups."

"The director wanted answers, yes, but he also didn't want us giving up any possible chances for advancement," Ray said and shrugged. "I've never cared, though, about rising in the ranks. I joined the Bureau to help bring down the bad guys and maybe dole out a little justice wherever it was needed. To know that some of our own were going missing and ending up dead if they were found? To know that *they* weren't being given any justice whatsoever?"

"As for me," Ethan said. "Well, I didn't and don't care. I'm closin' in on retirement age as it is, so in a few more years, it won't matter. Plus, with my last divorce, we had a ready-made excuse for an apparent personality change."

172

"Ah." Rick gave a knowing nod, at last understanding how Ethan, at least, had come to 'piss off the wrong people.'

"Appear to mouth off to a few people who are in the right positions and boom." He nodded back. "The director gives a call to a recommended acquaintance and tells him my supposed woes, and basically asks him to make me the liaison between his Department, which is supposed to be the one in charge of everything federal in the Mids, and the Bureau here in Sulivan to keep me out of trouble until things had either calmed down or I'm eligible for my pension." Ethan lifted a shoulder in an exaggerated half-shrug. "Whichever comes first."

"And that's how you came to be in Island Affairs."

"Yep." Sheer loathing entered Ethan's voice. "And I've never seen a bigger bunch of snakes."

"Corrupt?" Rick guessed easily.

"As sin." Ethan grimaced. "My supposed boss is the chief sinner, too, at least here in Sulivan. Harold Edmund Holloway is the Supervisor of this city, and he's the type that'll smile to your face just before he sticks a knife in your back." He gave Rick an apologetic look. "Fleischmann's the same, only nowhere near as good at it."

"Wonderful."

"Him, Holloway, and most of the rest of my supposed colleagues are of the firm opinion that the ends justify the means, and few of them seem to care what they have to do if it'll help get 'em what they want."

"Which is?" Rick wanted to know.

"Total and absolute control over the people of these islands," Ray said quietly. "Sulivan, Talfryn, Babineaux, Logan, and all the towns in between are supposed to be the fiefdom of Island Affairs. Nathaniel

Oliver, who sits in the Director's seat, is said to *hate* anyone he sees as bein' a threat to his Department accomplishing that."

"Sulivan's a hot seat of sorts," Ethan said. "Babineaux, by all accounts, is the furthest down the line of givin' Oliver what he wants. Talfryn and Logan are somewhat behind Babineaux, but Sulivan? This city gives Oliver the most headaches, or so I've heard. Bringin' Sulivan into line was part of why Holloway was put in charge here."

"The other reason he got the post of Supervisor is that his brother-in-law, David Daniel McClure, happens to be a Vice President with the DBJF," Ray said. "His sister, Regina, is also one of DBJF's top research scientists."

"Are they close?" Rick wanted to know.

"Tight as thieves," Ethan said.

"Lovely." Rick grimaced.

"It gets better," Ray said, in a tone of voice that let Rick know he meant the exact opposite. "It didn't take Ethan and me long to find out that our agents weren't the only ones who were going missing. It seems that quite a large number of others were *also* disappearing, and, in the course of our investigation, we've found that, while a good number of the adults who had vanished were found, the *children* who went missing have stayed that way."

He snarled those last words. Rick wanted to snarl with him. When he thought back to the evidence he'd seen, which Katherine Kincaid and William Wolfe-Wall had uncovered, it took almost everything he had to keep himself still and his mouth shut.

"It's the reason for that city code you were told about. As you might guess, our Director hasn't been happy with our reports either.

174

When he learned that most of the other missing people happened to be children?" Ethan blew out an angry breath. "Most of those files and records belong to Island Affairs. I knew they existed, but I didn't have the clearance or anything to access them since I was supposed to be just marking time. Ray, though, couldn't access them, either. The one time he tried, being the new SAIC of the FBI office here, every bell and whistle went off in alarm over in Island Affairs. Ray was able to play it off as an accident to Holloway when he went over to check on it and promised not to do it again."

"That's when they decided to bring me on board," Meg said. "Their Director asked if I'd be willin' to help out a little, and o' course, I said yes. We used the pretext of me bein' a bored and lonely housewife—" She rolled her eyes but still smiled. "So I could join my husband out here without anyone bein' any the wiser. Now, I have to figure out the computer programs they're usin' since the ones I'm used to aren't the most compatible with the systems the DBJF has developed. To do *that...*" She flashed an impish smile at Rick. "There's a couple o' courses I'm planning to take over at the university to, shall we say, pass the time here."

Rick chuckled. "I almost pity the people who'll be trying to teach *you.*"

Ray and Ethan joined in the chuckling. Meg was known not just for her wit and her brilliance with computers but for her inability to tolerate fools. If any of the classes she'd chosen had a professor who thought he or she was the end-all and be-all of computer knowledge, they were in for an unpleasant surprise.

Rick shook his head, bringing his mind back to the subject at hand when Ethan handed him the manila folders. "What's all this?"

"That's most of what we managed to collect so far," Ethan told him. "Including what little information we were able to collect on one Robert Kincaid."

"My client's son?"

"He was one of the last to go missing," Ray said softly. "Which means your case dovetails with ours."

"Which is why you said we might be able to help each other out?" Rick asked, at last understanding what had been meant. "So, if I can find Robert..."

"Then we may be able to find the others." Ray acknowledged. "Or at least find out what happened to them. The *official* belief is that the missing somehow crossed paths with the various criminal elements that exist in each of the Mid-Superior Cities. Each of the Mids, in fact, has something of a problem with street gangs, the Mafia, and other criminal elements. Babineaux is home to the Scordato Family, which is rumored to have connections to none other than The Commission. The city of Logan is home to the Ferra Family, a Chinese Triad calling themselves the Blood Dragons, and two street gangs—the Razors and the Diamond Street Devils. Talfryn has the distinction of housing the Agostini Family, the Tafano Family, no less than four street gangs, and what seems to be an offshoot of the Xiomar Cartel."

Rick stared at him. "The *Xiomars?* As in *Rodrigo* Xiomar? As well as his sons?"

"The same," Ethan confirmed with an unhappy nod. "And you know probably better than we do what they're like." He barely waited for Rick to nod before continuing, "Here, in Sulivan, we begin with the Pasquale Family, then the Three Strikes Gang, the Eighth Avenue Kings,

176

and finally the Arch Street Angels."

Rick blinked at the name and, despite everything he'd heard, felt the corners of his lips twitch upward. "The Arch Street...*what?*"

None of the other three shared his amusement. If anything, they seemed more inclined to grow more somber, more serious.

"Trust us, Rick," Ray said. "Despite their name, the Arch Street Angels were no laughing matter, and their actions were anything but angelic."

"Not unless we're talkin' angels of the *fallen* variety," Meg added in a dark, somber tone.

Her husband nodded in agreement. "There was a literal war on the streets here, from what I've heard and read about that time, just over four years ago—not that today is any better, with the new set of gangs that rose to mostly take the places of the original sets. While I'll admit that it would be possible to explain a lot of the missing, due to all of the violence, I doubt that explains *every*one."

The memory of what had been contained in the safety deposit box flashed through Rick's mind. The stories of the children he'd already seen were horrible. When he considered what could have happened to Victor's son had William Wolfe-Wall not gotten *to him before anything like that could happen?*

It made his decision easy. Rick's expression became uncompromising, and his jaw set firm. "Count me in."

Ethan and Ray both offered him looks of relief. Rick understood it. The two were no doubt constrained in many ways by the agency they were supposed to represent, as well as the Department that ran the Mid-Superior Islands. As a private investigator, Rick was free to do many of the things Ethan and Ray no doubt wanted to do but couldn't.

"Thank you, Rick," Ray said at length, offering him a small smile. "Where will you begin?"

Rick blew out a breath as he considered the question. "Honestly? I think I'd better start by learning about this city. I can't go 'round doing what I'd normally do until I manage at least a little of that."

"Good idea," Ethan said with the beginnings of a mischievous smile. "And, fortunately for you, we've got just the thing."

"Oh?" Rick glanced between the three. Ethan and Ray were both grinning while Meg was shaking her head, although she also had a smile on her face. "And that would be?"

"Since it's the weekend, and we've got off," Ethan said. "How'd you like a little tour?"

Rick arched his eyebrows. A tour would give him just the start he needed. "What are you planning?"

Ray became serious. "This city's a dangerous one, Rick, and not just because of its criminal elements. I do not doubt that Island Affairs is going to be watching us, especially since Ethan and I were there to meet you when you came off that plane. I don't think they'll try anything against us, not yet, but I want to see if we can spot anyone they might have following us, plus protect Meg in case things go south for some reason."

"I don't need a bodyguard," Meg said. While she still smiled, Rick detected a hard edge to her voice.

"I know you don't," Ray spoke in a soothing tone. "But Ethan and I have both seen enough of this city at work, Meg, even in the few short months we've been here, and I want to be extra cautious." His eyes were fixed on her face. "You're doing us a huge favor as it is by being here, and I

178

don't want to lose you."

"I know you don't, my love." Her smile softened, and she relented a bit. "And I certainly don't mind the idea of bein' escorted around by three handsome men, even if one of them *is* my husband."

He chuckled. "It'll be *four* men, not three."

"Oh?" Both Rick and Meg looked curious.

"Aaron's gonna be makin' a little extra money this year by playin' tour guide," Ethan told them. "So he'll be comin' along to get some practice."

"That sounds good to me," Meg said.

"I've got no problems with that, either," Rick said before a shadow passed over his face. "But what about Fleischmann? He's already threatened not just me but Quet and the kids as well. Hell, he had a *recent* picture of *my house*."

"I wish I could say we're surprised by that," Ethan said.

Ray nodded his agreement. "Unfortunately, Island Affairs can be very good at getting information. They've also got an array of off-island resources that they don't hesitate to use when they feel it's necessary. They won't worry about you taking a tour, though. In fact, they'll probably be expecting it." Ray shook his head at the look Rick gave him. "As I said, I just want to take precautions and see if we can't spot someone."

That did nothing to ease Rick's apprehension. Still, he had few options if he wanted to unite Victor with his son and find out what William had been involved in before his death.

"All right," he said at last. "Let's do it."

Chapter Seven: Sanguis Omnibus Imperare

Evening, the Department of Mid-Western Island Affairs

Brandon Fleischmann walked into the portion of City Hall that had been allocated to the Department of Mid-Western Island Affairs and headed directly for the Supervisor's Office. Despite it being just past the end of the business day, Brandon had a report to make in person rather than by phone or e-mail. He knew that Harold Edmund Holloway would not be happy about the fact that he'd allowed Rick Thorne into the city. He just didn't know what he could have done to prevent it. At least he'd followed his instincts and now had the private investigator being watched.

He took a deep breath as the Supervisor's secretary, a comely lady with a sweet face but a dragon's eyes, waved him inside. He had barely set foot into the office when Harold's quiet, controlled voice commanded him.

"Shut the door, Mister Fleischmann."

Doing his best not to show his sudden fear, Brandon did as instructed before taking the only seat placed in front of the large, oaken desk. Harold Edmund Holloway glared at him as he did so. His hazel-gold eyes were snapping with displeasure, and his voice held a definite growl.

"So you allowed Mister Thorne into my city?" he said. "After I distinctly remember telling you *not* to permit it?"

"I'm sorry, Mister Holloway," Brandon swallowed hard. "I couldn't think of a way to block his entry. He said he was here on a case, and SAIC Douglas *and* Agent Plumber were there with him."

"A case." Harold's voice was a snake's hiss. "Did he happen to say what *kind* of case?"

"No, sir," Brandon managed to say. "He claimed that was client privilege."

"Of course he did." Harold ground his teeth. "And now, because of your *incompetence,* I have a rogue investigator in *my* city, and I have *no* idea as to why he may be here. Can you *please* tell me why I shouldn't just strip you of your status as an officer of this Department and send you back to where I found you?"

Brandon gave him the satisfaction of squirming in his literal seat. Most of his career in the Department of Mid-Western Island Affairs had been as nothing more than a janitor. The only reason he'd risen to his current position was that he'd rescued some paperwork one of his predecessors had attempted to destroy and brought it to Holloway's attention. The man had been grateful to Brandon back then for his actions, which had enabled Island Affairs to 'clean house' of those opposed to its mission in Sulivan. It was the reason he'd rewarded Brandon with his current job.

Of course, he could also remove Brandon from it if given sufficient reason.

Brandon had no desire to give Harold that reason. He would do whatever it took to remain as an Island Affairs Officer. For the first time in his life, he had *significance.* He had *power.* People feared *him,* not the other way around.

It was the reason he revealed, "I made sure Mister Thorne was followed, sir, and he's being watched as we speak."

"You did?" Harold's tone turned more neutral. "Perhaps you aren't *quite* as incompetent as I had begun to fear." He leaned back in his seat, steepling his fingers in front of his chest. "Did you let Mister Thorne know about the sort of information we can acquire?"

"Yes, sir." Brandon gave a vigorous nod. "I asked him about his family, using their names to do so, and showed him the picture we'd received of his house."

"Good. It seems you can follow at least some directions." Harold still looked unhappy, but no longer quite as murderous as before. "And you said *both* SAIC Douglas and Agent Plumber were with him?"

"Yes." Brandon nodded. "They met him when he came off the plane and escorted him over."

Harold loosed a small, miserable breath. "Those two are rapidly becoming threads that need to be cut. If they weren't in constant communication with their Director, they would have been dealt with already."

Brandon didn't doubt it. His desk happened to be near the one that had been given to Ethan Plumber back when he'd arrived to take up his post as Liaison Officer between Island Affairs and the local FBI office. Brandon had overheard more than a few of the conversations Agent Plumber had had with the FBI's Director as a result, and he knew the man was no friend of Island Affairs.

"I'll be discussing them with Mister Oliver once he returns from DC," Harold said at last. "Hopefully, Mister Thorne will either be gone by then, or we'll at least know why he's here. In the meantime, who do you have watching him?"

"At the moment, Mister Espina and Mister Burnett," Brandon told him. "Although I'm thinking of adding either Mister Taylor or Miss Ells or someone from Veil-Tech to the detail."

182

"Mister Taylor and Miss Ells are working with Ms. Paulson and Mister Schomann regarding whoever's behind the *Project Enigma* posts. We need that thing shut down before it exposes us even more than it already has." Harold thought for a minute. "I'll assign Mister Brannigan and Mister Driar to the watch on Mister Thorne. They could use the experience. Reach out to Mister Renley on Monday morning, however, and ask him to have two of his security people on standby in case we need them."

"Yes, sir."

"Good. Now, how did Mister Locke take your replacing him at the airport?"

"He seemed happy with it, sir," Brandon said. "Especially when my taking his place allowed him to go home early."

"Hmm..." Harold's lips pursed. He'd known Glenn Locke for some time and was well aware of the man's easy-going, if sometimes lazy, nature. It had been the reason he'd ordered Brandon to replace him once word of Rick Thorne's arrival had come in. "You are working this weekend, am I correct?"

"I am, sir."

"Good. I'll want regular reports. I doubt Thorne will do much, at least for the next two days, but I'll want to hear about it if he does."

"I'll make sure that you do, sir." Brandon tried to temper his eagerness.

"Good." Harold glanced at the clock. "I have a dinner to attend tonight and will most likely be busy this weekend. In the unlikely event that anything with Mister Thorne or our two FBI agents happens and you cannot, for some reason, get hold of me, reach out to Ganesh. He already knows to be on-call."

"Yes, sir." Brandon nodded dutifully. "I'll touch base with both you and the Deputy Supervisor, in fact, if anything happens."

The wisp of an approving smile ghosted across Harold's lips. "Good man. Now, go."

Brandon scrambled back to his feet. A relieved breath escaped him as he exited the office, leaving a contemplative Harold Edmund Holloway behind. The City of Sulivan's Supervisor didn't like what Brandon Fleischmann had reported regarding Rick Thorne. He liked what he'd heard about Plumber and Douglas even less.

Sulivan's Supervisor leaned back in his seat. "It seems something may have to be done about Agent Plumber and SAIC Douglas much sooner instead of later. Rick Thorne, though..." His lips tightened. "He is the immediate threat."

Harold blew out a breath, then reached across to snag one of the files that littered his desk. Opening it revealed the dossier he'd compiled upon learning that Frederick Augustus Thorne, better known as Rick, had purchased a plane ticket to Sulivan.

Born on April 3, 1962, Thorne grew up in Philadelphia, Pennsylvania. While not a brilliant student, Thorne was not considered mediocre. He had gone to the police academy, becoming a patrol officer, and then had started attending a local university. Officer Thorne had majored in criminology and minored in criminal justice with the intent of becoming a detective with the police force. There, in a few of his night classes, he'd met one Jacquetta Clancy, who was attending a few of those same classes with an eye on becoming a criminal psychologist. They'd married in 1986 and been graced with their firstborn son almost precisely

184

two years later, with twins following nearly two more years after that. In 1990, just before his twins were born, Thorne achieved his goal of becoming a detective with the Philadelphia Police Force, beginning in the Robbery Division of his assigned precinct, then Homicide, and ending his career with them on a special Vice Task Force near the end of 2000. No one seemed to know where he'd been in the nine or ten months before he started his private investigations firm in late 2001. However, the file in Harold's hands suggested that family matters had come into play. After becoming a private investigator, Thorne had managed to finish a few solo cases before, in mid-2002, becoming partners with a former defense attorney, Edgar Cross, and a former tech-industry guru named Christopher Zeal.

Harold pursed his lips. Cross, Thorne, and Zeal Investigations had quickly gained a stellar reputation in their field for not only solving cases but also making it near-impossible to be defeated in a courtroom. Thorne had also done some favors for various federal agencies and was considered a force to be reckoned with.

So what sort of case had brought him *here*, to *Sulivan?*

Harold didn't know. He also didn't like it, and not just because of Thorne's reputation. The fact that he'd been met at the airport by none other than Ray Douglas and Ethan Plumber tipped Harold's suspicious mind into overdrive.

Rick Thorne wasn't the *only* one with a tenacious reputation, after all. Leonard Martel, the current Director of the Federal Bureau of Investigation, had become infamous for his relentless nature. Unlike his predecessors, Martel hadn't been willing to look the other way in regard to the numerous FBI agents and others who had gone missing in Sulivan. It didn't matter to him that many had been deemed embarrassments or mavericks, or worse. All that mattered in the mind of Leonard Martel was that the agents had gone missing and, in many cases, had turned up dead. Worse, and not long after he'd assigned Plumber and Douglas to Sulivan, Martel had begun to make little secret of his disdain for Harold, Harold's boss, and the Department of Mid-Western Island Affairs in general.

Had he gone to Rick Thorne? Or had Plumber and Douglas taken it upon themselves to involve the private investigator? Or was there another reason altogether for Thorne being in Sulivan?

Again, Harold didn't know. He meant, however, to find out, starting with—

"Sir?"

The voice of his administrative assistant, coming from the intercom on his desk, snagged his attention. "What is it, Pamela?"

"It's getting close to six o'clock, Mister Holloway. The dinner in honor of your sister is at six thirty."

Ah. Harold promptly returned the folder on Rick Thorne to his desk and stood. Most of the time, his work came first, but not tonight. Tonight would be about his little sister, and he couldn't miss the occasion that honored her promotion.

"Thank you for the reminder, Pamela. I'll see you on Monday."

"Yes, sir. Have a good weekend, sir."

"You, as well."

A minute or two later, after passing through the three security checkpoints that kept the Department of Mid-Western Island Affairs safe from the rabble they were supposed to be ruling, he entered the high-security garage and made his way to the depressingly plain, dark gray sedan

186

that he called his own. If Harold had had his way, he would have been driving something high-end, something that would have screamed out his importance. Unfortunately, he couldn't take that risk in the city of Sulivan, not if he wanted to remain among the living. As a result, he instead made do with his current car, which had a bullet-resistant body to protect him and tinted windows to hide his identity.

After making a quick detour to his penthouse apartment in the Cottonwood Tower Apartments in order to change into more formal clothing, Harold stomped on the gas pedal. If he wanted to make it to the dinner on time and spare his ears from his sister's anger, he'd have to drive faster than usual.

Fortunately, the Hetherington Marina and *Le Manoir Côtier* weren't that far away, and no one was inclined to stop him. At one point, he even passed a patrol car and saw it briefly turn on its lights as it made to follow him. That lasted for as long as it took the officers inside the vehicle to run his plates. They apparently thought better of their actions right after. Their lights went out in the next moment, and he had a clear drive to his destination, a fact that had him smiling smugly, secure in his perceived importance.

Le Manoir Côtier was an exclusive, very high-class restaurant that sat right on the upper East Sulivan coastline, where only the *creme de la creme* of Sulivanian society, such as it was, could afford to frequent. Dining in one of its private rooms meant that one had *arrived* at the very top of the proverbial heap, and Harold couldn't help but smirk as he pulled into the parking lot. This was just the sort of place his sister loved to experience, and he had little doubt that her husband had chosen the location for that very reason.

It was a far cry from how the two of them had grown up. Harold Edmund and Regina Eliana Holloway had spent their childhoods in the City of Logan's Trailer Park. Most of the Holloways' detractors had believed the two of them would never amount to anything. Despite his cleverness and ambition, and Regina's almost frightening intelligence, they had always been seen as 'less than' their peers.

Not anymore. If Harold had anything to say about it, it would never be like that again.

Really, he thought as he drove towards the restaurant in question. *I am happy. I should be feeling more pleased with myself.*

Most of the ones who had bullied, picked on, or outright dismissed him and his sister would never have the chance to eat at a place like *Le Manoir Côtier.* Most would be lucky even to see the outside of such an establishment and would have to remain content with places like *Blast O' Burger* or the *Sit-a-While* Diner. Some were lucky to have their own homes, but most lived in places like the trailer park that Harold and Regina had once called their home.

As the Island Affairs Supervisor for the City of Sulivan, however, Harold could eat where he liked and live far better. *He* wore the fine clothes now. *He* hobnobbed with all the *right* people. Most people *begged* to have even a moment of *his* time.

Hell, a few of those people had been the same ones who'd once made fun of him and Regina. Harold had taken a special delight in pretending to hear them out before sending them on their way without granting whatever requests they'd made. He was almost a King in the society of the Mid-Superior Islands. Once the Department of Mid-Western Island Affairs had the control it should have *always* had, he would be a King in truth.

Just as his sister would be a queen of sorts. Her promotion from the position of Head Scientist of the Genetics and Nanotechnologies Laboratories Division in the DBJF's Island Research and Intelligence Subdivision to Junior Vice President of the DBJF's Scientific Research and Development Division had been more than deserved. Doctor Regina Eliana Holloway-McClure now held both power and prestige. Her current work had received both the funding and backing it needed from the company's Board of Directors, despite the few setbacks she had suffered on two separate but related projects. Well, with luck, she'd soon be able to pick up one of those projects again in the near future and, with her brother at Sulivan's helm, nothing would be able to stop either one of them.

Yes, Harold decided, life was good. While there were still a few irritants that needed to be taken care of, he found he couldn't complain *too* much. As for those few issues? Well, perhaps Regina's husband would have some ideas. David Daniel McClure hadn't become the Senior Vice President of the DBJF's Accounting Department without reason, and he didn't crunch *just* numbers for his living. If anyone would have an idea about what to do about Rick Thorne, it would be David.

The two of them were waiting for him by the restaurant's entrance. A soft and genuine smile, unlike anything Harold usually plastered on for others to see, formed on his lips. Regina Holloway-McClure had put on the costume of an upwardly mobile socialite tonight, wearing a modest-cut, forest-green dress that matched her eyes. At the same time, sparkling dark topaz adorned both her slender neck and her carefully coiffed light brown hair. Her husband, David Daniel McClure, wore a tailored, dark-colored business suit with an off-white buttoned-up shirt that would not have looked out of place in the DBJF's boardroom—a place that David, as the Senior Vice President of the DBJF's Accounting Department, aspired to one day visit on a regular basis, as a member of the DBJF's Board of Directors.

Well, with luck and Harold's backing, that day might arrive sooner instead of later. Now that Regina had received the promotion she had always coveted, it seemed only right for David to move up next. The higher Regina and David rose within their company, the better for Harold himself and for Island Affairs as well.

Pulling up beside the curb in front of the restaurant's entrance, Harold waited for the valet to come over and present him with his ticket before exiting the car. He gave the boy a small tip, envisioning the day he'd be able to throw a hundred or more dollars on the ground for the other to collect, before going to greet his sister and her husband.

"Reggie." Harold gave her a quick embrace. "Congratulations, little sister."

"Thank you," she said, burgundy lips curling upwards. "Doctor DuBois thought it only right for me to take Doctor Sinaga's place, especially since I was the one to expose his disloyalty."

"Of course." Harold chuckled at Regina's feline smirk before extending his hand to her husband. "Good to see you again, David."

"Likewise, Harold." David returned the handshake. "Shall we go inside? I reserved The Amber Room for tonight."

Neither Regina nor Harold argued. The Amber Room of *Le Manoir Côtier* was considered its most exclusive private dining experience. It came complete with its own menu, a private serving staff, and the utmost privacy. Most people within Sulivan could do nothing except

190

dream of the mere *idea* of entering The Amber Room's doors.

It was yet more evidence that Harold and Regina, along with David, sat at the very top of Sulivanian society. Harold relished the moment when he walked through The Amber Room's doors. They were seated in mere moments, presented with the menus, and gave their orders soon after.

Almost as soon as their meals arrived, they were left to speak in peace. Regina sighed with delight as she took the first bite of her *magret de canard.* At the same time, her husband enjoyed his first taste of *poulet basques,* and her brother sampled his *steak au poivre* with a pleased smile.

"Only one thing could make this week achieve absolute perfection," Regina said. "And that would be the return of the seventh subject of Project Novum Genus."

David chuckled. "I do not doubt that your brother and I would arrange it if we could."

"That we would," Harold said. "Unfortunately, you'll have to wait a bit longer.

Regina laughed softly. "The two of you might not be able to arrange it, but Doctor DuBois thinks she might be able to do something that will result in giving me what I want."

Her husband and brother glanced at each other in slight shock before Harold spoke. "What do you mean she might be able to? Your brother and I have been trying for months to do just that. So how—"

"I know you have, Harry," Regina spoke in a soothing tone. "But Cassandra DuBois is in a position to pull a different set of strings than the two of you, and she's been working on it. I've been told that, by the end of next week, I may very well have Subject Seven back where he belongs."

"That is excellent news!" David beamed at her.

"Doctor DuBois thinks it to be only right, considering all the promise that particular subject showed, and the Board agrees," Regina said. "They're just waiting, I've been told, on one last piece of information before arranging it. No doubt we'll need to redo a few things to get the subject back up to the level he should be at, but I can spend the time it'll take on that while learning all my new responsibilities. With luck, I'll be able to impress Doctor DuBois even more than I already have."

David let loose another chuckle. Harold attempted to do the same in an attempt to conceal the pensive shift his mood had begun to take. The seventh subject of his sister's project worried him, mainly due to the fact that said subject was currently out of his and his sister's reach. Yes, Harold believed it was momentary, but at the same time, he couldn't help but ask *what if*.

What if Regina's seventh subject remained outside of their grasp? What if that subject was never returned to her?

And what would happen if Rick Thorne discovered the existence of Project Novum Genus alongside its seventh subject? The private investigator had achieved his tenacious reputation for a reason, after all. While Harold didn't know for sure what had brought Thorne to the Mid-Superior Islands, he could make a guess. Was he right, and had Thorne been called in to help investigate the Department of Mid-Western Island Affairs? Maybe himself, Harold Edmund Holloway, in particular? If he discovered what had been going on within the walls of the DBJF's laboratories, all of their lives would be over.

"Harry?"

"What?" Harold blinked and looked to find Regina and David

both eyeing him. How long, he wondered, had he been lost in his thoughts and fears? "Forgive me. The two of you were saying?"

"Why are you so melancholic tonight?" Regina asked. "We're supposed to be celebrating, and yet, you seem to be brooding."

"Forgive me, Reggie," he said and reached for the glass of expensive Cabernet that he'd ordered. "You as well, David. You're right. We *are* supposed to be celebrating." He saw the looks they gave him as he brought the glass up to his lips. As soon as he swallowed the three sips he permitted himself, he sighed. "It's just that a visitor arrived today in Sulivan, and it's put me on edge."

"Oh?" David inclined his head. "I take it this visitor could pose problems?"

"That would be putting it mildly," Harold told him. "Frederick Thorne has a reputation, and the fact that he's *here,* in Sulivan, bothers me."

The corners of Regina's lips turned down. She thought she'd heard the name her brother mentioned, but couldn't place the owner.

David, however, had no such trouble. "Are you *serious,* Harold? Frederick Thorne is *here?* In *Sulivan?*"

"He is." Harold nodded. "The idiot I put in charge of customs for the day was supposed to deny him entry. Instead, thanks to his becoming flustered at the sight of Thorne being escorted by our least-favorite FBI agents, he did the opposite."

Regina glanced between them, her mouth becoming a thin line that spoke volumes of her displeasure. "Excuse me, Harry. David. Who is Frederick Thorne, and why, exactly, are we discussing him during the dinner celebrating my promotion?"

"Frederick Thorne is a private investigator out of Philadelphia," her husband told her. "He has quite the reputation. Coupled with the fact that Plumber and Douglas met him at the airport, the man seems even more like a liability."

She waved an annoyed hand, cutting him off. "Private investigators can be bought off or persuaded to change employers with the right reward, so I don't see why—"

"Not this one," Harold said. "Frederick Thorne is known as much for his integrity and grit as he is for his success rate. He's also partly responsible for the removal of at least one of our Department's former allies. It's part of why I ordered that he be denied entry. If the idiot I left in charge of customs today had done his job, I wouldn't be this unsettled." He released a quick, explosive breath. "But as it currently stands, Thorne is in Sulivan, supposedly on a case."

"Do we know what sort of case brought him here?" David asked.

"No," Harold growled. "The idiot who spoke to him couldn't find out even that much. The *only* reason Fleischmann's still working as one of my officers is that he had the wherewithal to have Thorne followed. If he screws up again, though?"

"Fleischmann." Regina tilted her head. "He's the one who enabled you to clean the house before, correct?"

"Yes." Harold nodded at her. "He's a weasel of the highest order, without question, but useful most of the time." He saw her pout and rolled his eyes. "Sending him to you and your mentor for punishment isn't entirely out of the question, Reggie, but it can't happen yet."

"As long as you remember the option is available, Harry." Her pout changed into a small, shark-like smile. "Now, about this meddlesome

194

Frederick Thorne. You've said you don't know what case brought him here, but I'm assuming you still have an idea as to what it could be?"

"Why else would he have been met at the airport by Plumber and Douglas if he wasn't here to help them investigate me and my department?" Harold let another breath hiss out before shaking his head. "It's something I'll have to discuss with Mister Oliver when he returns from DC, but I'd like to have some answers before that time. David, you've dealt with this sort of thing on a few occasions in the not-too-distant past. What would you recommend?"

David appeared to think for a moment as he chewed another bite of his supper. "You say that your officer is having Thorne watched, correct?"

"Yes."

"Good. For now, we work on determining why Mister Thorne is here," David said. "It's indeed likely that he's here to assist Plumber and Douglas, but on the off-chance he's not?" He took a sip of his wine. "Do we know how Mister Thorne knows the two of them?"

Harold shook his head. "It wasn't in his dossier. Of course, I only had that thrown together when I learned Mister Thorne was coming to Sulivan, which was just yesterday, so it doesn't have everything it could about the man."

"Hmm. Send it over to me on Monday. I'll take a look at it, and we can discuss Mister Thorne more then. Right now?" David offered his wife a smile. "As you pointed out earlier, Regina, this is a dinner to celebrate your advancement. You were talking about some of the new responsibilities you would have before your brother sidetracked us?"

"I was, indeed." Regina smiled back before spearing that brother with a look that demanded his attention. "As I was saying..."

This time, Harry made sure to pay attention as his sister began to wax poetic about what her new position would entail. Most of the things she mentioned were, to be honest, well above his understanding. Harold dealt with politics and people, not experiments and theories. Still, what mattered was that Regina herself was pleased and that she seemed to be headed up her career ladder.

Such talk lasted well past the end of their actual dinner and through dessert. As they finished their last bites, all of them relaxed and joyful, but the mood was suddenly shattered when both Harold's and David's cell phones began buzzing insistently.

Regina's eyes narrowed with anger, while David's brow furrowed in annoyed consternation. The corner of Harold's lips turned downward, but he sighed and slipped a hand into his pants' right-hand pocket at the same time that David reached inside his jacket. A moment later, two sets of eyes widened, and David cursed.

"What is it?" Regina demanded.

Harold held his cell phone up so she could read the text. *The Ghost has struck again.*

All the air seemed to leave the room. Harold growled in anger. 'The Ghost' was a thief, someone who *shouldn't* have been worthy of his attention, or David's or Regina's. Thieves were annoying, to be sure, but they rarely went after anything that wasn't monetarily valuable. The loss of money, gemstones, works of art, and even technology was covered by insurance and, while regrettable, could be easily replaced.

The Ghost, however, did not steal those things. Instead, whoever The Ghost happened to be seemed to be seeking out information. Six or seven scientists' homes and a small number of laboratories had been burglarized, two of which were associated with the DBJF.

But most of those had occurred approximately five months ago. The Ghost had seemingly disappeared until just the month prior, when the last two scientists' homes had been robbed. It was distressing, without question.

Harold slowly retracted his phone and put it down. That The Ghost would have returned was bad enough. For The Ghost to appear to be escalating his or her activities was almost expected. But to strike *now?*

"Damnation!" David growled. "I'd thought—"

Harold held up a hand, silencing him, as his phone began to buzz again with an incoming call. Accepting it, he put the phone on speaker. "Holloway."

However, it was not his deputy supervisor's voice that answered him. It was, instead, his office's unofficial third-in-command who spoke.

"We're currently in pursuit of The Ghost, sir," Ira Utley snapped out.

Harold's eyes blazed. "Where are you right now?"

"Center Island, sir," Ira reported. "The DBJF's headquarters was hit."

"Are you *serious?*"

"Yes, sir. Unfortunately, I am. The DBJF's security teams, backed up by Veil-Tech's people, locked everything down but requested backup on the scene. It was a good thing they did, as The Ghost managed to get through their blockades and snag a car."

"I'm on my way." Harold rose to his feet. "Keep up the pursuit."

"Yes, sir."

He ended the call and gave his sister an apologetic look as he rose to his feet. "Forgive me, Regina, but this—"

"Go," she said. "You're right, this takes precedence."

"Just make sure to update us when you can," David added in.

"I will." Harold's lips twisted into an unpleasant smile. "And, with luck, I'll have the good news of having unmasked our thief."

Chapter Eight: The Grand Tour

May 26, 2007: Early Morning

Rick made his bleary-eyed way to the little restaurant that served the Mid-Lake Inn's guests, but not before stopping by the gift shop to purchase the local newspapers. He had close to an hour and a half before his party would arrive to collect him for the Grand Tour of the city of Sulivan. He planned to read as much as he could about local events while he ate breakfast.

The hostess took him to a small booth, handed him a menu, and told him his server would be there shortly, then left him to his own devices. It didn't take Rick long to decide what he would have, which allowed him to turn his attention to his papers. He soon found that it didn't matter which paper he looked at, however, as the headlines of the *Mid-Lake Gazette,* the *Sulivan Times,* and even the *Sulivanian Inquirer* were all the same.

'*The Ghost Strikes!*'

Rick almost chuckled at the melodramatic words before indulging his curiosity and reading each story. At the very least, he thought it would be a fascinating insight into what passed for news in this city, and maybe it would allow him to get his mind off the fact that he'd already been threatened.

The first of those stories, found in the *Mid-Lake Gazette* and written by a Jaxon Ortega, had most of the simple facts.

> Late last evening, the headquarters of the DBJF Alliance
> Corporation was broken into by the thief known only as The

Ghost. However, whatever The Ghost planned was interrupted by a security guard team, which locked down the Morana Building before calling for backup. Officers from Veil-Tech Securities, as well as police and the Department of Mid-Western Island Affairs, arrived to temporarily blockade the building. Still, The Ghost managed to escape their lockdown and steal a car. Officers gave pursuit, but The Ghost was able to lose them long enough to leave the stolen vehicle and grab a speedboat from the nearby docks before apprehension. The City of Sulivan Coast Guard was called in at that point, giving chase as The Ghost headed north. They lost sight of their quarry long enough for The Ghost to disappear once again. While the boat that The Ghost stole was recovered, no further information regarding the thief's identity was apparently discovered.

The story went on to give a brief description of The Ghost's previous appearances as a timeline of activity. It ended with a plea to the public to inform the authorities if they knew anything. Rick glanced over the stories in the *Sulivan Times* and the *Sulivanian Inquirer,* both of which added very little in the way of more information.

It was a fascinating tale, in any case. Rick could admit that much, and if he wanted to be honest indeed, it made the investigator within salivate at the idea of joining the hunt.

But no. Rick was there in Sulivan for a specific purpose, and hunting this Ghost wasn't it.

He heard approaching footsteps and set the papers aside before looking up to give a smile to his apparent waitress. She was a pretty girl with warm brown skin and raven black hair pulled back into multiple braids, and she possessed lovely, amber-honey eyes that, at the moment, held more than their fair share of fatigue. She seemed young enough to still be in school, and Rick guessed that she was probably around Emma's age. If so, she was either a high school senior or a freshman at the local university.

"I'm Alice," she introduced herself. Her voice had a musical quality, one that Rick could appreciate. "Cyndi will be your server, but she's runnin' a little late, so I'll be takin' your order."

"Thank you, Alice." Rick let his smile widen a little as he told her what he wanted. "I'd also like some coffee whenever you get the chance."

"It won't be a problem," she said before a short yawn escaped her. "Sorry 'bout that."

He waved the apology away, eyeing her in sympathy. "Late night?"

"Y'know how it is," she said and shrugged. "Ya meet up with some friends, party a bit, and the next thing ya know, it's past midnight." She smiled in self-recrimination. "Then I gotta get up early for work, so—" She was interrupted by a yawn. "Totally my fault. I'm here, just like I'm supposed to be when I'd much rather still be in conference with my pillows."

Rick chuckled. "I remember those days, even if they are a bit further away from me."

"Does it get any easier?"

"Honestly?" Rick tilted his head. "It depends on what you choose to do. The adage that if you love what you do, you'll never work a day is only partially true. You'll still have days where you don't want to get up, where you're just tired and need a break. I love to travel, usually, and my job often requires it. That doesn't mean I *always* want to be going somewhere, as home is where I'm happiest."

"Oh, yeah." She smiled back. "Lemme go ring this in."

Rick nodded just as his phone pinged with an incoming text. Glancing down, he saw the message from Ethan. *We'll be there in about an hour. We've got ourselves a boat tour first, then lunch, and, finally, a visit to the City of Sulivan's Crime Museum this afternoon. Tomorrow, we'll do a driving tour."*

It sounded good to Rick. After shooting off a quick reply, he spent the time waiting for his food by continuing to read the newspapers. Most of the other stories were nowhere near as interesting as the ones about The Ghost, not in Rick's mind, but there were two that caught his eye.

The first caught his attention strictly because of the headline. '*Black Death Headed For Trial!*' Rick blinked, then began to read.

> After months of waiting, the trial date for Temujin Alaric Lance, the fabled Black Death of the Arch Street Angels, has been set. Captured following his arrest for the attempted murder of the Deputy Chief of Police, Benjamin Baas—

Rick blinked again, rereading that name. Benjamin Baas. It seemed familiar to him, but he couldn't place it.

Shaking his head, he resumed reading the article, which briefly told the story of Temujin Lance, who had apparently been the Chief Enforcer of the Arch Street Angels. It listed only some of the crimes Lance would be on trial for, as the full count, according to the writer, would be too numerous to list line by line. June 18, 2007, was the trial's start date, and Lance, if convicted, faced nothing less than the Death Penalty.

That, once again, made Rick blink. While not as familiar with the laws in the State of Michigan, he knew enough to know that Michigan had abolished the Death Penalty back in 1846, with the last known execution being in 1830. So how could this Temujin Lance face being put to death despite his lengthy list of crimes?

Just one more example, he thought a moment later, *of how different the Mid-Superior Island Cities are run.*

Resuming his read-through, Rick's eye was caught by '***Iron Horde On The Rampage!***' It seemed that Sulivan didn't just have regular street gangs. The city also had a motorcycle gang problem, and the 'Iron Horde' seemed to be as feared now as the Arch Street Angels had once been. Led by a man identified only as 'Valente,' the Iron Horde had gone on a rampage the night before in the Sports and Arena District. A number of properties and businesses were damaged. At least five or six people had been reported as injured or killed after the fact. One had also been reported as being missing.

Rick felt his lips tighten into a thin line. As a former police officer, he'd seen more than a few scenes like the one being described in the article. Rick had hated it then, and he hated it now. Nonetheless, as Rick reminded himself, there was little that he could do about it. This wasn't Philadelphia, and he was a private investigator, not a police officer.

Blowing out an unhappy breath, he set the paper aside to wait for his food. Soon enough, another girl appeared, introducing herself as Cyndi. She was shorter than the first girl, blond and bubbly, and she set down his food with a flourish. Rick thanked her and learned in short order that she was the niece of the Mid-Lake Inn's owner. She and Alice would both be starting college in the fall; she loved her job and enjoyed talking to people. She was also super excited about *everything*.

Rick didn't mind it, though. Yes, Cyndi happened to be overly enthusiastic, at least in his opinion. Still, she also knew a lot about the city of Sulivan in general. She had no trouble answering any of Rick's fundamental questions. She left him to his breakfast, too, only when she saw new customers entering the restaurant itself.

Rick had finished eating and was paying for his meal when he spotted Ethan, Ray, Meg, and another younger man entering the hotel lobby. He grinned at seeing them, especially the young man, who had jet-black hair done in short cornrows and medium-brown skin. Joyful light brown eyes danced in the delight that their owner had in accompanying his father. Aaron Plumber was a good kid, one who corresponded semi-regularly with Rick's sons. He had a reputation for being outgoing but also well-mannered and respectful, and Rick had the feeling Ethan's son would go far in his life, regardless of whatever he decided to do.

Aaron grinned back when they were reintroduced. "You ready for your tour?"

"I am," Rick said. "And since you're the one giving it, you lead the way."

Aaron did so and brought them out to where a dark blue passenger van with chrome trim and large windows waited. "I got this baby when I decided to play tour guide. I'm going to need something that can accommodate both parents and students, and this lady does the trick. Hop on in."

He opened the passenger side van door as he spoke. Ray was the first to climb in, helping Meg up right after. The two took the back bench seat while Ethan claimed the front passenger seat, leaving Rick to sit in the middle.

He accepted his fate without argument, glancing out the windows

204

to see if anyone was watching and waiting until Aaron had settled himself in the driver's seat before asking, "Your dad said you were planning to give us a boat tour first."

"Yep." Aaron nodded, flashing him another grin. "The boat tour's great. It gives people an overview of Sulivan. I'll be able to point out a few landmarks and things, as well as some differences between the islands. I can also fill ya in a bit more about the various gangs, their territories, and almost anything else you want to know."

"Sounds good."

"We're currently in the middle of territory belonging to The Pharaohs," Aaron continued as he began to drive towards the hotel's parking lot exit. "They control most of the southern portion of West Sulivan, as well as all of Sellars and McCully Islands. If you see anyone in royal blue and gold wearing tattoos or jewelry that looks like it's straight outta Egyptian mythology, you know that they belong to The Pharaohs."

"Like the people I saw at the airport?" Rick asked.

"Yep." Aaron nodded. "They're a nasty bunch, so *don't* get into a fight with 'em, if you can help it."

"What about the other gangs?" Rick wanted to know. "What territories do they control, and what colors do they favor?"

"The Pasquale-Scordato wear mostly regular clothing, but their members can be identified by the Italian leather jackets they like to wear," Aaron said. "They always have a pin with Italian flags or colors attached to their jackets so they can identify each other. They're a mostly Italian gang, but not La Cosa Nostra."

"If anything," Ethan said. "They're more like La Camorra or maybe even 'Ndrangheta."

"What he said." Aaron flashed his father an impish smile, then continued. "They control all of East Sulivan, Principia di Italia on West Sulivan, and a bit of the Entertainment District, and there are a couple of other smaller islands under their control, too. That leads us to the Lords of the Wharf, who prefer purple and black, control the northern portions of West Sulivan, and make a lot of the illegal drugs currently being sold. The last gang is a motorcycle gang called The Iron Horde. Each member liked to wear dark gray leather jackets and chaps with a black or white shirt. They're not considered a rival to the others, interestingly enough, as The Pharaohs, the Lords, and the Pasquale-Scordato all use members of the Horde to make deliveries."

"Very interesting," Rick said as his eyes wandered before blinking as a sign came into view as they headed up the road. "The *Open-Fire Camping Grounds?*"

"Oh, yeah!" Aaron laughed. "Dad and Uncle Ray have already told you about Sulivanian humor, right? Well, that's another example. The camping grounds are considered part of Sinclair Park, which separates the hotels and market district from the rest of Sellars Island. One local weapons store is called *Pike's Carbines and Pistols.* It's better known as the PCP to the locals. Another is the *Slash and Bang Boutique.* The major pharmacy is called the *Drug-N-Drive*; there's *The Duelists' Den,* a gaming store and arcade; the *Packin' Meat Delicatessen;* and the premier burger place, *Blast O' Burger.* Their burgers are *explosively* delicious!" He grinned again. "Not that I'd argue with their motto. They really do have some of the best burgers I've ever tasted, and their rocket fries are amazing."

"What else?" Meg could be heard asking from the back seat.

"There's the *Sauce Shack,* " Aaron said. "It's a beer and liquor store over in West Sulivan. East Sulivan has *The Outpouring of Fine Spirits* Store. There's the *Stitch Itch* and *Flair Play,* which are both arts and craft stores found all over the islands. There's also the *Fur-abulous Pet Salon; Wing-Dings,* which is the mechanics' center for aircraft; *Go 4D Nuts (and Bolts) Hardware Store,* which is one of the local home improvement places; *The Frustrated Writer,* which is a cafe and bookstore run by, you guessed it, a frustrated, wannabe writer. Oh, and let's not forget *Fudge and Cooke's Accounting Services.* "

Rick snickered. "Anything else?"

"The *Novel Thoughts* bookstore is a really nice place to hang out in," Aaron said. "Then there's *Brass Dog Brewers* and *Ready Freddy's*—that last is the used car place where I bought my Fynd here."

"Your what now?" Meg blinked.

"*Fynd,*" Aaron repeated, spelling the brand name. "The cars in the Mid-Superior Islands may look a lot like the cars we have back home, but they're not the same. The main car manufacturers and dealers here are *Epona Automotive,* which names all their vehicles after various horse breeds; *Abra-Car-Dabra,* whose cars and trucks and everything are named after magic tricks and stuff; and then, there's *4A Steele* Cars and Boats, which was where my van originally came from. Those three make and sell just about every mode of transportation the Mids have, and despite being used, my Fynd runs better than the car I used to drive back home."

"Interesting." Rick almost shook his head in disbelief at it, then looked at Ray. "What were you driving when you picked me up?"

"They call it a *Norico* here," Ray said. "Epona Automotive makes it and just about every other official vehicle, not to mention the vehicles for construction, schools, and even taxis."

207

"Huh." Rick filed the information away for later review. "What else?"

"You've already seen the *Crash and Burn Bar,* but most students prefer the nightclubs or the movie theaters. Comin' up on your right, you'll soon see the *All D Cheese Restaurant,* which serves everything cheese-related. Doesn't matter if it's grilled cheese sandwiches, mac-n-cheese, lasagna, or anything else that has cheese involved. They'll make it fresh and serve it to you. Across the street from *All D Cheese* will be the *Troubled Waters Bar and Grill,* which has some delicious food for lunch and dinner, mostly pulled right from the Rousseau River and the Lake."

Everyone looked, and as the woods gave way to buildings and parking lots, they saw the two eateries in question. Aaron took another five or six minutes to reach a line of docks, where any number of larger boats seemed to be waiting.

"And we're here," he said as he pulled into one of the parking lots that had a sign announcing it to be free. "Ferry Landing. Let's get to the office before seeing if we can find our boat. Which one was it that you wanted to take, Dad?"

"*Sulivan's Lady,*" Ethan said. "That's the one Glenn recommended to me back when I first came to the islands. According to him, Herman Laine's a good guy, and he'll be able to answer any questions that you can't answer."

"Cool. Let's go."

It didn't take more than another minute to park and another two to get to the dock office. The passes proved relatively inexpensive, and a helpful young lady with blondish hair tied back in a ponytail directed them to the ship in question. It proved to be an eighty-one-foot, double-decked,

208

diesel-powered passenger ship. Its captain, a grizzled older man with a weathered face, waited next to the boarding plank and gave their passes the barest glance. His almost-white hair was half-hidden by his lopsided cap.

"How long before we set out?" Ray asked as he handed his over.

"We've got ourselves a few minutes yet," the captain said, his voice gruff. "This is the first tour o' the day, and sometimes people run a little late."

"Is anyone else on board?" Ethan wanted to know.

"A couple o' people," the captain said. "Most prefer the afternoon tours."

"How long will the tour take?" Rick asked.

"Usually, it takes 'bout three, maybe three and a half hours. You should be back 'ere in plenty o' time for lunch."

They all nodded in understanding and walked up the plank after thanking the captain. Heading towards the covered seating area that sat at the front, they found a pair of short benches they liked. Almost as soon as they sat down, Ethan gave his son a smile and a nod.

"Okay, kiddo," he said. "Dazzle us with your spiel."

Aaron chuckled and began. "The largest islands that make up Sulivan are West and East Sulivan Islands, McCully, and Aquitania. Sellars Island, Center Island, Pax Island, and Beaulieu Islands are all considered mid-size islands, and there's a bunch of small islands that make up the rest, which I'll be pointin' out. Mid-Lake University is on a small collection of islands known here as the Collegiate Islands. It is made up of the Marcellus, Wallace, Lark, Abram, Adrienne, and Fleur Islands."

"Are there any special sorts of islands we should know about?" Meg asked.

209

"Fort Kincaidia's one," Aaron said. "It's considered a historical site, sorta like Saint Augustine down in Florida, and comes complete with the preserved remains of the fort itself, a museum, and a gift shop. Pax is another. The locals call it Cemetery Island, and the two little islands next to it—Christianne and Jenevra—are reserved for family mausoleums. I'll be pointin' 'em all out."

"Any other islands here that we should know about?" Rick asked.

"Not really. There are the prison islands, which are up to the north and west of West Sulivan, and then the so-called Shield Islands, which are down around the southernmost end of McCully Island. The largest of those, Lighthouse Island, has the remains of Sulivan's oldest lighthouse. A lot of the homeless have supposedly made the Shields their home, too." Aaron thought for a minute. "There's also Arlette Island, which is a wildlife preservation island. People day-trip there for picnics, hiking, taking pictures, and all that. They've got a nature center out there that's really cool to visit. Students from the university often go there if they're studying biology, nature conservation, or similar subjects. Artists like goin' there, too, to sketch, paint, and draw."

A few moments later, as Aaron fielded a few other questions, the ferry's engines roared to life. Glancing at the windows, Rick could see when the ferry itself began to move, backing away from its mooring point before going forward into the open water. Had his brother-in-law's son ever, he wondered, taken this sort of tour? Or had Robert Kincaid not needed to, as he'd grown up in Sulivan? What had that been like growing up in this city? Given what they'd all been told the previous evening, Rick had trouble imagining it and hoped that Robert would open up to him about his childhood in the city if and when they met.

210

He also had to wonder if he and the others were being followed at all. He hadn't seen anyone at the hotel taking an unusual interest, nor did there seem to be anyone on the ship. Yet, there remained a nagging sense of eyes being on them.

Well, there wasn't much Rick could do, other than pay attention to Aaron and keep watch. With luck, he, Ray, Ethan, or Meg would spot someone.

That having been decided, Rick meant to return his full attention to Aaron and the tour. To help Victor and his unknown son, he believed he would have to get to know the city.

Instead, he was distracted by the ringing of his cell phone. The others glanced at him as he pulled it out.

"Keep talking," Rick told them. "I'll do my best to listen in, but I know better than ignore Quet's call." As soon as they nodded their acquiescence, he went ahead and accepted the call. "Everything all right, Quet?"

"With the exception of Victor pacing around like a caged tiger whenever he's not in your office, or talking with his former partners, or helping run training exercises?" Jacquetta sighed. "I've already threatened to kick him out if he doesn't find something more useful to do."

"Be kind to him, Quet," Rick chided. "He's got a lot on his mind right now."

"We *all* do, especially with what happened to Dad," Jacquetta said, then sighed once more. "I shouldn't be complaining, I know, but I really wish you were here instead of out there."

"I wish I were, too." Rick smiled. "This place is interesting, but..." He tilted his head, glancing at Aaron and following his gesture off the starboard side. An eclectic mix of Spanish, German, and even Asian architecture, which were indicative of West Sulivan Island's Barrio, Germantown, and Chinatown Districts, was visible. Inclining his head, Rick lowered his voice so as not to interfere with Aaron's planned speech and to make it harder for anyone not in the know to listen in. "Has anything been found about our mysterious photographer?"

"Nothing," Jacquetta told him. "I'm thinking Vic's arrival, plus that of his former partners and their apprentices, drove off whomever it might have been."

"It's possible," Rick allowed. "Keep your eyes open anyway."

"Planning on it."

"Good. Anything else?"

"So far? The only issue we've had is Phillipe's student."

"Oh?"

"He's having some trouble with the fact that three teenagers and one civilian woman have been able to outwit all of his attempts to trap us."

There could be no mistaking the faint smirk in Jacquetta's voice. Rick almost chuckled as he listened to Aaron point out Fort Kincaidia in the distance, on the boat's port side, complete with a statue of its founder, one William Kincaid, near its docks. There had been a small number of Rick's enemies who had thought they could take Jacquetta, or Charlie, or Emma, or Josiah hostage, to use against him, only to discover far too late that they were anything but helpless.

"How have the other two taken it?"

"They're not exactly thrilled about it, either," Jacquetta told him. "But they're taking us as more of a challenge than as an insult." She sighed again. "I know I should be pleased about that, and about the fact that we've gotten a chance to sharpen our own skills, but I hate the fact that it's been necessary."

"I know."

Rick knew how much Jacquetta longed for a quieter life. The upheavals of her childhood, due to her father's work, and the issues that had plagued her adulthood, due to Rick's profession, had left Jacquetta with a desire for the peace and quiet of a more ordinary life. Rick couldn't give her that, no matter how much he wanted to, but that didn't mean he couldn't try to balance out the dangers of his work with some much-needed downtime.

"After this is over," Rick said at last, barely glancing at the rows of fishing vessels that lined the coast of what Aaron called Fisherman's Wharf. However, he did blink at the gigantic wooden stave church that could be seen perched on the nearby cliffs that overlooked the Wharf itself. "I think we could use a vacation."

"An *actual* vacation?" Jacquetta asked, the faintest hint of hope in her voice.

"Yes," Rick said, smiling once more. "It's almost the summer, after all." He followed the others back over to the port side once more to see Arlette Island not too far off. It proved a pretty little place, with a pristine beach and a gentle hill rising up in the back, and Rick found himself strangely reminded of the place where he and Jacquetta had honeymooned, so many years ago. "Maybe we can take a trip down to Mexico or, if you'd prefer, we leave the kids with your brother for a bit, we can visit that little island in the Caribbean we went to after we got married."

"Oh...." Jacquetta breathed. "I'm *really* tempted to take you up on that."

Rick chuckled. "The kids are old enough, too, to be on their own for a little while, if you'd prefer them not to be more influenced by Victor than they already are."

Jacquetta gave a soft laugh before asking, "Do you think it'll take you very long to track down the one you went there to find?"

"I hope not." Rick honestly did hope it wouldn't take him all that long to locate Victor's son. "But we'll see."

He continued to talk with Jacquetta for another half hour. During that time, Aaron pointed out other notable aspects of the city of Sulivan. There was Morwill Beach and Amusement Park, which Aaron swore was a fun place to visit; the Hetherington Marina, which showcased some of the wealthier citizens' fancy yachts and sailboats; Pax Island, which was better known as Cemetery Island to the locals, along with Christianne and Jenevra Island, where the citizens of Sulivan were all laid to rest sooner or later; little Stephen Island, which housed the Pasquale Estate, and was the seat of the Pasquale-Scordato Crime Family's power; and Suellen Island, which was where the Mayor's House happened to be.

They were passing the cliffs and crags that marked the far end of Sulivan's largest island, Aquitania, which was home to Sulivan's Farmer's Market, when Rick at last said his good-byes to his wife. He couldn't hide the troubled expression that crossed his face as he put his cell phone away.

Ray arched a questioning eyebrow, having noticed. "Everything all right at home?"

"About as well as can be expected," Rick said and shook his head when Ray looked about ready to inquire further. "We'll talk later. I'd like to hear the rest of what Aaron has to say."

214

Ray glanced back at Aaron, who had started talking about the soon-to-be-visible Mid-Lake University, which made its home on the Collegiate Islands, and lowered his voice. "I haven't seen anyone watching us so far."

"Maybe they stayed on the land?" Rick said.

"It's more than possible." Ray seemed about to say something else when Aaron's voice cut him off.

"That's Mid-Lake University's Stadium," he said. "Home of the Sulivan Sturgeons and other school-related events. Sulivan's also got the DuBois Dome, at the southern tip of East Sulivan Island. A lot of different events are featured there, including a concert in honor of Founders' Day—which is one of the biggest celebrations in the Mid-Superior Islands—as well as a demolition derby and also the Mid-Superior Island Motorcross Championship, both of which will be held later in the summer."

The tour boat soon passed the Collegiate Islands and, once again, they were looking at the open farmland of Aquitania. Aaron pointed out one of the farms in particular, Bramblewine Farm, which was connected to Bellerose, Philomena, and Brambleberry Islands, as being considered a major local landmark and business.

"They sell some of the best sodas, wines, and a ton of fruits and candies," Aaron told them. "You have to be careful when going there, though, as some people have had run-ins with the Iron Horde."

"The motorcycle gang?" Meg said. "Out there?"

"Yes, ma'am." Aaron nodded. "No one knows what they might be doin' out on Aquitania, but rumor has it they've been using a couple of the farms as hideouts. The Horde also loves hanging out at the Sickle and Scythe Bar, by the Farmers' Market."

Which could make it a place to avoid, Rick thought, or a place to find out information that he couldn't find anywhere else. He made a note of it as the tour boat again headed past the island's border. Aaron informed them that they were coming to the end of the tour, with just the tips of McCully Island and West Sulivan to go before they would be heading towards Sellars Island once again.

"Already?" Meg said.

"None of the Mids are huge, not in comparison to some places," Aaron said. "They're maybe a little bigger than Hawaii, but not by much. Like I said earlier, the boat tour's more of an overview of Sulivan, which is why we'll be doing a driving tour tomorrow." He pointed out the collection of docks that were now becoming visible. "McCully Island is home not only to the airport, but also to the shipyards and docks." His voice lowered. "There are a lot of rumors about what the Pharaohs might be smuggling in and out of there."

"I remember you saying that they were in control here," Rick said.

"Yep. It's believed that one of the shipping companies is partnered with them somehow," Aaron said. "There are similar rumors about the Lords of the Wharf using some of the boats docked at Fisherman's Wharf to bring in and move their own products, but no one has been able to prove it about them or the Pharaohs."

One last major landmark, Saint Asteria's Cathedral in the Principia di Italia District of West Sulivan, was pointed out as *the* place for weddings, funerals, and other significant events. After that, as Sellars Island came back into view, Rick felt his eyebrows shoot up. Instead of seeing the sculpted gardens and grounds that belonged to the hotels, or the bit of wilderness that belonged to the nearby Sinclair Park, he saw several

216

massive buildings and manufacturing structures that were the hallmarks of heavy industry.

He wasn't the only one doing a virtual double-take. Meg looked shocked, and even Ray and Ethan blinked in astonishment.

"Remember what I told yas earlier?" Aaron said when asked about it. "Sinclair Park divides the various industrial sections of Sellars Island from the Hotels and Market here."

It didn't take long for the various buildings to give way to an apparent forest on their starboard side, while the shipyards off the port side transformed into the airport. Before fifteen more minutes had passed, the ferry was docking.

"All right, folks," Aaron said after they'd disembarked. "It's time for lunch, then we'll head to the Crime Museum. Where d'yas want to eat?"

"What would you recommend?" Rick asked, glancing around and feeling frustrated when he failed to spot anyone watching them. He was supposedly one of the best private investigators in the business, and he knew eyes were on them.

But where?

"Honestly? It doesn't matter to me. Most of the restaurants around here are really good," Aaron said. "It just depends on whether you want fast food or a sit-down type of restaurant."

"I think I'd like to try this *Blast O' Burger* you were talkin' about earlier," Meg said. "You said they were explosively delicious?"

"I did!" Aaron chuckled and looked at the others. "Any objections?" When none were raised, he grinned. "Great. There's one just a couple of streets away. Let's head back to the van, get our grub, then head to the museum."

Ten or so minutes later, they were pulling into the parking lot of a smallish, tan-colored building with a picture of two burgers and a carton of fries flying through the air, as though caught in the cartoonish explosion behind them. The inside looked like any other burger place, but the names of the products made Rick gape and Meg snicker.

"T-n-T burgers?" Rick asked, all but doing a double-take. "And chicken *grenades*?"

Meg almost giggled. "Along with a beef-bomb burger, dynamite chicken strips, and The Landmine."

Ethan and Aaron both grinned. Ray chuckled as they joined the short line. "I seriously don't know why we don't have one of these in each state."

Rick soon found himself in agreement as he bit into the T-n-T burger he'd bought, alongside an order of Rocket Fries and a large cup of Astrolite soda. Even *Meg* seemed impressed by the food's quality.

As they ate and talked, Rick allowed his eyes to roam. Not quite a minute, he finally found another set of eyes that seemed abnormally focused on them. They were a smoldering near-onyx that belonged to a man with light brown skin and pitch-black, short-cut hair. He didn't look out of place, but the fact that his attention seemed to be focused solely on them caused Rick to give Ethan a slight nudge.

"Two o'clock," he murmured. "Our right."

Ethan's eyes dutifully slid over, then back, narrowing a fraction. His voice dropped to a near-whisper. "That's Luis Espina. He works in Island Affairs, and he's usually with—" Ethan's eyes went from side to side, searching. "Ah. I thought so."

"Ethan?" Ray kept his voice low.

"Marcus Brannigan's here, too," Ethan said. "And Ed Driar. Espina's been helpin' to train them."

"Huh." Ray glanced at Rick. "They're pulling out all the stops for you."

"All three of them are Island Affairs?" Rick asked. When Ray and Ethan both gave subtle nods, he blew out an unhappy breath. "What should we do?"

"For now?" Ray said. "We do what we planned and go to the museum."

Rick didn't like it, but he also didn't see the point in arguing about it. He was now aware of his followers, though, and that was what mattered.

"All right," he said at length. "Let's finish up and get to driving."

About thirty minutes later, they were back on the road. Like Ray and Ethan had the previous day, Aaron headed for the closest on-ramp to the expressway, which meant they reached Center Island in a matter of minutes. They were at the Crime Museum shortly after and, once the van had been parked in a nearby public garage, Aaron led the way over to the building.

Its former life as a police station proved evident, as the lobby had been remade to look like one. Pictures of Sulivan's former 'Most Wanted' covered the walls, even behind the ticket counters, which had been constructed to resemble how they'd once been.

The first display hall proved to be more of a history lesson, focusing on the period when the region's natives referred to the Mid-Superior Islands as the Exile Islands or even the Ghost Islands. If a member of any one of the tribal peoples who had inhabited the coasts of Michigan, Minnesota, or Wisconsin, or the Canadian Provinces that lined Lake Superior's shores, was believed to have committed a crime and could escape to any one of the Mids, then they were considered 'as dead' to their former tribes. Such things hadn't, according to the information provided in the exhibit, happened all that often, and the islands had apparently been empty when the first European settlers had arrived.

Those first settlers were the subject of the second room, which detailed the founding of the Mid-Superior Island cities in general. The ancestors of what had become the Mid-Superior Islands' Old Families were gone over, along with how they had founded the Mids. Yes, they had been considered outlaws during their time, committing acts of piracy and the like, but some of their crimes caused more than one member of the group to shake their heads. They were escaped slaves; supposedly fallen women; men who had stood against the so-called nobles that had ruled at the time and were in danger of paying a high price for their supposed insolence; and various other people who had escaped a hangman's noose, some simply for trying to survive. Apparently, the ancestors of the Old Families had not only banded together but decided to make the Mids their home.

Rick noted a man named William Kincaid, recalling the statue Aaron had mentioned at Fort Kincaidia. The First of the Kincaid Family had fled the shores of his native land alongside the woman who had become his bride after he'd helped her escape the machinations of her family. According to the placard of information underneath their portraits, they had pledged themselves to Henry Sullivan after the man had helped them escape again when the lady's family tracked them down. The Kincaid Family became as inextricably intertwined with the Mids' society

220

as the Sullivan, the Rousseau, the Chevalier, the Beaufort, and the others who had made up the Old Families, and the Kincaids had, in fact, become known as the 'Guardians of the Mids.'

Was that, Rick wondered, why they had been taken out? If so, why hadn't they been dealt with sooner? Why had Island Affairs, if they were indeed the ones behind the Old Families' near-extinction, waited until the nineteen eighties to end most of the Kincaid Family?

He didn't know. Not yet. *Hopefully, I can find that out. But first, I need to find Victor's son.*

With that thought firmly in his mind, he followed Ethan, Ray, and Aaron as they led him and Meg through the following rooms. The third, fourth, and even fifth exhibit halls dealt with the sort of criminals that all societies seemed to have, no matter their origins. Murderers, con artists, bank robbers, and the like were all showcased, but in nowhere near as positive a light as the Old Families' origins had been.

The sixth collection of exhibits dealt with the first wave of street gangs that had plagued Sulivan's streets. Titled 'The Gangs of Sulivan', it first detailed the rise of the Pasquale Family under its former patriarch, Alphonse, and his children: Alberto, who had disappeared and was believed to be dead; Giovanni, who was seen as the next in line before his death; Bruno, a known killer who acted as his family's Chief Enforcer before his death; and, finally, Lorenza, the daughter, who had returned after her marriage to pick up the pieces of her family's legacy.

Next had been Los Demonios de Olegario. Named for the neighborhood they were founded in, deep within the Barrio District of Sulivan, they were headed by Lucero Escarra, a known criminal who saw the opportunity to form a gang. Backed by Flavio Merino, a towering giant of a man who was better known to most as 'Machado', Amaro Quijada and Jasper Velasco, all of whom had been met during Escarra's time in prison, Escarra's gang became a force to be reckoned with for a time.

After them had come the Eighth Avenue Kings. That particular gang had been headed by Ernesto Cardoso and his cousins, Ignacio and Maricela Valdez. The three had been orphaned due to the actions of the Pasquale Family, and naturally, they had all wanted revenge. The uncle who had taken them in, one 'Big Bentley' Gomez, had encouraged their endeavor, as he had apparently wanted a piece of the Pasquale Family's pie.

Third on the list was the Three Strikes Gang. Headed up by three brothers, the Three Strikes had been small but incredibly violent. Tyrell Howard was the leader, known for being tough and a thinker. Rick knew that combination could be deadly, but, according to the exhibits, Tyrell had been held back by his youngest brother. While Tyrone Howard had been loyal and intelligent, Tyrese Howard had been a hothead who had tended to take everything personally, and, more often than not, he'd drag his two brothers down with him. Worse, he'd been sleeping with Tyrell's girlfriend, Desirae Frost, which led to the gang unraveling and, eventually, being destroyed.

According to the information provided, each of those four gangs would meet their various ends because of the fourth gang that arose on Center Island itself. That gang would be none other than the Arch Street Angels.

Their portion of the museum exhibits proved to be the largest of the various collections. Rick found himself stunned by the sheer size they faced. Created to look much like the Center Pointe District of Center Island had, about five or so years ago—or so the entrance to the Angels'

222

exhibit read—the collection contained a vast wealth of information, ranging from the weaponry the Angels had used to the vehicles they had driven to police reports about the Angels' activities and brief biographies of the principal players.

To Rick's astonishment, he recognized one of those players. He *knew* he'd heard the name Benjamin Baas before. Now, upon seeing the man's picture, the various pieces clicked into place. The one thing that stood out most in Rick's memory, however, was that Benjamin Benedict Baas had *not* been a gangster. Back in Philly, he'd been a *cop*.

What in the hell was he doing *here,* in Sulivan? And what had he been doing in the *Arch Street Angels?*

Rick felt his mind whirling with sudden shock. He barely noticed it when Ethan stepped up beside him.

"Rick?"

The FBI agent spoke in a quiet, questioning tone, having caught the other's quick shift in expression. He had been keeping close to the private investigator as they'd wandered the museum, never quite letting Rick out of his sight. Ethan had learned enough about Island Affairs in the short time he'd been installed in his position to not want to take chances, especially now that they knew for sure that Rick was being watched.

The last thing Ethan had expected, though, was for Rick to look like he'd been suddenly bludgeoned.

"I don't believe it." The private investigator continued to stare at the picture in question. "What is *he* doing here?"

"What?" Ethan's eyebrows rose, and he looked over. A moment later, he frowned. "Ben Baas? He was the officer who was undercover in the Arch Street Angels. When his assignment ended, as a great success, I might add, he was leap-frogged into the position of the Deputy Chief of Police."

Rick's face snapped over. "Are you *serious?*"

"I—"

Ethan blinked. His frown deepened. Why wouldn't he be?

His brow furrowed as Ethan struggled to remember what little he knew about the City of Sulivan's Deputy Chief of Police. Benjamin Benedict Baas was about five feet ten inches tall and had dark hair and brown eyes. He was known to smoke like the proverbial chimney, had a sarcastic streak as wide as a canyon, and was from Philadelphia, Pennsylvania.

Oh. A sudden realization struck Ethan like lightning. *No way.*

Inclining his head, focusing intently on Rick's expression, he asked, "You know 'im, Rick?"

"He was a patrol officer with the precinct I was a detective in. He was transferred a few years before I left to become a private investigator."

Rick couldn't help his disbelief any more than Ethan now could. The Benjamin Baas that Rick remembered had been a young man with a definite attitude that had rubbed Rick, along with a number of others, the wrong way. Baas had also possessed a strange, wary hardness, which Rick could remember mocking alongside his partner. It had seemed too out of place on such a young officer, one who hadn't experienced half the things the detectives had yet.

What in the world, Rick wanted to know, was Ben Baas doing out *here*, in the Mid-Superior Island City of Sulivan? How had he made it to the rank of detective, and how in the *hell* had Ben managed to get put undercover in the Arch Street Angels? And then, to discover that he now

224

happened to be a *Deputy Chief of Police?*

Rick's thoughts raced, trying to fit these new facts in with what he knew about Ben Baas. He soon found he couldn't, and he had no answer to the questions he now, not yet.

"We'll tell ya the story tonight," Ethan told him when Rick finally managed to give voice to his thoughts. "So far as we know it, that is. In the meantime, do you wanna continue through the exhibit?"

Rick almost shook his head. He had learned more than enough about the Mid-Superior Island City of Sulivan that day, and wanted to leave the Museum posthaste.

Instead, as he looked up to answer Ethan, another picture caught his attention. Rick's eyes, which had been filled with disbelief, grew wide with another shock. His feet moved almost of their own accord, taking him past a bewildered Ethan to bypass a large video screen that featured a number of newscasts from the Angels' time. Within seconds, he was standing in front of the picture in question.

It was of a young man with blazing, coppery red hair. A hardened expression made his already thin lips thinner while his jaw and square chin were set in defiance. Icy, blue-gray eyes glared out at the visitors as though daring them to say something the young man would disagree with.

There could be no mistaking him, not in Rick's mind. "Oh, fucking *hell!*"

Chapter Nine: The Call

May 26, 2007: Evening, Harold Edmund Holloway's Office

Harold loathed paperwork. It was one of the few aspects of his job that he could be said to despise. The tedium of filling out form after form ruined the joy he had in ordering his subordinates around or in being admired by various women. If he could have had someone else to do all of the paperwork that was so prevalent in this job, then he thought he would have been delighted.

Of course, there was one thing he hated more than filling out paperwork. Working on the weekend whenever emergencies cropped up made him more than just irritable and angry. It made him downright hateful.

And, all thanks to that damned Ghost, he was stuck in his office, being forced to endure both of the things he hated at the same time.

He gnashed his teeth as he scribbled out the details of the previous day's events. It wasn't enough that The Ghost had struck again. Oh, no. *This* time, The Ghost had managed to appear at the *headquarters* of the *DBJF Alliance Corporation.*

He stabbed at an inoffensive lowercase 'i with his pen, growling at the thought. As bad as it had been that The Ghost had been inside the DBJF's headquarters itself, the fact that he or she hadn't been noticed for at least a full hour was *worse.*

"An hour!" Harold spat at the paperwork in front of him. "Sixty minutes of doing *something,* and *no one* knows what!?"

Another growl, this one mixing fear with anger, escaped him.

Granted, so far, the detailed inventory that had been taken after The Ghost's appearance had revealed nothing. A small handful of custodial uniforms had been logged as missing, but no one could be certain whether they had been taken by The Ghost or misplaced.

Harold didn't care about the actual truth of the matter. He preferred not to take any chances and had advised the DBJF's Board of Directors to take action. They had listened, much to his relief, and had ordered all of their custodians to return their uniforms for replacement. They had also gone so far as to contact the laundry services they used to destroy whatever uniforms were out for cleaning or repair.

Even if The Ghost *had* taken a uniform or three, he or she wouldn't be able to use it. That was the good news.

The bad news? All of those precautions would cost both the DBJF and Harold's Department thousands of dollars. Money was just burned away, all because some freak in a mask wanted to play games.

Even worse was the fact that The Ghost had somehow managed to escape. Harold hissed at the thought of it. *How*, he wanted to know, *was it even possible?* Hundreds of questions assaulted his mind. *How could The Ghost have gotten past the armed blockades? How had The Ghost managed to steal a car before hightailing it to the docks to take a boat? How the hell did the slippery bastard even get hold of a vessel that was supposed to be moored, let alone get it to work? It was supposed to be disabled!*

Harold didn't have a clue. He also seemed to have no way of getting any answers, at least not at the moment. While the stolen boat had been recovered, it hadn't offered anything that might give the investigators a solid lead or direction. The first forensic team had been over the ship for at least three hours and had found *nothing*. A second team had been flown in from the mainland at great expense, and they had literally torn the boat apart, but again, they had discovered nothing. There hadn't been any fingerprints, fibers, shoe imprints, or even an *eyelash*.

It should have been impossible. It certainly was, at the very least, improbable. The Ghost had quite literally vanished from the boat he or she had taken. The vessel had been recovered in the middle of Lake Superior, far enough away from Arlette Island, the Prison Islands, and much, *much* too far away from any of the other Mid-Superior Island Cities and towns that were close by. Unless The Ghost had managed to grow flippers and gills or had access to a submarine of some sort, there should have been absolutely no way for The Ghost to disappear as thoroughly, as ultimately, as he or she had. Yes, the Coast Guard had lost sight of the boat during their pursuit, but only for a matter of *seconds*. Not minutes.

So how had The Ghost done it?

Who the hell is able to pull off something this elaborate? Harold wondered. *And who would be able to get away with it?*

Again, he didn't know. Not yet, but he intended to find out.

Immersed as he was in those thoughts, Harold found himself caught off guard by the sudden, shrill ring of the phone by his elbow. He jerked, nearly falling out of his seat, and stared at the device in shock before shaking his head. Cursing, he reached for the handset. *When I find out who the idiot is who has the gall to disturb me now, they will rue the day, I promise!*

"Holloway!" he barked into the speaker, making no effort to hide or disguise his impatience.

"Ah, Harold."

"Sir."

Harold's attitude shifted from resentful rage to immediate subservience. He sat up in his seat, his spine stiffening. Nathaniel Oliver was the Director of the Department of Mid-Western Island Affairs and Harold's immediate superior. There weren't many people who could make Harold afraid, but Nathaniel happened to be one of them.

"You sound stressed, Harold," Nathaniel said, the faintest hint of what Harold took to be a concern in his voice. "Is everything all right?"

"N-not really, sir," Harold said, bracing himself. Nathaniel would not, he knew, be happy about what had happened the previous night.

Before he could begin to speak, however, Nathaniel interrupted with a light-hearted tone. "Well, I have some good news that might help relieve a portion of the strain you're under."

"Oh?" Harold felt his eyebrows rise before giving quick thanks that he could put off telling Nathaniel about what had happened, at least for a few minutes. "Believe me, sir, I'll take anything at the moment, no matter how small."

"You should particularly like *this* piece of news," Nathaniel told him. He cleared his throat, then announced, "The Wall has been brought down."

Harold felt the breath catch in his lungs. His head almost swam as he remembered the absolute worst day of his life. After all this time, spent living in the dread that it would happen again, he no longer needed to fear. "Truly?"

"Yes. I wanted to inform you personally, as I know what the Wall had you endure," Nathaniel said. "My assistant is in the process of calling the others. We will *finally* be able to start making moves in the *right* direction now."

"Towards the end game?" A hint of anticipation tinged Harold's voice. "Are you serious, sir?"

"I am." Nathaniel sounded smug. "Granted, we still haven't heard from the team that was sent for his second, but he was in a more remote location."

"Which means it'll take longer to hear from them?" Harold nodded in understanding, although he needed to fight back a shudder at the thought of the man Nathaniel had called The Wall's second. "You're certain that he didn't know anyone was being sent?"

"There's no question that he doesn't—" Nathaniel's voice abruptly cut off. "Forgive me, Harold, but my assistant is calling me."

"Of course, sir."

Harold allowed himself to lean back, letting a wave of relief wash over him as he listened to the 'on-hold' music. At long last, he would be able to sleep without fear. He could enjoy a whole night of blissful rest, joyful dreams, and have a peaceful awakening, all without the worry of finding a certain someone in his home.

Releasing a large breath he didn't realize he had been holding, one that mixed respite with satisfaction, Harold felt a smile form on his lips. Not only would he be able to enjoy a whole night's rest, but perhaps he would also *finally* be able to deal with the greatest threat to his rulership of the city of Sulivan.

Before he could begin to celebrate his triumph, however, the music disappeared. He heard Nathaniel's voice again, but the previous pleasantry had vanished. Instead, there was now a subtle anger, much like a darkening sky that hinted at a coming storm.

"Is there something," Nathaniel asked, "that you wish to tell me,

Harold?"

Harold blinked, momentarily taken aback, before his eyes dropped back down to the report he had been writing. His relief dissolved. *Ah, shit.*

"I'm afraid there is, sir," he said. He swallowed and drew in a deep breath, preparing for the fallout he felt certain would be coming. "The Ghost struck the DBJF last night."

Nathaniel was silent on the other end of the line. "Was anything disturbed?"

Harold looked over his report again, his words failing him for a moment as he skimmed the report quickly. Where to begin?

At last, he said, "The Ghost was in the DBJF's headquarters for about sixty minutes. Nothing seems to have been touched except for a few maintenance uniforms. I've already ordered them all to be destroyed and replaced. The new uniforms are being made as we speak."

Nathaniel sucked air in through his teeth. "Maintenance workers, you say?"

Harold found himself nodding stupidly as if Nathaniel could see him. "Um, yes. Sir. Three were unaccounted for. I decided not to take any chances."

Nathaniel was silent for a moment before he said. "Very good, Harold. You are using your head, but I fear it will not be enough. There is a good chance that one of the custodial staff has already been compromised. Yes, we got lucky this time, but I want every single maintenance worker's background checked and alibied, and I want it started *yesterday*. If one of them is The Ghost, we have him trapped now."

Harold refrained from correcting Nathaniel's assumption. It

made sense to suspect that The Ghost was a man, given how easily The Ghost had outpaced seasoned agents and officers.

"Yes, sir," he said. "I'll get that done right away. I'll call every available agent in, and we'll make sure we track down The Ghost. No matter how long it takes."

Nathaniel began to sound a bit happier again. "Very good, Harold. Is there anything else?"

Harold almost said no. He nearly decided to say his 'good-bye'; but his eyes fell upon the dossier he still had out, the one detailing Rick Thorne's life. Harold swallowed once more before speaking.

"Actually, sir," he said. "There is. It seems that Rick Thorne has come to the Mids."

There was a heartbeat of silence. Harold tried to keep his breathing calm and even as Nathaniel processed what he'd just said.

"Rick Thorne." At last, Nathaniel's low and dangerous voice reached Harold's ear. "As in the private investigator from Philadelphia? The one who not only danced with, but outsmarted a few of our mainland operatives?"

"Unfortunately, yes," Harold said. "The same."

"What is *he* doing there? In the Mids?"

"A case, or so he told Mister Fleischmann."

"And he wasn't denied entry?"

"I'm afraid Mister Fleischmann became flustered," Harold said. "As Agents Plumber and Douglas met Mister Thorne at the gate and escorted him to customs."

"They did?" Nathaniel asked. "*Both* of them?"

"Yes, sir."

"This complicates things."

Harold waited, hoping that Nathaniel would have some idea as to what could be done. He didn't believe that the usual methods of bribery and persuasion would work on Rick Thorne. As Harold had told Regina, Rick's integrity and grit were well-known, at least to certain people.

Nathaniel knew it as well as Harold did, but he still thought they were worth a try. "Are people watching him?"

"Yes, sir," Harold acknowledged. "There are."

"Good. Try what we know usually works first. I know that in Mister Thorne's case, they probably will not, but try anyway. If they fail, then you will have permission to do something else."

Harold's brow furrowed. "May I ask why, sir? Why bother attempting something that won't work, and why give Mister Thorne any warning as to what will happen if he doesn't cooperate?"

"Mister Thorne has many useful contacts that several of our superiors covet," Nathaniel told him. "His reputation as an investigator is a sterling one, as well, and that would allow us to move a bit more openly against those who would oppose us if we were to get him onto our side."

Harold held in a sigh. He disagreed with his superiors on this but would act as they wished. He had little choice in the matter, to be honest.

"What of Agents Plumber and Douglas?" he asked instead.

"They are untouchable at the moment." Nathaniel's voice held a sullen edge. "Their Director is too insulated to move against, even through them. If whatever cover story we choose isn't absolutely perfect, we stand to lose a lot more than we would gain." He could be heard to sigh. "We should have liquidated them when they first came to the Mids." Another sigh was heard to escape. "It's too late now, though, and their director would be suspicious if they also went missing."

"Understood, sir."

Nathaniel sighed again at hearing Harold's equally glum words. "Let's try to look on the bright side, Harold. We have removed the Wall. This means we can begin moving against Deputy Chief Baas and all of those under his so-called protection."

Harold blinked, then smiled. It was not, he knew, his most pleasant expression. He had never liked the current Deputy Chief of the Sulivan City Police, Benjamin Benedict Baas. The man was not an ally of the Department of Mid-Western Island Affairs. In fact, he had long ago proven himself to be the proverbial thorn in the sides of Harold, Nathaniel, and their various supporters, standing in their way on more than one occasion and getting away with it, all thanks to his association with The Wall.

But now that the Wall was gone?

A new thought caused Harold to lean forward in his seat. "Does this mean we will be able to retrieve my sister's lost subject?"

"Indeed, you will," Nathaniel confirmed, sounding a bit happier again. "We may even be able to take care of Lance before his trial."

Harold's smile widened, even as he said, "And spoil Judge Dicks' planned fun? We made certain he'd be appointed to oversee it, and I know for a fact that he's looking forward to the assignment."

"Ah." Nathaniel chuckled. "Well, far be it from me to ruin the good Judge's entertainment. Has he confirmed that the prosecutor will be pushing for the maximum allowable sentence?"

"He has."

"Excellent. You see, Harold? The tide is turning in our favor once more. I'll be letting the Senator know. No doubt he'll—"

A knock at Harold's door caused him to look up to see his secretary poking her head in. "Forgive me, sir, but could you hold on for a moment? It seems Pamela wishes to speak with me."

"She does? Very well. I know she would never interfere unless it were something important."

"Thank you, sir." Harold waved the woman in after putting Nathaniel on hold. "What is it?"

"Mister Utley has something he says you need to see, sir," she said. "He has Mister Ringewald with him."

"He does?" Harold went on alert. Ira coming to see him would not be surprising, as he no doubt would have a report to make following his pursuit of The Ghost. For Sean Ringewald to accompany him? That caused all manner of alarm bells to go off within Harold's mind. "Send them in."

She nodded, opening the door to allow the two men to enter. Ira Utley was a tall, well-muscled man in his fifties who had served the Department of Mid-Western Island Affairs for almost three decades. His dark eyes resembled twin flakes of obsidian that, at the moment, held a hurricane of anger. Sean Ringewald, on the other hand, had the appearance of a slightly built Neanderthal. The wispy beard and mustache he'd somehow managed to grow did nothing to make the young man look older, and the coke-bottle glasses he currently wore made his gray-green eyes look wider than they actually were. He carried a laptop computer with him, and his expression alternated between fear and dismay.

"Well, gentlemen," Harold said as soon as Pamela had shut the door. "What do you have?"

235

"This." Ira nodded at Sean. "Put it down and show 'im."

"Yes, sir." Sean placed the laptop in front of Harold and opened it, showing what appeared to be security camera footage. "This is from the DBJF's security feed. I've isolated all the video that shows The Ghost and spliced them together."

"You have? Excellent work, Mister Ringewald," Harold praised. "Let's see what we have."

"Yes, sir."

With a single press of a key, Sean began the playback. Harold focused on the screen, watching as the masked figure of The Ghost appeared.

The Ghost seemed to be a tall figure, although Harold couldn't tell if the person in question happened to be male or female. The Ghost's outfit and mask were jet-black, lightly armored, and just baggy enough to conceal anything that might be used to narrow the field of suspects.

Harold leaned back a little in his seat. His lips pursed. So far, The Ghost had taken care to make sure he or she could not be identified. It was highly irritating, to be sure, but expected.

As expected, Harold was watching The Ghost duck into the custodial locker rooms. As he had suspected, The Ghost took three uniforms after messing about the area for a few minutes. The uniforms themselves were neatly folded before being placed into a small bag that The Ghost slung over his or her shoulders.

What Harold, Sean, and Ira did *not* expect to see was where The Ghost went next. Instead of wandering around aimlessly, as they had half-anticipated, The Ghost headed towards a particular area.

Harold felt the blood drain from his face when he saw The Ghost enter the liaison office that existed between the DBJF Alliance Corporation and the Department of Mid-Western Island Affairs. *This* could not be good.

His heart sank as he watched The Ghost cross over to sit behind the desk. With a deft hand, The Ghost turned on the computer and began to do *something*. What that something was, Harold didn't know. The footage revealed nothing.

It was enough, however, to know that The Ghost *had* done something. Harold hissed under his breath as The Ghost remained at the computer in question for no less than a full twenty-six and a half minutes before getting back up.

"Do we know what was done?" he finally demanded.

"Not yet, sir," Sean said. "We've got people currently working on it."

"Good." Harold nodded. "This is your top priority. *Nothing* else matters in comparison to this."

"Yes, sir."

Ira nodded back before he and Sean were dismissed. Harold blew out an angry breath as he watched them leave. Whatever The Ghost had done, whatever programs or files he or she had gone through, uploaded, or downloaded. They needed to know these things *yesterday*.

His eyes fell back to the phone. Harold knew he would have to tell Nathaniel all of this. He wasn't looking forward to it.

He drew in another breath, this time in preparation, and picked the handset back up. "Are you still there, sir?"

"I am," Nathaniel said.

He didn't, Harold noted, sound irritated about having been kept waiting. Only curious. *If only it could last.*

"It seems The Ghost did more than just take a couple of custodial uniforms," he said. "I just watched footage that was taken from the security cameras. It shows The Ghost entering the office of the liaison officer we have stationed with the DBJF and doing something with the computer there."

Nathaniel's tone became low and dangerous as he snarled, *"What?"*

"I have my best people working on it, sir," Harold swallowed past the lump in his throat. "It's been labeled priority one."

For one eternal heartbeat, there was silence. Harold waited, a droplet of sweat trickling down his spine.

"I have two more meetings that I will need to attend this week with the Senator," Nathaniel said at last. "But I'll be on a plane immediately after they've wrapped up. I hope you will have the answers we need by the time I reach Sulivan's shores."

Harold blinked. Nathaniel would come to Sulivan? He wouldn't head to the primary office Island Affairs had over in the Mid-Superior Island City of Babineaux?

"Yes," Nathaniel told him when he asked. "I'll also have my assistant start on the paperwork to transfer your sister's seventh subject back to her custody. We'll put a rush on it, so you should have it by Tuesday morning, most likely."

"Yes, sir. Do you want me to call the Warden and let him know?"

"No. I'll do that. You concentrate on finding out just what the hell The Ghost did while on that computer."

"I will, sir," Harold said.

238

"Good."

Not a moment later, Harold heard Nathaniel hang up. The dial tone proved ominous to his ears.

Relax, Harold, he told himself. *Yes, Nathaniel Oliver will be on his way here, and chances are slim that you'll have any more information on The Ghost and what he or she was doing last night. However, the Wall is gone, and you'll soon have one less problem to worry about now that Reggie will at last have her seventh subject back under her control.*

With that thought, he returned his attention to the paperwork. The sooner he finished, the sooner he could head home to tell his sister and her husband that piece of good news.

Chapter Ten: Sulivanian Prison Blues

May 28, 2007: Morning, Thomas G. Burfield Prison Hospital

The young man with coppery-red hair lay, unmoving, on the hospital bed. His chest rose and fell with even regularity as his oxygen was supplemented by the nasal cannula he wore. Various pieces of equipment monitored his heart rate, brain activity, and more.

He never stirred, not even a little, as Doctor Kim Hana examined him. He didn't flinch when she lifted his right eyelid to expose one blue-gray orb, then used a pen light to check that eye's pupil to see it dilate. He didn't wince when she repeated her action with his left eye. He made no sounds or movements to protest the doctor as she worked, giving every appearance of sleeping through it.

Not that anyone in the room seemed to expect anything different. Not Doctor Kim, not Deputy Chief of Police Benjamin Benedict Baas, and certainly not Prison Warden Euphrates Moorehead. Why should they? It was well known that the young man on the bed had been trapped in a coma for just over four years now, and he was never expected to wake up.

The warden huffed in irritation, irked at what he believed was an unnecessary waste of time and money. Every two weeks for the past nine or so months, the Deputy Chief had made this trip out to the City of Sulivan's Prison Islands to check in on this particular young man. Every two weeks, Euphrates Moorehead had to make time to accompany Ben down to the ICU ward of the Thomas G. Burfield Prison Hospital and stay at least a few minutes before being dismissed back to his duties. He didn't see the point and hated having his time wasted.

This particular visit, however, was earlier than expected—almost a whole week earlier, in fact. The abnormality of it all finally caused Euphrates to give voice to his frustration.

"I don't know why you're botherin'," he grumbled. "All the docs have said he'll never wake up. You should pull the plug and be done with it all."

Ben flicked granite-brown eyes over to him. His tone proved deceptively mild. "Did I ask you for your opinion, Warden Moorehead?"

Euphrates snorted. "You never do, Baas. Normally, I hold my tongue, too, but *he*—" He nodded at the man on the bed. "He has been here, like this, for four full years now. He's a criminal, while you're a cop. Why should you care about a *thug* like Liam Alastor? You bein' undercover in the same gang doesn't explain why you fight for him."

Again, Ben's eyes slid over to where the warden stood, huffing like an angry bull. They were complete opposites in almost every way. Euphrates Moorehead was a large, even corpulent man with an oversized brow and a near-constant sneer. His uniform was stained with sweat despite the air conditioning, and he mopped at his forehead every so often with an old, equally stained handkerchief. Piggish, watery blue eyes glared daggers at the lean man leaning against a nearby wall. Ben Baas showed no apparent signs of discomfort, anger, or even anxiety despite what he'd claimed had brought him out to the prison islands. His uniform proved as clean as the ICU itself, and not even the smallest drop of sweat marred his skin. Ben's entire appearance seemed crafted to be as professional as possible, with only his eyes giving away his irritation with the warden's attitude.

"Tell me, Euphrates," he said at length. "Have *you* ever been deep

241

undercover?"

Euphrates heaved a long-suffering sigh. As a boy, he had dreamed of being a detective and putting away the bad guys. Unfortunately, he had also earned a well-deserved reputation as a bully, and his ease with excessive force put an end to that particular boyhood dream. Only his willingness to play ball with the Department of Mid-Western Island Affairs had allowed him to remain employed. However, he'd been forcibly shunted off into the Corrections Department to allow Sulivan's police department to escape the whiff of scandal he'd brought to them. Yes, he'd worked hard to earn his current post, but being the warden of the Mid-Superior Islands' Prison was a far cry from the sometimes-dubious distinction of being a detective.

It galled him, even now, especially when it was pointed out by someone like Benjamin Benedict Baas, who *had* lived out Euphrates' boyhood dream. Ben Baas wasn't a native of the Mids like Euphrates was. Yes, Ben had family in The Mids, but he was from Philadelphia. He was an *outsider* of the Mids, not a native, and the warden growled at him as a result.

Still, he took care to confine his words to this latest irritation. Euphrates caught enough flak as it was, and he didn't need Ben running back to his Chief with the claim that Euphrates couldn't play nice with outsiders, too.

"You know I haven't," he bit out.

"Then you couldn't possibly understand," Ben said in quiet retaliation. "I'm only here, still walkin' this planet, because of this *thug*, as you called 'im. The two of us were once cornered by Giovanni Pasquale and his favorite band of killers. They were huntin' us, lookin' to kill the both of us in as gruesome a way as possible, to take revenge for what we'd

242

done to Giovanni's brother and their father. If it wasn't for *his* quick thinking, I know for a fact that neither of us would've made it outta there. I owe 'im for that, and for all the other times he saved my ass." Brown eyes glared at the other, boring a hole into Euphrates' thick skull. "D'ya understand *that?*"

The warden huffed again but chose to say nothing more, in part due to Ben's glare but also due to the fact that Doctor Kim had glanced up and over their way. She was a tiny woman, barely five feet in height. Yet, she had already managed to terrify the entire prison staff in the few short weeks since her arrival at the prison islands. No one in their right mind wanted to upset someone who had regular access to large needles and other equally frightening pieces of equipment, nor did they want to annoy the one who had been responsible for hiring Doctor Kim or promoting Ben Baas. Chief of Police Makoto Akiyama was *scary* when he wanted to be, and not even Prison Warden Euphrates Moorehead wanted to try and piss him off.

Chief Akiyama was the sole reason, in fact, that Euphrates continued to make time for all of Ben's visits, even the unannounced ones. Still, he had his limits, and Ben was rapidly reaching all of them.

"You can see that nothing has changed." He spoke through gritted teeth. "The guards and I have all been following Chief Akiyama's orders, and no one has attempted to visit. The doc and her team haven't let anyone without authorization get near him, either."

"Good," Ben said. "I'm glad, as it shows you're still capable of following *some* orders, at least. Now, be good enough to follow one more and be quiet so that Doctor Kim can speak."

Euphrates glared at him but did as asked when Doctor Kim

stepped away from the young man on the bed. She showed no discomfort, despite the tension in the air, and went over to stand before Ben.

"My patient is in excellent health, sir," she said. "Despite everything he's had to endure. Beyond that, I'm afraid he is just as he was when I arrived to take over his care earlier this month."

Ben arched an eyebrow at her, eyes sliding to the young man on the bed. A moment later, he inclined his head. His tone softened, just perceptibly.

"I'm glad," he said. "Keep up the good work, Doctor."

"Of course."

The warden huffed again. "Are you satisfied now? Can we leave?"

Ben's gaze hardened as he turned his head. A winter's chill once again permeated his voice. "Oh, we're leavin'. But I'm a *long* way from bein' satisfied. With Lance's trial comin' up, many things'll need to be tightened up around here, which means that you and I are gonna be havin' a little chat, *Euphrates*. Doc? I'll be seein' ya again. Warden? It's time we paid a visit to your office."

An irritated sigh slipped past Euphrates' thick lips before he gave a curt nod. "Fine."

He led the way out of the ICU, not quite slamming the doors on the way out. Ben followed him at a more sedate pace, glancing back only to offer the doctor a slight nod of gratitude. He saw her incline her head back at him before the doors closed.

Euphrates did his best not to grumble even more as he led Ben down several short hallways through two more doors and two more checkpoints before finally leaving the hospital. He ignored the Deputy Chief's casual glance back, as well as the slight dip of his head that occurred

244

before Ben turned his attention back to the path. It was bad enough that he had to humor Ben on his regularly scheduled visits. The idea of also potentially having to deal with him outside of those visits *and* listen to all the criticisms Ben would no doubt have regarding *his*, Euphrates Moorehead's, domain rankled. He wished the slack-jawed idiot would stop yammering on about security risks, staying vigilant, and treating even the worst offenders with some degree of humanity. These *animals* were locked up in cages for a reason.

Still, maybe he couldn't blame the other man. At least, not entirely. As Ben himself had pointed out, the trial of Temujin Alaric Lance was coming up, and there were many, *many* former members of Lance's gang inside the prison's walls. Hell, Liam Alastor happened to be one of them, and Ben had been using that bit of information to keep the comatose young man alive. Who wanted to kill the one person, comatose or not, who was keeping Lance from starting a riot within the prison's walls? When he took into account all of the other Arch Street Angels who were locked up, no doubt just itching for a chance to vent their frustrations about their jailers, the warden was happy that the Deputy Chief of Sulivan's Police Department was willing to take on the responsibility.

I sure as hell don't want it, Euphrates admitted, if only to himself.

To be honest, the thought of Lance, or any of the other gang members currently locked up in his prison, creating even the most minor disturbance made Euphrates nervous. As much as he wanted to believe that he and his fellow officers were ready for anything, the truth was that they would probably only be able to handle what the less violent and dangerous inmates could throw at them. A total riot would definitely end in deaths and injuries, followed by extensive and damning investigations.

People would turn their attention to the City of Sulivan's correctional system and start looking deeper into some things than they otherwise would. If someone discovered certain less-than-ethical activities that were being conducted, the ones that were decidedly *not* above board, Euphrates knew that not even his association with Island Affairs would save his career or maybe even his freedom and life.

In all likelihood, that association would only further condemn him.

Euphrates risked a glance at the Deputy Chief walking beside him. Ben Baas and his backers would no doubt be the first ones in line to boot Euphrates out of his current position, too. Ben had made no secret of his desire to do just that.

Ben would have loved to do more, including giving the warden over to the proverbial wolves. Unfortunately, and despite Euphrates Moorehead's association with the Department of Mid-Western Island Affairs, Ben's allies had found Euphrates to be more useful in his current position. The warden was a moron in Ben's eyes, without question, one who missed more than he saw, heard, or was told, but that had allowed Ben and his allies to sneak many things past him. Replacing him would run too many risks, at least for the moment.

Ben already faced too many of those risks to want to add to them. He could only hope that what he'd said back in the ICU had been understood. They had only one shot at doing this *right,* and the weeks to come would be made that much more onerous if his message hadn't been received.

He held in a sigh as the main administration building came into view about twenty minutes later. Despite where he'd grown up, Ben had never been a fan of heat and humidity. He knew he would welcome the air conditioning when he and Euphrates stepped into the lobby before heading up to the warden's office.

Until Euphrates opened the door so they could step inside. Ben recognized the two men waiting for them, and his stomach dropped. *Shit!*

Ben recognized them immediately, as did Euphrates. Robert DiGirolamo and Zohar Ontonagon Kavanaugh were both officers in Island Affairs. They were also both well-built men, and each had the reputation of being authoritarian as well as no-nonsense. Robert was younger and was known to have a temper. Zohar had the same copper-brown skin as his Native American mother. He was one of the few agents who could keep Robert DiGirolamo in check.

No doubt the ones who'd sent Robert knew how much he and Ben despised one another, and wanted Zohar to play the buffer. Ben could respect that much.

Still, the knowledge that they were there and that they were also loyal to Harold Edmund Holloway was enough to make Ben almost miss the step up into the building. *Show no fear, Ben. Lean on your training. Be a Wall. You've got this.*

He did his best to school his face, pretending that this was just like any other day, even as his mind raced. What reason, other than a specific prisoner, could these two men from Island Affairs have to be at the prison islands?

Ben didn't know and prayed that if they'd seen his flash of surprise, they'd mistake it for being a natural reaction to almost tripping over the step. He could appear unconcerned, or at least unfazed, by even the worst scenarios. That ability had served him well over the years he'd spent undercover. Most people saw a man who remained calm under pressure, a man who would give nothing away, including the fact that his organs were currently doing their best to turn themselves into a pretzel.

Neither of the men from Island Affairs seemed to think anything was amiss. They were smirking, yes, but Ben expected that.

"Warden." Robert flashed his badge, sneering as he approached and making Ben's title sound like an unpleasant joke. "*Deputy* Chief Baas. We're here to take a certain prisoner into our custody and to transfer him to a more *comfortable* location." He chuckled, the sound ominous, while Zohar rolled his eyes. "Well, comfortable for the city. We could actually care less if the prisoner is comfortable or not."

Euphrates wanted to cheer in relieved joy. At last, one of the most significant spots of cancer in his prison would be removed!

Ben, on the other hand, met Robert's smirk with a cold, expressionless face. He had been warned that this was coming, and it was why he had made the trip out to the prison islands earlier than usual. Still, he hadn't expected it to happen quite so fast.

Of course, as both the warden and Ben knew, Island Affairs could move with lightning speed to dissolve red tape when necessary. Ben hated it but could play his part with relative ease.

"As the Deputy Chief of Police—" he began.

"You have no authority over Island Affairs, Baas," Robert cut him off, stepping closer and leaning in. "In fact, we've got a message for you. The Heads of the Table have left the party, and now, we've got you by the balls. There's not a damn thing your so-called boss can do about it, either, Bennie-boy." He jammed a finger at Ben's chest. "Why don't you go and take your happy ass back to Sulivan? You can hide under covers there!"

248

He snickered at his lame pun. Zohar heaved a long-suffering sigh.

"Forgive us, Deputy Chief Baas," he said in his quiet bass. "But orders are orders."

"I know," Ben said, forcing a look of reluctant understanding to his face. *Relax, Ben. Let 'em think your side's been defeated. It'll be all right, no matter what happens. You can find out later what DiGirolamo means when he says the Heads are no longer at the table, too.* "I assume you're here for Alastor?"

"We are, yes." Zohar inclined his head in acknowledgment.

"Well, we just came from there." Ben nodded to where Euphrates stood, watching the exchange with interest. "We can both report that he is still very much in his coma, according to the doctor. In fact, we would be happy to escort you back there so you can do what you have to do."

He looked over at Robert, who stood glaring. No doubt the man thought Ben would kick up a fuss. Under other circumstances, Ben might have, but not right now. Instead, he pretended to play along.

Although he couldn't resist getting in at least one slight dig at the other. "I'm sure you want to get back to your extortion and bullying behavior as quickly as possible, so let's get this over with. Shall we?"

The veins in Robert's neck bulged with anger at Ben's placid yet venomous tone. His face turned red, and he would have no doubt said something stupid when Zohar placed a restraining hand on his arm.

"Thank you, Deputy Chief Baas," Robert managed to bite out instead. "We *appreciate* your cooperation."

Zohar nodded approval before turning his attention back to Ben and the warden. "If you would lead the way, gentlemen?"

Euphrates agreed without hesitation. He all but skipped back the entire way to the infirmary, happiness surging through him as he believed that, at last, the Deputy Chief and his allies were defeated. He would no longer have to deal with the presence of one comatose young man.

He ignored Ben's blank mask, believing the man was concealing his anger and helplessness. Robert seemed to feel it as well, given the snide remarks he kept muttering under his breath. Even Zohar appeared to think the same way.

The hospital came into view once again. Euphrates pulled out his key ring and made a short show of selecting the current key, then opening up the steel door.

Ushering the others inside, he couldn't help but sneak a glance at Ben's face, hoping to see something. It wouldn't have mattered to him what it was so long as he saw it.

He was disappointed, however. Ben had made sure that his expression would be blank, calm, and cool as he repeated to himself, *Be a Wall. Show no fear, no concern. Let your enemies think they've won.*

It wouldn't do for the others to see even the tiniest hint, the briefest glimmer of the emotions swirling within him. Not now.

Especially if the message he'd taken pains to deliver hadn't been understood.

He and the two from Island Affairs followed the beaming warden to the ICU ward. No one but Ben seemed to notice the strange quiet. No one but Ben had time to prepare for the discovery about to be made.

Euphrates led them all through doorways, checkpoints, and halls to the room that he and Ben had left just over forty minutes before. He couldn't help but grin as he placed a hand on the curtain that had been drawn to conceal the bed.

250

"Gentlemen," he said, mimicking a side-show announcer. "I give you the Scourge of Sulivan, the Red Angel himself. Liam Alastor!"

Euphrates yanked the curtain to one side, expecting to see the young man on the bed once more. Instead, his world fell apart.

The bed was *empty*.

For the most minuscule fraction of a second, Ben felt himself smile in utter relief. If he'd been alone, he would've celebrated, maybe even pumped a fist into the air in jubilation.

I can do that later, he told himself. *Right now?*

He quickly schooled his face to mirror the others' genuine shock. Euphrates, in particular, looked almost ready to collapse from sheer consternation. He and Ben had been there less than an hour before, after all. They had both seen that the man who'd been on the bed had been comatose and incapable of anything!

"Where?" Euphrates finally managed to get the word past thick, stunned lips. "Where did he go?"

"That is an excellent question," Robert snarled and rounded on Ben. "Where is he?"

"I..." Ben feigned complete disbelief with his eyes wide and his lips gaping. "I have no idea!"

"Really?!" Robert rounded on him. "Everyone knows, *Deputy Chief* Baas, that you have spoken against something like this happening! So who's to say if you didn't move him already so that *we* couldn't take him to where he belongs!"

"And just when would I have done that? I didn't even know you were comin'!" Ben snapped back at him, lying about that last and letting his hatred, his disdain seep into his voice. "Ask the warden. I haven't left his side since I stepped foot on these islands today."

Euphrates glanced between the two, feeling helpless and not wanting to get in the middle of things. Zohar also glanced at the two before asking a simple yet essential question.

"Where is Doctor Kim?" he asked.

Ben blinked as though suddenly becoming aware of her absence and feigned a slight frown. "She was here when we were. Maybe she took Alastor to run a test or something?"

He made sure to sound as perplexed as he was trying to look. Zohar nodded at him, apparently believing his words, while Robert continued to seethe and glare. Euphrates took the offered cue.

"I'll call her number," he said. "Even if she's in the laboratory or a bathroom, she—"

He didn't get the chance to finish. A strange, quiet tap interrupted him.

The four men glanced at each other, then around the room when it sounded again. It repeated once, twice, even three times before Robert and Euphrates followed the sound to the maintenance closet just outside. Robert looked over, motioning to Zohar and telling the warden to get back.

"Stay here, Baas," Zohar told him in a quiet rumble. "Just in case."

Ben nodded, not about to argue, and watched as the two positioned themselves in front of the closet door. He almost held his breath, in fact, as Robert and Zohar prepared to open the door. *Give 'em the show you want them to see, not the show that'll lead to any suspicion.*

Slowly, at a cue from Zohar, Robert turned the knob and pushed the door back. Not a second later, his eyes went wide, and he was scrambling forward.

"Doctor Kim?" he could be heard to say, surprise coloring his voice. "Holy... Give me a second, we'll getcha outta there."

Before another heartbeat had passed, he was bringing the woman out. Ben took note of the zip ties that had been used to bind her hands and ankles together, as well as what looked like a torn bit of pillow case now hanging around the doctor's neck—used as a makeshift gag, no doubt—and immediately moved to assist.

"Easy, doc," he said in a soft voice as he and Robert moved her to a nearby chair. "Warden? Kavanaugh? We got something to cut these things off of her?"

"Hang on," Zohar said. "I'll check her desk."

"I'll look in the cabinets, back in the room." Euphrates was already on the move as he spoke.

"Don't worry about me." Doctor Kim shook her head, her eyes wide with apparent terror. "Alastor." She swallowed. "He woke up."

The words were a bombshell. Euphrates froze, his face bleaching with sudden fear. The two men from Island Affairs stared at the woman in disbelief.

"How?!" Zohar demanded. "How is that *possible?*"

Ben kept his eyes carefully trained on her, his mask of bewilderment and dread concealing the relief he felt. "What happened? Take it from the top, doc."

She nodded, swallowing again. She did so once more, then again before speaking. "I was working on the board for the upcoming shift change, so my back was turned. I didn't hear anything that would have made me turn around, either. Alastor came up from behind me, and he had a scalpel."

By this point, Zohar had found a scalpel of his own and made his way back over. Gently, he worked to free her wrists. She put a freed hand up by her throat soon after, swallowing once more as if in memory of a blade being held there.

"Someone get her some water," Ben demanded before once again softening his voice. "Take your time, doc."

To his credit, Robert obeyed without the slightest hint of snark. A few heartbeats later, he had a glass in his hands. "Here, doctor."

"Thank you." Doctor Kim offered him what looked like a tremulous smile before she resumed her tale. "Alastor demanded I tell him where he was. Once I did, he forced me out to the office and found some zip ties, as well as one of the pillowcases that had just come back from the laundry. He tied me up, used the scalpel to tear up the pillowcase to gag me, and then put me into the closet. I have no idea where he went after that."

"We'll sound the alarm," Euphrates said. "There's no way he can get off these islands if he can't get to a boat and—"

His walkie-talkie crackled without warning. Even Ben looked over at that, watching as Euphrates frowned and brought the device up.

"What is it?" he demanded.

"Prison fight, sir," one of the guards answered. "A pretty big one."

Euphrates froze, his face turning white. Alastor waking up and escaping was terrible. A potential riot would be far, far worse. If *Lance* escaped alongside Alastor?

The absolute worst-case scenario left him shocked and his mind blank. It didn't help that Robert's bravado fled with the news.

254

"What do we do?" he almost begged Zohar. "If they find us, we're dead!"

Before Zohar could answer, Ben moved. Guided by training and instinct, he surged upright and snapped orders.

"The two of you, finish gettin' the doc free. Warden, tell 'em to lock the prison down, and let's get to the armory." Ben glared when Euphrates looked at him, mouth opening but seemingly unable to move right away. "Oh, for—" Ben snatched up the walkie-talkie, playing up the need to move quickly. "This is Deputy Chief Baas. Lock down the prison and have all available guards who are not already involved get over to the armory. We gotta stop that fight before it becomes a full-scale riot."

"Yes, sir!"

"Also, be on the lookout." Ben barely managed to keep the smirk off his face and out of his voice. "Liam Alastor has not only woken up, but he's also escaped. Someone get to Lance's cell and make sure he stays put. Got it?"

"Are you—" A note of panic entered the guard's voice. "Are you serious, sir? *Alastor's* awake?"

"And gone, yes," Ben confirmed it. "Now, *move*. The warden and I will be joining you as soon as we can."

"Yes, sir!"

Ben looked back at Zohar. "As soon as the doc's free, I want the three of you to barricade yourselves in here. While it's not likely any of the prisoners will make it down here, it's best to be safe. Do *not* open the doors unless you can confirm it's the warden or me. Got it?"

"Yes." Zohar gave him a short nod. "Be careful, Baas."

"We'll do our best." Ben offered him a tight smile, then looked at

Euphrates. "Snap out of it, Euphrates! Let's *go!*"

Chapter Eleven: The Return

Immediately after the departure of Ben Baas and Warden Moorehead, Thomas G. Burfield Prison Hospital

Doctor Kim Hana watched as the warden and the Deputy Chief left the ICU and waited a single minute after their departure to head back to the young man in the hospital bed. Sliding a hand into the right-hand pocket of her scrub pants, she withdrew a capped syringe. Carefully, she slid the needle into the young man's arm, injecting the contents.

As she waited for the results, she couldn't help but think back to when she had first accepted this assignment. Liam Alastor was known throughout the city of Sulivan as one of the leading figures in the Arch Street Angels street gang. He'd been notorious for his judicious use of violence against law enforcement and his enemies, but, strangely enough, had also garnered a reputation with the regular men and women of the city for his apparent desire to help them.

Of course, knowing what she did now, she thought she understood the discrepancies. 'Liam Alastor' was merely an alias, one that the young man before her had taken to try to protect himself. Robert William Henry Nicholas Alastor Kincaid had already dealt with members of the Department of Mid-Western Island Affairs and their various allies. He'd known, even then, what they would likely do to him if they caught up with him. As a result, he'd felt he had no choice but to join with the Arch Street Angels in an effort to avenge his mother, as well as to try and protect the city he saw as his own.

Considering what the Department of Mid-Western Island Affairs had been doing and was *still* doing, Doctor Kim found that she couldn't blame him or the people he'd gathered to his banner. When she thought of everything Island Affairs and their allies had attempted, including some of the things she'd seen with her own eyes?

She heard a deeper-than-usual breath being taken from the young man on the bed. Doctor Kim returned her attention to him and felt rewarded when she saw blue-gray eyes flicker open, then focus.

"Welcome back, Mister Alastor," she said.

She didn't dare to call him a Kincaid, even here in the privacy of his ICU room. Too much was dependent on secrecy, including his actual state of health and mobility.

"Thank you." His voice proved to be the barest whisper, and he glanced around with wary eyes. "We're clear?"

"We are." Doctor Kim smiled at him. "I wouldn't have given you the wake-up juice, as you like to call it, otherwise. Do you wish me to brief you now? Or would you prefer to have a snack first?"

"Briefing."

She nodded, utilizing her eidetic memory—the main reason she had been chosen for this assignment—to recount everything that had happened from the moment Ben Baas had arrived with the warden. Liam made sure to pay close attention as he recovered from the light sedation he'd been given to help him simulate still being in a coma. It was something he'd become used to, although he didn't necessarily like being incapacitated, regardless of the reason.

When he heard Doctor Kim relate the story Ben had told about the encounter the two of them had once had with Giovanni Pasquale and his crew, he sat up. "Repeat that. The story Bennie told, exactly as he told it."

Doctor Kim arched a questioning eyebrow at him. He knew, as did a select few others, of her gift, but still, she did as she had been asked. Liam's brow furrowed as he listened. His lips became a thin, unhappy line.

The doctor couldn't help but notice. "What is it?"

"That's not how it happened," he said. "Not quite."

"It's not?"

"No. I remember that day very well." Liam's tone darkened. "The Pasquale did have Bennie and I cornered, but they weren't looking to kill me. Anyone with me, yes. Me, personally?" He shook his head. "They had orders to return me to the custody of Island Affairs."

"They did?" Doctor Kim frowned. "Why did Deputy Chief Baas tell it that way, then? Because of the warden?"

"In part? It's probable, but..." Liam let his voice trail off. The furrows of his brow deepened with thought, and he shook his head a moment later. "No. It was a message. I need to leave."

"Leave?" She studied him, noting the certainty on his face as he reached up to begin removing the various pieces of equipment that were monitoring his health. "Now? We're currently right on schedule, Mister Alastor. How do you know that story was a message telling you to go now instead of when you originally planned to escape?"

"Why else would Bennie have brought up that particular story?" Liam asked. "Only the Pasquale ever worked with Island Affairs back then, too. Who better for them to go to, to get what they wanted? Bennie and I *heard* them as they came after us, and Giovanni Pasquale gave specific orders for me to be taken alive so that I could be given to Holloway and Beringer."

"And it's well known that Mister Holloway's sister has been attempting to regain access to you," Doctor Kim murmured. "Do you believe she has succeeded?"

"Either her or someone she knows," Liam said. "Which means I need to get moving and get outta here."

"Very well," Doctor Kim agreed. "Give me a moment to summon your escort."

"Escort?" Liam frowned. "Why would I—"

"Unless, of course, you wish to take the chance of getting shot, something which would either put you back in that bed or the morgue? Not to mention the fact that you would lose the element of surprise?"

He did not look pleased, she saw. Still, he chose not to argue, knowing that time was of the essence. "Fine."

Doctor Kim gave him a small smile and reached into her left-hand pocket. Pulling out her cell phone, she made a single call. "It's time."

To her surprise, less than a full minute later, and just as Liam began to fidget, a short young man with light brown skin, short-cut black hair, and wearing a maintenance uniform walked into the ICU. "I got the nod a couple of minutes before you called and made sure the cameras would be out. It'll look like the same glitch that's been plaguing the cameras for the past year or so now, so the guys watching the feed will wait a few minutes to see if the picture comes back up before sending someone down."

"Good job, Miguel," Doctor Kim said. "You have the rest of it?"

"Of course."

Miguel put down the toolbox he'd carried inside as Liam swung his legs over the side of the bed and slowly stood up. A moment later, he

260

caught another maintenance uniform that Miguel tossed over, as well as a bandana and a cap.

"Put those on as quick as you can," Miguel instructed him. "Doc, we'll need your ID and keys."

"You have the zip ties?" she asked, handing over the items he'd requested.

"And the gag." Miguel looked apologetic, even as he came over with them. "Sorry, Doctor, but to make it look real, we need to do this."

"I know." She glanced over at where Liam now stood, having shed his hospital gown and now in the process of replacing it with his acquired uniform. "Mister Alastor, will you do the honors?"

The redheaded man stepped over as soon as he'd finished redressing, taking the zip ties that were held out for him. Before he bound the doctor's wrists and ankles, however, he surprised her by giving her a quick hug of gratitude.

"Thank you, Doctor Kim," he told her, offering her a warm smile. "For everything."

"You are more than welcome, Mister Alastor." She smiled back. "Now get on with it. Don't forget to gag me, too."

"I'll do that." Miguel gently tied the ripped-up pillowcase over her mouth, then carried her into the closet once Liam had finished. As soon as he locked her inside, he stepped back and turned his attention to the man he had enlisted to rescue. "Ready?"

"Almost." Liam nodded, then held up a finger. "One moment." He headed towards the doctor's desk and held up a scalpel a few seconds later. *"Now* I'm ready to go. *Doc!* I grabbed one of your scalpels!" He heard a tap from the closet door, grinned, and began to follow Miguel out of the

ICU. "Good. She said that you are Miguel?

"I'm called Miguel Hidalgo Costilla here," he said. "My real name, though, is Hector Carlos Hidalgo. My brother was in the Angels, and I was one of the last to earn my wings. When word got out that your cousin was lookin' for someone to help with this?" He shrugged. "I kinda leaped at the chance, and your grandfather set everything up."

Liam's voice held nothing but sincerity. "Thank you."

"Don't thank me yet," Hector said. "We gotta get outta here first."

Liam couldn't, and wouldn't, argue with that. This moment had been a long time in coming. Granted, it was earlier than initially planned, but it was happening, and that's what mattered.

"So how are we going to do that?" he asked, lowering his voice at a signal from the other as he followed Hector past a door that sat at the back of the ICU instead of the pair that were at the entrance. "Without getting spotted and shot?"

Or, in his case, worse.

"Watch and see." Hector glanced back with a mischievous grin that faded after seeing Liam's unhappy expression. He became more serious as a result, his whisper laden with gravity. "The prison islands are riddled with an old series of underground tunnels that date back to when they were used as a military fort. The tunnels were designed to allow the soldiers to move around without being seen and even make it down to various docking points to escape if needed."

"Like us."

"Yep," Hector nodded. "Most people don't know about 'em, which we're going to use to our advantage. We just have to get to them."

262

"Where are we right now?"

"In a maintenance hall. It's why I brought you the clothes I did," Hector said. "Workers like me use 'em to travel all over to do various jobs easier and without getting in the way of the guards. This one happens to let out near a tunnel entrance."

"Are the exit points watched?" That, in particular, concerned Liam. "And do the guards themselves ever use these halls?"

"Some are," Hector said. "And yeah, some of the guards use the maintenance halls if they think they need to get someplace quicker."

Which could be a problem, Liam thought with a frown. *We're walkin' louder than a whole herd of stampeding horses, thanks to the tiled floor, and who's to say if a whisper couldn't carry in a hallway like this? If any guards are nearby, they'll hear us without a problem.*

Hector noticed his expression. "We don't have far to go, and, again, there's a reason I gave you a maintenance uniform. The chances of us running into a guard right now, especially with the Deputy Chief of Police visiting, are slim to almost none."

But it's still there, Liam thought as they continued. He strained his ears to listen for any potential trouble, ignoring the slight pressure he felt emanating inside his skull, as well as the way his muscles trembled with the strain of remaining upright. Instead, he did his best to focus on his surroundings and brought up a hand to tug the brim of his cap down in an attempt to hide the color of his eyebrows. *And if someone spots us and identifies me, then this could be over before it begins.*

Nothing happened, however, as they made their way past no less than three more doors before, at last, coming to stand before the fourth. Hector looked over.

"The entrance to the tunnel is about seven or eight feet away," he whispered. "Once we make it into the tunnel, we shouldn't have any problems escaping to Sulivan proper."

We can hope, at least, Liam thought. "What if we run into a guard?"

"Follow my lead."

Liam nodded, steeling himself for whatever they might find waiting for them on the opposite side of the door. To his surprise, they entered what looked like an oversized janitor's closet. There were shelves, a bunch of cleaning supplies, toolboxes, buckets, sweepers, and even a few extra uniforms. No guards waited for them here, nor did any other members of the prison maintenance personnel. Hell, there weren't even any rats, mice, or cockroaches visible.

"C'mon." Hector motioned him over to a corner, just past a pair of shelving units that obscured an ancient-looking metal door that appeared coated in rust. "In here."

Much to Liam's surprise, the door swung open without a problem or even the slightest sound. He stepped inside at Hector's urging, on alert for any potential issues, and wrinkled his nose at the almost overpowering smells. *Mold, rust, dirt, and old rock. This is going to be a fun trip. Too bad I don't have a choice.*

At least Hector didn't seem bothered by it. Liam wondered a bit at the other's lack of reaction but put it down to the younger man having been in the tunnel before. *He's probably used to it, while I haven't been anywhere outside of the hospital ICU for years.* He nodded to himself at the thought. *I won't complain. This'll keep us out of the guards' way, which means we can do as Hector said and get back to Sulivan proper without a*

264

problem. That's good, seeing as how the only weapon we have to defend ourselves if we get caught is a single scalpel.

As it turned out, he'd thought that last bit a little too soon. A good ten minutes later, after rounding a bend in the tunnel, Hector brought them to a halt and bent down next to what looked like a small, dug-out space in the tunnel wall. A moment later, he'd brought out a duffel bag. Liam found himself blinking in shock when Hector unzipped it.

"*Madre de Dios*," he murmured at the sight of the pistols, extra clothing, wallets, and even knives. "How...?"

"Your grandfather, your cousin, and the others in the know have been puttin' this stuff here for the past few months," Hector told him. "They figured it couldn't hurt to be prepared in case we needed to move things up."

Liam couldn't help his grin. "They plan for everything."

"That they do." Hector grinned back. "How fast can you change clothes?"

"Give me one minute. I won't need more than that."

Just over a literal minute later, now clad in dark blue jeans and a t-shirt, with a plain gray bandana tied around his head to hide his tell-tale red hair, Liam again followed Hector, who sported his pair of lighter blue jeans and t-shirt, as well as a flannel shirt, through the tunnel. It would take close to ten minutes for them to journey the entire length, but, in the end, Liam saw they had reached their destination.

The chosen dock proved to be small. In Liam's eyes, it looked more like four planks of wood that had been nailed together before being set just above the water. Still, it was enough to tie a boat there, and the smallish fishing vessel that waited for them wouldn't look at all out of place on the waters that surrounded Sulivan. Painted gunmetal gray, it bobbed gently in the water, which lapped a quiet rhythm against both the boat and the nearby rocks.

It beckoned, enticing them with the promise of freedom. Hector took a step, intending to head out to the boat and untie it. Liam, however, grabbed him by his shoulder to stop him, holding up a finger for silence when Hector opened his mouth to speak.

His brow furrowing, Liam listened with an intensity that few could match, turning his head to the left and then the right. He once again ignored the pressure that was inside of his skull and, four or five heartbeats later, was rewarded with the sounds he'd been waiting to hear—the paired crunch of footsteps walking on gravel. They sounded so close by that Liam couldn't help but believe that they were right outside, right by the dock, but out of sight.

One more heartbeat passed before Liam heard the voices.

"Man, I do *not* wanna be in the Warden's shoes when the Deputy Chief discovers the officers that Island Affairs sent over," one of the voices complained. "Holloway's either gotten stupid or developed some massive balls to be movin' to take possession of Alastor now. If the Angels that are here find out, we're gonna have a riot on our hands, and if Lance gets loose?"

"I don't even wanna *think* about that," the second moaned. "I accepted bein' assigned here 'cause there's not as much paperwork, and, at the end of my shift, I can head back to my bunk and play my games. By the way, did you see that new one that's gonna be released at the end of the year? *B&E: Larceny City?* It looks terrific!"

"We're surrounded by incarcerated criminals, and you want to get a game where you play as the criminal?"

"Why not? The *B&E* games are fun, and it's not like—"

A tinny voice, no doubt coming from the man's radio, cut off the guard's words that no doubt came from the man's radio. *"Disturbance in Cell Blocks A and B. Repeat, disturbance in Blocks A and B."*

"Shit," the first guard muttered as the radio again crackled to life.

"Per orders of the Deputy Chief, we are to lock down the prison. All available guards not already involved in containing the fight are to report to the armory. Also, be on the lookout. Liam Alastor has woken up and escaped."

"Ah, fuck." The second guard groaned. "There goes the rest of our day."

"Orders are orders," the first said. "C'mon!"

A moment later, Liam heard the pounding of their footsteps recede as they no doubt ran to the prison armory. He let out the breath he hadn't realized he'd been holding in relief.

"What is it?" Hector whispered, frowning at the look on Liam's face. "You okay, Boss?"

Liam frowned back. "You didn't hear all that?"

"Hear what?" Hector shook his head, eyeing him in confusion. "I didn't hear anything."

He hadn't? Liam's frown deepened, wondering how it could be possible that Hector hadn't heard what he had. Those guards had practically been on top of them!

After a moment, he pushed the thought from his head. He could puzzle over it later. For now, what mattered was the fact that they had apparently escaped detection and that it was time to get out of there.

"Never mind," he said. "Let's go."

"Sure thing, Boss."

"Don't call me that." Liam grinned to take the potential sting from his words. "I'm not your Boss."

"Not yet." Hector grinned back as they headed to the boat. As soon as they'd both climbed in, he directed, "Sit down and buckle in."

"Anything else?"

"Hold on tight."

Right. Liam did as directed, bracing himself.

A moment after Hector had sat down up front, the boat's engines were purring to life. The vessel rocketed forward, away from the prison islands.

Glancing back to make sure no one was coming after them, Liam caught his first glimpse of the place he'd spent the last five or so years in. *Mon Dieu. What a depressing place to be in. I am never comin' back here.*

Of course, if anyone came after them, he might not have a choice.

Liam narrowed his eyes and, again, strained his ears as he searched for any signs of pursuit. There was none, however. No helicopters had yet lifted off. No watercraft could be seen launching to head out after them, either. They had escaped, and soon, they would actually be *free.*

Another breath of relief escaped Liam's lips before he looked at the young man who had helped to free him. Hector had said he'd already earned his wings and was, therefore, already a member of the Arch Street Angels. He'd also, of course, spoken of Liam's grandfather, cousin, and the others who were their allies, which meant that he was 'in the know.' Once they made it back to Sulivan and reunited with the others, Liam would make sure that Hector rose in the Angels' ranks as a result.

268

Of course, first, they had to get to the city, and that brought a question to Liam's mind. "Where are we heading?"

"Fisherman's Wharf," Hector said. "No one will look twice at us there."

"True enough." Liam couldn't argue against that logic, but he still had at least one question. "What about the docks around Center Island, however? No one would look even once at us there."

"Four years ago, they wouldn't have," Hector said. "Today? Oh, yeah. They would."

Another trickle of dread dripped down Liam's spine. "What do you mean?"

A small sigh escaped Hector's lips. "Look. A lot has changed in the time you've been out of the game. The DBJF Alliance Corporation took over Center Island and made it into its corporate headquarters. With the fall of the Angels—"

"*What?*" Liam stared at him, incredulous. "What did you just say?"

Hector's sigh, this time, proved more audible. "Without anyone to lead them, the Arch Street Angels basically fell apart. Michael Roi had been killed, and you were in a coma."

"What about The Prince?" Liam demanded to know. "I know he disappeared. It's why I was made second! But—"

"No one knows what really happened to him," Hector said. "But seein' as how he happens to be in Island Affairs—"

"I know he was in Island Affairs," Liam cut him off. "He got kicked out, though." He caught the look that passed over Hector's face. "What is it?"

"He didn't get kicked out," Hector told him quietly. "It turned out that he was undercover, just like Bennie."

He what? Liam felt his head beginning to swim. Granted, he had never truly liked Emmett Emil Prince when the man had been Michael Roi's second-in-command, but Liam had never once considered the idea that Emmett Prince would have been a traitor. His temper started to boil as he thought about how long Emmett had been undercover *for* Island Affairs!

"He was transferred out of Sulivan, but no one knows where he was assigned." Hector glanced over. "He hasn't been back once since giving his testimony, not even when Temujin Lance was arrested. Russell Jamison dropped his colors not long after you were almost killed, and he went to work for Veil-Tech Securities. No one was left to pick up the pieces after that."

Liam growled at the thought. The red haze continued to color his vision. Why hadn't he been *told?*

"That's just fucking *wonderful,*" he growled. "And the Arch Street Angels are gone? Completely gone?"

"They did their best to survive," Hector said. "And rumor has it that they're not entirely gone, but I have no idea where any remnants might be holed up."

He didn't, but Liam did. He forced himself to relax as a result. *Worry about it all later. For now, concentrate on the next step: getting yourself and Hector here to the others. Hopefully, they're where you think.*

Finding them would likely be too challenging otherwise.

"What else has happened in the time I've been gone?" he asked, doing his best to keep even the hint of a growl out of his voice. "Have any new gangs formed?"

"Quite a few," Hector told him. "It was a near literal bloodbath for almost two years, in fact. The Angels fought against I don't know how many others who tried to rise before the Pharaohs, the Lords of the Wharf, and the Iron Horde established themselves. The Pasquale Family has also made a comeback, although they're callin' themselves the Pasquale-Scordato now."

Liam almost snarled at the news. *I am going to* kill *my cousin! Maybe my grandfather, too! Why couldn't they have* told *me any of this before now?*

"Look." Hector's soft voice recaptured Liam's attention. "I know for a fact that your cousin and the others wanted you to be told, but your grandfather thought otherwise."

Of course. Liam blew out a slow, angry breath. As much as he loved his grandfather, there were times—many times, in fact—when Grandpa Will would treat him as the child he'd been rather than the man he'd become. It frustrated him, to say the least, and he would have words with both his grandfather and his cousin, as well as a few others, about it.

But that was for later. First?

"I tried." Hector's voice derailed his thoughts, and Liam looked at him. The young man bit at his lower lip before continuing, "I tried to find them. The other Angels, I mean. I'm pretty sure at least *some* would have survived, but I'm pretty sure only your grandfather knew where they would've holed up."

Liam drew in a deep breath. They'd find out soon enough. For now, they needed to concentrate on the immediate tasks at hand. That meant shoving aside the thoughts he now had of cheerfully murdering his grandfather and also his cousin in favor of making it to safety. There was a lot that he, in particular, had to do before he rescued Temujin Alaric Lance.

Starting with getting to shore. Fortunately, Hector was soon guiding their boat to an available dock. Liam followed him as he hopped onto land as soon as the boat's engine was shut off.

To his surprise, though, Hector didn't just abandon him. In fact, the guy seemed intent on staying at his side.

"They've no doubt noticed I'm gone by now," he explained when Liam asked. "If I go back, there are going to be many questions asked, and it'd be too easy for me to slip up. I never wanted to work there, but in order to help out you and the other Angels that are on the inside?"

Liam nodded in both sympathy and understanding, but he wanted the other to be certain. "Are you certain? It would probably be safer back at those islands, and we could continue to use you there."

"Yes. I'm beyond sure, in fact," Hector said. "My brother believed in what the Angels were doing, enough so that he gave his life tryin' to defend their Tower before it fell." He paused, drawing in a deep breath before speaking again with steely resolve. "I need to make sure he didn't die for no reason."

"He didn't." Liam's face proved somber, and his voice's rumble echoed with distant, incoming thunder, even as he winced internally. How many others, he wondered, had also died doing the same as Hector's brother? "We had this city once, and we'll retake it. If you're certain that this is what you want to do, then follow me."

Hector's lips parted in a wide smile. Without argument or hesitation, he did as Liam asked, and the two moved away from the docks into the broader city of Sulivan.

Chapter Twelve: Questions and Suspicions

Mid-Afternoon, Approaching the City of Sulivan's Prison Islands

Harold Edmund Holloway glared out at the prison islands from the co-pilot's seat of the helicopter. Of all the phone calls to receive, the one telling him that Liam Alastor had woken up had been both dreaded and unwelcome. The news that Alastor had also managed to *escape?!*

He growled under his breath. He had believed, earlier in the day, that he would have cause to celebrate, given how quickly the transfer order had arrived, which awarded Regina's seventh subject back into her dubious care. But now? When Liam Alastor had managed to not only wake up but flee?

Harold growled again. How that could have happened, he didn't yet know, but he meant to find out.

"We're almost there, sir," the pilot reported.

"I can see that," Harold bit out. He didn't, for once, take pleasure in the fact that the other man winced. His sole focus was on the warden of the prison and how Euphrates Moorehead could have missed the signs of Liam Alastor waking up, let alone letting him somehow *get away*. "Just fly, don't talk."

To his credit, the pilot followed his orders. It didn't take more than another seven-and-a-half minutes to reach the prison helipad on Farris Island and a bare thirty seconds more for Harold to notice the person waiting for them to land.

His eyes narrowed when he recognized Sulivan's Deputy Chief of Police. Harold despised Benjamin Benedict Baas. The man stood in the way of many things, all thanks to his vaunted connections. Ben Baas was part of why Liam Alastor had been kept alive. He had also been one of the reasons Regina's seventh subject had been removed from her custody. He had been part of the driving force behind every Judge ruling against Harold or his sister regaining that custody, as well as refusing to pull Alastor's plug, all because Ben had pointed out that no one in their right mind wanted Temujin Alaric Lance to cause a riot.

There were other things, too, that Harold had lost out on due to Ben standing against him. Seeing him here and now?

Harold's vision was tinted red. Could it *really* be a coincidence that Ben Baas had arrived before the two men from Island Affairs had, and for Liam Alastor to have escaped right after?

Harold didn't believe it, not for a second. Of course, *proving* it would be another matter, but without his most excellent protector, enabler, and supporter to help keep Ben safe from any and all retribution?

The thought of finally being able to bring Ben Baas down allowed a vicious smile to form on Harold's face, which temporarily blotted out his anger. *Soon, Baas. Your Wall of Protection is down, and it won't be long before you and all of those you've been protecting will fall, as well.*

Almost as soon as the helicopter landed, Harold slipped on his sunglasses and stepped out onto the pad. He smirked, seeing Ben's dark look.

"Well, now. Deputy Chief Baas." Harold made certain his tone would be as condescending and disdainful as possible. "What an *unexpected* pleasure."

"I'll bet." Ben's tone proved more acidic as he hissed, "You moved too soon, *Harry*."

274

"Did I?" Harold kept his cool, at least for the moment. He didn't need or want Ben to know just how rattled he happened to be, thanks to Alastor's escape, but he also wanted to shake the other up. Leaning forward, lowering his voice just enough so Ben alone would catch his words, he said, "You and yours are *done,* Deputy Chief Baas. *We* will own this city, along with its sisters, and there is *nothing* you can do to stop that now."

Ben snorted, but the worry in his eyes gave him away. Still, his voice kept its bite. "We'll see about that."

"I'm sure."

Harold stepped around him with a smirk, only glancing back when he heard the crunch of gravel. Ben Baas was no fool, but he'd been known to let his temper get the better of him on occasion. If Ben attempted to give Harold a physical blow, then Harold would get the chance to defend himself and show Ben just who happened to be the better.

But no. To Harold's semi-disappointment—he would have loved to see Ben put behind the same bars as the gang members the Deputy Chief had put away—Ben was moving to the helicopter. *Ah, well. There's always next time.*

Continuing down the path from the helipad, Harold met Euphrates Moorehead at the halfway point. Once again, his displeasure surfaced.

"Your office," he snapped. "Now."

Euphrates swallowed but didn't argue. Harold let him stew as they walked. The warden deserved much more than that, considering how badly he'd dropped the proverbial ball. Still, Harold had questions that

275

needed to be answered before anything else.

The moment they stepped into the warden's office and closed the door, Harold rounded on him. "How in the *hell* did you allow this to happen?"

"S-sir, I—" He swallowed. "I didn't—"

Harold waved away the man's stuttering attempt to say something, anything, that might deflect at least some of the potential blame. He didn't want excuses. He wanted *answers.*

"You're fucking *useless,*" he bit out, stepping around the warden to go and sit behind the man's desk in Euphrates' chair. The move was not only to show Harold's contempt but was also a subtle threat. Euphrates Moorehead was replaceable. He was now a guest in his own office, and Harold could choose to keep him that way. "Tell me *everything.*"

"Yes, sir."

Over the course of the next fifteen minutes, Euphrates did just that. From the moment of Ben Baas' unanticipated arrival, ostensibly to check on the preparations for Temujin Lance's upcoming trial, to their visit to the prison hospital and Alastor's apparent comatose state, to their meeting with the two men from Island Affairs, and finally to their discovery of Alastor's escape, Euphrates related everything he could. Harold listened intently, growing more perplexed by the second.

It was *impossible,* he thought. Regardless of what Hollywood and the entertainment industry wanted people to believe, no one woke up from a multi-year coma to get out of bed and escape prison. Harold would have denied the possibility of it all, even called Euphrates a liar, if he hadn't remembered what Regina had told him of the experiments she and her fellow scientists had conducted on Liam Alastor. She had been working on

276

modifying the young man, making him less vulnerable to certain things and enhancing other bodily functions.

Perhaps her experiments had backfired, in a way, leading to this moment.

He didn't know. It was something he would have to discuss with his sister, but first, he had a few other questions to answer. For example, why hadn't the attending doctor noticed if Liam Alastor happened to be in better shape than a coma patient should have been?

"She's new," Euphrates explained when Harold asked about her. "Both to Sulivan and to the prison hospital. She replaced Doctors Violeta Ruiz, Thomas Arwen, and Patrick Elliot just a few weeks ago, and Doctor Kim was still getting familiar with everything. It wouldn't be surprising that she might have missed something."

Ah. Harold inclined his head in agreement while wanting to rant and rave at the universe. "Is anyone missing that you know about? And what happened to the hospital's security cameras?"

"The cameras have been glitching out for the past year or so," Euphrates said. "They went out again just after we, Deputy Chief Baas and I, that is, left the hospital." He hesitated for the briefest heartbeat of time. "The officers watching have gotten so used to the cameras going in and out that they waited almost fifteen minutes before calling maintenance." Another hesitation. "That's when we discovered one of our staff from that department had disappeared."

"Disappeared," Harold repeated the word, his tone becoming low and dangerous.

Euphrates winced. "I'm afraid so. Miguel was sent out earlier today to check on an electrical issue in the Maximum Security Section of

Randel Island, so no one noticed his absence until after the fight between those former Three Strikers, Angels, and Kings had been dealt with. He hasn't responded to all of the attempts to contact him, either. He's usually a good kid, from what I've heard, so not hearin' from him is unusual, to say the least. I've got my people looking for him right now, but so far? He's still missing."

"Didn't you have this Miguel person *vetted* before he started working here? Or *think* of having someone come out here to get the cameras fixed?"

"Um." Euphrates looked distinctly uncomfortable. "It was Island Affairs that did the vetting for Miguel, sir. As for the cameras? We, ah..." He swallowed at the dark glare he received. "We've had technicians come out several times, and they haven't found anything wrong. The head of Prison IT told us it's probably due to the wet and wind from the Lake. Sir."

"And did you *think* to requisition a full replacement?"

Euphrates swallowed. "We, uh, did. Three times, in fact. We were told that, due to the money and the time it would take, getting a new security system for the prison would have to wait."

Harold snarled. "Get me this Miguel person's file and the doctor's. Show me the requisition forms, too!"

Euphrates scrambled to obey, heaving his large bulk out the door of his office and all but running down the short hallway to where the records of everyone on the prison islands, from inmates to correctional staff, were kept. Harold was tempted to throw something after him, but decided it would be a waste of energy.

Instead, he chose to *think*. The Wall had surrounded his grandson

278

and their allies with innumerable protections that Harold had, until now, been unable to surpass. With The Wall gone, however, Harold believed that he and the rest of Island Affairs would at last be able to begin dealing with their enemies.

One question, however, kept repeating itself, over and over, in his mind. Just how long had Liam Alastor been *awake?* Had he truly just opened his eyes that morning? Or had he, in fact, been awake for far longer?

The thought chilled Harold right down to his bone marrow. If the boy's eyes had opened just that day, and if Regina's experiments had been more successful than any of them had hoped, then while they had plenty to worry about, they didn't have as much to fear. If, however, Liam Alastor had been awake and moving before this morning's events, then what had the boy been doing?

A shudder ran down Harold's spine. Harold knew just how cunning Liam Alastor could be when the boy wished. He knew Alastor could be devious, too, and more than capable of putting on a good show. How many times had he been in the hands of the police during his time with the Arch Street Angels, only to be let go each time before Island Affairs could be alerted? Harold was well aware that the young man *thought* and *plotted* before doing most things, and that Liam Alastor rarely did anything 'on the fly' if the situation didn't require it.

So, again, what might he have been doing?

Fear of the answer to that question caused Harold to break into a sweat. There were *so* many possibilities, ranging from simply recovering from his coma to being able to conduct surveillance and gather information, even to conducting covert operations against any number of targets that Liam Alastor might have deemed to be worthy—

Harold's thoughts halted on that last. A new idea entered his brain, one that simultaneously shocked and frightened him.

The boat that The Ghost had stolen had been abandoned in the middle of Lake Superior. At the time, Harold had believed it to be too far away from the prison islands, or anywhere else, for someone to escape to, but what if it hadn't? What if it had been just close enough to the prison islands for Liam Alastor to swim back to it and, somehow, return to his bed before his absence could be noticed by those who mattered?

Thinking back to The Ghost's previous strikes, Harold felt a different sort of chill wash over him. Could it be possible, he wondered, for *Liam Alastor* to be *The Ghost*?

His brow furrowed. His lips pursed. His hands balled into fists. His eyes narrowed. The *idea* caught hold of his brain and began to whirl about inside it.

Harold knew that the experiments being conducted by Regina and her team had been interrupted by The Wall and Ben Baas the previous July 4. The Ghost's first strike had been on September 10, when the home of one of the junior scientists who had been involved on the periphery of those experiments had been burglarized. Could Liam Alastor have recovered enough by that time, due to whatever Regina's team had done, to accomplish such a thing?

It would explain so much, Harold thought. Most of the scientists who had been robbed had been involved, at least a little, in the experimentation. The labs targeted by The Ghost were known to be associates of the DBJF Alliance's Research and Development Division. If Liam Alastor and his allies were looking for information on what had been

280

done to him, then there could be no better targets.

Harold sat back in the warden's chair. He needed to find out. When he returned to his office, he would pull everything his office had managed to obtain on The Ghost's activities. He would also pull every report he had received on the condition of one Liam Alastor. If there were *any* correlations to be had, he would find them.

Don't count your cluckers yet, Harold scolded himself. *Investigate. Make the necessary connections if they're there. Do your due diligence. Sew them up tight. Now that the Wall is dead, Baas and Alastor and their allies aren't as protected. However, you also can't let them have even the tiniest bit of room to wriggle their way out of facing the consequences of their actions against you and Island Affairs.*

He took a deep breath, willing himself to be calm again. He would have the answers he wanted, he knew. He just needed to be patient for a little longer, and he would have everything he ever wanted.

When Euphrates returned, Harold appeared as he had before the warden had left the office. There were no signs of the tempest that wanted to rage or of the volcano that wanted to erupt. All Euphrates saw was the placid, yet dangerous, sheet of ice that was Harold Edmund Holloway waiting for the things he had requested.

"I have what you wanted, sir," he gasped out.

"Good." Harold took them. "I want you to double, even triple, check every officer and member of staff on these islands. If there's even a *hint* of unbecoming conduct from *anyone* who's not an inmate, you and I will be having another discussion. Understood?"

"Yes, sir." Euphrates swallowed. He wasn't looking forward to the amount of work that would be involved, but he knew it could be worse. "I do."

"Get me copies of the visitor logbook, too," Harold ordered. "I want to know everyone who has visited Liam Alastor or the hospital ICU, going back to July 4 of last year."

Euphrates grimaced but nodded. "Yes, sir."

"Good. As soon as I have *that,* I'll be heading back to Sulivan. I don't think you're off the hook, however. I plan to review everything myself before presenting it to Mister Oliver."

"M-Mister *Oliver,* sir?" Euphrates went pale.

"Yes." Harold smiled, the expression cold, as he spoke. "I'll be updating him the next time we speak, and he has already indicated that he will be flying out here as soon as he's done with his business in Washington." He paused, noting the warden's terror-stricken look. "You'd best hope that we have at least *some* answers before he gets here."

"Y-y-yes, sir!"

Harold glared at the man, then rolled his eyes when Warden Euphrates remained where he stood. "Where are my copies?"

"Oh!" Euphrates blinked and began to move again. "Right. I'll get them for you!"

He fled the office once more. Harold shook his head, exasperated. He wanted, *needed,* to get back to his own office, where he could start cross-referencing dates and events. If Liam Alastor happened to be The Ghost, he would not find out here.

He reached for the warden's phone. Harold had a number of fires to light, and what better time than now, while he waited for the warden to return?

"Pamela, I'll need all of the incident reports regarding The Ghost put on my desk," he said without preamble when his assistant answered the phone. "I'll need to review them when I get back."

"Yes, sir."

"Also, let Ganesh know I'll need to speak with him about what just happened on the prison islands. Has it slipped out to the media yet?"

"Not that I'm aware of, sir," Pamela said. "The phones haven't been ringing more than normal."

"Good. That means we have time to fix things. Has Fleischmann or any of the others he has with him reported in?"

"They have, yes, sir," she said. "Apparently, Mister Thorne has been busy visiting the FBI office and the city's library."

Harold frowned. Given that Ray Douglas had met Rick at the airport, Harold couldn't be surprised by Rick visiting Ray's office, but what reason would he have to see the city's library? Could it be something to do with his nebulous case? Could he be trying to learn the city better by studying the public maps at the Sulivan City Library? Or was this city's unique history clamoring for attention? Or was it something else, something that Harold couldn't think of at the moment?

It was another thing he would have to look into after he left the prison islands. There were things that someone like Rick Thorne couldn't be allowed to learn.

"I should be back at the office in another hour or two," he said. "Make sure those files are on my desk and that Ganesh knows I'll want to meet with him as soon as I'm back."

"Yes, sir."

Good. Harold ended the call and then began to dial his sister's work number. She would not like what he had to tell her, he knew, but it would be better if she heard the news from him before anyone else. He would also be able to ask about the experiments she and her team had performed on Liam Alastor during the first half of the time he had reportedly spent comatose.

To his frustration, however, his call went straight to his sister's voicemail. Harold blew out an irritated breath, then made sure to inject the right amount of urgency into his tone when he spoke. "Give me a callback, Regina, as soon as you can."

With that having been accomplished, Harold hung up and leaned back in the warden's chair. His forehead furrowed again with thought. They needed to recapture Liam Alastor, and the sooner, the better.

Of course, that brought up the question of *how*. Now that the boy was free, he would no doubt go to ground, which would make the efforts to recapture him all the more difficult. Harold hated to admit it, but he knew that Liam Alastor had known the city of Sulivan far better than he or most others had four years ago. He would most likely still know most of the best places to hide, even in plain sight, and he would undoubtedly still know where to go in order to evade capture if he happened to be spotted. Harold would need to counteract these things, but again, the question was *how*.

It was a question that preoccupied him during the forty-five minutes he waited for the warden to return with the copies. It would be a question that plagued him for the entirety of his flight back to Sulivan proper, then throughout the drive to his office at the Department of Mid-Western Island Affairs.

How could they recapture and once again imprison Liam Alastor?

Ganesh Khan, who was waiting for Harold's return inside his

office, noticed his distraction and sought to refocus him. "Sir? Is it true? About Liam Alastor waking up?"

"And escaping? Yes." Harold loosed a sigh before dropping down into his chair. Much as he'd expected, the files on The Ghost were piled on his right hand—Pamela was nothing if not efficient at her job. "I want him recaptured immediately, and preferably without having the Sulivan PD and its Deputy Chief involved."

"That could be difficult," Ganesh said. "Even with the Wall gone, Deputy Chief Baas will no doubt remain tenacious."

"I know," Harold acknowledged. "But we need to make it happen, regardless." He loosed a sigh. "Have Kavanaugh, DiGirolamo, and a couple of others stake out the Mausoleums on Christianne Island. There are a few graves out that way that Alastor might wish to visit."

"Yes, sir."

"Good." Harold thought a moment, the corners of his lips turning down. "Where else might he go? Where could he hide?"

"I have no idea, sir. Finding out such information will mean finding those who know or knew Alastor and who might have an idea as to where he might go," Ganesh said, and saw Harold nod. "Temujin Lance? We could work a deal with him, perhaps?"

"Not until after the trial," Harold grunted. "Even then, I'd hesitate. Lance is not someone I'd want to owe a favor to, even if he agreed to help in this matter."

Ganesh nodded in agreement and thought a moment. "There's exactly one other person I know off the top of my head, sir, other than Deputy Chief Baas or Temujin Lance, who might know Alastor well enough to point us in the right direction at least. Unlike the Deputy Chief and Mister Lance, I do not doubt that Russell Jamison would be only too happy to help us."

"Russell Jamison?" Harold frowned. He knew he'd heard the name before, but couldn't place it.

"He currently works for Veil-Tech, sir, but he was once a member of the Arch Street Angels," Ganesh said. "A lieutenant in that gang, if I'm not mistaken. If there's anyone other than Baas or Lance who might know Liam Alastor's preferred hiding places, it would be him."

"Good. Call Mister Jamison and Mister Renley and set up a meeting," Harold ordered. "Preferably for tonight, but tomorrow or the day after will do as well. That will hopefully give me enough time to go through all of these and then, to *think.*"

He nodded at the files on his desk. Ganesh looked and almost frowned.

"The Ghost, sir?" he said.

"How likely is it, Ganesh," Harold asked, "for Liam Alastor to have woken up from a four-year-long coma and then managed to escape the same day?"

"Real life is not Hollywood, sir," Ganesh said, his expression darkening. He glanced again at the files before putting the pieces together. "You suspect that Mister Alastor and The Ghost are the same?"

"It makes more sense than Alastor snapping awake and escaping just before my people arrived to collect him," Harold said. "After four years in a coma, his muscles should have been too atrophied for him even to turn his head, let alone to get off his bed, grab a scalpel, sneak up on his doctor, and then disappear."

Ganesh nodded, thought again, and then hesitantly opened his mouth. "What about what your sister and her team of scientists did to him while he was comatose, sir? Could whatever they accomplished have allowed Alastor to do what he did today?"

"I don't know, but I'll be finding out just as soon as she returns my call. In the meantime, I'll concentrate on The Ghost's files and work on correlating them with certain things that happened while Alastor was supposedly still trapped in his coma."

"Good idea, sir."

"I know." Harold nodded to his door. "Go, Ganesh. Speak to Kavanaugh and DiGirolamo, then call Veil-Tech and set up that meeting."

"Yes, sir."

As soon as Ganesh left his office, Harold opened the top left-hand drawer of his desk to retrieve a pad of paper and a pencil before turning his attention to The Ghost's files. Again, the experimentation being conducted on Liam Alastor had been prematurely halted on July 4, 2006, thanks to interference from The Wall and Ben Baas. Opening the first of the files dealing with The Ghost, Harold confirmed that the first robbery attributed to The Ghost had occurred on September 10 of the same year. It wasn't much time for Alastor to wake up from his coma and recover enough to start conducting any clandestine operations. Still, perhaps, depending on what Regina and her team had been doing to the boy before being interrupted, it had been enough.

The Ghost's first run was between September, October, and November 2006. The homes of four scientists and three laboratories, one of which had been connected to the DBJF, had been hit. Most, although not all, had been interconnected, at least in some small way, to the experimentation that had been going on at the prison, if not on Liam

287

Alastor himself.

The last to be hit in 2006 had come on the heels of Thanksgiving. No doubt, The Ghost had thought the target in question, Intra-Genetics, would be an easy job, thanks to the holiday. Instead, due to the sensitive nature of several ongoing experiments, the laboratory had been under intense scrutiny, and The Ghost had nearly been caught. Two separate teams of security guards had even sworn that they'd scored a hit on The Ghost.

Was it a mere coincidence that Liam Alastor had supposedly taken a brief turn for the worse around that time?

Harold now thought it might not be. He also thought it might not be so coincidental that The Ghost had reappeared just the month before, when Liam Alastor's medical team had been changed.

His mouth became a thin line as he thought about it. Perhaps Doctor Kim wasn't as much a victim as she had pretended.

He reached for her file. Yes, he still needed to speak to his sister to find out what the chances were that Liam Alastor could awaken in one breath and escape in the next. Until that time, he could discover more about the good doctor and fill in a few more blanks.

On the surface, nothing seemed too out of the ordinary, at least not to Harold's eyes. Doctor Kim Hana was born on the Island City of Talfryn, the daughter of Kim Ji-Hun and Suwabe Kazumi. They were prosperous, even well-to-do, and had been able to afford to send not only their daughter but two of their three sons to top-level mainland universities. Doctor Kim had scored top marks in medical school and had more than earned her diploma, according to her file. Yet, she was still young and had come home to the Mid-Superior Islands to help her parents

288

after her father had suffered a serious injury.

The move had put her career on hold for almost a year, and it seemed the job of prison doctor had been the first position she'd taken after she had been able to return to work. Her father was well enough that she could move to Sulivan to take the job, and there didn't seem to be any red flags or any reason for Harold to remain so suspicious.

So why did he?

A few minutes' worth of thought produced no answers, causing Harold to close Doctor Kim's folder. It would come to him eventually, he knew.

While he waited for both his sister to return his call and for his mind to produce the answers he wanted, Harold decided to read the other file the prison warden had given him. It wasn't quite as thick as the doctor's was, and he felt confident he would be able to put it aside if Regina called or something else developed that required his attention.

Much like the doctor's, the file on Miguel H. Costilla seemed to have no red flags or anything that would cause alarm bells to ring in anyone's mind. A native of Sulivan, he was apparently an orphan who had been raised by an aunt and uncle with far too many children and far too few financial means to afford much. Despite being raised in the Barrio District of Sulivan and surrounded by Eighth Avenue Kings and Pasquale Family members, Miguel claimed to want nothing to do with any gang due to how his parents had died. He had accepted the maintenance job at the prison not only for the money he could earn, but also because it allowed him to attend classes at Mid-Lake University remotely. His supervisors had nothing but praise for him, and those who worked with him would not say anything negative about him.

This is what made his disappearance so concerning. Had he run into the escaping Liam Alastor? Perhaps he'd been injured? Or even killed? If so, why couldn't anyone find him or his body?

Harold didn't like it. Once again, he thought there was something he was missing. He couldn't put his finger on it, whatever it was, but he *knew* something wasn't right.

Before he could spend too much time thinking about it, his phone rang. Harold snatched it up. "Holloway."

"You asked me to call you, Harry?"

"Yes, Regina, I did." Harold drew in a deep breath. "There was a problem today out at the prison hospital."

Regina's voice sharpened. "My seventh subject?"

"He woke up," Harold told her. "And escaped."

"What?" Her tone proved incredulous. "That's impossible."

"Is it?" Harold asked. "Given what you and your team were doing to him?"

"That doesn't matter," she said. "Even with what we did, it would take *time*, Harry, for my subject to recover enough to do anything physical. His musculature had atrophied almost to the point of non-use. Without the proper nutrition and exercise, even with the regenerative features we introduced into him, his muscles would still need weeks, if not months, before they could be used again."

It was precisely as Harold had feared. "How likely is it that a doctor would not know this?"

"A first-year medical student would know this," she said. "As would any full-fledged doctor worth their proverbial salt."

Which meant it shouldn't have mattered that Doctor Kim was

relatively new. Harold would need to talk to the woman himself and find out just why she had missed such an obvious indication that not everything with Liam Alastor was as it might have seemed.

And if she happened to be an accomplice?

He almost stood, ready to go charging out the door and back to the prison hospital to find out. Instead, his eyes flashed to the clock, and he found himself blinking. It was already past six thirty in the evening.

An irritated breath escaped his nostrils. He had too much to do at that precise moment to take the time to go back to the prison islands right then. *Tomorrow,* he promised himself. *I'll go first thing tomorrow morning. If she is an accomplice, then she most likely believes they've gotten away with it, and my return might shock her into admitting something. Even if it doesn't, if Doctor Kim's answers aren't to my liking when I question her, I'll make her pay.*

"Harry?" Again, Regina's voice echoed into his ear. "You said my subject has escaped. What is being done to recover him?"

Ah. Harold drew in a breath, preparing himself to upset his sister. Before he could open his mouth to begin, however, a thought came to him.

"Will you and your husband be free tonight?" he asked instead. "I'd like to come over. Chances are good that I'm going to need yours and your husband's help to reacquire your subject and get him back into your custody."

"We'll make ourselves free for this," Regina promised him.

"Good. I'll be leaving my office soon, and I'll head straight over," Harold told her. "Between the three of us, I do not doubt that we'll have him back with you before the week is out."

Chapter Thirteen: A Meeting Between Two Men From Philly

May 29, 2007: Morning, Outside Police Headquarters

Rick walked up the steps of the City of Sulivan's Police Headquarters building, doing his best to ignore the already oppressive heat and humidity, as well as his trepidation. Finding the answers to the mystery that seemed to surround the possible son of his brother-in-law warred with the idea of possibly meeting with Benjamin Benedict Baas again.

It would not, Rick suspected, be a happy reunion. Again, they had worked together in the same precinct, with Ben being a patrol officer and Rick being a detective. Rick had taken issue with Ben's temper, as had many of their fellow officers. Again, Ben had been strangely wary of people, which Rick and a number of others had found to be disconcerting in the best of times, as well as irritating.

But now, Rick had to wonder what reasons Ben had had for acting that way. According to what Ray and Ethan had told him, not long after their return from the City of Sulivan Crime Museum, Benjamin Benedict Baas had transferred out to the Sulivan Police Department in the hopes of finding out what had happened to a cousin of his, who had gone missing. He'd made his detective's shield just before heading to Sulivan. He had been tapped by none other than the Police Chief at the time, Franklin James O'Connell, for his undercover assignment in the Arch Street Angels.

But when had Ben's cousin gone missing? Had the cousin already been missing when Ben joined the Police Academy back in Philadelphia? If so, why hadn't he said anything? His fellow officers would have been far more understanding of Ben's attitude back then if they had known.

Unless Ben had believed he couldn't take the risk of telling them? Rick could well remember that Ben had been one of the very few who had viewed Detective Norman Hornsby with a distrustful eye. Norman Hornsby had been charismatic and personable, and Rick would have gone so far as to call him a friend back then. Like so many of his fellow officers, Rick had believed that Ben had disliked Hornsby for the detective's willingness to call Ben out for his mistakes and his temper, but given the fact that Hornsby had turned out to be a predator, one who had preyed on *children*, doubt now started to form in Rick's mind.

Had Ben somehow known? Or had he at least suspected as much about Hornsby?

Memories of that bygone time tickled the back of Rick's brain. However, he ignored them for the moment as he entered the thankfully air-conditioned lobby. He could tease out the memories later after he completed this visit. For now, he needed to focus on the reason he'd come to Sulivan's Police Headquarters.

The young officer assigned to the front desk smiled at him as he walked up. "Welcome to the Sulivan Police Department. How may I help you?"

"My name is Rick Thorne." The private investigator gave her a small smile in return, forcing the apprehension he felt to the back of his mind. "I'm a private investigator, and I was hoping to talk to one of your detectives or maybe even your Chief of police about an ongoing case of mine. I'm hoping they'll have some information I can use or can at least point me in the right direction."

"Of course." She nodded. "If you'll sign in and have a seat, I'll see if anyone is available to assist you."

"I appreciate it. Thank you."

Close to fifteen minutes would pass before a lean man wearing the full uniform of a Police Chief appeared. Rick sat up in his seat, eyeing the man as he approached the front desk. He was of average height, seemed to be in his mid-forties, with Japanese features, short-cut black hair, and sharp, dark eyes. He had a no-nonsense expression, but his voice held nothing but curiosity as he spoke to the officer on desk duty.

"You said we have a private investigator visiting us today?" he said.

"Yes, sir, Chief." The officer nodded toward Rick, who took it as his cue to stand. "He's right there."

"Ah." The Chief stepped over, extending his hand to Rick. "I am Makoto Akiyama, Mister Thorne."

Rick took the hand and shook it as expected. Akiyama's grip proved a solid one, and Rick thought he detected the faint hint of gunpowder residue. Makoto Akiyama was not a lazy man, he suspected, or one who tolerated much in the way of foolishness.

"I believe you said you were working a case?" the Chief asked. "And you are hoping that we can help you?"

"Yes, sir," Rick said. "I'm new to the area and am hoping you could at least point me to the right people, as well as give me a heads-up as to the ones I should avoid."

"Very wise." The Chief gave him the barest flicker of a smile. "Please, come with me to my office, and we can discuss things there. Cassie?" He looked to the officer on desk duty. "If there are any calls for me, please direct them to Ms. Sutton. She will be able to deal with them."

"Yes, sir."

"Good." Akiyama turned back to Rick and inclined his head towards the right. "This way, please, Mister Thorne."

"Call me Rick," the private investigator said. "Whenever I hear Mister Thorne, I'm reminded of getting sent to the principal's office, although most of the time now, it's due to one of my kids."

"Understandable." The corners of Akiyama's lips quirked upwards a little. "You will have to go through a few security measures first."

"Of course." Given everything he had already learned about the city of Sulivan, Rick had no problems with it. "Point the way."

Turning on his heels, the Chief walked over to the door that Rick suspected would lead into the rest of the station. Anyone going through would need to walk through what looked like a metal detector, and Rick didn't hesitate to step up when Akiyama waved him on. When no alarms sounded, the door was opened, and Rick was permitted to go through.

"Thank you, Rick, for your cooperation," Akiyama said as he followed him. "It is most appreciated. Let us head to the elevators."

"Sounds good."

Within the span of seconds, they had boarded one. Rick watched as Akiyama pressed the button for the third floor and opened his mouth to speak.

To his surprise, however, Akiyama shook his head at him. Rick almost frowned but nodded. Why wouldn't they at least make small chit-chat now?

It bothered him, but he kept his peace. No doubt, this Makota Akiyama had his reasons for not speaking as they rode up to the third floor.

The doors opened with a quiet *ding,* and Rick followed Akiyama out, glancing around as he did. He knew that Sulivan's Police Headquarters building was no less than six stories high and included not only a parking lot but a helipad. The third floor housed not only the Chief's office but apparently the various Detective Divisions, including Vice, Robbery, Narcotics, and Homicide. They passed a break room as well before rounding a corner and entering the Administration section.

Before long, they were entering the Chief's office, with Akiyama gesturing to one of the two chairs in front of his desk. "Please, have a seat. Now. How can I help you?"

Rick had thought long and hard about how much information he should give. Ray and Ethan had both told him that Makoto Akiyama was anything but a fool, and he had gained a reputation for spotting a lie from miles away. The trick for Rick would be to keep everything as vague as possible while also giving as much information as he could to find out what he wanted and needed to know.

"I'm looking for the son of a client," he said. "Up until recently, he didn't know that he had any children, but a letter he received just a week ago informed him otherwise. He'd like to meet his son, of course, and if at all possible, and maybe get to know him. It's why he hired me and why I flew out to this city. I'm hoping to find out as much as I can, and then I guess you could say I'll test the waters, if you get my drift."

"I do." Akiyama inclined his head. "And I find it commendable of your client, as well as wise. Do you know the name of the child in question?"

Rick pulled out his notepad. He didn't really need it as he had a fantastic memory for all sorts of detail, but he liked having people underestimate him. "Not really a child, Chief. More like a young man, who would be named...ah. Robert Kincaid."

Akiyama's eyes widened for a split second in shock before hardening. His expression became stone-like. He leaned forward a little, steepling his fingers in front of him. "Mister Thorne. Rick. This is a challenging subject to bring up. I am unsure of just how much I can say, but I *can* tell you that *that* name is dangerous, at least in this city."

Rick frowned, aiming to look puzzled. He didn't doubt the Chief's words, not after what he'd seen in the crime museum. If Robert Kincaid happened to be the young man in the pictures and videos there, Victor was in for an unpleasant surprise.

The way Akiyama spoke, however, added a new layer to the thoughts swirling in Rick's brain. He scribbled *'conspiracy'* in his notebook, with a question mark beside it. He had the feeling that whatever was going on was significant, even if he didn't yet know what that something was or just how big it could be.

"How so, Chief?" he asked. *Play dumb, Rick.* "Is he a criminal of some sort?"

Akiyama sat back again, eyes focused with laser precision on Rick's own. His hands went to the edge of his desk as if he were steadying himself.

Rick recognized the move as a stalling tactic, one he would sometimes use when trying to decide what to hide and what to reveal. Depending on Akiyama's decision, their conversation could become more insightful.

At last, it seemed as if Akiyama had made his choice. Leaning forward once more, he crossed his arms in front of his chest and lowered his voice.

297

"Mister Thorne," he said. "What I am about to tell you is not to leave this room. The man you call Robert Kincaid is—"

The door flung open without warning, cutting off the Chief. Rick's head snapped over as an angry, red-faced Benjamin Benedict Baas charged inside.

"Chief!" Ben's eyes were burning bright and fierce. "We've got ourselves a prob—"

As luck or fate would have it, he happened to glance over at Rick at that exact moment. Rick saw the other man stop and blink, cutting himself off before looking closer. Ben's hands became fists, and he snarled.

"What the *fuck*," he spat out, advancing on the private investigator, "are *you* doin' here?"

Rick swallowed, feeling a strange fear surge deep from within him at the glare he now received. The sheer *enmity* he saw in Ben's eyes! He had known things would be rough if he and Ben met again. Still, somehow, Rick hadn't expected to see anything other than maybe some surprise and disbelief, even a little resentment. Not this full-blown *rage*.

He opened his mouth to try and say something, anything, that might cool the other's anger, but nothing made its way past his throat. What, exactly, could he say? Ben had been known back in Philly for letting his temper get the better of him, and if Rick said the wrong thing now?

Well, Ben had also been known for having one of the heaviest fists in all of Philly. There was a reason for that.

Much to his shock, however, Akiyama seemed unruffled. He spoke with both measured authority and power, and Ben did not, could not, ignore him.

"Why, yes, *Deputy* Chief Baas," Akiyama said, his annoyance

298

clear. "Do come into my office. You are more than welcome at this time."

"Ah—" Ben blinked as if just realizing that Akiyama was still there. Furthering Rick's surprise, the fury on Ben's face slid away, and he took a deep, calming breath. His fists uncurled a heartbeat later. "Sorry, Chief."

Rick couldn't help but stare. The Benjamin Baas he'd known would never have calmed down so easily or quickly. He had once cursed out their precinct's captain in Rick's hearing before throwing a punch at Rick himself, an act that had resulted in Ben being suspended and transferred.

That was about fourteen or maybe fifteen years ago, Rick, he reminded himself. *Baas isn't a rookie anymore. He's a Deputy Chief of Police, as strange as it might seem, and he's no doubt learned a few things.*

No doubt thanks to Makoto Akiyama, who was nodding at said Deputy Chief. A glimmer of understanding lurked within his eyes. His voice gentled. "It has been a trying week for you, Ben, I know. I would appreciate it if you didn't bring it into the office, however. Perhaps you should take a break and head to the helipad. As soon as I am done with my visitor, I'll join you, and we can chat a bit."

Ben, however, did not move. A faint hint of steel lined his voice. "Why is he here?"

Rick, again, opened his mouth, this time to explain. Akiyama once again beat him to it.

"He says he is here to look for the son of a client," the Chief said. "A Robert Kincaid."

If Rick hadn't been watching so closely, he might have missed the way Ben froze for the slightest moment. Why that would be, Rick had no idea.

And Ben didn't try to clear up the mystery. "Rob...?"

He shook his head a moment later. Granite brown eyes flicked back at Rick, then focused on Akiyama.

"I don't care who he's in town for," Ben bit out. "I don't trust 'im. You know how I feel about that, Chief, and, most importantly, you know *why.*" Again, his eyes slid over to Rick and back. "We were warned, too, about not lettin' just anyone get involved in things, *especially* in regard to that name."

Rick allowed a slight frown to form on his face, even as he filed away what Ben had said. He would investigate that later, if possible. For now?

He cleared his throat. "I'm not here to step on anyone's toes. I'm only here to find the son of my client, and the best lead I have so far is his name, which I was told is Robert Kincaid."

"So you say," Ben's eyes narrowed at him. "I just find it incredible that you would happen to show up *now,* at this exact moment." He turned back to Akiyama. "I don't think we should give any information, no matter how small, about certain people to those we can't fully trust. Wil—I mean, The Superintendent warned us against doin' just that."

Ben's verbal slip-up was yet another thing he would have to check into later, Rick thought as he turned his attention to Akiyama. He could see the Chief was weighing Ben's words, and he didn't like the idea that the past could interfere with a present investigation.

At length, Akiyama proved that it would. "Forgive me, Mister Thorne, but I find that I am unable to provide you with any information regarding who you're looking for. However, I would caution you against

300

discussing who you are searching for outside my office. Doing so could lead to *unhappy* consequences."

Rick pursed his lips, unhappy at this reversal. Before Ben Baas had entered his Chief's office, it had seemed as though Akiyama had been predisposed to reveal something. Now? Akiyama was sending Rick away with only a warning.

He might have argued the point if Ben hadn't spoken at that moment. "I would be *more* than happy to escort him out, Chief."

Akiyama glanced at him and saw the way Rick blanched. "I know you would, Deputy Chief Baas, which is why I'm not going to allow it."

"Ah, c'mon—"

"No. You and I still need to have a chat, remember?" Akiyama reached for his intercom. "Ms. Sutton, could you please have..." He thought a moment. "Officer Scofield, come to my office. Thank you."

Ben's brow furrowed. "Scofield?"

"Yes," Akiyama said, a faint smile ghosting over his lips. "I can't think of anyone better for something like this."

Rick felt a twinge of something like dread. Why would Akiyama think this 'Scofield,' whomever he or she was, would be the best to escort him out? Was yet another threat incoming?

Apparently not. A knock at the Chief's door heralded a young man with a startlingly familiar shade of red hair and pale, bluish-gray eyes poking his head in.

Rick sat up in his seat. Who was this, and could it be possible that Liam Alastor *wasn't* Robert Kincaid after all?

"You wanted to see me, Chief?" the young man said.

"Yes. Come in, Officer." Akiyama waited until he was inside the office. "Officer Alan Scofield will escort you downstairs, Mister Thorne. Officer, you are to make certain that this man, Mister Rick Thorne from Philadelphia, is seen out."

"Rick Thorne?" The young man's eyes went wide. "You mean *the* Rick Thorne? The private investigator?"

He sounded both impressed and excited, and Rick found himself hard-pressed not to smile as he stood. Of course, he also found himself hard-pressed not to react to Ben's roll of the eyes.

"Of *course* he'd be a fan," the Deputy Chief could be heard to mutter.

"Yes, Officer." Rick kept his attention firmly on the younger man. Alan Scofield also had an oval face, a square chin, and large, round eyes, and Rick felt his hopes surge. "That would be me."

The young man looked positively giddy. "This way, then, sir!"

Rick followed him out of the Chief's office without complaint, and a new set of plans was forming. First, he meant to determine if Officer Alan Scofield could be Victor's son. Second, if Akiyama wouldn't talk, and regardless of whether Alan was or wasn't Victor's unknown child, perhaps the young man could provide some information.

Of course, before he could do any of that, Rick needed to set the young man at ease and begin a dialogue between them. "You don't have to call me 'sir,' officer. Rick is fine, or, if you're not comfortable with that, then Mister Thorne will do."

"Really? You're serious, sir? I mean, Mister Thorne?"

"I am, yes." Rick saw Alan's face light up even more and suppressed a chuckle. The young man *had* to be new to the police force, he thought, which meant that Rick's idea of getting information from him

302

could work. "I'll be more than happy, too, to answer any questions you might have about my work."

As he'd expected, the expression Alan wore shifted to resemble a kid's on Christmas morning. Excitement flooded the young officer's grayish-blue eyes and—

Grayish-blue? Rick stopped, focusing on the young man's face. *Not blue-gray. Damn.*

He soon discovered that there were a few more, equally subtle deviations from the one he was searching for could be seen—Alan's nose wasn't straight but had a slight upturn; his lips, while thin, weren't *as* thin as that boy's in the painting; and his cheekbones weren't as high, and they were slightly more prominent.

That could all but eliminate him, Rick knew. *Unless he either had plastic surgery in the past few years or the painting wasn't* entirely *as accurate as it seemed.*

He gave his head a mental shake. He could find out for sure if Alan Scofield had any chance of being Robert Kincaid in the course of a conversation with the young man.

Fortunately, Alan had no problems with asking questions and talking. Rick did his best to satiate the other man's curiosity, waiting for the right moment to ask a few questions of his own.

Alan rewarded his patience when, at last, he asked, "What brought you to Sulivan? A case?"

"Yes." Rick nodded, smiling inwardly and lowering his voice. "A client has asked me to look for the son he never knew he had. A Robert Kincaid."

Alan's eyes went wide. "Are you *serious?* You're looking for a

Kincaid? Robert Kincaid?"

"Yes." Rick made sure to act bewildered. "What is it? Why does that name have some people so on edge around here?"

"What do you mean?" Alan inclined his head with a slight frown.

"Your Chief just warned me not to say that name outside the walls of his office," Rick said. "And your Deputy Chief looked quite worried when he heard who I was looking for."

"Oh." Alan nodded. "Yeah, I can understand that."

"Could you explain it to me?" Rick inserted a pleading note. "I have no idea what's going on, and I just want to find my client's son."

"Understandable, Mister Thorne." Alan thought a moment. "Follow me."

Okay. Rick almost frowned, but followed regardless. The officer led him through a few corridors, then down a set of empty stairs, before heading towards what looked like a small, lobby-like area next to what Rick recognized as an empty press room. The lobby, too, proved empty, except for the collection of photographs that hung beneath a *Most Wanted* placard, which sat between a pair of doors.

To his shock, Rick recognized one of the photos. He moved forward, all but ignoring the officer at his side.

The man in the picture had a chiseled, light brown face with stylized black hair. Vibrant dark eyes, so dark they almost looked like chips of obsidian, stared back. A pair of scars ran down the left side of the man's otherwise handsome face.

Rick *knew* he'd seen the man before. But where?

"Sir? Um, Mister Thorne?"

Alan's uneasy voice brought Rick out of his reverie. The private

304

investigator blinked, then looked over, feeling a slight pang of guilt for having ignored the younger man.

"Sorry," he said. "What can you tell me about him?"

Alan also blinked, then looked up at the photograph Rick had indicated. "That's the leader of the Iron Horde, a motorcycle gang that's one of the four groups that commit most of the major crimes here in Sulivan. He's known only as Valente and is best described, along with his two main lieutenants, as bestial."

He nodded to two other photographs that hung right beside Valente's. There were two men, both muscular and glaring. One had a chiseled face and long-looking blond hair, with dark, storm-cloud gray eyes, while the other had dark brown skin, a shaved-bald head, and what seemed like soulless, almost black eyes.

"That's Jax and Zale," Alan said quietly. "All of them are known to be nasty, to say the least. There isn't a crime they haven't committed, it seems." He glanced over and saw the look on Rick's face. "Do you know them?"

"Not Jax or Zale," Rick murmured. "But Valente? I might. He looks familiar, at least. I'll need to check my files, though." He drew in a deep breath, trying to think where he might have seen the man in the photograph before, then shook his head. It would no doubt come to him later. "Never mind. I'm pretty sure this isn't why you brought me here."

"No, it's not," Alan said. "I figured we could talk a little more here without too much risk of being overheard or disturbed. The last thing I want to do is get in trouble with the Chief and the walls...some of the walls have ears, y'know?"

Rick nodded. News, whether real or not, had always traveled

faster than lightning at his old precinct, and he didn't doubt it would be the same here. Getting the young man in front of him into trouble would do no one any favors.

"I understand," he said. "Would you prefer if we met elsewhere, maybe for lunch or even dinner? You could tell me everything then, and I can answer any more questions you might have."

"We should be safe enough here," Alan told him. "And you need to know a little more about things, especially when it comes to the Kincaid Family."

"All right?"

Alan took a deep breath. "The Kincaids were part of what's called the Old Families. They were part of the descendants of the original group of people who settled the Mids."

Rick could remember Ray telling him that, back when he'd first called. "Go on."

"The Old Families used to be powerful here until the Pasquale Family and others wiped them out," Alan said and bit his lower lip in hesitation, glancing around as if to ensure they really were alone. Rick waited, letting the younger man take his time, and, at last, his patience would be rewarded when Alan continued, "Some say that the Department of Mid-Western Island Affairs was actually behind it all."

Again, Ray and Ethan had said the same thing. Rick nodded, encouraging Alan to continue.

"The Kincaids were among the last to be taken out," Alan told him. "The last known patriarch of the family, Robert Joseph Kincaid, along with his wife, Anne Elizabeth, and their two sons, William and Alastor, were all killed in a single drive-by."

306

"A drive-by?" Rick repeated, incredulous. Drive-by shootings were loud and chaotic, to say the least. Why wouldn't this Department of Mid-Western Island Affairs go with something more subtle?

Alan nodded. "It was one of the Pasquale Family's favorite methods for dealing with people they perceived as enemies since they thought it sent a message."

Rick nodded in sudden, grim understanding. He'd seen such things happen before, back during his days with the Philadelphia Police Department. However, despite what Ray and Ethan had also told him, he had a question.

"What makes you believe this Department of Mid-Western Island Affairs had anything to do with what happened to the Kincaids? And the other Old Families?"

"It's said that they were looking into things that Island Affairs didn't want revealed," Alan said. "Most of the Old Families who were wiped out didn't want to play ball with Island Affairs, but the Kincaids had always been seen as being more on the neutral side. Their family was seen as the Guardians of the Mid-Superior Islands and, until they began to look more closely into certain things, Island Affairs had left them pretty much alone."

"And what is it that you believe?"

"That if Robert Kincaid is still here, on the shores of Sulivan, Island Affairs will do anything to remove him," Alan told him. "They'll use you, if it's possible, to find him and then take both of you out." He glanced around again. "You'll need to be really careful. Island Affairs doesn't mess around."

"I understand," Rick said. "Is there anything else you can tell me?"

Alan hesitated again, brow furrowing as he thought. Again, Rick waited, wondering what else the young man might have to tell him.

"Where are you staying?" Alan finally asked.

Rick blinked. "Over at the Mid-Lake Inn near the airport."

Alan grinned without warning. "I have family down that way, so no one would question me heading over there. If you still want to meet up later, that is."

"I'd be more than happy to. Say around dinner? Six or so?"

"That sounds good." Alan's grin widened a little. "I'll be off work by then, plus I know a few things about the Old Families that might help in your investigation."

"Just tell me where to meet you."

"My dad owns the *Balance of Flour Pizzeria*, which is in the Sellars Island Market. I'll give him a call, and he'll let us have the back room to eat and talk in private."

Rick smiled. "I'd appreciate that."

"It shouldn't be a problem. I can clue you in on a few other things, too, and—" Alan's eyes snapped over to the nearby door as it opened. His grin morphed into a sneaky sort of smile, one that reminded Rick far too much of Charlie and Josiah. "Maybe give you a tour of the islands?"

Still, he couldn't argue with the other's precaution when another officer, a big and burly-looking man wearing the insignia of a sergeant, entered. "There you are. I was wondering where you'd gotten off to after the Chief had ya kidnapped."

"Sorry 'bout that, Sarge," Alan said. "Got caught up in asking Mister Thorne here some questions. He's a PI from Philadelphia and—"

"You decided to torture him?" The sergeant cut him off,

chuckling and eyeing Rick with a mixture of sympathy and good-natured humor. "I can save you."

Rick chuckled back. "It's okay, sergeant. I can handle a little curiosity."

"It's better than bein' shot, am I right?" The sergeant laughed again and shook his head. "Unfortunately, Alan, you gotta get back to your desk to finish up the paperwork from yesterday's little, uh, adventure."

Alan sighed dramatically. "Do I *have* to? Right now? I have so many questions I still have to ask Mister Thorne!"

"Sorry, kiddo," the sergeant said. "It's part of the job."

"As much as I might hate to admit it," Rick said. "Your sergeant's right. But before I go—" He extracted a business card from his breast coat pocket, flipped it over, and made a small show of writing his cell phone's number on it. "Text me anytime you're free, and we can chat more."

"Thanks!"

"It's not a problem." Rick looked at the sergeant. "If you can point me to the way out, I can let you and Officer Scofield get back to work."

"I appreciate it," the sergeant said. "C'mon. It's this way."

A few moments later, Rick stepped back out into the heat and humidity. Glancing around, he began to head down the street to where he knew Ray and Meg, who had dropped him off, would be waiting.

"Well?" Ray asked when Rick finally slid into the back passenger seat. "How'd things go?"

"I'm pretty sure Akiyama was going to tell me something," Rick said. "But Baas came in."

"I take it he wasn't happy to see you?" Meg said.

"Not in the least." Rick shook his head. The memory of Ben's hands curling into fists as he'd advanced on Rick lingered in the private investigator's mind, and he needed to shake his head again to dispel it. He preferred to dwell on another, hopefully more productive, meeting that would soon take place. "Still, something good did come of it. I met a young police officer named Alan Scofield. Akiyama asked him to escort me out, and we started talking. It seems he may know a few things."

"Such as?" Ray wanted to know.

"He told me a bit about the Old Families," Rick said. "And about how Katherine Kincaid's parents and brothers were killed. He also warned me to be careful, as Island Affairs just might use me to help find Robert Kincaid and then take both of us out."

Ray's expression became grim. "They would do something like that, at least from what Ethan's told me."

"So Officer Scofield said." Rick also looked grim. "He and I are meeting later, by the way."

"Is that wise?" Meg wanted to know.

"He said he had some more information he could tell me about the Old Families, which could assist in my investigation," Rick said. "We'll be meeting at the *Balance of Flour Pizzeria* near where I'm staying. Apparently, it's owned by his dad."

"What time?" Ray asked.

"Around six."

"Good. Ethan should be off by then, and the two of us can be there to provide backup in case things go south."

"We'll be meeting in the back room, so we can talk in private," Rick said. "And how is it that you could get off work, but Ethan couldn't?"

"I'm the SAIC here," Ray reminded him. "And my wife's just gotten into town. It's only natural that I would take a couple of days off in order to show her around." He glanced back. "I don't know if I like you meeting this Officer Scofield in private. Island Affairs has a lot of the local police force in its pocket."

Rick's brow furrowed. "You think it could be a trap of some sort?"

"Maybe, maybe not." Ray thought for a minute. "Ethan and I'll be there, regardless. If you'll consent to wearing a wire, then we can still help out if needed."

Rick thought about it, then nodded. "If that's what you think we should do, then we'll do it."

"Good." Ray leaned back in the driver's seat, looking relieved.

Meg glanced between them. "Well, now that that's been settled, how 'bout you boys treat me to some lunch?"

They looked at her, and her husband grinned. "I think we can handle that. What d'ya think, Rick? Want to try *Those Crazy Quesos?*"

Chapter Fourteen: Revealing Secrets

5:47 pm, Just Outside of the Mid-Lake Inn

Rick stepped out into the warm, humid evening air just as a light drizzle began to fall. He almost frowned as he began to walk over to the Sellars Island Market, which was just a couple of dozen feet away.

The weather was a near-perfect reflection of the day's events. It had gone from sunny and somewhat promising to gray and bewildering, then frustrating, and finally dark, rainy, and possibly worrisome.

He sighed, hunching his shoulders in a vain effort to keep the falling drops of water from making their way down his neck and back. Ray and Meg had driven him back to his hotel room sometime after lunch, with Meg dropping them off. Ray had intended to help Rick go over what little they had as they waited for Ethan to join them.

Instead, they had found themselves a new mystery. While Rick had been out, someone had managed to sneak into his room. That by itself might not have been strange, as hotels in general could be subject to thieves and the like, and out-of-town visitors always seemed to be favorite targets.

This particular occurrence, however, was bizarre because it seemed nothing had been taken. Instead, something had been *left*.

Rick could still feel the surprise that had lanced through him at the discovery of the file that had been sitting on his bed. He could still see, in his mind's eye, the shock that had caused Ray's mouth to fall open. The plain Manila folder, thick with papers and with a crudely drawn eye on it, had all but begged for their attention, and after a few minutes of debate, they'd given in.

The astonishment they'd felt after opening the folder exceeded everything else they'd felt up to that point. Inside had been copies—*so many* copies—of paperwork from a local law office. On the surface, they seemed to be random, detailing various things that neither Rick nor Ray had any idea about.

It wasn't until they had read through everything that they had found several small, but essential, links that appeared to connect the DBJF Alliance Corporation's Board Members to none other than the murders of Sulivan's Old Families.

The absolute disbelief that Rick and Ray had felt upon making the connections had been shared by Ethan when he'd joined them just after four o'clock. Just the *idea* that the DBJF's Board could have been involved flabbergasted each of them. It had taken the better part of forty-five minutes for them to at least attempt to come to terms with it all before the questions had started. Where had the folder and its files come from? Why had it shown up so unexpectedly in Rick's hotel room? Was it a warning? Or did someone want him, and by extension Ray and Ethan, to investigate further?

None of them yet knew. To be honest, none of them had a clue as to how to proceed.

All of which made Rick's upcoming meeting with Alan Scofield a welcome distraction despite the worries surrounding it. Right now, Ethan and Ray were both watching Rick from his room at the Inn, listening in via the device they had fitted him with. The private investigator could only hope the rain didn't complicate things. If he needed help and couldn't speak, and they couldn't see his signal, he would be in some *significant* trouble.

Well, they wouldn't be able to see him after he crossed over the *Balance of Flour Pizzeria's* threshold, either. With luck, the rain would remain a drizzle, too.

The Sellars Island Market wasn't strictly a large strip mall. Still, as Rick had noted back when he had first arrived, it had just about everything the hotels themselves couldn't provide, including the pizza place. Soon, if all went as planned, Rick knew he would have not only a slice or two of hopefully good pizza but also information regarding the islands and, hopefully, one Robert William Henry Nicholas Alastor Kincaid.

Ethan's voice grumbled from the tiny earpiece that was in Rick's left ear. "You've got no idea how badly I want a couple o' slices."

Rick almost smiled. "Be good, and maybe I'll pick you and Ray up a large pie. No one should question me bringing back a pizza, especially if this place is as good as the two of you say it is."

"I'm always good," Ethan said. "So I'll be holdin' you to that."

"Your ex-wives might have to disagree 'bout you being good," Ray could be heard to say. "But I want pizza, too, and I *was* the one who made sure you got your concealed carry permit here, Rick."

"Then I'll make sure to bring back one large pie, half with extra cheese and hamburger, the other half with pepperoni and garlic," Rick promised. "I'm almost there now, in fact."

"So we can see," Ethan acknowledged. "Be careful, Rick."

"You know it."

Having reached the edge of the sidewalk beside the *Packin' Meat* delicatessen, Rick stepped up and gave silent thanks for the oversized awning that stretched out over his head. Yes, he still needed to walk down to where the pizzeria happened to be, but at least now he would be out of

314

the drizzling rain.

Of course, first, he needed to get past the *Crash and Burn Bar*. As luck would have it, two men in dark gray leather vests happened to exit just as Rick walked past. He and one of the two almost collided.

"Yo!" The one Rick had almost hit spat at him. "You almost spilled my beer!"

Rick held up his hands in an apologetic gesture, eyes raking over the two. The one he'd almost walked into proved to be tall and muscular, with light brown skin and a multitude of tattoos. The other had darker skin and was shorter and broader. They both looked drunk already, yet were carrying open bottles of beer. *Excellent—the last thing I need is more attention, thanks to two drunken idiots.*

"Careful, Rick," Ray's quiet voice said. "The tall one's known as Ti or Tiago, which is short for Santiago. Last name is Torres. He's originally from Mexico. The other one goes by Zev. He's a local boy, full name Zevulun Darby. They're both Iron Horde."

Iron Horde? Ah. Rick held in a sigh. Of *course,* he would run into members of Sulivan's biker gang.

"Sorry, guys," he said. "I didn't see you."

"You hear dat, Ti?" Zev said. "He didn't *see* you."

The newly named 'Ti' snorted and spat on the ground. "Maybe you should be watchin' where you're goin', *ese.* Or maybe someone should teach you, eh?"

The man reached into his biker's cut. Rick took a step back, his instinct driving him to go for the gun he carried.

"I'm not looking for trouble," he said. "And I don't think you are, either."

'Ti' upended his beer, pouring the rest of the liquid on the ground where Rick had been standing just the previous moment. "Maybe trouble's lookin' for you."

Before he could do more, his companion spotted Rick's firearm. One hand shot out to stop 'Ti' from stepping forward.

"He's gotta piece, bro," Zev said. "He's heat."

Heat? Rick glanced at him before realizing what he'd meant. *Oh, for heaven's sake. One look, and they peg me to be a cop. Wonderful.*

Ti squinted at him, beginning to smile in anticipation. "That's even better. I don't suck to the bulls. We gonna make this donut-swillin' piggy disappear and—"

"Get outta there, Rick," Ethan's voice hissed in his ear.

No shit. Rick shook his head, drawing on some of the things his father-in-law had once taught him. *Time to sell a story.*

"I'm no cop," he said, lowering his voice and adding a dangerous tinge to it. "I have a *different* sort of employer."

"Not heat?" Zev sounded incredulous, even as he ignored Ti's growl. "But you packin', man. If you ain't heat, then—" He rubbed the tip of his nose as he thought. His eyes went wide a moment later. "Forget it, bro. Valente don't want no static with the dagos."

Ti growled again but subsided a little when Zev glanced at him. Still, he leaned in. "Your time comin', *ese.* We gonna take you to class, and I'll be lookin' for ya *personally.*"

"C'mon, Ti. No static, 'member?" Zev shook his head as Ti stepped forward to give Rick's shoulder a hard butt before heading over to the parking lot. "Watch yer back. Even the dagos won't be able to stop everythin'."

316

Rick inclined his head, watching as Zev went to join the other. Only when they'd climbed onto their bikes, laughing at something that was no doubt at his expense, did he let loose a relieved breath. He could hear Ethan and Ray doing the same.

"Good job, Rick," Ethan said. "Not even members of the Horde want to mess around with what they think is an out-of-town hitter for the Pasquale."

It wasn't precisely the tale Rick had aimed to sell, but that didn't matter. All he cared about was the fact, "It worked."

"That it did," Ray said. "Like Ethan said, good job."

"Thanks." Rick drew in a deep breath, held it a moment, then released it. "Time to go and get some pizza."

He heard the other two chuckle in his ear before heading to the *Balance of Flour*. A middle-aged yet muscular-looking man with reddish-brown hair and blue eyes greeted him as he walked in.

"Good evening, sir, and welcome to the *Balance of Flour*," the man said. "Will you be eating in tonight?"

"I'm meeting someone here," Rick said, smiling at the other's pleasant demeanor. "So, yes."

"Oh?" The man inclined his head, eyeing him for a moment or two, then lowering his voice. "Rick Thorne?"

"Yes?" Rick eyed him in sudden suspicion and was surprised at the other's nod.

"Oskar Scofield," the man introduced himself. Nervousness now tinged his words. "Alan's my son." He grabbed one of the multitude of menus that were next to him. "If you'll please follow me?"

Rick nodded, wondering at the other's sudden and apparent

jittery state. He followed, regardless, intending to ask Alan during their meeting.

The back room proved quiet and was decorated in a faux-Tuscan theme. There were a few tables and chairs, most of which were empty.

Only two chairs at the center-most table were occupied. Rick recognized Alan and smiled, though he was puzzled by the woman sitting next to him. He was even more surprised by the number of Manila folders stacked on the table.

The younger man grinned back at him. "Oh, good! You're here! See, Dad? I told you he'd show up!"

"I have," Rick said, taking the seat that was directly across from Alan and taking the menu Oskar offered him. "I know I said I wanted some information, but you seem to have gone above and beyond."

Alan offered up a slight shrug, glancing at the woman. She was a pretty enough lady, with dark brown hair and green eyes. She had almost the same nose as Alan did, as well as the same chin and forehead, leading Rick to conclude that the two were related.

She, in turn, eyed Rick. Her expression proved difficult to read, while her gaze never wavered as she studied him.

Alan continued. "We figured that you'd need to learn as much as possible about the actual situation here in Sulivan, so that if you *do* find the one you've come for, you'll be able to protect him better."

"I still don't think this is wise," Oskar interjected, worry and disapproval written over his face. "I know what you said he told you, Alan, but—"

The lady raised a hand, and Oskar fell silent. Her posture conveyed authority. "We need help to deal with this, Oskar. You know that

318

as well as I do, and I, for one, am tired of constantly looking over my shoulder."

Rick's eyebrows rose. Oskar glanced at him. "Amelia, do we really need to be having this sort of discussion with an *outsider?*"

"Island Affairs used outsiders to hurt and nearly eliminate the Old Families," the newly named Amelia said with a hint of bitterness sliding into her tone. "Mister Thorne's reputation is a good one, at least according to the information we've been able to collect."

"*Outside* of the Mids, he may be." Oskar crossed his powerful arms. "But here? *In* the Mids?"

"Sometimes we have to take a chance," Amelia said and flashed an unexpected, impish smile. "Didn't I take one with you?"

"That was different," Oskar grumbled. "My family had been here for generations. We weren't Old Family, but we knew enough to know which side to take." He glanced again at Rick, then refocused on Amelia. "And if you're wrong?"

"I know." Her voice became soft. "It's not just me that'll pay the price. However..." She nodded to Rick. "He *is* here. We should at least give him the chance to prove himself."

"Amelia."

"No, Oskar." She shook her head. "We've had this discussion before, and my mind is made up."

Oskar held her gaze for one, two, three, even four heartbeats before sighing in defeat. "On your own head be it, then, if he proves less than worthy of the reputation Alan says he has. I'll be back in a few minutes for Mister Thorne's order."

He stalked from the room. Rick looked quizzically at Alan and the lady. Alan shrugged while Amelia shook her head and offered him a small smile.

"Oskar can be a bit overprotective," she said. "Especially of his wife and his children."

Rick blinked, leaning back in his chair as surprise swam through him. *His wife and children?* "You and him? And Alan?"

"Alan's our oldest," Amelia said, shifting her smile to her son. "He's also the one who researched you."

"The Deputy Chief *did* say I was a fan," Alan said, lifting up one of the folders and opening it to show Rick the various newspaper clippings that highlighted some of Rick's own cases. "And he wasn't kidding. Between a couple of computer-literate friends, a good VPN, and the internet, there are few things Island Affairs can conceal about the outside world anymore." The smile disappeared, and his expression became tired. "Not that most of the people here care about the world outside of the Mids."

"Why not?" Rick wanted to know.

"Island Affairs may not be able to control everything," Alan told him. "But they're doing a good job of trying. That and most of the people of the Mids don't really care what happens beyond our borders, so long as it doesn't affect them."

"Isolationists?"

"To a degree," Amelia confirmed. "Being isolated kept the Mids safe for centuries, and many people still think it will, despite all of the evidence to the contrary."

"Including your husband?" Rick probed.

She hesitated, but Alan nodded. "Among other reasons. If Dad

320

sees that we can, in fact, trust you, then maybe we'll be able to tell you *every*thing, not just what we're planning on for tonight."

"Smart people," Ethan murmured in Rick's ear as the private investigator nodded his agreement.

"Understandable," Rick said. "Where do we begin?"

"You figure out what you want and order it," Alan told him. "After that, we can get down to business."

Less than ten minutes later, Rick had placed an order for two slices of Margherita pizza. Giving back the menu, he looked back at Alan and his mother, opening his mouth to ask his next question. Amelia cut him off before the first words could leave his lips.

"Do you wish to enjoy your meal first, Mister Thorne?" she asked. "While I know from the newspaper articles and things I've read that you're made of stern stuff, the *true* story behind the magistrates of the Mid-Superior Island Cities is quite grim."

Rick thought back to the documents, binders, and notebooks he had taken from the safety deposit box in Pennsylvania, as well as what Ray, Ethan, and Meg had told him, and then considered the folder left in his hotel room. He didn't—couldn't—doubt Amelia's words.

But, as she had pointed out, he wasn't precisely a wilting violet. Few things could be said to throw him off his feed, too, no matter how horrible they might be.

"Worst case scenario is that I end up taking what I ordered back to my room at the hotel," he said. "If what you tell me helps me to unite a father with his previously unknown son, I'll stomach it."

Amelia studied him a few moments longer before nodding. "Very well. If it helps Robbie, then I have little choice."

Robbie? Rick inclined his head at her. "Did you know my client's son?"

"He was born a few months after my Alan here," she said. The faintest smile ghosted over her lips as she glanced at her son. "They grew up together, went to school together, and even played together as boys." The would-be smile vanished. "Katherine and I were also friends."

"Do you know what happened to her?" Rick asked softly.

"The official explanation was a home robbery gone wrong," she said. "Of course, that didn't explain Robbie's disappearance, which is why their explanation was never accepted."

"Understandable." Rick eyed her. "What is the *un*official explanation, the one that most people believe?"

"That Katherine got too close to certain truths, and the ones who don't wish those truths to be known killed her," Amelia said. "They also most likely took her son."

"Do *you* believe that?"

"To be honest?" Amelia studied him again. Her face clouded. "Yes. I *know* it's true, just like I know it's my fault that she's dead and Robbie went missing."

"Mom." Alan laid a gentle hand on his mother's arm, watching as Rick rocked back in his seat. "You couldn't have known how she'd put that information you gave her to use or what would happen afterward."

"Oh, yes, I did," Amelia said, shaking her head. "I knew why she came back to Sulivan, and I also knew how she wouldn't rest until she'd brought everything to light." A small, quiet sigh escaped her. "Katherine had always been the brave one, and I knew *exactly* what she would do with everything I told her."

322

Alan looked ready to object to his mother's words. Rick interrupted before he could begin.

"What did you tell her?" he wanted to know.

Amelia sighed again. "About the reality of who is *really* in charge of the Mids."

Rick frowned. "What do you mean?"

She hesitated long enough for Rick's order to arrive. Oskar still did not look pleased by his continued presence, even as he placed the two slices of pizza in front of the private investigator. He stepped back from the table but didn't leave right away, his eyes flickering from his wife and son and back to Rick.

Rick, for his part, decided to utilize the silence and lifted one of the slices to his mouth. Taking a bite, his eyes widened as the flavors danced upon his tongue. He hadn't, to be completely honest, expected much. Having had authentic New York pizza and the famed Chicago Deep-Dish pie, Rick knew quality pizza.

Balance of Flour had, in his mind, just taken first prize. He looked up at Oskar with admiration.

"This," he said, holding the bitten slice, "is *amazing.*"

"Well, it seems we can at least trust your taste buds." Oskar's wintry look thawed just a little, even as he caught his wife's expression. "Amelia? Are you all right?"

"I will be," she said, smiling at her husband through shadowed eyes. He eyed her, nodded after a moment, and left the room. Amelia refocused on Rick. "Most people throughout the Mids believe that the Department of Mid-Western Island Affairs is to blame for everything, that they are the source of all the evils that plague our islands. They are the

323

outsiders, after all, and therefore, they *must* be the reason behind every bad thing that has happened since their arrival." Amelia took a deep breath. "The truth is a bit more complex. Most aren't ready to hear it. You may be an outsider, as my husband says, but with your history?" She tapped the folder that held the newspaper clippings covering Rick's career. "It indicates you would not only hear us out but believe us."

"I'm more than willing to listen," Rick told her. "Especially if what you have to say can help lead me to my client's son."

"I hope so. I'll have to ask that you bear with me, as I'll need to go through a bit of my personal history first." Amelia's eyes took on a faraway gleam. "After I graduated high school, I chose to go to Mid-Lake University and pursue a business degree. At the time, I thought only of rising high in the Mids' Corporate World, which the DBJF Alliance dominates. They like to present themselves as trying to be neutral, as though they are doing their best to stave off Island Affairs' interference. I believed that at the time, and when I was in my junior year at the university, I accepted an internship that would have fast-tracked me into their junior executive levels. It was a very coveted spot, and I counted myself as fortunate to have gotten it. Only twenty-three others received it as well, out of over fifteen hundred applications."

"Very selective," Rick said.

"It was." Amelia nodded once more. "But not for the reasons you might think. Yes, they wanted the best and the brightest, but they also had another criterion that few can meet."

Again, she hesitated. Rick didn't pressure her, choosing instead to let her take her time and tell her story in her own way. At the same time, he couldn't help but wonder what that 'other' criteria Amelia had

324

mentioned happened to be.

Finally, his patience was rewarded. "The others who had applied to be fast-tracked were accepted into a slightly different program. They would be able to start in slightly higher-than-entry-level positions and rise with hard work. Despite what the DBJF's people might tell them, however, they would not and will never rise beyond the position of Vice President. Not unless they marry in a selective fashion."

"Selective fashion?" Rick asked, not understanding.

Alan glanced at his mother before asking, "What do you know about the Old Families?"

"Only that they founded the Mid-Superior Island Cities and Towns, used to have power, but were either killed or died off," Rick said. "Oh, and that Katherine Kincaid and her son were considered Old Family. Most of the information I received came from the City of Sulivan Crime Museum. I went to the library but couldn't find anything more about them."

"That's not surprising," Alan said and tapped the other folders that were on the table. "The Sulivan Library sponsors the official narrative. Anything else has either been cleansed or removed from public consumption." He offered Rick a slight smile. "I'm not sure if you'd find anything at the Records Office, either. The Department of Mid-Western Island Affairs and the DBJF both seem determined to erase the memory of the Old Families from recent Mid-Superior Island history."

Rick arched his eyebrows. "Oh?"

Alan glanced again at his mother. She bit her lower lip but nodded. Slowly, he pushed one of the stacks of files forward.

"These contain the full histories of each of the Old Families," he said. "Including their fates and any remaining survivors that we know about. One of the things you'll notice is that three Old Families are not only still around but thriving: the DuBois, the Jourdain, and the Fowler."

"Why would—" Rick cut himself off in sudden realization. "The DBJF?"

"Yes. Those particular Old Families are the founders of the DBJF Alliance Corporation," Amelia said. "They were never considered the best of the Old Families, but that no longer matters to most people. The fact is that they *are* all still Old Families, and that wins them both clout and influence. It is the benefit of the doubt in the eyes of most of the local people. With the fall of the other Old Families, the DuBois, the Jourdain, and the Fowler have all become the leaders in Mid-Superior Island Society. Their words carry *weight*. More than most realize, in fact." Her lips thinned. "The Department of Mid-Western Island Affairs could not have accomplished even half of what it has without their backing."

Rick leaned back in his seat, connecting the dots. He wasn't the only one. In his ear, he could hear Ethan's low whistle of realization.

"Why, though?" Ray wanted to know. "Why would the DBJF turn on the other Old Families?"

"Power," Amelia said when Rick passed along the question. "The DuBois, the Jourdain, and the Fowler families were always hungry for more power, more money, and more influence. Island Affairs made use of that and helped them to secure all three. In return, they push much of what Island Affairs wants to do." Her lips pressed together, and she inhaled deeply. "They participated in the destruction of the other Old Families and now use the power their company holds to root out the last remnants. Those who do not fall in line?" She hesitated for a moment before

326

continuing, as if not saying it would make it less real. "They're taken care of."

"You know this for a fact?" Rick asked.

"I do." Amelia's look hardened, and her dark look had all the intensity of a spear in the gut. "This information goes no further than this room. Understood?"

Rick blinked but nodded, feeling only the slightest guilt in lying. Ethan and Ray were two he trusted with his life, but Amelia couldn't know that. Under other circumstances, Rick might have said something to clue her in that the two were listening in. Still, he didn't want to take the risk of not having information that could help him find Robert William Henry Nicholas Alastor Kincaid.

That internship program I told you about?" Amelia said at last. "It was open *only* to members of the Old Families."

Rick blinked, trying hard to ignore the faint gasps he heard in his ear. "Are you saying—"

"That I am Old Family?" Amelia nodded. "Yes. I was born one of the LeRoux, Mister Thorne. That was why the DBJF chose me for the internship program I told you about. *Only* those who are Old Family or married into Old Family will ever be part of the DBJF's Board of Directors."

Alan's head whipped over. "You never told me that part!"

"There was no reason to," she said, giving her son an apologetic smile. "When you first began discussing career options, you made no secret that you wanted nothing to do with the corporate world. Out of all my children, only your sister has ever thought about going down that path, but she wants to take over the restaurant one day, not run the DBJF." She looked back at Rick. "I was never so relieved as I was on the day my youngest told me he wanted to fix and restore cars, boats, and planes, not be in a boardroom."

He gave her a small smile. "I hear that. I wish I could get my three to understand I don't want them anywhere near my line of work."

"You don't want your kids to follow in your footsteps?" Alan sounded incredulous.

"No," Rick said. "I don't. Given everything I've seen and experienced both as a detective and as a private investigator?" He shook his head. "I'd prefer for my children to keep some of their innocence, if at all possible."

"Understandable," Amelia said. "Oskar and I would've preferred all of ours wanting to work here forever, but Alan made it clear he wanted to follow in the footsteps of his uncle, Oskar's brother." Another shadow passed over her face. "And despite all of the warnings that Lukas gave him."

"Many of my fellow officers are on the take," Alan said when Rick looked to him for an explanation. "Between Island Affairs, the DBJF, and the gangs, the few good cops there are just aren't enough. I know for a fact that both the Chief and the Deputy Chief are two of those good ones, and they're doing their best by the rest of us, but they need to step carefully. *Very* carefully."

"As do we," Amelia said. "The official reason I chose to drop out of the internship program is that I burned out. The *real* reason is a class that I took. It's mandatory for everyone in that particular internship, and it's more about *indoctrination* than *education."* Her expression became dark, troubled. "The DBJF's board aspires to nothing less than royalty. They present the other Old Families, with few exceptions, as being weak-

328

minded fools. They fully believe that they are meant to *rule* the Mid-Superior Islands. If the Department of Mid-Western Island Affairs ever outlives its perceived usefulness, the DBJF will turn on it. They've helped to direct any number of events within the Mids, and they did all but celebrate their tactics in that class." Her lips became a thin, white line. "They also made it clear that the goals their Board of Directors has supersede everything else. Even Family loyalty is no match when compared to what they want to accomplish."

"You told all of this to Katherine Kincaid?" Rick asked.

"I went into excruciating detail about everything I had learned," Amelia said, her voice soft with old grief and regret. "I *knew* Katherine, after all. We'd grown up together, gone to the same schools, and were friends with the same people. Once I told her what I knew and, more importantly, what I suspected..."

Her voice had trailed off. Rick inclined his head. "What was it?"

Amelia breathed out a sigh before admitting, "That the DBJF was the *real* perpetrator behind the drive-by that took the lives of Katherine's father, mother, and brothers. *Not* Island Affairs, as so many people believe."

"Holy *shit*." Ray's voice breathed in Rick's ear. "If it were the DBJF instead of Island Affairs, then it's no wonder that nothing was done. Almost no one wants to go up against *them*."

"Why?" Rick wanted to know. "What made you believe that?"

Amelia hesitated again, but only for a moment. "Katherine's father, Robert, was the Deputy Chief of Police at the time of his death. It was known that he was investigating the links between the Pasquale Family and Island Affairs. What *isn't* known is that he discovered a powerful

329

connection between the DBJF and the DIA. The last time I spoke to Katherine, she said she'd found what her father had and had sent it on to the two people she trusted most." Amelia grimaced. "Not even a week later, she was dead, and Robbie was missing."

Damn. Rick took a deep breath. "You believe that, in order to find my client's son, I'll need to lock horns with the DBJF?"

"It's a very real possibility," Amelia said. "I do not doubt that the DBJF and Island Affairs both have every reason to be afraid of whatever Robbie might know." She touched her hair. "There's a reason I've dyed my hair, Mister Thorne, and wear colored contacts. Amelia LeRoux supposedly died a number of years ago in childbirth. Oskar is reputedly married now to *Amalia Rojas.*" She offered up a sad smile. "We're lucky that only Alan took after me in his looks."

Rick blinked, then smiled his own sad understanding. "I'll do my best to be careful, I promise you. Is there anything else you can tell me? In regard to the possible whereabouts of my client's son? Do you suspect him to be in the DBJF's custody or that of Island Affairs?"

"It's possible, but I can almost guarantee you he's not." Alan shook his head.

Rick did his best to look puzzled. "What do you mean?"

Another stack of files was passed over. Alan explained, "Robbie Kincaid is distinctive in his looks. I know that he and I look a lot alike, and there are a few other people within the Mids' territories who could pass as him. I've put together a few dossiers of the people who could pass as him here in Sulivan. There are only two who could be a true match, in my opinion, at least, and not including myself. One is Zedekiah Thomas. He works over at Veil-Tech Securities. He's the right height, has the right look,

330

and is around the right age. If he's Robbie, then I have no doubt he'd be undercover or something to get to the truth behind what happened to his mother and the rest of her family. As to the other?"

He hesitated. Rick could easily guess why.

"I've been to the crime museum," he said quietly. "I assume you're speaking of Liam Alastor?"

Alan nodded, looking both relieved and unhappy with the idea. "Yes. The files I have on him are the official ones; they are the only ones I could get my hands on. There's rumored to be quite a few more, but only the Chief and the Deputy Chief are said to have access. If Liam Alastor *is* Robbie Kincaid—"

"He had to have come back for revenge," Amelia said, her voice a whisper. "While I understand it, I'd prefer that he live. The DBJF doesn't play nice with those they believe are their enemies, and neither does Island Affairs. If your client truly is Robbie's father, then maybe he can somehow spirit him away from here."

Rick heard the heartbreak in her voice. He kept his own voice quiet as a result and put as much sincerity into it as he could. "I'll do my best to confirm his identity, and if it's possible, I'll arrange to have him taken to safety."

Amelia offered him the ghost of a smile. "I would appreciate that."

They conversed some more as Rick ate the rest of his pizza, then ordered the large pie he'd promised to Ethan and Ray. Alan offered to escort him out of the restaurant when, at last, the time came for Rick to head back to his hotel room.

"There's something else," he said as they left the back room, his voice too quiet for anyone else to hear.

"Oh?" Rick looked over as they walked.

Alan glanced around, then pulled out another file. "You thought Valente looked familiar, so I thought I'd bring you a copy of his police file. It might jog your memory in regard to him."

Rick took the offered manila envelope with his right hand, balancing the carry-out pizza box and the other files on his left. "I can't promise I'll take a look at it right away, but I'll definitely check it out."

"Finding Robbie comes first." Alan nodded. "I get it."

"I appreciate the effort, though," Rick said. "And I'll fill you in if and when I figure it out."

"Thanks." Alan grinned at him, then looked over his shoulder at his father's call. "I gotta get back. I'll talk to you again?"

"Give me a call," Rick told him. "Any time."

Alan flashed him a thumbs-up. A moment later, once again alone, Rick stepped back outside. The rain had stopped falling, and he let out a deep breath.

"Ray," he muttered as he began the walk back to the Inn. "Ethan? I think we're going to have a lot to talk about between Island Affairs and the DBJF."

"Yeah," Ethan muttered back. "No shit."

Chapter Fifteen: "I Know What You Did"

Late Evening, Harold Edmund Holloway's Office

Law Offices Targeted!

No longer content with scientists and their labs, the mysterious Ghost is now targeting lawyers. The law offices of Chamberlain, Ainsworth, and Shearer were broken into late on the night of May 28. While nothing has been reported taken, many files were apparently reviewed. The law firm has several big-name clients, including the DBJF Alliance Corporation and the estate of the late Lionel Quentin, who went missing five years ago. Our readers may recall that The Ghost targeted the DBJF's headquarters just days ago. While it is likely that this latest activity by The Ghost is related, there is still a small measure of doubt.

Before going into corporate law, Dexter Ainsworth worked as a Prosecutor. Not only does he still maintain ties with several of his former colleagues, but he was also responsible for the prosecution of several former gang members, including members of the Arch Street Angels. With Temujin Lance's trial on the horizon, one cannot help but speculate if a former Angel or two aren't responsible, at least in part, for The Ghost's activities...

Harold smiled as he read the rest of the would-be article. It was near-perfect, in his opinion, keeping The Ghost a mystery while planting the seeds of suspicion in people's minds. When the news of Alastor's escape was at last released, people would be more likely to jump to the conclusion that Harold wanted them to reach.

He leaned back in his seat at last and turned his smile on the author. Summer Lambert, the Media Relations Officer for the Department of Mid-Western Island Affairs, smiled back.

"Well?" she said, her hazel eyes reflecting confidence but also a hint of worry. While she had faith in her ability to spin a story, she was still young and sometimes second-guessed herself. "Does it pass muster?"

"It does."

Harold nodded, his smile widening at Summer's pleased expression. She was a pretty young woman, just twenty-five years old, and eager to rise in their world. With her strawberry blond hair, model-like looks, clever and intelligent mind, sharkish nature, and willing attitude, she had all the hallmarks of a future star. If she hadn't already accepted the sponsorship of Archibald Woodford, one of the executive producers at Channel 3, Harold might have attempted to cultivate a relationship with her himself.

Especially since she reminded him so much of Katherine Kincaid, both physically and intellectually. Summer even happened to be a polyglot, as Katherine had been, and she had a similar sort of fire.

Unlike Katherine, however, Summer was always willing to play proverbial ball. So long as it advanced her in the eyes of her peers, she would do whatever—and whoever—it took.

"Are there any edits you'd like me to pass along?" Summer asked, her tone carrying just the slightest hint of honey.

"No." Harold shook his head, stifling the desire he felt stirring within him. While he might have enjoyed Summer's company in a less-than-professional way, the last thing he wanted was to offend Archibald Woodford. The man was too rich and too powerful, at least for the moment. "You can send it along to your media contacts."

"Excellent." Summer took the article back when Harold slid it back over. "Is there anything else you'd like to discuss?"

He ignored her flirtatious hint. "Not at the moment, no. Thank you, Summer."

"Of course."

She rose from her seat and sashayed towards the door, making sure to put a little extra swing to her hips. Harold permitted himself a brief moment of fantasy, one involving Summer and himself, before his phone ringing recaptured his attention.

Grabbing the handset, he barked, "Holloway."

"It's Fleischmann, sir," Brandon Fleischmann said. "I'm at the Sellars Island Market. Rick Thorne just left the *Balance of Flour Pizzeria*."

"I'm not exactly interested in what he's eating," Holloway said, irritated that anyone would call to give him such mundane information.

"I know you're not, sir," Brandon told him. "However, just before he left, we spotted him talking to a young man that Mister Driar recognized as a police officer who is currently assigned to police headquarters."

Holloway sat up in his seat. Rick Thone had met a police officer who worked at the Sulivan PD's headquarters. The same office where Ben Baas worked?

A knot of fear formed in the pit of Harold's stomach as he asked, "What did they discuss?"

"Unknown at the moment, sir," Brandon said. "But Thorne was handed a file before he left. He added it to what looked like several others."

Fear turned to terror as Harold considered the information Rick Thorne could now have in his possession. "Do we know what these files contain?"

"Not yet, sir," Brandon said. "Thorne seemed eager to get back to his hotel room, though, no doubt to share whatever he received with Plumber and Douglas."

"Plumber?" Harold's left hand balled into a fist. His right hand tightened on the phone's handset. "*And* Douglas? They're both there?"

"Yes, sir," Brandon confirmed it. "Douglas came back with Thorne after Thorne had gone to Police Headquarters this morning. Agent Plumber arrived about a couple of hours before Thorne went to the pizza place. They did not accompany Thorne to the restaurant but remained inside the hotel. Thorne brought them back a large pizza, but he was at that particular *Balance of Flour* for almost three hours. It does *not* take that long to get a single pizza, no matter where it's ordered."

"No." Harold did his best to swallow back his trepidation. "It does not." His mind began to race. "Did anyone else show up?"

"No, sir."

Not that it mattered if no one else had appeared in the physical sense. Thanks to phones and other communication methods, it was more than possible that Baas or Akiyama had still talked with Thorne, Douglas, and Plumber. Depending on what was in the files that Thorne now had, Harold knew he could be in for a world of proverbial hurt if he didn't find a way to retrieve whatever information Thorne had been given.

Brandon's voice in his ear derailed that train of thought, at least for the moment. "The only thing of note that I'd like to add is that Thorne had an encounter with a pair from the Iron Horde. Again, I'm not sure what was said, but the bikers looked ready to brawl until Thorne showed them his weapon."

Harold's ears pricked. "He's carrying?"

"It seems so, sir."

The corners of Harold's lips curled upward in a sudden, small, satisfied smile. Thorne no doubt had a concealed carry permit, but it wouldn't be legal here, in the Mid-Superior Islands. Harold had used other, similar minor things to have people brought in for a 'chat'. What better excuse could there be to have Thorne brought to him so that Harold could find out the reason for the private investigator's visit to the Mids? Just as soon as he verified there was no permit in the system, Harold would order Brandon to pick Thorne up and bring him to the office.

Except that there *was* paperwork on file. Harold felt his smile vanish when he saw the order for a temporary concealed carry permit that had been signed by none other than Raymond Douglas. His expression became thunderous with anger.

"*Damn* it," he snarled under his breath.

"Sir?" Brandon's voice held a tremor.

"He has a temporary permit," Harold growled. "Signed for by SAIC Douglas." He sighed, mind turning over the rest of the information that Brandon had given him. "Which Iron Horde members did Thorne run into?"

"I believe they were Santiago Torres and Zevulun Darby," Brandon said.

"Hmm."

Harold thought a moment. He didn't know Darby, but he had heard of Torres. The man had come up from Mexico and was known to be a nasty piece of work who hated all forms of legal authority. He had been feared even by the cartels and wouldn't hesitate to kill a cop, an FBI agent, or even an officer from Island Affairs.

But there *were* a few he wouldn't tangle with if he didn't need to do so. Harold knew one, thanks to some of Island Affairs' connections.

"I need to make a call," he said at last. "Keep watch on Thorne and stay by the phone if it's possible."

"Yes, sir."

As soon as he heard the dial tone, Harold punched in the number he knew. One, two, three rings later, he heard a quiet, masculine voice.

"Palladino."

"Isidoro," Harold greeted the other. "How are things?"

"Mister Harolds." Isidoro Palladino had a note of surprise in his voice as he used Harold's alias to greet him. "It has been some time since we last spoke."

"And I apologize for that," Harold said. "Business concerns have kept me busy."

"Understandable," Isidoro said. "May I ask if this is business, as well? Or merely social?"

"Business, I'm afraid," Harold said. "A man has recently arrived in Sulivan and had a run-in with two members of the Iron Horde this evening."

"The Iron Horde, you say?" Isidoro said. "Perhaps two members in particular?"

Harold blinked. "Yes. Santiago Torres and Zevulun Darby."

"You calling about this is interesting," Isidoro said. "I got off the phone not three minutes ago with Mister Valente. Two of his people apparently had some words with a man they mistakenly believed to be an out-of-town contractor for some friends of mine. I, of course, corrected them, as my friends have no need at the moment for someone like that.

338

Perhaps the Pharaohs or the Lords would, but not us." A questioning note entered his tone. "Was I mistaken in assuming this? Is he one of yours?"

"He is not one of mine, any more than he's one of yours, one of the Pharaohs or one of the Lords," Harold told him, his voice darkening. "His name is Rick Thorne. He's a private investigator from Philadelphia, in town supposedly on a case."

"Interesting. I don't suppose you know what Mister Thorne's case would entail?"

"No. He's refused so far to divulge that information. However, he has been seen quite frequently with SAIC Douglas and Agent Plumber. Earlier today, he was also at Police Headquarters."

Isidoro's voice became a venomous hiss. "Baas?"

"I have no proof, but I suspect he may have met with our Deputy Chief," Harold told him, smirking. Isidoro held a definite grudge against Sulivan's Deputy Chief of Police, not only thanks to what Ben Baas had done against the Pasquale Family during his time undercover with the Arch Street Angels, but to Isidoro himself. "What would they have discussed? Again, I have no proof, but I have my suspicions."

Silence fell and lasted for a single pair of heartbeats. Isidoro Palladino had never been a fool, Harold knew, and he knew the other man would soon reach the same suppositions that Harold himself had.

"You believe," Isidoro said, quiet and confident. "That this Mister Thorne has been brought in to help root out the connections between your Department and my friends?"

"Among other things," Harold said. "There has to be a reason as to why he would be met at the airport when he arrived by both Plumber and Douglas. As you most likely know, I believe the two of *them* to have been planted by their director."

"Would you like for some of my, shall we say, friends, to have a chat with this Mister Thorne?"

"Not yet," Harold said. "I'd like instead for you to utilize some of your contacts. Find out as much as you can from your end about why he's here."

"An easy feat to accomplish. Consider it done." Isidoro paused. "And if we discover what you believe, we will?"

"Well." Harold smiled. He knew his expression, if he could have seen a reflection of it, would have proven unpleasant. "It wouldn't be the first time something unfortunate befell a visitor to this city. If it so happens that Deputy Chief Baas were to be caught in the crossfire..."

Harold let the unfinished thought speak for itself. He was rewarded when he heard the quiet, malicious chuckle that escaped Isidoro. Most likely, he was now imagining the worst sort of fates for Ben Baas.

"It would be *such* a shame," Isidoro said after a few moments. "If something like that were to happen."

Harold's smile widened. If Isidoro and his *friends* were able to remove two proverbial thorns together, instead of one at a time, from his and his department's side, then he could switch more business back over to them. Island Affairs had once dealt with them exclusively before certain events curtailed the relationship. Perhaps, though, if they accomplished what Harold wanted now, then one day soon, Isidoro and those he called his friends would again be the sole outside arm of Island Affairs' will.

"I'll keep in touch," he said.

"As will we, Mister Harolds."

340

Hanging up the phone, Harold leaned back in his chair. He felt the beginnings of a good mood stir within him, and his smile grew warmer and more genuine.

Of course, it couldn't last. A tiny *ding* from Harold's computer captured his attention. Harold reached for the keyboard, expecting a notification of some incoming report.

Instead, he found a notification that the *Project Enigma* blog had been updated. His eyebrows rose. He had followed the blog to stay current with what its author dared to say, so that when Island Affairs at last managed to shut it down, they would be able to prevent it from starting back up or another similar blog from taking its place.

He never expected to read now what he did now.

```
Project Enigma
Post # 353
Written by The Haunted


Title: For the Birds?


One of the places I love visiting in the city
of Sulivan is pretty little Arlette Island.
It's a relaxing place, one right off the
northern coast of West Sulivan, near
Fisherman's Wharf, Little Norway, and
Morwill Beach and Amusement Park. It's a
little slice of nature next to the city, a
haven for all sorts of wildlife, and a
beautiful place to visit.
However, there are a few things about Arlette
Island that are strange. No, for once, I'm
not talking about the weird little tales of
beasts and beings that have popped up on that
```

Island Sanctuary. Instead, I'm talking about
money.
Not that long ago, when I revisited the
island, I discovered a portion that had been
essentially roped off. While it's away from
the main hiking areas and off the proverbial
beaten path, it's still close enough to
reach. Many people would no doubt love to
visit this area for its wildlife and
previously unexplored trails. Unfortunately,
they're not able to, as the area is closed
for 'construction.'

Harold felt the first stirring of dread. Arlette Island wasn't just a
pretty piece of wilderness that had been kept pristine. The place held a few
secrets, ones that couldn't or shouldn't be leaked. Whomever the blog's
author was, he or she was stepping into worrisome territory.

Again.

I, of course, was curious and decided to
explore it. It's an easy enough thing to slip
past some ropes and signs. I thought I'd find
some decking if the area proved to be more
marshland or perhaps materials for an
overlook or two, given how close the area is
to the little hill they like to call Mount
Eliraz.
Instead, I found nothing.
Yes, you read that right. I found nothing
except more wilderness, a few seagulls, and
some rocks. There was no sign of any
construction anywhere or of any other human
presence. Yet, it's been like this,
according to a few of my acquaintances, for

more than a decade.

So, what was going on? Why should this area of Arlette be closed off if nothing is happening there? It piqued my curiosity, and I decided to look into it further.

The whole of Arlette Island is maintained and preserved by the Arlette Island Wildlife Fund. People from all over the Mid-Superior Islands donate to it, as do various businesses. These funds help support the Arlette Island Nature Center, the walkways and overlooks, the wilderness, the beaches, and Mount Eliraz itself. They also fund wildlife education programs, a small rehabilitation center for injured or ill animals, and similar activities. It's a noble cause, and millions of dollars are raised each year.

Not all the money, however, is put towards the above, nor does it go to the workers. Most of it, in fact, doesn't. I discovered this when I began to look a little deeper.

One of the most significant contributors to the Arlette Island Wildlife Fund is OrenLi, Incorporated. On paper, this is a small technology firm. In reality? OrenLi, Incorporated doesn't seem to exist. Neither does SybFile, LLC, nor Kydain, Co., nor do three other supposed firms that contribute. They each hold thousands, if not millions, of dollars in their accounts, but…

The blood drained from Harold's face as he continued to read. He knew the companies the blog mentioned, as they were, in fact, shell companies for the DBJF Alliance. For 'The Haunted' to have as much

343

information about them as he or she did was troubling at best, and could prove destructive at the worst.

Memory stirred, and Harold grabbed at the reports he had on The Ghost's latest activities, concentrating on the raid on the DBJF's headquarters and the more recent attack on Chamberlain, Ainsworth, and Shearer. Among the data stolen from the DBJF were the names of a few of the shell companies the DBJF Alliance Board of Directors regularly used. When Harold considered what those companies helped fund, beyond the various charities the DBJF used as tax write-offs, he couldn't help but reach for the phone again.

If Liam Alastor did happen to be The Ghost, it was now beyond urgent that they found him. They couldn't afford for him to remain free.

He intended to call his brother-in-law and tell him to give the Board a heads-up. He may have even requested a meeting to go over everything with them, fill them in on his suspicions, and come up with a solution.

Instead, just as his fingers reached the telephone, it rang.

Harold froze. He wasn't expecting anyone to call.

Taking a deep breath, he picked it up as it rang once more and barked, "Holloway."

"I know what you did. I've *got* you, you fucker."

Chapter Sixteen: Panic Button

Late Evening, Harold Edmund Holloway's Office

Harold felt sudden terror course through him, leaving him frozen in his seat. *Who in the hell?!*

The question screamed at him. Alarm bells began to ring loudly within his mind, all but drowning out the fierce pumping of his heart. His eyes shot back up to the screen. His breath quickened.

No, he thought in desperation, wondering who was on the phone with him. *There's no way. He can't know.* How *does he know?*

"What's the matter, Harry?" The voice taunted him after the silence began to stretch out into the second-longest minute of Harold's life. It would never match the first, of course, but The Wall had seen to that. Harold swallowed hard as the voice continued, "Cat got your tongue?"

Again, who—wait. Harold stopped before he could truly panic and forced himself to take a deep breath. The effort, though small, allowed him to regain some semblance of composure and clear his mind enough to recognize the speaker on the other end. The bitter taste in his mouth sharpened while dread began to churn the acid in his stomach.

"Baas." He hissed the name with as much hatred as he could muster, wishing he could reach out through the phone line to throttle the other. "What are you talking about?"

Ben Baas chuckled, the sound ominous on the other end of the line. Most of the time, whenever Ben and Harold needed to speak, Ben's tone would hold a strained quality, as though Sulivan's Deputy Chief of Police had to struggle in order to manage even the most basic, polite nonsense. Now, though?

The churning in Harold's stomach became worse. Red flags began to wave in his mind. Ben Baas was many things, he knew, but the Deputy Chief never sounded so *happy,* not unless he had reason. He'd never once, in all of Harold's experience in dealing with him, been so confident, either.

So what had changed? What reason could Ben have to sound as he did now? And just what did he mean by saying he *knew* what Harold had done?

"You've been a naughty boy, Harry," Ben told him, the smile he no doubt wore evident in his voice. "A *very* naughty boy, and now? I *know.* I have *all* the evidence I need."

Harold's eyes once again slid up to what his monitor displayed, then dropped down to the files on his desk. They stopped at the report on The Ghost's last-known strike and what was taken. He felt the blood drain from his face as the pieces started to click together.

Oh, shit. Baas knows. He freaking *knows!* Harold almost screamed at him in denial before forcing himself to take another deep breath. *No. He* suspects. *If he knew,* truly *knew, he wouldn't be bothering to make this call. He'd be* here, *arresting you.*

Struggling to make himself sound both bored and confused, Harold spoke. "I have no idea what you're talking about, Baas. I'm sure you think I do, but I don't. Whatever this is about, you don't have a leg to stand on."

Another chuckle came from the man on the other end. Ben sounded all too pleased with himself, and the sound grated. "Oh, that's where you're wrong, Harry-boy. You thought you could hide it. Hell, knowing you, you probably thought you'd hidden it so well that no one

346

would ever be able to find it. I did, though. I've got the evidence sitting right here in my hands, and I'm going to use it to bring your smug ass *down.*"

Harold felt the bubbling in his stomach escalate, and he needed to swallow back the bile that wanted to rise. Dots were connecting at a furious pace in his mind. The hand not holding the phone snapped back to the computer's keyboard, tapping at the keys to flash through some of the previous entries in the *Project Enigma* blog. Mentions of Arlette Island were replaced by speculations regarding the ties between the DBJF Alliance Corporation, the Department of Mid-Western Island Affairs, the Pasquale Crime Family, and more. There were mentions of various murders, of people going missing, and...

His eyes stopped abruptly on one entry. Post Number 342 listed several examples. Still, the one that grabbed and held his attention was none other than the murder of Katherine Kincaid and the disappearance of her son, Robert. Worse, it contained a kernel of information that had *never* been made public: the security cameras Katherine had installed had been tampered with, rendering whatever footage they'd captured unusable.

Oh, hell. Harold had the sinking feeling that Ben wasn't joking around this time. He needed to get off the phone, do more research, and see if what he feared proved to be true.

Gritting his teeth, he tried to make himself sound more bemused and annoyed instead of afraid. "Of course, Baas. You may enjoy whatever little victory you think you have, but remember that, sooner or later, you could find yourself in a tough position."

Even to his own ears, Harold's voice sounded more flat and sterile

347

than anything else. Ben, of course, picked up on that.

"Sounds like I've touched a nerve." Ben seemed positively giddy at the thought. "No worries, *Harry*. I'm sure we'll be talking again soon. *Real* soon."

The *click* of the other's phone being hung up would have normally caused Harold to snarl into the mouthpiece, but not this time. Instead, he slammed his own handset down and grabbed a nearby notebook. With pencil in hand, he set about raking through the blog in front of him.

Almost three hours later, he put the pencil down. His hands were shaking. Nearly every single blog entry contained sensitive information. A good many contained information that could only have been gotten from a scientist or a computer at the DBJF.

Again, Harold's eyes flashed, this time skittering over to the blog author's tag. *The Haunted.* Was that more than a simple pseudonym? Perhaps it could be a clue to who was feeding the author information. Or even an indication of the author's actual identity?

His lips thinned. His brow furrowed. A ghost would haunt a person, or people, or places. The Ghost had broken into scientists' homes and laboratories, as well as the DBJF's headquarters and their lawyers' main office. The Haunted had obtained information that could only have come from The Ghost or the police. Who did Harold know who would have the skills to operate as The Ghost did? Who did Harold know who happened to have connections with at least one high-ranked member of the City of Sulivan Police Force? Who would have the utter audacity to dangle everything right underneath Harold's nose while making it next to impossible for the people Harold had working for him to find anything definitive about that person's identity? And *who* might have been able to escape suspicion until very recently?

The knife of realization stabbed into his brain. Harold felt understanding begin to burn within him. Dread became terror.

There was precisely one man Harold could think of that matched each of the points raised by those questions. One man, and one man only.

Liam Alastor.

Harold almost cursed. It *had* to be him. Liam Alastor *had* to be The Ghost.

Shooting up from his seat, almost toppling the chair in the process, Harold began to pace his office. The experiments Regina and her team conducted on the young man calling himself Liam Alastor had been forcibly discontinued just over ten months before. Ben Baas had been named Alastor's guardian immediately after. The Ghost had shown up just eight months ago. The Haunted had started publishing around that time as well.

Fuck! Harold screamed silently, hands curling into fists. No doubt Alastor had woken up not long after the experiments had ceased and had taken the barest amount of time necessary to recover before taking up The Ghost's mantle. *Damn it all! He's been escaping from the prison for the past eight months at* least, *then passing along whatever evidence he acquired to Baas, who had to be* covering *for him! Shit, shit, shit!*

No wonder Ben had sounded so confident just now. He had what he needed to put not only Harold away but a good portion of the Department of Mid-Western Island Affairs and the DBJF's higher-ups into prison alongside him. Hell, for all Harold knew, Ben had enough to implicate Harold's *own* boss.

Nathaniel would be furious when he found out. He might go so far as to demote Harold or even worse—put Harold's head on a very literal pike.

Unless, of course, Harold could fix it. He would need to do that as soon as possible, too, to make sure everything was taken care of before Nathaniel returned from D.C.

But how?

He blew out a breath, coming to a standstill in the center of his office, right in front of his desk. He needed to think. He needed to *plan*.

Stalking back around his desk, Harold dropped back down into his chair. First, he'd outline all of the evidence and highlight each connection. He would list each possible question and seek an opening to reel in Alastor and expose Ben Baas as the actual criminal.

It was slow, methodical work. Worse, Harold soon realized there was almost nothing he could put to his advantage. With Alastor trapped in a supposed coma, the idiot warden hadn't positioned any guards in and around the hospital. Doctor Kim might have been a good candidate to question, but when Harold called the warden to set up a meeting, he was informed that she had already left.

"Understandable that she would need the time off, all things considered," Harold repeated, mimicking the warden after hanging up the phone in disgust. "How stupid can the man be? If the doctor was telling the truth about everything, then maybe I could see it, but if that was the case, then how in the hell did she not notice that Alastor's muscles weren't atrophied?"

The words of his sister came back to him. *A first-year medical student would know, as would any full-fledged doctor.*

350

Doctor Kim had known, then. She must have. She had known, aided, and abetted Alastor's recovery, as had the doctors before her, and then continued to help him in his actions as The Ghost.

And I let her slip away. Harold wanted to scream. He wanted to wring the warden's neck for letting her go before Harold could interrogate her.

But that wasn't the worst of it. No, Harold reserved *that* for the still-missing maintenance worker.

He growled, then reached into his desk for the relevant file. Harold had been right to be suspicious about Miguel Hidalgo Costillo's file. After setting some of his people to dig a little deeper, it was discovered that Miguel Costillo didn't exist. Not as the young man who had been working at the prison, at least. There *were* people named Miguel Costillo, including an eighteenth-century Catholic priest who was considered the father of Mexican Independence. Still, none of them had lived in Sulivan. The aunt and uncle did not exist at all, and the address given? It belonged to the old Santa Caterina Catholic Church, which was deep in the Barrio District of Sulivan.

So, who was Miguel Hidalgo Costillo in reality? No one seemed to know, and the young man himself had yet to be found, let alone made to answer.

The lack of actual, proper vetting made Harold angry. He wanted heads to roll over it, and he had ordered another investigation to find out just what, exactly, had gone wrong and where.

He leaned back in his chair, his right hand coming up to massage his forehead. Things were spinning out of control, unraveling before his eyes. Ever since Rick Thorne had shown up in Sulivan, it had been like this.

He slammed on the mental brakes. Thorne had visited Police Headquarters earlier that day, then had met with a police officer that evening. He'd been given at least one file before disappearing back to his hotel room to confer with SAIC Douglas and Agent Plumber.

And now Ben Baas dared to call and taunt Harold, saying he *knew!?* That he had *evidence?*

It had to be connected. All of it!

Harold drew in another deep and shuddering breath. He couldn't, he thought, waste time by offering Thorne a deal that the private investigator would undoubtedly reject despite what Nathaniel had said. He needed to be taken care of quickly and in a far more permanent manner, along with Ben Baas. Harold could then ensure that any evidence they had was disposed of properly so it could never be used again.

The question became how.

Drumming the fingers of his right hand against the top of his desk, Harold began to think. Dealing with Rick Thorne and Ben Baas separately wouldn't be easy. Granted, Harold could use Rick's newness to the city against him. As Harold had already said, it wouldn't be the first time something bad happened to a visitor. Granted, Rick hadn't survived as long as he had without reason, even during his dances with a few of the operatives who had worked for Harold's superiors. Still, he was a newcomer to Sulivan's shores.

That, in Harold's mind, made the private investigator vulnerable. Still, it would be best to be cautious, given Rick Thorne's record and reputation.

It was too bad he couldn't say the same thing about Benjamin Benedict Baas. Ben knew all too well how Harold and the rest of Island

352

Affairs operated. He'd spent enough time in Sulivan to learn to be on his guard, to be cognizant of his surroundings at all times. He'd survived and even thrived during his time undercover. He'd danced with the likes of Isidoro Palladino and others, and had come out on top. He had survived any number of other attempts on his life, too, before being elevated to the position of Deputy Chief of Police. He had the backing of his Chief and others, like William Andrew Wolfe-Wall.

Granted, Harold no longer had to worry about The Wall, but the others would do whatever they could to protect Ben. Bringing him down would never be easy. Eliminating him? It would be near-impossible.

Unless, of course, he had help.

A slow smile appeared without warning on Harold's face. Yes, he could go after Rick and Ben separately. He would probably succeed in having Rick removed from Sulivan's board. Still, he knew from bitter experience that whoever he sent against Ben would almost certainly fall and serve to put Ben even more on guard than he already happened to be.

But what if they were *together* when someone came to deal with them?

"Hmm."

Harold leaned forward, steepling his fingers in front of him as he considered the possibility. As he'd told Isidoro, it would be *such* a shame if Ben happened to get caught in some crossfire by someone attempting to take out Rick. But was that actually the answer? Would it, in fact, be easier to remove both of these two proverbial thorns in Harold's side at the same time?

His smile began to widen. It would take some planning, to be sure, but the *possibilities!*

Harold reached for the phone once more. He had some people to contact and plans to make. If everything worked out the way he believed it would, then it would be a mere matter of days before Liam Alastor would become his *only* problem.

ᑌᔑ ᑌᔑ ᑌᔑ ᑌᔑ ᐱᑎᒪᔑ ᛣᖽᗰ ᐸᕼᒪᗰ ᔑ ᐅᔑ ᐅᔑ ᐅᔑ ᐅᔑ

Police Headquarters:

Ben Baas grinned as he put the phone's handset down. He had heard the tension, the worry, even a hint of fear in Harold Edmund Holloway's voice before Ben ended their call. There could be no question that Ben had scored a few proverbial hits, given how rattled Harold had sounded.

Despite his best attempts to sound unconcerned. Someone else might have been fooled, but Ben had known Harold for a long time. He'd studied the Supervisor of the City of Sulivan, too, in the hopes of one day bringing Harold to justice.

Well, with luck, he had unnerved the other enough for Harold to make a stupid move or two. If that happened, then maybe Ben would be able to add to the case he was putting together, and perhaps, just perhaps, he'd be able to fulfill a promise he'd once made some years ago.

His smile faded as he reached for the pair of files that were in front of him. As much as Ben wanted to bring Harold Edmund Holloway down, to put him in the prison cell where he belonged, he hated what the man had done to give Ben the opening he now had to do so.

Pushing away from his desk, Ben stood up. With the two files in hand, he left his office to visit with the Chief.

A few steps later, he knocked on Akiyama's door and waited for acknowledgment, as the Chief had requested he do after the events of that morning. Much to Ben's relief, Akiyama did not waste time by making him wait.

"Enter."

"It's me, Chief," Ben said, stepping inside and pausing just long enough to give the two women in the room another, more friendly smile. The closer of the two proved to be short and curvaceous, with long dark hair that reached almost to her waist and blue-green eyes that, at the moment, were shadowed with weary fear. The other was taller and leaner, with shoulder-length ash blond hair and sapphire eyes that sparked with protective anger, even as she smiled back. "I've got the files you wanted."

"Good." Akiyama's voice held a distinct edge of fatigue as he took the files from Ben's hand. "Have a seat." He looked over at the brunette. "I'm thankful, Miss Rhys, that you decided to listen to Mrs. Harvey."

Lydia Rhys offered him a tremulous smile. Her expression was, again, one of fear. People who stood up to Harold Edmund Holloway tended to have their lives cut short, and Lydia knew the stakes better than almost anyone else. She had been forced to walk away from her job as Harold Holloway's assistant due to his predatory actions. She had nearly lost her home, her family, a majority of her friends, and more as a result.

Despite all of this, there remained a spark of fire in her blue-green eyes. Ben suspected that spark would transform into a blaze of righteous fury if the young lady were ever given enough reason.

He sneaked a glance at Adeline. She was his cousin—second cousin, to be more precise—and Ben suspected that she might have given

Lydia that reason. She had been one of the very few who had stood at Lydia's side, had sat with her when Lydia had been at her lowest, and had coaxed Lydia's story from her before propelling Lydia into visiting Ben and then Akiyama.

Now, faced with not just Adeline's encouragement but Akiyama's and Ben's, Lydia found that she could speak. "I am, too. As Addie pointed out, if I allowed him to get away with what he did to me, it would let him do it to others. I can*not* permit that." She swallowed. "No matter what it might cost me."

"We shall do our absolute best to make certain it does not cost you more than it already has," Akiyama told her in a gentle voice. "We will also do what we can to make sure he has no more opportunities to do as he did." He glanced at Adeline. "I understand that she is staying with you, Mrs. Harvey?"

"Yes." Adeline nodded, her tone matter-of-fact. She had rarely suffered much in the way of foolishness before the death of her husband. After what had happened to him, she had become even less inclined to do so. "And you already know where I live."

"I do." Akiyama nodded back. "Ben will be escorting both of you there just as soon as he and I finish with this paperwork. In the meantime, while you're waiting, why don't you take Miss Rhys and yourself to the cafeteria? I know the food there isn't the best and, to be honest, our coffee is abysmal, but at least they'll tide you over until you're home."

"Yes, sir." Adeline stood, recognizing the dismissal. "C'mon, Lyddie. Let's see what they have. We'll see you in a few, Ben."

Ben nodded, keeping the pleasant smile plastered on his face until after the two had left. As soon as the door closed behind them, his

356

expression dissolved into something more complex. His tone became angrier.

"She's the *third,*" he spat out. "At least accordin' to those files, Chief. Who knows how many others there might have been, too, who *didn't* come forward."

"We can't do anything about the ones who chose not to come to us, Ben," Akiyama reminded him quietly, even as the corners of his lips turned downward. "Who handled the two before Miss Rhys?"

"McDuff." Ben's eyes smoldered with granite-colored fire. "And, funnily enough, both ladies who previously came forward met with rather convenient accidents shortly after makin' their statements. The one who lived refused to cooperate afterward."

A low, angry growl escaped Akiyama's throat. "That will *not* happen this time with Miss Rhys."

"We can hope," Ben said. "But you know as well as I do what'll happen if McDuff hears about this. Same for the others whom we suspect are on Island Affairs' payroll."

Akiyama's lips became a thin, disgusted line. Ben watched as his left hand curled into a fist before the Chief reached for a nearby stress ball and all but squeezed the life out of it.

"Seal the file," he ordered, dark eyes snapping. "Again, I will *not* allow something like that to happen."

"And neither will I," Ben agreed, his lips twisting into a wintry smile. "Not to her and not to Addie."

There was something in his tone that caused Akiyama to look at him. "What do you mean by that, Benjamin?"

Ben lifted his right shoulder in a half-shrug. "I figured that if

357

Holloway wants a target, it should be me."

Akiyama closed his eyes for a moment, cursing in Japanese before demanding, "What did you do?"

"Made a call."

"Please tell me you don't mean that in the literal sense."

"I'd be lying, then." Ben saw the look Akiyama gave him. "I want him to make a mistake, Chief. Holloway's arrogant. He likes to think he's smarter and better than almost everyone else. Stoke his temper, though, and he gets stupid." Ben stood. "I want him to be stupid."

Akiyama sighed. He couldn't disagree with Ben's words or his stated reason. He knew just as well, if not better, than Ben about what Harold Edmund Holloway would do to an enemy.

It was why he feared for Ben's safety. The Department of Mid-Western Island Affairs had the reputation it did for a *reason*. Too many of those who had stood against it had ended up either dead or missing. Akiyama had no desire to see Benjamin Benedict Baas confined to a slab down in the Police Department Morgue or be posted alongside several others in Missing Persons.

Harold Holloway, on the other hand, would no doubt do everything he could to ensure one of these outcomes would happen. He disliked yet tolerated Akiyama, but it was no secret that Harold Edmund Holloway *despised* Ben Baas. If Holloway believed that Ben had something that could be used against him, then chances were good he'd stop at nothing to remove the information or Ben from the planet.

After a moment, Akiyama breathed out a sigh. While not ideal, Ben did have one good point to continue his scheme. It would be far better if Harold Holloway went after Ben than someone like Lydia Rhys.

Still, he needed Ben to make a couple of concessions first before he could give even the tentative approval. "Please do me two favors, Benjamin, if you decide to continue with this insanity. First, make sure Mrs. Harvey knows it was *you* who came up with this idea, not me. I have no desire to be on the receiving end of her anger, should anything happen to you."

Ben winced but inclined his head in assent. "I can do that. What's the other favor?"

"Be careful." Akiyama saw his Deputy Chief's expression. "A frightened animal can be just as dangerous as an injured one when it's backed into a corner, Benjamin. I do not wish to have to find a new Deputy Chief any time soon."

Ben almost grinned. "Oh, c'mon, Chief. What's the worst he might do?"

"Do you really wish for me to answer that?"

"Not particularly. No."

Despite his words, Ben remained unrepentant. Akiyama leaned back in his seat, eyes spearing the other man where he stood, and sighed once more when Ben's expression stayed unchanged.

"I do not like this," he said at last. "I, in fact, almost wish that Mrs. Harvey had brought Miss Rhys in next week instead of this one."

Ben blinked. "Why?"

"Because then I would be able to assign you a protective detail, and no one would raise an eyebrow at it."

"Again," Ben said. "Why?"

"Temujin Alaric Lance." Akiyama saw Ben wince again and inclined his head. "Or perhaps I should use Mister Alastor's escape as a reason to assign you one right now."

"That hasn't been leaked to the press, Chief."

"No. Not yet, it hasn't," Akiyama said, then pointed to the door. "Go, Benjamin. Take your cousin and her friend home. Just please be careful. Holloway will not take your call lightly, and you're not bulletproof."

"I know," Ben said. "But better men than him have tried to take me out and failed."

"There's always a first time, though, Benjamin. Remember that, and please. Again, be on your guard."

Chapter Seventeen: Finger on the Trigger

May 30, 2007: At the City Records Office

Rick couldn't remember feeling so frustrated in all of his life. He had spent the whole of his morning at the City of Sulivan's Records Office, searching for something, *anything*, that he might call helpful. Despite what Alan Scofield and his mother had told him, Rick still expected to find, at the very least, birth certificates, marriage licenses, and death certificates for various Old Family members on file.

Instead, he had found nothing. Absolutely and literally *nothing*.

It should have been impossible. A record or two going missing wasn't unheard of, but entire collections? *That* was the sort of thing that only happened in certain disasters, such as fires or floods. Yet, the officer he'd spoken with earlier had taken pride in telling him that such events had never taken place in this section of the city.

So then why couldn't Rick find anything? He didn't, couldn't, understand it. Shouldn't there have been at least a *hint* of someone's existence? One Old Family Member's life?

For not the first time, he gave thanks for having met Alan Scofield and, through him, Amelia LeRoux. If not for them, Rick wouldn't have had anything at all.

It *should* have been impossible, he knew. Rick knew for a fact that Robert William Henry Nicholas Alastor Kincaid had existed. He had a copy of the birth certificate to prove it, alongside photographs, letters, various mementos, and more, all courtesy of William Wolfe-Wall.

And yet, according to the City Records Office, no one by that name or any similar name had existed in the past century. It was as if Katherine Kincaid's son and father had both been erased, as had Katherine herself and so many other Old Family members.

It was the reason he approached the Records Officer at the desk. She was a young and pretty woman who had greeted him with a smile when he'd first appeared.

"Have you found what you're looking for, sir?" she asked as Rick again approached.

"Unfortunately, no," he said. "But maybe I'm not looking in the right places. Would you be able to help?"

"I can try," she said. "Give me the name of the person you're looking to get records for."

"Kincaid," Rick told her, deciding to start with the reason he'd come to Sulivan. "Robert Kincaid."

The moment the name left his mouth, he saw her freeze. Her smile fled. "I'm afraid I can't help you, sir."

Rick blinked, not so much at the speediness of her reply but the faint hint of fear he heard. "Ma'am?"

She shook her head. "I can*not* help you, sir. Not with that name."

"Okay." Rick frowned. "What about—"

"I can't. Sir, *please.*"

"Is there a problem here?"

Another Records Officer appeared. Rick almost stared at him in disbelief. He was tall, broad with muscles on muscles, and had a face that reminded Rick of a very unhappy pit bull.

"No problems," Rick said. "I'm simply trying to find information and was hoping she could help me discover what I'm looking for."

362

"I'll deal with him, Linda," the pit bull said. The moment she fled, he turned back to Rick. "What sort of information did ya need?"

"Robert Kincaid," Rick said. "He would have been—"

"There's no one by that name in the Records here."

Rick frowned, taken aback once more. "You haven't even looked."

"I don't need to," the man said. "You're done here."

"Excuse—"

"You. Are. Done." The man glowered at Rick from his superior height. "You can either leave on your own, or I'll help you."

The threat was clear. It made Rick's blood boil, but he had no desire to create a scene. That would help no one.

"Fine," he bit out. "I'll go."

"I'll see you out."

Just a few moments later, Rick was being walked down the steps of the Records Building. The pit-bull gave him what would have looked like a smile, if not for the vicious twist it had.

"Word of advice," he said. "Don't keep lookin' into this. You won't have a happy ending if you do."

"Right."

Rick glared, watching as the man turned and climbed back up the steps. Anger at being stonewalled warred with the incredulity of having been threatened over wanting to look at documents belonging to Robert Kincaid. Alan's words from the previous evening, about how those in charge seemed determined to wipe out the memories of the Old Families, came back to him.

"You weren't kidding me, kid," Rick muttered and sighed. "So, where do I go from here?"

Blowing out a breath, Rick glanced down at his watch. *Almost noon. All right. I'll get lunch and go from there.*

Glancing about, he saw a *Packin' Meat* deli just down and across the street. Soon enough, Rick was sitting at a table. The tray he carried held a turkey club sandwich, seasoned fries, and a medium soda. Still, he barely tasted any of what he ate or drank, being too focused on what he had been learning.

Along with Ray and Ethan, Rick had spent much of the previous night going through the files Amelia had given to him. He'd made several pages of notes, as well as compiled the list of names he'd attempted to plug in at the Records Office. While the Records Office apparently had nothing on any Old Family past the 1950s, apart from the DuBois, the Fowler, and the Jourdain, Amelia's files had given names, occupations, birth and death dates, and more.

Much more, including the fates of a good majority of various Old Family members. Just as Ray and Ethan had told him, there had been drive-by shootings, a few execution-style assassinations, at least three different car explosions, and one *house* that had been blown up. Amelia's files had added to that tally, revealing a few 'accidental' poisonings, apparent muggings and robberies that had 'gone wrong', and other Old Family members who had simply disappeared.

There was also one name that caught Rick's immediate attention, alongside Ray and Ethan. Michael Roi had been the founder and leader of the Arch Street Angels for almost nine years before. He had led his gang throughout their rise. His death, following their takeover of Sulivan's underworld, had preceded the Angels' fall. According to the exhibit at the Crime Museum, the Angels' former leader was killed in a supposed escape

364

attempt.

What the Crime Museum *hadn't* revealed was that Michael Roi had been Michael *Sullivan*-Roi. His mother had been the last daughter of the Sullivan Old Family.

"Which brings the whole official narrative into question," Rick muttered to himself. "What better or easier way could there be to get rid of a potential problem? I've never been into conspiracy theories or anything like them, but in a case like this one?"

How did official records and documents vanish from a City Records Office without either a disaster taking place or the collusion of government officials? Rick had the sinking suspicion that they didn't. How was he to prove it?

And what about Michael Sullivan-Roi, Liam Alastor, and the Arch Street Angels? *If* Liam Alastor turned out to be Robbie Kincaid, why had he joined the Angels? Amelia had believed it was for revenge—for himself and his mother. Rick didn't like it, but he thought he could understand it. But why had Sullivan-Roi started the gang? Had he felt as though he had no other choice? Did the fact that he happened to be a member of an Old Family play into the Arch Street Angels' rise to power? Was that why all records containing his full name had been, at the least, hidden?

Rick didn't know. Not yet. How he could find out was, for the moment, uncertain.

Think, Thorne, he told himself. *You're supposed to be an investigator. The Records Office was a bust, so there is no question about that. Where else can you go to find more information, maybe? What's something that the Powers in Sulivan might have overlooked?*

He thought about it as he continued to eat. The obvious answer came as he finished the last bite. He had already visited the Sulivan City Library once to learn as much about this place as possible. Whatever Aaron Plumber hadn't covered in his tours, he had tried to find out. Libraries usually had collections of old newspapers, too.

Bingo. Rick smiled. *Let's see what that can teach me.*

Leaving the deli behind, he set off for the library. As it happened to be only two streets away and the weather was beautiful, Rick opted to walk.

He felt eyes on him the entire way. *You'd think this Department of Mid-Western Island Affairs would have better things for its officers to do than to continue to follow me.*

But apparently not. Rick sighed, eyes glancing at the windows in the various storefronts he passed, trying to catch a glimpse of them. He recognized two of his followers almost as soon as he saw them. Ed Driar had been watching him since he'd taken the tour, along with Marcus Brannigan. Rick didn't know who the blond woman now following him happened to be, but the fact that she *was* following him told him everything he needed to know.

Let 'em follow. Rick shook his head, feeling a small wave of anger rippling through his mind. *I'm only going to the library to look through some old newspapers. It's not like I'll be giving 'em anything to be alarmed about.*

He didn't think so, at least.

Less than half an hour later, armed with several reels of microfilm, Rick sat down at a reader and began his search. Since Robbie Kincaid had been born in the last week or so of 1982, he started with the newspapers of

366

that time.

To his minor frustration, he noticed that none of the papers contained a birth announcement section. Granted, most newspapers had discontinued issuing birth announcements back in the late 1990s, but in the early '80s?

He inclined his head in thought. Perhaps, he reasoned with himself, the city of Sulivan, and maybe the other Mids, had discontinued the practice much earlier due to the many children who had gone missing. Could not announcing a birth have been seen as a way to protect the newborn?

It seemed a satisfactory answer, one Rick could accept. The lack of obituaries proved harder to explain away. Still, again, Rick attributed the lack of death notices to people not wanting to be reminded of how many people were supposedly dying.

Not finding engagement or marriage announcements proved harder to rationalize. Discovering that there wasn't even a single article on the murder or suspicious death of even one Old Family member?

Rick's lips drew into a thin, angry line. Between the lack of official files at the Records Office and now newspaper articles detailing the events that Amelia had described, there could be little doubt that either Amelia was making everything up or the Department of Mid-Western Island Affairs, likely in conjunction with the DBJF Alliance Corporation, was actively covering things up. He didn't want to believe either one, but at this point, he felt as though he had little choice. When he remembered what his father-in-law had collected, as well as what Victor's letter had said, and then put it all together with what Amelia and Alan, Ray and Ethan had told him, Rick knew which scenario he was more inclined to believe, regardless of how far-fetched it might have seemed.

But how can we find even the smallest kernel of information if both official records and newspaper articles aren't helpful? Rick racked his brain, trying to think.

A page from the scrapbook he'd found in the safety deposit records ghosted through his brain. There had been a cut-out article there about a boys' soccer game, with a brief note about a ten-year-old Robbie Kincaid making the winning goal. Rick's eyebrows rose at the idea, but he took the chance.

It took him close to half an hour to find it. Buried all the way in the back of the *Mid-Lake Gazette*'s Local News section, the article recounted the junior league soccer game and the winning shot of one Robbie Kincaid, the son of Katherine Kincaid. Rick felt a broad smile spread over his lips.

"Gotcha," he murmured. "Let's see what else I can now find."

A small collection soon began to form. An award ceremony honoring Katherine Kincaid's father was discovered on page 16 of a 1978 copy of the *Sulivan Times*. There was a brief article recounting the charity work being done by Katherine Kincaid, in league with Amelia LeRoux and three other ladies—an Olivia McIntire, a Constance Sinclair, and a Maxine Martin—which was buried in the back of another *Mid-Lake Gazette*. Another small article recounted the results of a school science fair in which Robbie Kincaid had placed third.

There were a few others, all at last corroborating the existence of a few of the Old Families. They were all small but also just the sort of things that would be missed by those looking to erase someone from more official records. Rick printed them out, then turned to finding articles about the

368

Arch Street Angels.

Those were easy to find. Rick didn't bother to print out the articles. Instead, he concentrated on photographs of Liam Alastor, selecting those that clearly showed the young man's face. If Liam Alastor *was* Robbie Kincaid, Rick would hopefully be able to determine it. He knew that Chris Zeal, whenever the man wasn't working on their cases, was developing more advanced facial recognition software. Perhaps Rick could ask Chris to use his program to try to find out whether the boy in the newspaper articles, together with the boy in the painting Rick had found in the safety deposit box, was, in fact, the same person as the young man labeled 'Liam Alastor.' Yes, it was a long shot, but what if it worked?

At last, gathering up the printouts, Rick stood. It was getting close to five o'clock, and Rick planned to meet with Ray and Ethan one more time before Ethan took everything to Pennsylvania to show Victor. Rick had wanted to do that himself, but didn't think he could take the chance of being denied re-entry. Ray was the SAIC, and he didn't believe he could take the time off yet. Meg offered to do it, but would need to wait another two days to avoid conflicting with her class schedule. Ethan, on the other hand, could make an excuse to call out and board a plane. They wouldn't be able to deny him re-entry, either, not without risking suspicion.

Going up to the front desk, he paid for his printouts, then stepped outside to summon the taxi that would take him over to Ray's apartment. He never noticed one of his watchers splitting off from the others and going over to speak to the librarian who had accepted Rick's money.

ᑲᏽ ᑲᏽ ᑲᏽ ᑲᏽ ᒐᏕᑎ ᖿᏒᎷ ᖿᒐᏒᎷᎷᏕᒐ ᒐᒐᖮᒐᑎᎢᏒᖿᏞᎷᎷ ᗷᏕ ᗷᏕ ᗷᏕ ᗷᏕ

Harold Holloway rubbed his eyes as he finished the final report of the day. It had been a long day for him, between the regular running of the Sulivan Office of Island Affairs, coordinating various upcoming events with a few out-of-office contacts, and waiting for the people he had watching Rick Thorne to call in. He found himself looking forward to heading back to his penthouse apartment, where he could take a long, hot soak in the special jacuzzi tub he had installed before turning on the television to indulge in one of the sitcoms he favored since they made him laugh and could make him forget the problems of the day for an hour or two.

He reached down, intending to shut his computer off for the night. The phone rang before he could. Harold's head snapped over to it, and he didn't hesitate to reach over.

"Holloway."

"It's Fleischmann, sir."

"What do you have for me?"

"Thorne spent the entirety of the morning at the Records Office. He was escorted out around noon."

"Escorted out?"

"Yes, sir. Apparently, he was getting frustrated due to not finding what he'd gone there for."

"And that would be?"

"Information, sir." Brandon seemed to hesitate. "About Robert Kincaid and several other Old Family members."

Kincaid? The Old Families? Harold felt the blood drain from his face. It seemed as if all his worst fears, barring one, were coming true. While The Wall would never bother him again, the same could not be said about the man's grandson or allies.

Could this week get any worse? He bemoaned silently. *First, Thorne shows up in Sulivan. Then, Alastor manages to get free. Baas calls to tell me he knows and has evidence. Now, Thorne shows up at the Records Office, trying to find information on the Old Families.*

At least there was nothing for him to find. Harold had made sure of that long ago at the behest of his predecessor, Patrick Beringer.

Brandon, however, wasn't done with his report. "He went to the Packin' Meat deli that's near the Records Office for lunch. We kept an eye out to make sure he wasn't meeting with anyone, and he didn't. However, as soon as he'd finished his lunch, Thorne went to the library again."

Harold frowned, struggling to keep his panic from reaching the surface. "Why?"

"The same reason he went to the Records Office, sir," Brandon told him. "He again tried finding something on the Old Families."

"Ah."

The panic receded just enough for Harold to shake his head. There would be nothing at the library, either. Again, thanks to Harold's former boss, there would be nothing in the library about the Old Families, either.

Right?

"Not quite, sir," Brandon said when Harold asked. "He managed to find a few small things. Articles and the like, which were all buried at the back of the old newspapers he was searching through."

Panic once again spiked. "What things?"

"A kids' soccer game that had an Old Family member on the team. An article about some charity work that Old Family members had done.

Things like that."

Shit. Small things, without question, and the sort of clues that Harold and the rest of Island Affairs, including Patrick Beringer, had never thought to erase. The articles weren't much, to be sure, but in the hands of someone like Rick Thorne, they could be enough.

"Anything else?" he barked.

"Yes, um, sir." Again, Brandon hesitated. "Thorne also spent some time looking up articles on the Arch Street Angels. He printed out a few pictures, too." Another moment of hesitation. "They were all of Liam Alastor."

Harold froze. Why in the world would Rick Thorne have printed out pictures of Liam Alastor? Unless...

The memory of the conversation he'd had the previous night with Ben Baas swam to the forefront of Harold's mind, together with The Haunted's blog post, number 342. The blog had talked of Katherine Kincaid's murder and the disappearance of her son. Ben claimed to have evidence that could put Harold away. Rick Thorne was apparently investigating the Old Families, most likely at the FBI's behest. He had visited the police headquarters where Ben worked, then met with another officer who happened to be there. He had been given files, and now, Rick had printed out photographs of Liam Alastor.

Fuck! Harold had the sinking feeling that things were starting to unravel. If he didn't put a stop to it quickly, it could spiral out of control. That could put the Department of Mid-Western Island Affairs on a literal chopping block in the city of Sulivan and, where Sulivan led, the other Mid-Superior Island Cities and Towns might follow.

That was something Harold could not permit. He needed to deal

372

with Ben Baas and Rick Thorne. To do that, he needed to reestablish control.

But first, he needed to confirm a few things. "Continue to follow him and let me know what he does next. Right now, I need to make a call."

"Yes, sir."

As soon as he heard the dial tone, Harold punched in a new number. Three rings later, his call would be answered.

"McDuff."

"Good evening, Detective," Harold said. "I have a favor to ask."

"Oh? What sort?"

"First, information. Someone paid a visit to Police Headquarters yesterday, a man named Rick Thorne. I'd like to know whom he spoke with."

"Rick Thorne? Oh, you mean the PI?" Damien McDuff said.

"Yes."

"The Chief took 'im to his office," McDuff told him. "I don't know what they talked about, but Baas joined them for a brief time. Thorne left about...an hour and a half later."

It wasn't much time, Harold thought, but it might have been long enough. As a result, a plan began to form in his mind.

McDuff gave him an idea with his following words. "I know that Baas wasn't happy at seein' 'im. Not sure exactly what the story is there, but scuttlebutt says Baas was practically foaming at the mouth when he saw Thorne."

"Really?" Harold thought a minute more. A slow smile began to creep across his face. He could make use of that in more ways than one. "Do me a favor and find out what you can, then let me know."

"Will do. Time frame?"

"The next couple of days, if it's possible."

"It'll be done," McDuff said. "You can expect to hear from me."

"Good."

Harold's smile widened as he ended the call. Not only would he be able to use whatever information McDuff gave to him, but he might even be able to finally deal with one longstanding rat who was still in his office.

With that thought in mind, Harold turned back to his computer. Yes, he wouldn't get home on time tonight as he'd hoped, but that no longer mattered. The only thing that mattered was laying the groundwork that would, Harold hoped, remove one of the most significant problems in his life, as well as Rick Thorne.

Chapter Eighteen: Flushed Out

June 1, 2007: Late Evening, Pasquale Family Estate

The four of them stood before the lady's desk. Two were grim, while the third looked eager. The fourth, an old man with a head full of silver hair, leaned a bit on the cane in his right hand. His face proved a solemn mask.

"We've come for your blessing, *piccina*," Isidoro Palladino said in a gravelly voice. "That we may at last begin to avenge the wrongs committed against this Family."

The dark-haired woman leaned back in her seat, closing her onyx eyes and bringing up her manicured hands to lightly massage her temples. This was a day Lorenza Pasquale-Scordato had long awaited, and to hear those words now, from her uncle, almost made her smile with delight. Yet, the worry of possibly losing him, as she had lost her father and brothers, kept the joy from surfacing.

Still, she gave him what he had asked for. "You have it, uncle. May you find nothing but success as you wreak vengeance upon our enemies."

He offered her the smallest of smiles in an attempt to reassure her. Isidoro knew his niece well and knew what she now feared.

"We will return to you, *piccina*," he told her. "I swear this to you."

"See to it that you do," she said, opening her eyes and fixing them on his leg. "How is it today, uncle?"

Isidoro's small smile became vicious. "The thought of visiting the pain I've had to endure these past few years upon my sworn enemy has made it throb less."

One of the other three, a young man barely out of his teenage years, glanced between them. "May... May I ask a question? Ma'am? Sir?"

The other toughs rolled their eyes at his quiet, nervous voice, but Lorenza offered him a graceful nod of her head in approval. "Speak, Zeno."

Zeno Bondesan, one of the newest recruits of the Pasquale-Scordato Family, looked both relieved and curious. "Thank you, ma'am. I was wondering—please take no offense, Mister Palladino, but I am curious. Who is it that we're after, and what did they do to make you so angry?"

"No offense is taken," Isidoro reassured him. "Yes, I do not like to speak of it, but considering what we now seek to do? You have the right to know." He looked at the others. "Erminio. Leandro. Go outside and tell Mister Scordato that we will be along shortly."

They inclined their heads before leaving the office. Isidoro opened his mouth to once again speak, only for Lorenza to cut him off.

"Sit, uncle," she said, pointing to a well-cushioned chair. "You're not as young as you used to be."

"None of us are," he retorted before sighing at her raised eyebrow and going to do as he had been instructed. As soon as he had seated himself, he looked at where Zeno still stood, waiting with anxious, eager dark blue eyes. "How much do you know of the Arch Street Angels?"

"Very little," Zeno admitted. "I was in Babineaux until last year."

"Ah." Isidoro inclined his head. "That's right. You came to us on Mister Scordato's recommendation."

"Yes, sir."

"Not even ten years ago," Isidoro said. "The Pasquale Family, with

376

the blessing of the Department of Mid-Western Island Affairs, ruled the islands that make up the City of Sulivan. Island Affairs has a certain order it would prefer to implement and maintain. We were, and are, a vital piece of that order."

"Of course, others did not see it that way," Lorenza said, eyes snapping and her expression offended. "Los Demonios de Elegario, the Eighth Avenue Kings, and the Three Strikes Gang were irritations, to be sure, but my father and brothers were told to allow them a brief reign, so that people would beg Island Affairs to remove them."

"Indeed, they did," Isidoro said. "And it is why we allowed those two gangs to exist." His face darkened. "But then the Arch Street Angels began their own rise." He breathed deep, eyes smoldering with suppressed anger. "They were upstarts, a group of misfits who *dared* to stand against us, against the other gangs and against Island Affairs itself. Michael Roi, their leader, returned from a stint in the armed forces and believed he knew better than his superiors here in the Mids. His second, Emmett Prince, was a sycophant who nevertheless knew how to move and strike against his enemies. Russell Jamison, Temujin Lance, Ellie Knight, and others all flocked to Roi's banner, searching for another way to the top of the Sulivanian Society. None of them respected Island Affairs' edicts or the Pasquale Family."

He took a moment, then, to draw in another deep breath. His eyes grew cold and sharp, like flakes of obsidian.

"Bad as they were, they were small," he continued at last. "Almost insignificant. We found them to be nuisances, much like fleas on a dog, although they did do us the favor of removing Los Demonios." His lips drew together in a thin line that revealed volumes about his displeasure.

"Until Liam Alastor arrived."

An unladylike growl escaped Lorenza's throat. "That boy was *nothing* but trouble."

"Indeed, *piccina,*" Isidoro said. "He is the one who took the Arch Street Angels from being mere inconveniences to a force to be reckoned with."

"He is the reason my father, my brothers, and so many of our people no longer remain among the living," Lorenza said, her tone quiet, but thrumming with restrained fury. "Island Affairs demanded we take him alive, however, as they wished to have *words* with him."

She almost spat out the last. Zeno's eyes were wide.

"But why?" he wanted to know. "If this Alastor is such a threat to their order, why not have him killed and be done with it?"

"That is something we do not know," Isidoro said. "But it is what Island Affairs wished, and what we attempted to facilitate." Again, his face became dark with anger. His voice became a wrathful hiss. "It was a mistake. Worse, due to the interference of Benjamin Baas, we not only failed, but our Family *suffered.*"

Zeno blinked, and his brow furrowed. "The Deputy Chief of Police?"

"He was not the Deputy Chief, not then," Lorenza said, her voice low and brimming with rage. "He was undercover, sent in by the police to do whatever he needed to bring down the other gangs."

"Baas was given literal *carte blanche,*" Isidoro growled. "Unfortunately, he believed that his assignment included taking down the Pasquale along with the Los Demonios, the Three Strikes, and the Kings, and no one apparently corrected this." Isidoro snarled. *"He* is the reason I

378

now need this cane." He hefted it, knuckles white as he gripped it tightly in his right hand. "Alastor and Lance led a raid upon one of our former properties, over on McCully Island. Baas, or Bennie Brown as he was known back then—" Isidoro sneered. "He accompanied them. I attempted to defend our property, as did several other members of our Family, including my *piccina's* brother, Bruno. While Bruno faced Lance and Alastor, I attempted to speak with Baas." Fury sparked in Isidoro's eyes. "He carried a bat and proved quick to strike." He rubbed at his knee absently. "He was unwilling to listen."

"Bruno died that day." Lorenza's voice proved to be a deep well of grief. "My uncle here nearly followed, thanks to Mister Baas and his bat. Now, uncle suffers with every step he needs to take."

Isidoro looked over, giving her a gentle smile, but before he could speak, Erminio reappeared in the doorway. His expression held a dark joy.

"Forgive me, but Mister Scordato has requested your presence, Mister Palladino," he said. "Now."

"Ah." Isidoro bent his head in acknowledgment. Planting the tip of his cane on the floor, he struggled to rise to his feet. "Forgive me, *piccina,* but your husband—"

Lorenza held up a hand. "Go, uncle. Be careful, and please. Come back breathing."

"I will do my absolute best." Isidoro at last managed to stand. "Come, Zeno."

"Yes, sir." The young man also rose, his face. "Thank you, too, for taking the time to explain things."

"Of course. Never be afraid to ask a question, Zeno. We may not always give you the answers you seek, but you won't know unless you ask."

"I'll remember that, sir."

They said nothing more as they left the home office. Passing by the large family room, then through the spacious gourmet kitchen, which had been done in Italian marble, before turning right into the mudroom. From there, they went through the small door, which connected the house to the five-car garage.

Carmine Scordato waited for them there, a cat winding its way around his legs before fleeing at the sight of the newcomers. To Isidoro's slight surprise, however, Erminio and Leandro weren't his only company. Harold Edmund Holloway turned to see them when Isidoro and Zeno entered, while Ira Utley, muscles bulging inside his ill-fitting suit, forced another man to kneel before them.

Isidoro looked at the kneeling man in curiosity. He didn't yet know who had happened to him, as his head was covered with a cloth sack.

"Isidoro," Harold greeted him. "How is your leg today?"

"It has been better, Mister Harolds," Isidoro said. "As I have told Mrs. Scordato, I am hoping that it will hurt a bit less after tonight."

"I also hope that it will," Harold said. "And, to that end, I have brought you and Mister Scordato a gift." He motioned to the kneeling man. "Ira? If you would?"

"Sure."

Ira whipped the cloth sack off the kneeling man's head. Isidoro's eyebrows rose. Despite the gauntness of the other's face, his crooked nose and blonde hair gave him away. Joseph DeLuca had been a former, low-level soldier for the Pasquale Family before the Arch Street Angel had dismantled them. He had walked away from the Family to go to work for the Department of Mid-Western Island Affairs, and no amount of

380

bargaining from Lorenza or Carmine had secured his return.

Until, apparently, now.

"Mister DeLuca." Isidoro's voice held vicious satisfaction. "It has been some time since we last spoke to each other."

"Not long enough." Joe DeLuca looked around and blanched, seeing where he was and whom he knelt before. His nose twitched. "Shit."

"Indeed, Mister DeLuca." Harold Holloway inclined his head, smiling. "You are deep in that."

Joe glanced around again before closing his eyes. "Can we just get this over with?"

"Now, now, Mister DeLuca," Carmine said, his voice quiet and sinister. "A drowning rat does not choose when it dies. You still have one purpose left to fulfill."

Again, Joe's nose twitched. His voice sounded resigned. "And that would be?"

One of Ira's meaty hands produced a cell phone. "You're gonna make a call."

A wary look entered Joe's eyes. "To whom?"

Harold looked down on him, false sympathy on his face, but an all-too-satisfied gleam lit in his eyes. "You are not *entirely* stupid, Mister DeLuca. Oh, and don't worry about not knowing what to say. We've prepared a script for you to follow. You may, of course, ad-lib a bit. Too much so, however? And if you try to warn the one you're calling? We'll *know*, and your end will *not* be swift as a result."

Joe paled, then went completely white when he saw the prepared script and who it was intended for. "M-mister Holloway—"

Harold's hand rose in a sharp gesture. "I don't want to hear it,

Mister DeLuca. You have a history of betrayal, and this will be just one more act of treachery in your long experience of selling others out. Of course, if you would *prefer* to do this the hard way..."

Ira cracked his knuckles, as if in preparation. He was a brutish man, with a thoroughly unpleasant reputation, as well as a long record of service to the Department of Mid-Western Island Affairs. Isidoro respected him, and Ira Utley was one of the very few who had made even Alphonse Pasquale, back when he had been alive, act with caution.

He also made people such as Joe DeLuca live in terror. Joe had always been something of a coward, and now, his eyes widened at Ira's display. His voice shook with terror.

"Fine," he managed to say. "I—I'll do what you want."

"Excellent," Harold purred. "Mister Rinaldi? Mister Natale? Would the two of you mind taking Officer Utley's place? He needs to dial a number for Mister DeLuca. Unless—" Harold looked over. "I know this is something you've waited a long time for, Isidoro. Would you like to have the honor of dialing? Or would you prefer to hold the script?"

Isidoro's smile proved unpleasant. "Either will do, Mister Harolds."

"Excellent. Please give Mister Palladino the phone then, Officer," Harold said.

Ira nodded and handed the cell phone over before taking the brief script and holding it up in front of Joe. Isidoro relished each number he hit with his fingers before turning on the speaker and holding the phone out.

One ring. Two rings.

On the third, there was a click as a receiver was picked up. A weary voice answered. "Baas."

"B-Bennie. It's Joe."

Ben Baas' fatigue seemed to disappear in the heartbeat it took him to speak again. "What's up, Joe? You got somethin' for me?"

"Y-you could say that," Joe said, his anxiousness palpable. Isidoro almost growled, both at his display of fear and at the sound of Ben's voice. "H-Holloway's gonna be meetin' with some out-of-towner tonight. Don't know what it's about, but with the way Holloway's actin'?"

"You think it's gonna be about something important?"

"Yeah." Joe's eyes met Isidoro's, then slid to Harold's. His voice became tinged with something approaching sadness. "No question 'bout it."

"When?"

"About a half hour from now. Maybe forty-five minutes, if the guy he's meeting runs a bit late."

"Where?"

"A-at the parking garage. The one right across the street from your headquarters."

Outrage flooded Ben's voice. "You sure, Joe? That asshole's meetin' someone *here?*"

"Yeah. I know it for a fact. Holloway's meetin' some guy named... Vic?" Joe squinted at the script, his voice becoming more uncertain. "Maybe Nick?"

"*Rick,* maybe?" Ben's fury became cold, much to Isidoro's joy. "Rick *Thorne?*"

"Yeah," Joe confirmed it. "I think that's it."

A nasty chuckle could be heard before Ben said, "You just made my entire day, Joey. See if you can't escape Island Affairs tomorrow, and I'll spring for lunch."

"Bennie..." Joe swallowed at the looks he received. Any thought he might have had of at least attempting to clue the man on the other end of the line in died. "Be careful. Holloway's been on the warpath."

"Not as much as *me*."

The call ended. Joe breathed deep as Isidoro handed the phone back to Ira. Carmine smiled down at him, the expression dark and unfriendly.

"Well done, Mister DeLuca," he said. "It's almost a shame you couldn't have put your acting skills to a better, more productive use."

"Indeed," Harold seconded. "It truly is a pity." He looked over at Isidoro. "Will you be leaving soon?"

"Right now, in fact," Isidoro told him. "Or at least this is what I hope." He looked at Carmine. "Mister Scordato? Do we have your blessing to proceed?"

"You do, Mister Palladino." Carmine nodded at him. "You may head to the car now, if you wish, as can the rest of your crew. Mister Harolds?"

"I'd like to walk Mister Palladino out."

"Very well. Might I keep Mister Utley for a few more minutes?"

"So long as he does not object."

Ira smiled, his eyes fixed on the quivering Joe DeLuca. "I don't."

"Good." Harold turned to Isidoro. "Shall we?"

They headed out of the garage, with Erminio immediately heading to the driver's seat of Isidoro's personal car. Leandro pointed Zeno to the front passenger seat before going to open the driver's side back door

384

for Isidoro himself.

Isidoro, however, waved at him to get in as he turned to first face Harold. "You wish to speak, Mister Harolds?"

"Yes. Were you informed of The Wall having been brought down?"

"I was, yes." Isidoro allowed a faint smile to take hold of his lips. "Alberto has been avenged at long last, and now, I intend to avenge myself as well as deal with your issue."

"Good." Harold returned the smile. "I've already contacted one of my people who is inside the Sulivan Police Department. Mister Thorne should be on his way shortly, which will allow my officers to go inside Thorne's room to recover the information he's been collecting without worry. I just wanted to thank you, Isidoro, for your assistance with this."

"Of course, Mister Harolds. I am only too happy to help in this matter, as you well know. If there are other matters you happen to need assistance with..."

"I'm glad to hear that, Isidoro," Harold looked relieved at the offer. "There is indeed something else I may soon need your help with."

"Oh?"

"Alastor is missing."

Isidoro drew in a sharp breath, his pale blue eyes becoming twin chips of ice. The man who had helped bring down Alphonse and Bruno Pasquale, and who had personally killed Giovanni Pasquale, had *disappeared*. "How?"

"He awoke," Harold said, voice soft and regretful. "And escaped."

Shock filled Isidoro's being before being blotted out with fury. *"Quel figlio di puttana...* When did this happen?"

"A few days ago."

"You should have killed him when you had the chance!"

"Perhaps we should have," Harold acknowledged. "But as it stands right now, Alastor is awake, he is free, and we don't know where he is."

"Ah." Even in the midst of mind-altering rage, Isidoro had never been a fool. "You would require help in tracking him down?"

"Yes. You have more contacts than I do with certain groups. If you can make some inquiries, I would greatly appreciate it," Harold said. "Discreetly, of course. We have yet to release this news to the media, and I'm hoping we won't have to take that step."

"Understandable." Isidoro inclined his head. "I would be more than happy to help you in this matter, as would the rest of this Family."

Harold allowed a small breath to escape. His expression became more relaxed. "Thank you, old friend."

"Of course." Isidoro bowed his head. "Perhaps, too, Baas' death will provide a lure, with which we may achieve that goal."

"Let us hope so."

Before either man could say any more, a loud *crack* grabbed their attention. A moment later, Ira came out of the garage and returned to Harold's side.

"It's done," he said. "Mister Scordato will get rid of the rat and is planning to send a message at the same time."

"Good." Harold's smile widened. "Let's return to the office, then. Isidoro, I'll expect to hear from you soon."

Isidoro nodded as he went to the open door of his car. "And you shall, Mister Harolds. Count upon it."

386

Chapter Nineteen: Smoking Guns

10:47 pm, Rick Thorne's Room

Rick sighed as his head hit the pillow. It had been a *long* two days, and he was just about ready to pass out.

That wasn't to say that the past two days had been wasted. No, in fact. Now that Rick knew what to look for, he had been able to find quite a few more small tidbits of information about the Old Families, the Kincaid Family in particular, by visiting various news organizations and looking through their archives.

Even better? Ray had decided to dive into the FBI Office's own archives. The files in the computer system had curious blips where a file *should* have been, but wasn't. As the SAIC, Ray couldn't be barred from entering the FBI Archives, where all the hard copies were kept.

As a result, he had discovered a small but near-literal treasure trove of information. Granted, most of the paper files for the missing computer ones weren't to be found, as the archivist, when Ray asked, had muttered something about being ordered previously to 'clean things up.'

However, the files created during the tenure of Ray's immediate predecessor were still available, and the archivist could do nothing to prevent Ray from removing them for study. Rick almost grinned when he remembered what the SAIC had said.

"I never thought I would be so happy about that man's laziness." Rick snorted, repeating Ray's words. "To be honest, I never thought I'd be happy at *anyone's* laziness, but I am today."

Especially since the recovered files had confirmed not only the existence of Katherine Kincaid's father and his role in the Sulivan Police Force, but a small number of other Old Family members who had been working in law enforcement and city politics. The discovered files not only confirmed the reality of those people's lives, but they also showed the way the Old Family members had all died.

Not to mention the lack of investigation that had been made into each of those deaths.

Rick's lips thinned. Anger, tempered by exhaustion, bubbled up from deep within the private investigator. A file or two going missing spoke of carelessness, but nothing malicious. For *so many* files to be supposedly mislaid and almost certainly destroyed smacked of out-and-out corruption.

Rick hated it. Corruption was something he despised. To find it to such an extent anywhere would have been enough to spike his fury. Finding it during his attempt to locate the son of his brother-in-law?

He growled. The idea that a city's corruption would get in the way of helping a family member reunite with the child he'd never known ate at him. *If this keeps up, I may have to sic Victor on them. They can hide things from a simple PI but not an agent of SIN. Of course, that means finding a reason for Victor coming here, one that he can tell his fellow agents and his director.*

Well, with luck, at least one of the files Ethan had in his possession would give Victor the excuse he needed to head out. Rick could hope for that much, at least.

Breathing out another sigh, Rick allowed his eyes to close. They were shut for only a few minutes before he heard his cell phone ring.

The hell? His eyes snapped back open, and Rick reached over to the nightstand. Grabbing his phone, he jabbed at a button and held it up to his ear.

"Rick Thorne," he said.

He halfway expected to hear Ethan or Ray on the other end. Rick almost hoped to hear Jacquetta's voice or maybe Charlie's, Emma's, Josiah's, or even Victor's, despite how late it was.

Instead, he heard a voice he didn't recognize. "Mister Thorne? This is Officer O'Malley, down at Sulivan HQ."

Rick felt his fatigue vanish. He bolted upright. "Officer, I wasn't expecting your call, especially now, when it's so late."

"Yeah, sorry about that, sir." The voice on the other end gave a weak chuckle. "I wouldn't be calling, though, especially at this hour, without reason. The Chief asked me to let you know that he wants to meet with you. He said to, and I quote, 'let Mister Thorne know that I have important information regarding his case.'" There was a pause before the voice, sounding a bit perplexed, added, "Does that mean anything to you?"

"Yes, Officer." Rick grinned. "It does. Where and when did he say he wants to meet? Tomorrow morning?"

"No, sir. If possible, he hoped to meet you right away, despite the hour. How fast can you get downtown?"

Rick felt his heart leap. "I can be there in about thirty or so minutes. I gotta get dressed and then get a ride."

"Would you like me to send a squad car out your way?"

Rick considered it, then shook his head. "No, Officer, but thank you. I'll be down there in about thirty, maybe thirty-five minutes. Will I be meeting him at his office?"

"No, sir, not at his office." The officer rattled off an address. "It's a parking garage that's kitty-cornered on the street across from headquarters. Go up to the second level, and he'll meet you there." A note of humor entered the officer's voice. "He said there's less of a chance of bein' interrupted that way."

Rick chuckled back, remembering what had happened the first time. After thanking the officer, he hung up the phone before sliding out of bed to get dressed. As he slid his legs into his pants and pulled on a t-shirt, he thought about who, exactly, he could call for a ride. Ethan should already be stateside by now. He could call Ray, but Rick hated the idea of interrupting whatever sleep Ray was getting. The SAIC was already spending far too much time in his office, away from Meg, as it was. That left only one option.

As soon as he finished dressing, Rick reached for the phone again. A droll voice answered.

"Front desk."

"This is Rick Thorne in Room 201. Could you have a taxi come pick me up and take me downtown, Marty?"

"Not a problem, Mister Thorne." The clerk at the front desk sounded pleased to hear from him. "My cousin drives a cab. I'll give 'im a call and see if he can't be here in ten minutes, max."

Rick grinned. He'd made a habit of talking to the staff of whatever hotel or motel he happened to be staying at, as one never knew the sort of connections they had or how they could be turned in one's favor by simply being polite. "I'd appreciate it, Marty. Thanks."

"Sure thing!"

Hanging up the phone, Rick grabbed his wallet and his weapon. After another moment's thought, he also grabbed two extra magazines. He put them into his right-hand pocket before leaving his room.

Within the space of a mere two minutes, he walked into the front lobby. Marty Favior dipped his head in greeting when Rick walked over.

"We got lucky," he said. "I got my cousin just as he dropped off his last fare. Tim should be here in maybe two minutes."

"Thanks, Marty." Rick smiled at him. "I appreciate it."

"Of course, Mister Thorne. It's not a problem."

He made some small talk until he saw a black-and-white *One Star Taxi* pull up out front. The cab looked a few years old, with the white portions showing quite a bit of gathered dust and even a few specks of dirt. An old Scooter Dog decal could also be seen stuck to the back bumper. This fact caused Rick to chuckle again as he walked outside, glancing at the time to know that it was just about eleven o'clock.

As he got in, the driver turned around to grin at him. "Where to, boss-man?"

Rick almost did a double-take. Marty and Tim looked eerily similar, although Marty had never once smiled in the few days that Rick had known him.

"Ah, downtown," Rick said. "To the garage by Police Headquarters." He pulled out a twenty-dollar bill and passed it over. "There's your tip."

Tim's eyes widened. "Whoa, thanks, boss-man! I'll get you over there in no time whatsoever."

Turning around, he flipped the fare flag. A second later, his tires peeled as he drove Rick away from the hotel.

At just five minutes past eleven thirty, the taxi came to a screeching halt beside the entrance of the parking garage. Rick took a deep breath, thankful that they'd made it there in one piece—Tim's driving skills were, in the private investigator's opinion, excellent for a racetrack, not a city's streets. Still, there was an upside, as it seemed none of those following Rick had managed to match the taxi driver's skills. Rick paid the fare, added another twenty-dollar tip as thanks for getting him to the garage so quickly, then stepped away from the cab.

The parking garage towered over him in the darkness. The building was easily five stories tall and composed of light brown concrete, currently shadowed by the trees lining the sidewalk next to it and by the night itself. Two nearby streetlamps were trying to shed some light on the area, but one of them was sputtering as its bulb struggled to stay lit.

A glimmer of unease made Rick hesitate to step inside the building. He couldn't remember another city where he'd been threatened as soon as he'd set foot onto its shore. The fact that he'd been followed since his arrival only heightened his concern, making him feel on edge.

How different would it have been, Rick asked himself. *If I'd been born and raised here, as Victor's son was?*

He didn't know. At the very least, he believed he would have been more familiar with Sulivan's various idiosyncrasies, its history, and everything associated with it. He might even have been able to fly under the radar of the Department of Mid-Western Island Affairs as he hunted for Robbie Kincaid, but maybe not. Katherine Kincaid and her son had no doubt known Sulivan far better than he did, having lived there for most of their lives, and it hadn't saved them. It hadn't saved any other member of their family, nor had it saved the other Old Families that Rick had been researching.

Except for the DuBois, the Jourdain, and the Fowler. Rick

breathed out a sigh, pulling a small bottle of water out from a coat pocket. He took a couple of sips before, at last, daring to enter the garage. *With luck, Akiyama can shed some more light on that subject.*

Much to his surprise, he found the parking garage to still be quite full. Granted, Philly and New York rarely ever had an empty garage of any sort, but Sulivan was nowhere near as large as either of those cities. Apparently, and if his assumption proved to be correct, Sulivan's police department remained busy even at this late hour of the night.

And why should that surprise you? He asked himself that question as he made his way up to the second floor. *You've seen the crime museum, Rick. Not too many other cities have one of those, let alone one as large as Sulivan's. You were a detective, too, back in Philadelphia. The night shifts there weren't exactly quiet, so why would you think Sulivan's would be?*

Rick almost chuckled to himself at the absurdity of his thoughts as he reached the second level. Glancing around, he spotted a small, out-of-the-way alcove. The small area would allow him to see the rest of the garage while still having concrete behind him.

Perfect, he thought as he moved to take up a position inside of it. *Now, I just need to wait for Akiyama to get here and hope that whatever he has to tell me will give me the answers I need.*

He didn't need to wait for very long. The sound of footsteps alerted Rick to the fact that he was no longer alone.

It wasn't, however, Makoto Akiyama that he spotted coming towards him. Instead, it was none other than Benjamin Benedict Baas.

A malicious smile formed on the face of Sulivan's Deputy Chief of Police the moment he spotted Rick. His tone, when he spoke, held nothing but rage.

"There you are, you son of a bitch!" Ben snarled. "Did you really think that I'd let this go? After you all but ruined my life back in Philly?"

The hell? Rick's jaw worked as he tried to figure out how, exactly, he should respond. He'd thought he'd be meeting with *Akiyama,* not with *Ben.* What in the hell, then, was the Deputy Chief doing here? Had it actually been *Ben* who had gotten Officer O'Malley to call Rick earlier? If so, why? Did he really hate Rick that much?

His brow furrowed as he struggled to think of a way to de-escalate the situation. Ben's accusation of Rick having all but ruined his life back in Philadelphia touched a nerve. *Ben* had been the one to throw that punch, back in their shared captain's office, which had gotten him suspended and transferred. Rick had simply been doing his job by taking those files that Ben had given him to their captain—

Oh. The floodgate of memory opened, and Rick blinked, recalling exactly what had led up to that moment where Ben had thrown his punch. *Oh, shit. Ben gave you those files on Hornsby to look over, after asking you not to show them to the captain. And just what did you promptly do, Rick? Precisely as he asked you not to do. Fuck.*

It was no wonder that Ben hated him. In his eyes, Rick had betrayed him in order to protect a *predator* of *children.*

There could be no worse crime, no worse sin.

Taking a deep breath, doing his best to prepare to talk to the other, Rick stepped out from the alcove. He raised his hands, both in surrender and in an attempt to calm Ben down. Rick was the taller of the two by almost two full inches, but Ben's anger, coupled with his broad shoulders and barrel-like chest, made him seem much more intimidating at the moment.

394

"Look," Rick spoke in a quiet, even tone. "Ben."

"That's *Deputy Chief Baas* to you, fuckhead." Ben snarled back, his face red and his mustache bristling. "And did you *really* expect me to allow you to *waltz* into *my* city to make trouble?"

Rick grabbed a deep breath, doing his best to keep a hold on his own temper. Losing it, he knew, would help nothing. He and Ben were both consummate men of the law, he reminded himself, and Ben had a very real, very legitimate reason to be angry with him.

"I am not here to cause you any trouble, Deputy Chief," Rick said. "The past is the past. Yes, I made a mistake back in Philly, and you turned out to be right about Hornsby. I apologize for not believing you about him. I also apologize for going to the captain with those files instead of doing as you asked and reviewing them to see all the evidence you'd collected. I know I should have." His words seemed to have no effect, as Ben continued to stomp towards him. Rick almost sighed, then brought himself back to business. "That's not why I'm here now, though. I only came to Sulivan for my client. I keep runnin' into roadblocks, and—"

"I don't give a *shit,*" Ben roared back. "Not about your client or about whatever roadblocks you happen to be facing. You not bein' able to do what you want to do makes me *happy*. It shows just how unimportant you are in comparison—"

He continued his rant, and Rick felt a swell of anger rise up into his throat, despite his best efforts to fight it back. Yes, Ben had a reason to despise him, but his refusal to listen, to at least allow Rick the chance to try and explain things, caused Rick to grit his teeth. He had a job to do and, if Ben wasn't going to help, then Rick needed him to just get out of his way.

"I can see that coming here was a mistake," he grated out at last, when Ben at last needed to draw a breath. "Your temper, though, is *not* my fault, *Ben.* You could have handled things differently in Philly, too, not just me."

"I *told* you, I'm *Deputy Chief Baas* to you, *Mister* Thorne," Ben snapped back. "I *outrank* you here, and you *will* give me the respect I *deserve.*"

Rick rolled his eyes, preparing to tell Ben to just shove it. He didn't need to endure the other man's tirade about past wrongs, real or imagined.

Instead, he tried to concentrate on the call that had brought him there. Officer O'Malley said the Chief wanted to meet him and that he had *important information* about Rick's case. O'Malley could have meant Ben, and had dropped the *Deputy* portion of Ben's title, but...

Movement caught his eye at that moment and drew his attention. A car was creeping up the ramp towards the second floor. It moved slowly, far slower than Rick thought it should.

That by itself might not have seemed too unusual. Many people, in search of a closer parking spot, tended to drive slowly.

But the fact that this car's headlights happened to be off? In the dead of night and in a place that didn't have much in the way of interior lighting?

Ben didn't, couldn't, see it. The car happened to be coming up behind him. All of Rick's instincts, however, were screaming at him that something was off, that something wasn't *right*.

"Ben—" Rick tried to draw the other man's attention to what was behind him, keeping his eyes fixed on the car.

The Deputy Chief ignored him, still too fixated on his hatred.

Rick grit his teeth, doing his best to return the favor when a sudden thought struck him.

Set-up.

He almost reeled back with the realization. If that *was* the case, then Rick had no time to continue listening to Ben's rant. He reached into his jacket pocket as the vehicle slowed down further, cresting the top of the ramp. Rick had the bizarre sensation of time itself freezing just before the car's tires peeled out.

His hand found his gun at the same time that the tires screeched. The sight of Rick drawing his firearm, combined with the sound of a vehicle suddenly speeding nearby, caused Ben to whip around. His eyes widened, now seeing the car that was speeding toward them directly.

"Ah, fu—"

The rest of Ben's words were drowned out in the roar of the oncoming car's engines. Life itself seemed to slow as the car spun around the corner, near where the two stood. Rick could see that the front and back windows closest to them were down, and two rifle barrels were beginning to slide out, aiming at both him and Ben.

Yanking his gun free as the first shots were fired, Rick almost cursed as he ducked down. Out of the corner of his right eye, and as he sighted down the barrel of his weapon, Rick could see Ben also ducking and drawing out a gun of his own. Bullets whizzed around, dinging the nearby cars, as both the private investigator and the Deputy Chief of Police fired back.

But as Ben shifted his focus, aiming his weapon at the car's front windows, Rick saw one of the two enemy barrels adjust its aim. To his horror, he saw the line of sight move directly to Ben's head.

There was no time for Rick to think. Ben wouldn't, he knew, be able to duck out of the way in time, even if he noticed what was about to happen. Reacting quickly, the private investigator darted over.

Rick's shoulder struck Ben, pushing him to the side and down, just as the crack of a weapon being fired reached Rick's ears.

He felt one of the rounds tear into his side, but Rick felt no pain. Not yet. Adrenaline surged through his body as he brought his gun up. He didn't aim, but his finger stroked the trigger and squeezed off a few rounds in retaliation.

The bullets struck the car in quick succession. One shattered the front windshield; another struck the passenger-side mirror; and still another gouged out a line in the passenger-side door.

Rick could hear a roaring in his ears, a pounding that sounded as though his heart had leaped up into the sport where his brain should have been. He ignored it as he tried to aim, still trying to fire, but his magazine proved empty. He reached for one of his spares and, to his shock, his hand met something wet.

He blinked, looking down, not noticing either Ben's pained expression or the cannon-like booming from Ben's own gun. When, Rick wondered, had his side turned red? Why was it wet?

He decided it didn't matter. He felt no pain; therefore, he must have been all right. He couldn't understand why he needed to grit his teeth as he reached back into his jacket's pocket for the spare magazines of ammunition that he wanted.

Managing to wrap his hand around one, he pulled it out. At the same time, he thumbed his gun's magazine release button with his other hand, allowing the spent one to fall to the ground. Both proved to be more

398

difficult than they should have been. It was even harder to slam the new one into its predecessor's place. How was it, he wondered, that every movement had become slower, heavier, more challenging to accomplish?

His vision swam as Rick struggled to raise his pistol. He tried squeezing the trigger once more, but his finger could barely move. *What the hell?*

He tried to speak, but no words came out. He tried again to say something, anything. He even tried to call out to Ben to warn him, but his mouth had gone dry.

Rick felt his vision spiraling. His mind went numb, and he just barely managed to mouth the only thing he could still think about.

"Quet..."

ᚤᚷ ᚤᚷ ᚤᚷ ᚤᚷ ᛋᚱᚿᚱ ᚱᛗᛖᛁᛖᛏᚱᛁᚲᛗ ᛁᛖ ᚠᚱᚱᚿᛁᛖᚾ ᚥᚥ ᚥᚥ ᚥᚥ ᚥᚥ

Ben cursed himself as the bullets flew by, feeling the burgeoning pain that came from his chest. He'd been hit, and he could only blame himself for having been so focused on getting even with Rick Thorne that he had failed to notice the car, which had apparently been tailing him. Now, he knew his inattention had been a significant mistake.

Possibly even a fatal one.

Stupid! He chastised himself as he hunkered down to return fire. *Stupid, stupid, stupid! You* know *better than this, Baas! Never lose yourself to your surroundings! It'll get you killed!*

He breathed deep, fighting hard to refocus. This was life or death. He had no time to question anything, only to act.

Remember, Ben. His mentor's most important words ghosted

through his mind. *There's only you, your weapon, and your target. Everything else is irrelevant.*

Right. Eyes narrowing, Ben did his best to obey those words. Nothing else could be allowed to matter, not if he wanted to keep himself and his unexpected companion from being killed.

The sound of the bullets whizzing by to strike concrete and cars did not distract him from his purpose. Ben had been in numerous firefights over the years, and he knew enough not to panic. It was how he had managed to survive throughout his years undercover, not to mention so many other attempts on his life.

But he wouldn't, couldn't, survive everything. Ben knew the moment he saw one of the rifle barrels poking out from the assailant's car's window shift towards him that his luck was about to run out. It now pointed directly at him, and it wouldn't matter that he happened to be ducking down and returning fire. He had nowhere to go, no place to move—the nearby parked cars had made sure of that. His own aim couldn't shift fast enough, and Ben knew that he would likely be hit again, this time in a place not covered by the bulletproof vest he'd made sure to wear.

Once that happened... Well, that would be the end of everything.

Just as he felt certain that death had at last come for him, Ben felt *some*thing slam into him without warning. Rick Thorne knocked him down just as the enemy's weapon sang out.

Ben needed only an instant to recover. Rolling back up to his knees and bringing his gun back up, he emptied his LK-26 handgun's magazine into the car as it flew past them.

The car didn't slow down as it reached the end of the short turn and spun around, tires squealing, to make another pass. Ben cursed again, dropping his now-spent pistol to the ground before reaching back to his rear holster to grab his much more powerful MRD-85. He steeled himself, aiming at the car's windshield. As the vehicle hurtled towards him, Ben steeled himself and fired.

The gun *roared.*

Glass shattered an instant later, and the car's windshield disappeared. Ben smiled grimly at the sharp cry he heard directly afterward from one of those within the vehicle itself. Its wheels screeched as its driver no doubt slammed a foot down on the gas pedal. Ben fired once more, hearing an even more satisfying scream as the round traveled through the air to strike one of the car's passengers.

Again, the car spun around, its wheels screaming before finding traction. The car shot away in the direction opposite to Ben and Rick once more.

Ben thought about getting up and chasing after it. He'd done several similar things before, and there were a number of cars near him in the garage that he could have hot-wired to chase after the escaping vehicle.

He chose to shake his head instead, feeling the pain in his chest. He knew he would need some serious backup to do something like that, and one lone private investigator wouldn't suffice.

Grabbing a deep breath, Ben listened as the sound of squealing tires faded away into the night. The adrenaline began to drain away as he climbed back to his feet, wincing as he moved. *That was too close. If it hadn't been for Thorne, I'd be dead.*

It was a realization that didn't sit well with him, but there could be no getting around the fact that if Rick hadn't shoved him out of the way at precisely the right second, Ben wouldn't be alive now. No matter how much he hated the idea of owing the other, Ben knew that he did.

Turning around, he opened his mouth to thank his unexpected savior, no matter how reluctantly. Instead, Ben's eyes went wide when he found the other.

Rick lay sprawled out on the hard ground. A pool of red could also be seen underneath him, growing wider by the second.

"Ah, shit."

Ben didn't hesitate, even as he swore. The idea of anyone, even Rick Thorne, saving his life at the possible cost of his own did not sit well with Sulivan's Deputy Chief of Police.

Swiftly holstering the weapon that was still in his hand, Ben reached for the cop-turned-private investigator, planning to use his limited experience as a field medic to hopefully save the other's life. He grabbed at his radio, too, as he moved. He kept his voice steady, but there could be no mistaking the urgent undertone.

"All units! This is Deputy Chief Baas. Shots have been fired in the parking garage at the corner of Kaller and Jacobsen. Suspects have fled the scene. We have a man down. I repeat, we have a man *down*. Again, this is Deputy Chief Baas! Initiate Code Blue and get the paramedics here, *now*."

Epilogue: The Coiled Serpent

June 1, 2007: 8:03 pm, Thorne Residence, Pennsylvania

Victor sank into his chair at the dining room table, grateful for the break. It had been a long day, spent not only watching for strangers who seemed overly interested in his sister's property, but also aiding his sister and her children in the 'training' of his former partners' trainees.

Rick's warning that the Department of Mid-Western Island Affairs had somehow obtained recent pictures of his and Jacquetta's house had lit an angry fire in Victor. Together with his former partners, they had walked the property's perimeter, then set up a few small, but high-end electronic devices that would alert them to any possible trespassers. If anyone *did* show up unannounced, then they would know and could confront them.

In the meantime, Jacquetta, Charlie, Emma, and Josiah had kept the apprentice agents of SIN busy. None of the three had expected much from Victor's civilian family until, over the course of the week, Jacquetta and the kids had shown them what William Andrew Wolfe-Wall had taught them.

Victor almost smiled at the thought as, over a simple dinner of soup and sandwiches, he listened to his sister, niece, and nephews plot as to how they would continue surprising his former partners' trainees. Seth Yago and Annette Prior, who were under the mentorships of Maria Fuentes and Ronald Kohler, had, according to Emma, 'upped their game' seriously after getting over the shock of the challenge Jacquetta and her children were presenting to them.

Apparently, they hadn't taken the fact of The Wall being Jacquetta's father and the kids' grandfather all that seriously. Not until they had been outwitted, outmaneuvered, and outdone just by Charlie, Emma, and Josiah no less than seven times in a row.

Victor's would-be smile faded. Yes, Seth and Annette had taken the challenge being thrown at them to heart, once they had realized the three teenagers could run near-literal rings around them, and with*out* any help from Victor. It was too bad the same couldn't be said about Phillipe Depardeaux's student, Korey Smithson. While the young man had been just as shocked as his fellow two SIN trainees by the competence Jacquetta and her children were showing them, he had quickly gotten angry about it. His attitude seemed to be worsening, too, with every 'victory' that Charlie, Emma, Josiah, and Jacquetta pulled off, no matter how minor.

"Civilians," he'd been heard to mutter more than once, "should know their place."

Nothing Phillipe said to Korey had any effect, either. He had apologized to Victor more than once as a result.

Victor had waved the apologies away each time. He and his former partners had all seen attitudes like Korey's before. A small but potent number of new agents within the Special Intelligence Network and other intelligence agencies seemed to believe themselves superior to the people they were meant to protect; only time and experience ever worked to cure them, and some never seemed to learn.

Hopefully, Korey wouldn't be one of those who didn't. Victor could hope for that much, even as he ran interference for whenever Jacquetta or Emma or Charlie or Josiah had needed it. Thanks to Korey's attitude, that had become more frequent than Victor liked.

Still, he had found the time to wonder how Rick was doing in his search for Victor's son. Was he having any luck? Victor didn't think he'd found anything—he felt sure that Rick would have called otherwise—but was he maybe closing in?

Victor couldn't remember another time when he'd felt so anxious. It was part of the reason he had begun, whenever he wasn't helping his family, train his former partners' students, to investigate the upper echelons of power at the Special Intelligence Network. Not only did he wish to discover if they could be compromised, as William Wolfe-Wall's letter had insinuated, but it also allowed Victor the chance to get his mind off of whatever Rick might be finding out.

Of course, finding anything beyond names and brief, official blurbs on people such as Ryan Dominick, Vera-Faye West, Philip Evander, Dexter Ibarra, and the others who were considered the higher-ups of the Special Intelligence Network was near-impossible. Victor had expected that. Information on any or all of them was *supposed* to be hard to come by. None of them would have remained safe, let alone alive, for very long otherwise.

But Victor had found a couple of irregularities, which had raised several small but powerful internal alarm bells.

To start with, and according to the official blurb he'd read, Vera-Faye West had taken a year off between her time with the CIA and coming on board with the Special Intelligence Network due to a 'family issue'. The problem with that? Victor knew for a fact that Vera-Faye West *had* no more family. She had been a foster child, something that Victor had discovered about her by accident. She had been passed from family to family until she was eighteen, when she enrolled in a prestigious university on scholarship.

So where had she been during that year? What had she done? Victor didn't doubt that whatever it was must have been considered essential and kept quiet, but...

Philip Evander's information also seemed off. In the provided list of places where Philip had supposedly been assigned, Victor saw that he had allegedly been in Austria for one year in 1991. The problem with that was that *Victor* had been in Austria on assignment in 1991. The office there was small, with no more than fifteen agents of SIN stationed there at any one time, and he knew that Philip Evander had not been among the agents with him in Austria back in 1991.

Victor could have dismissed it as a simple mistake or typo if Philip had been there in 1992 or '93, but he hadn't been. Victor himself had been stationed there for five years, starting in 1989, so he would have known if Philip had been there then as well.

So, again, where had Philip actually been? What had he actually been doing?

He didn't know. Not yet.

Just as he didn't know how *two* years could be 'missing' from Rolanda Brogan's work history. They weren't consecutive, but had been about five years apart. The reason for her first 'missing' year was, like Vera-Faye's, a 'family-related issue'; the second 'missing' year had no explanation given—it was just missing.

By themselves, these oddities weren't much. Victor didn't doubt that each one could be explained away if they were asked about. The fact that they were *there,* however...

406

He leaned back in his seat, thinking hard as he chewed the final bites of his sandwich. Before his father's letter, Victor would have put the oddities down to classified activities that couldn't be discussed. Now?

Were they among those who tried to hand my son—my son—over to the people who had murdered his mother? Did they witness my father's firing when he refused to cooperate back then? What else might they have done in order to get to where they now are?

Again, Victor didn't know. Yes, Vera-Faye, Philip, and Rolanda hadn't been in their current positions back when William had rescued Victor's son, but they *were* being groomed for them. What had they seen, if anything? Had they secured their current positions in the Special Intelligence Network by their willingness to 'play ball' with whoever had made those decisions? Or...

"Victor?"

Jacquetta's soft voice derailed his train of thought, and he looked over. "Yes?"

His sister offered him a small, sad sort of smile. No doubt she thought he was remembering their father and, now, sought to distract him.

"The kids and I were hoping you could give us some extra insight," she said. "So we can continue winning the, uh, games."

"Especially against Smithson," Emma said with a little, feline-like smile. "I like cutting him down to size."

Charlie nodded, grinning. Josiah also nodded, but his expression proved more solemn. Victor almost frowned at his younger nephew, wondering why.

"I don't like him," Josiah said when asked. "His whole attitude just sorta *reeks*."

Jacquetta frowned, her expression morphing into concern. "Like Detective Hornsby?"

"No." Josiah shook his head, decisive. "Nothing like *him*."

"Is it because he's so angry all the time?" Charlie wanted to know.

"He's only acting like he's angry," Josiah said. "But I don't think it's anger we're actually seeing. If anything, I'd have to say he's more, y'know, disappointed."

He shrugged when everyone but his uncle looked at him with incredulity. Victor alone proved more curious.

"Why do you think that, Sy?" he wanted to know.

Josiah seemed to hesitate before explaining, "A couple of times, when I've managed to sneak around him, I caught sight of his face. He seemed more.... intent. Measured and calm, but also... It's like he's frustrated that a couple of kids have been able to get the better of him, time and time again. You know?"

Victor nodded, thoughtful. Was it possible that Phillipe's student wasn't suffering so much from arrogance but from self-recrimination? He was supposed to be an intelligence agent, one of the best and brightest, in order to be recruited by the Special Intelligence Network. Yet he found that it meant little when faced with the unorthodox methods that Jacquetta, Charlie, Emma, and Josiah were all employing in their 'games' against Smithson and his fellow trainee agents.

Jacquetta's expression likewise softened as she considered what her younger son had said. Her eyes went to her brother's face.

"You might want to talk to Phillipe about that," she said. "That could be just as dangerous, in a different way."

Victor nodded. "I'll talk about it with him tomorrow, see what he says, and maybe we'll need to adjust the training a little. The last thing we'd want to do is cause his student to pull out because he overthinks something and then blames himself. That can kill an agent as much as—"

A quiet knock at the front door caused him to break off. Victor's eyes flashed over to each of the three teenagers, then his sister. Each one looked surprised.

"I take it no one expected that?" he asked.

"Definitely not." Jacquetta shook her head.

Victor stood. His face remained calm, even placid, but his eyes were stormy. "Quiet, get one of the guns I know Dad and your husband gave you. Kids, get to the safe room."

His voice was quiet but firm, brooking no disobedience. Neither boy argued, standing as they watched their mother move to the dining room hutch, which had a concealed panel near the back, from which she pulled out a small handgun. Emma swallowed as she stood with her brothers.

"You really think the bad guys would try something?" she asked. "Even with your former partners here?"

Victor wished he could reassure his niece that, no, he didn't think anything of the sort, but experience had taught him that the truth was best. Even the most extraordinary precautions were sometimes useless against someone who *really* wanted something.

"Let's hope not," he said instead. "It's best to be on the safe side, though, especially right now." He nodded to the opposite dining room door. "Go."

None of the three teenagers argued. Victor and Jacquetta watched them go, then waited another pair of heartbeats. When another knock came from the door, more insistent than the first, Victor looked at his sister.

"Ready?" he asked.

"Do I have a choice?" she retorted, her own eyes flashing with angry displeasure. "Let's do this."

The siblings moved towards the front door. Victor stood on the left side and put his hand on the doorknob when they reached it. Looking over to where Jacquetta stood on the opposite side, he gave a slight nod of approval. Jacquetta's feet were apart in a ready stance, the gun pointing towards the ground. A finger rested alongside the pistol, exactly as their father had taught them.

His own weapon was also in his hand, but in his *off* hand. Victor's lessons had been more profound than his sister's. While she had wanted to know only the basics of defense, he had wanted to know *every*thing that could make him a better field agent. Whether it was shooting with his off hand, or wielding dual weapons, or field stripping his guns... All the things Victor had learned had been meant to improve his efficiency, his safety, and his ability to deal out death, if needed.

The Wall had been nothing, if not thorough, in training his Wolfe of a son.

It was the reason Jacquetta took on the role of his backup. When she nodded to him, signaling that she was ready, he opened the door.

A surprised-looking, middle-aged black man with a duffel bag slung over his shoulder stood on the other side. Both of his hands were up, showing they were empty. His expression gave Victor the impression that

410

the man would have liked to have been anywhere but there, at that precise moment—an understandable desire, considering the fact that Seth Yago happened to be right behind and to his right, his gun out and pointed directly at the unknown man's spinal column. All it would take was a single twitch, and the man would most likely end up in the hospital with a serious injury.

Victor had to give the young agent credit. He didn't look nervous. Anxious, yes, but he wouldn't hesitate to do whatever he needed if it proved to be necessary.

His eyes slid over to Maria Fuentes, who stood on their unknown visitor's other side. Her weapon seemed to lie loose in her hand, giving the impression that she would not be ready for any kind of action, but Victor knew better. The fact that Maria's weapon was out and in her hand meant that she was not only ready for action but also anticipating it.

And yet, while her own expression proved impassive, her brown eyes with the gray irises held the faintest hint of bewilderment. Apparently, and if Victor was reading the situation correctly, this unexpected intruder held some kind of position that had caused Maria and Seth to bring him to the door instead of running him off.

She smiled when Victor arched an eyebrow at her, then tossed a small leather wallet—the kind, Victor realized, that was issued to government-employed people. Catching it one-handed, he flipped it open to reveal both the badge and the identification inside.

FBI Agent Ethan Chase Plumber... Victor almost frowned, comparing the photo in the wallet to the man standing before him. The two matched, even though the photo looked to be at least five years younger. "Agent Plumber?"

"Yeah." The man glanced at Maria, nervousness evident, then at Seth and back to Victor. "Shit, this is the last time I do Rick a favor. *Ever.*"

Under other circumstances, Victor would have chuckled and returned his weapon to its holster. Given what Rick had said the last time he'd called, however?

Victor slid his eyes to Jacquetta. "You know him?"

"Not personally." She shook her head. "Rick's mentioned him, though. Called him, and I quote, a damned good agent."

The agent of SIN breathed out a relieved sigh, visibly relaxing and reholstering his gun. Jacquetta smiled, following her brother's lead, and moving with catlike grace to return her own weapon to its hiding spot before going to call her children to rejoin them. Maria relaxed as well, once Victor's gun vanished, and she motioned to Seth. He frowned, not catching the hint right away.

"*Madre de Dios,*" she snapped. "Put it away!"

Sheepishly, Seth reholstered his gun. "Sorry."

Maria rolled her eyes, then winked at Victor. "We'll be heading back out, since you look like you have this under control, *Lobo.* Let us know if you need help, and don't forget, Phillipe and his *aprendiz* will be taking our place at zero hundred."

"Got it." Victor nodded. "Careful out there, *Ojos.*"

"Of course."

Not a second later, she and Seth had both melted into the darkness. Victor turned back to where the FBI agent still stood, still looking uneasy.

"Sorry about that, Agent Plumber," he said, moving to allow the other inside. "But you can't be too careful nowadays."

412

"Yeah." Ethan swallowed, then crossed over the threshold. "I guess not." His eyes met Victor's, and his brow furrowed, eyes narrowing ever-so-slightly. "You would be?"

"Victor Wolfe," Victor introduced himself. "I'm Rick's brother-in-law."

"You're a lot more than that, I suspect," Ethan said. "With everything he gave me to give to you, plus what just happened."

Victor inclined his head at the other, doing his best not to show his sudden anticipation. What had Rick found regarding Victor's son?

"Come over to the dining room," he said. "We can spread everything you've brought out there."

Ethan nodded, still looking on edge as he followed Victor back. He said nothing, however, as he unzipped the duffel bag and began laying out file after file.

There were a *lot* of files, Victor realized, but the ones that caught his immediate attention all had a single label. *Kincaid.*

He picked up the one closest to him. Katherine's picture met his eyes the moment he opened it.

For a brief moment, Victor forgot the world around him. It didn't matter how much older she seemed. Her eyes still caught him, still held him in their grasp. It was just him and her once again, and the world was theirs...

"Vic?"

Jacquetta's quiet voice broke the spell. Victor took a deep breath and put the folder aside. His voice, when he spoke, held a rough edge.

"Yeah?"

She pretended not to notice, waving Victor over to the file she had opened and ignoring the way Ethan looked over, a quizzical expression on his face. Victor didn't set down Katherine's file, bringing it with him instead as he walked the short distance over. When he saw what Jacquetta had opened, he wanted to deny the image before him. The angry young man with the blazing red hair and the cold, blue-gray eyes in the mugshot *couldn't* be his son.

And yet, who else could it be? Victor began shaking his head in denial when a portion of his father's letter about Robbie came back to him. **Don't believe everything you might read or hear about him. Not everything is as it seems with the life he now leads.**

Was this what William Wolfe-Wall had meant? What in the hell had happened to Robbie Kincaid, if the young man in the mugshot *was* him, to make him a criminal? What had he done, or been accused of?

What, Victor wanted to know, *was going on?*

His expression must have given something away. The newcomer glanced from him to the picture of Katherine Kincaid, then the mugshot, and blinked.

"Are you the client?" Ethan asked. "The one who sent Rick to find his kid?"

Victor looked at him, while Jacquetta glanced between them. The SIN agent initially wanted to deny it. He didn't know this man, this Ethan Plumber. How did he know if he could be trusted, especially with information like *that*?

But, after a moment, he reconsidered. Rick had proven himself an excellent judge of character, at least most of the time. Victor knew he wouldn't have sent this FBI agent to them without being certain that he could be trusted.

It was the reason he nodded after breathing out a sigh. "I am. Yes."

Ethan let out a low whistle. "Damn. I don't envy you, 'specially if he *does* turn out to be who Rick suspects."

He nodded at the mugshot. Jacquetta arched her eyebrows as her brother sighed once more.

"I was, uh," Victor said in resignation, "hoping that you *wouldn't* say that."

"Sorry," Ethan said, shaking his head. "I can't even begin to imagine what you'll go through if—and I stress the *if*—he turns out to be who you're lookin' for. He's not the only one Rick's lookin' at, though." He gave Victor the weak beginning of a smile. "Don't lose hope?"

"He won't." Jacquetta smiled back. "We'll make sure of it. And if the young man in that picture does turn out to be who Rick suspects?" She glanced at her brother. "Well, we'll figure everything out, no matter what." She eyed Ethan, taking in the slight fatigue she saw. "Have you eaten?"

"A few hours ago, ma'am," he told her. "On the plane here."

"Let me get you a sandwich," she said. "Turkey and cheese on rye, all right?"

"Sounds good to me," Ethan said. "We can go through everything here as I eat, if that's okay with all of you."

"I take it there's a reason he sent so many files, then?" Victor asked.

"Oh, yeah." Ethan nodded. "It's quite the story, too, but before we start in on everything..." He laid one more file down on the table. "Rick

415

wanted you to take a look at this. It has nothing to do with your possible kid or any of *that*." He nodded to the other files. "He thought this guy looked familiar, though, and wanted to see if you'd recognize him."

Victor picked it up, all too glad for any potential distraction. Another mug shot met his eyes when he opened the folder in question. This time, he saw a man with a chiseled, light-brown face, stylized black hair, and vibrant dark eyes, wearing a biker's vest and what looked like a T-shirt. A pair of scars ran down the left side of the man's face, and Victor frowned. The man seemed familiar. He couldn't yet place him, but Victor knew that he had seen him before.

"I know him," he murmured. "I just don't know where I know him from."

"Rick said pretty much the same thing," Ethan said. "We know 'im as Valente, the leader of the Iron Horde. It's a motorcycle gang, back in Sulivan."

"Huh." Victor's brow furrowed as he studied the photograph, mouthing the name. He *knew* it, but how? Where had he seen and heard of this man before? "I'll think on it, if that's all right?"

"Sure." Ethan turned his attention back to Jacquetta as she returned with a plate piled high with no fewer than three sandwiches, each loaded with meat, cheese, lettuce, and more. "Oh, man! That looks tasty!"

"Of course." Jacquetta gestured to a chair. "Sit down and eat. We can wait until you're done, if you prefer, too."

"We've got a lot to go through," Ethan told her, then looked at Victor. "Unless, o' course, you—"

Victor shook his head, knowing what the man thought. "She's my sister, so this affects her as much as it does me."

416

"All right, then. Let me give you the rundown on the history of the city of Sulivan, the Mid-Superior Islands, and the Old Families, including the Kincaids."

 басьбасьбасьбась BMPⱯRM TNM XRⱯ↲ ঌ৺ ঌ৺ ঌ৺ ঌ৺

The clock struck midnight as the man ahead of him droned on. The young man following had stopped listening some time before, his eyes flashing with irritation at the other's voice, although his face gave nothing away.

The night had proven quiet. The two stalked along the edges of the property before moving towards the house. Only the chirping of a cricket could be heard somewhere in the hedges, complementing the older man's quiet attempts at instruction.

The younger man breathed deeply, struggling to contain his impatience and anticipation. They had been at this place for a week and a half without anything to show for it, except bruised egos. Now, not even two full hours of strenuous exercise, going through every physical labor he could think of, could take the edge off of his restlessness. Sleep had begun to elude him, and soon, he knew he wouldn't be able to stomach even the smallest bite of food.

But it is always this way, he reminded himself, *just before a hit.*

Up ahead, the older man continued to speak. The younger permitted himself the luxury of rolling his eyes.

Fool. The younger man's lips tightened as the older man mentioned their supposed duty. *I am well aware of what I am meant to do. Soon, you will know as well.*

As if on cue, the young man felt the soft buzz that came from the ancient pager he carried with him. His lips parted in a thin smile as he reached into his left-hand pocket.

The tiny screen lit up when he thumbed a small button. A moment later, adrenaline surged through him at the simple message. *8463. Go.*

At last. The assassin's teeth bared in a hideous mockery of a grin. Replacing the pager, his eyes went to his companion's back. The old fool was still talking, still going on about something regarding the protection of the innocent. *As if I would care about that.*

The young man kept his eyes trained on the other, even as his right hand slipped into his modified pants' pocket. There, his favorite weapon was sheathed, waiting for just this moment.

As the two rounded the corner, near where a tree's shadow cast their path into blackness for the briefest moment, the younger man struck. His companion jerked once, eyes bulging. He let out the faintest gasp, then slid to the ground.

"You were not ready for La Plaga," the young man said, his voice the barest whisper. "But then, no one is."

Stepping over the body of his former companion, the young man paused only to wipe the bloody blade of his knife on the dead man's shirt before looking up at the house. The lights had shut off about an hour earlier. Movement had ceased soon after.

"It is time indeed," he murmured.

A moment later, he took a key from the dead man's pocket. Moving forward, he crept towards the steps that led up to the front door. He walked carefully, making sure to avoid the places that creaked ever-so-slightly. Once he stood at the door, he tested the knob and found it to be locked.

It is no matter. La Plaga almost chuckled. Gently inserting the key he had liberated, he turned the knob again, ever-so-slowly. The deadbolt moved with the merest whisper of sound, unlocking with an almost inaudible *click.*

Hesitating just long enough to ensure that no one had heard, La Plaga slowly opened the door. He ran his thumb along the handle of the knife as he moved inside. It was the only reminder he had kept of his previous life. La Plaga had taken it from the body of his first-ever kill, and he had used it in almost every mission since. The knife had become his signature weapon as a result, and he considered the blade to be his most faithful friend.

Creeping through the foyer, the assassin ventured into the short hall and then the living room. He glanced around, remembering the exact path he had taken to each bedroom on the previous evenings he had spent preparing for this specific moment.

Soon, he promised himself. *Blood will cover each pillow. It is now only a matter of time.*

Another step. Two. La Plaga all but salivated at the prospect as he continued to move forward.

The unexpected click of a gun's hammer caught his attention. La Plaga froze, then wheeled around, his dark eyes searching the darkness. There wasn't supposed to be anyone here, in the living room. They were all supposed to be sleeping in their beds!

"Who the fuck are *you?*" A lamp clicked on to reveal a middle-aged black man sitting up on the couch, holding a weapon that La Plaga recognized as having been issued by the American Federal Bureau of Investigation. "Start talkin', asshole, or I'll end you. Right here, right now."

La Plaga did not speak. His face hardening, he simply and quickly inverted the grip on his knife, lowering into a fighting stance. As he had been taught so long ago, there were no words in situations such as this. There was only action.

The agent sighed in response. "Fine, then. Let's do this."

La Plaga smiled. Light glinted off his sharp and deadly steel blade before it blurred into action.

To Be Continued...

...in The Gathering of the Blood.

Acknowledgments

To Greg, who was a constant source of encouragement and support from the very beginning.

To Jaxon and Eric, both of whom lent their time to read through the first draft and make suggestions to better the story.

To Jamie, Linda, Ann Marie, and Bryon, all of whom read the story before almost anyone else and encouraged us to reach for the proverbial stars.

422

Prentice Derian Fowler clung to the various shadows that were scattered throughout the bit of woodland. Brown eyes slid from left to right as he carefully picked his way through the underbrush.

Despite wearing dark clothing, he tried his best to avoid those spots where the moon's light penetrated the trees. This particular mission required the utmost secrecy for the moment. Alerting his prey before he and the others who were with him were ready to move in wouldn't just be unacceptable. It could spoil everything.

He kept his breathing steady and even, not betraying the way his heart raced with excitement. As the Commander of the East Sulivan Precincts, he was rarely permitted to come along on operations like this one. Setting up a sting operation was one thing. Him actually getting to participate in one?

No. It was generally considered too risky for one of his rank.

Prentice didn't agree. Yes, he happened to be one of the youngest Police Commanders in all of Mid-Superior Island History. In his mind, that meant he should be leading from the front, not hiding back in his office, only to trot out to take credit in front of the cameras whenever there was a press conference. He didn't care about all of the toes he had stepped on to get where he now stood, nor did he care about the criminals he had helped to put away, who might want to take an opportunity to get revenge. Prentice still retained some of the arrogance of his relative youth, and chafed at the restrictions that usually came with his position in life.

Both professional and personal.

He held in a sigh at the thought. Police Commanders were meant to be supervisors, directing and overseeing various activities within their assigned areas of control. Members of the Fowler Old Family, however, weren't meant to be police officers at all. Prentice happened to be a third son, one who was ignored if not outright dismissed by most members of his family. His DuBois aunt had been the only one to pay any attention to him, and it was thanks to her that he had been able to follow his dreams of being a police officer instead of working for the DBJF Alliance Corporation, like the rest of his family. When she had asked him to help her chosen protege in this, what else could Prentice do but say 'yes' and handle it himself?

The fact that his target happened to be The Ghost, that mysterious thief who had caused his family and their allies so many headaches? It was imperative, Prentice felt, that he be on-scene for The Ghost's capture. He not only wanted to use this moment to prove his worth to the rest of his family, but be the first to remove the mask of the one who had dared to stand against them.

The earpiece he wore crackled softly. "Doc's almost in position, Commander."

"I see that," he murmured back. Up ahead, just a few feet away, Prentice could see Doctor Yuri Orav entering a small clearing. "You in position, Hauke?"

"Yes, sir," Police Lieutenant Vincent Hauke said, making Prentice smile.

Vincent was almost twice Prentice's age, a fact that should have irritated the man; yet he seemed content to act as Prentice's own second. As he himself had told Prentice, being a Lieutenant gave him rank while still permitting him out in the field enough to take off the edge that came from being forced to be mostly behind a desk. He had the age and

424

experience that Prentice lacked, no apparent desire to move up further, and all the willingness to teach Prentice what he needed to know.

For that, Prentice couldn't help but be grateful and had not only named Vincent his official second, but had used his Family's assets on occasion to help the other. Sometimes, at least in Prentice's opinion, a little judicious force was necessary, regardless of who it was used on and no matter what others thought about it.

Such reasoning had also allowed him to bring the other two he had with him under his control. "McDuff? Passerini? The two of you ready?"

"I'm all set, Commander," Damien McDuff reported. "Just say the word."

"Same," Bernardo Passerini said, voice low and gruff.

"Good." Prentice smiled. "Stay alert."

He positioned himself just out of sight near the treeline. His eyes never left Doctor Orav, even as he recalled what he'd been told about the scientist.

Doctor Yuri Orav worked under the supervision of Doctor Regina Holloway-McClure, who was the protege of Prentice's DuBois aunt. He was a short man, standing barely five foot six in height, with nervous, darting blue eyes. His skin resembled marble in the best of times, and his thinning brownish hair hung limp around his head. Thick, coke-bottle glasses perched on a short nose. The man sniffled as he walked, sometimes stopping to blow a stuffy, allergy-ridden nose.

Prentice almost shook his head at the sight. If not for the man's supposed intelligence, Yuri Orav would no doubt have been confined to the dust heap of history.

He *was* intelligent, however. According to Doctor Holloway-McClure, the projects that Yuri worked on all showed remarkable promise. The man had a gift for biotechnology, and it had been a paper the scientist had done while still in *junior high school* that had led to the DBJF taking an interest. They had awarded the boy with multiple scholarships, first for a private high school academy for the gifted, then for university. The DBJF had even taken the highly unusual step of sending Yuri to one of the best universities in the world so he could study, then had hired him as soon as he had graduated.

Was that why The Ghost had decided to contact him? Or was it due to one of the projects that Yuri had worked on in the past? Perhaps one he worked on now?

Prentice didn't know. At the moment, he didn't believe it mattered. All he cared about was bringing the mystery of The Ghost to an end. If he and his hand-picked team did that, then no one, not even Chief of Police Makoto Akiyama, would be able to hold them back from getting what they wanted.

He glanced about the woods, trying in vain to spot the ones who had come with him. His lips curled upwards. Much to his satisfaction, he couldn't. *Of course I can't. Why would I bother picking them for this if they couldn't do their jobs?*

Vincent Hauke had the most experience out of all of them, but Damien McDuff and Bernardo Passerini had their own talents. Prentice had scouted the two for various reasons, then had bought their loyalty through various favors and offers of protection.

Damien had spent a great deal of time undercover and knew how to blend into almost every sort of background. He was a short man, lean and dark-skinned. He possessed a nasty temper, which Prentice often worked to point in what he considered to be the 'right' direction. It was part of the reason Damien had been trained as a sharpshooter, part of the reason he had been taught how to box and also jujitsu. Still, Damien's temper both at his home and on the job had forced Prentice to protect him from a multitude of repercussions, and the man owed Prentice not only his career but his freedom.

Bernardo Passerini, on the other hand, was a giant bear of a man. He possessed some military training, could sneak up on a cat and kill the animal before it was aware of his presence, and had few scruples when it came to getting a job done. Few at work trusted him because of that and the ties he was known to have to the Pasquale-Scordato Family. Prentice thought those things only added to Bernardo's worth, however, and had taken pains to not only bring him into his group, but to advance him in the eyes of the others.

If The Ghost did show up to meet Yuri Orav, then he or she would have little chance of escape. Prentice's smile widened at the thought. Capturing The Ghost meant a multitude of rewards, which Prentice wanted to collect.

As such, he focused on Yuri. The little scientist had walked to the center of the clearing and, now, came to a halt. He glanced around, clutching the folder he'd brought with him as though his life depended on it.

Knowing my aunt, Prentice snickered. *It probably does.*

Cassandra Madison DuBois was not a person to be crossed lightly. Neither was Regina Holloway-McClure.

Flicking his eyes down at his watch, Prentice saw that it was nearly midnight. The Ghost, from what Yuri had said, would appear at exactly midnight; but would he or she? Perhaps The Ghost would wait a bit first, to try and make certain that the scientist had come alone, as requested?

Prentice soon found out. At just one minute past midnight, a figure emerged from the opposite line of trees.

It was a tall person, whoever it happened to be. The Ghost wore tactical gear, which Prentice had been warned to expect, and a mask to conceal his or her face. That won't matter for much longer. *The moment The Ghost is in our custody...*

A quiet, static-tinged voice hissed into Prentice's left ear. "Do we move now?"

Prentice rolled his eyes at Damien's impatience. It was a long-standing problem for the other, one they could not afford him giving into right now. "No. We wait for the hand-off, McDuff. You should already know that."

"Fine."

Again, Prentice rolled his eyes but refocused as The Ghost approached Yuri. The scientist looked relieved when he saw the masked figure coming towards him.

"Oh, good," he said. "You're here."

"I said I would be."

Prentice blinked. The Ghost wore a voice changer? *Damn. Can't ascertain anything more about identity. Not yet.*

"You did," Yuri said and lifted the folder he carried a little. "I've got the evidence you wanted."

428

"Good." The Ghost came closer to the scientist. The helmeted head never moved, but Prentice had the feeling that the concealed eyes were darting back and forth, searching for enemies. "Is it as I'd hoped?"

"Yes," Yuri said as The Ghost reached his side. "It's everything."

"Excellent."

There could be no mistaking the joy in The Ghost's voice, despite the voice changer, or the faint relief. Prentice almost frowned. Why should The Ghost be relieved?

After a moment, he decided that it didn't matter. Not to him. The only thing he cared about was The Ghost's imminent capture.

As soon as The Ghost took the folder Yuri handed out, Prentice acted. "Go!"

Almost as one, Prentice, Vincent and Bernardo surged forward, out of the trees. Their weapons were out and already pointing at the scientist and The Ghost.

"On the ground!" Prentice ordered. "Now!"

Yuri seemed to freeze before he obeyed. The Ghost, however, did not.

A single curse could be heard before The Ghost, faster than Prentice or any of his fellow officers could almost believe, took to his or her heels and darted back towards the woods. A pair of shots from Damien's position rang out.

To Prentice's disbelief, both missed. One was barely an inch away from The Ghost's shoulder before said Ghost appeared to dodge it; the other missed The Ghost's foot by bare centimeters, gouging out a small furrow into the ground instead of in flesh.

Snarling an oath, Prentice headed after The Ghost in pursuit. Bernardo was beside him, with Vincent dropping back to cover Yuri and waiting for Damien.

There hadn't been many sports Prentice had favored during his time in school. Unlike his oldest brother, the quarterback; his middle brother, the baseball star; or his sister, the cheerleader, he'd preferred things like chess and the book club. His father had all but forced him to choose something athletic, however, and Prentice had reluctantly chosen Track and Field. He'd already been used to running, after all, from various bullies. Track had felt like a natural fit.

It had served him well, too, allowing him to develop the endurance and stamina to go longer distances at a full run. Prentice had been particularly successful in those sort of races, in fact, and that talent had served him well when he'd become a patrol officer, then a detective. Granted, as a Commander, he had little opportunity to get involved in a physical foot-pursuit; but Prentice had continued his training regimes regardless.

Such training and exercising showed their worth now. It didn't take long for Prentice to out-pace Bernardo. He kept his eyes on The Ghost's retreating form, not letting anything distract him from his goal of bringing The Ghost to a halt. Slowly but surely, he began to gain ground.

The Ghost glanced back once, then twice. Again, thanks to the mask, Prentice couldn't see the other's expression, but he thought he could smell The Ghost's fear. He even believed that he could hear The Ghost's thoughts.

'Run faster, run faster! Please, let me run faster!'

He almost snorted with laughter, but controlled himself. He was gaining more and more ground on his quarry. Laughter would do nothing except take precious oxygen and concentration away from the pursuit.

A few more footsteps, and Prentice was now within arms' length. He could hear The Ghost muttering in a mounting panic.

"No, no, *no*." Despite the voice changer, The Ghost's voice seemed to become higher-pitched and Prentice could hear the other beginning to gasp. The chase was almost at an end. "Go, go, *go*, damn it!"

"You're mine," Prentice said.

Reaching out with one hand, he made ready to grab The Ghost and bring the chase to a quick halt. He smiled as his fingers brushed the fabric covering The Ghost's shoulder...

Only to find nothing but air in the next second. "The *fuck*—"

Prentice blinked, unable to believe what he now saw. The Ghost had somehow managed to accelerate, so suddenly and so quickly that he or she had slipped literally from Prentice's fingers. Now, The Ghost was flying farther and further forward, outdistancing Prentice in the space of mere heartbeats.

It was *impossible*.

He pushed himself harder, running faster than he had in years. His lungs burned. His heart pounded. The muscles in his legs felt like they were on fire.

And The Ghost was *still* moving faster. Prentice snarled in anger, as leaves and branches whipped by him. He blinked once.

In that instant, The Ghost was gone.

Prentice felt his mouth fall open. He slowed down, going from a dead run to a mere jog, then a quick walk as he stared ahead at the bizarrely empty space.

How, he wanted to know. How in the *hell* could something like this be possible?

He came to a stop at last. His breath came in short, wheezy gasps. His eyes darted about as he spun in a slow circle, searching in desperate disbelief.

Where could The Ghost have gone? How could he or she have just...*disappeared*?

Again, it should have been impossible. Prentice couldn't believe it, couldn't understand it. First, he had been close, so *very* close, to capturing whoever The Ghost happened to be and now...

"Damn it," he whispered as he tried to search in a vain effort to find his quarry. "God-*motherfucking*-damn it!"

There was *nothing*. No one. No matter where he looked, he saw nothing except trees, bushes, and shrubs. He heard nothing but cricket-song. Even trying to strain his eyes and his ears produced nothing.

He was alone.

He shook his head in denial. He had been so close. He'd been within *millimeters* of making the capture!

But The Ghost was gone. Prentice couldn't deny it, no matter how much he wanted to do so.

Contributors (or People this Book Would Not Exist Without)

Greg Steele: Thank you, Greg. You've been there since the beginning, when this was more fanfic and less original fiction. Many of the characters and some of the setting names you helped with making these your children, too.

Violet J. Jacobs: As an encyclopedia of names, many of the stores and businesses were the result of Violet's unflinching and meticulous work. Thank you, Violet.

J.A. Callin has been weaving stories since the age of seven, guided by Tolkien, *Star Wars*, and the many adventures found in books, games, and life. An editor, researcher, and graduate of Rutgers University, she's also a rescuer of animals, a builder of worlds, and a lover of the strange and unexpected. Her first novel was a test run; *Discovery of the Blood* is where the real journey begins.

Wolfgang Jacobs is a writer, product designer, and (depending on who you ask) a possible wizard. Raised on a steady diet of Greek myths, Tolkien's elves, and Michael Crichton's science gone wrong, he has been telling stories since he could first hold a book. When not conjuring worlds and characters who refuse to behave, Wolfgang can be found plotting elaborate board games, tinkering with design projects, or attempting to prove that coffee is, in fact, a form of spellcraft. *Discovery of the Blood* is his debut novel.

434